THE
TROPHY BRIDE'S
TALE

8 - 15 - 2010

THE
TROPHY BRIDE'S
TALE

CYRILLA BARR

BASCOM HILL PUBLISHING GROUP
Minneapolis

Bascom Hill Publishing Group
212 3rd Avenue North, Suite 290
Minneapolis, MN 55401
612.455.2293
www.bascomhillpublishing.com

The Lute Player (c.1612/1620) by Orazio Gentileschi. Detail.
Ailsa Mellon Bruce Fund, Image courtesy of the Board of Trustees, National
Gallery of Art, Washington, D.C.

ISBN - 978-1-935098-28-7
ISBN - 1-935098-28-4
LCCN - 2010903206

Printed in the United States of America

BASCOM HILL
PUBLISHING GROUP

CONTENTS

A ciascun'alma presa e gentil core

(To every captive soul and gentle heart)

Dante Alighieri, *Fedele d'Amore*

IN MEMORIAM

TITUS

TERI

MY END IS MY BEGINNING…

Florence, Piazza Sant' Apollinare,
10 August 1549

I have never seen an execution! I am terrified and tremble uncontrollably now as I stand on the fringes of the restless crowd desperately hoping that no one will notice me in my shabby pilgrim's weeds. Then, as is my custom when faced with a difficult decision, I speak aloud to myself: It steels my resolve, so I believe. "Admit it," I say. "You are terrified, and you want to run away." But finer sensibilities tell me I dare not flee.

Even so I hear his voice now as clearly as if he were at my side. "It will be dangerous for you," he had warned, "you must not come." But not even the strident cries of the mob in the *piazza* can drown out his voice now thundering in my head: "You must not come! YOU MUST NOT COME!" I know he means well but… what matter now? I have come, and I will stay—for her.

My quaking nerves belie the resolve of my words. Although I am not usually given to such spontaneous expressions of piety, I suddenly cross myself and, without pause, step into the bedlam to be swept along in the tide of milling bodies. I stumble now on the uneven paving stones and struggle to remain upright. I cannot see or easily keep my balance while men much larger than myself push their brawny shoulders into my back and sides. Bawling fishwives jab my ribs as they elbow their way through the surging crowd. Finally I am forced to surrender to the unrelenting tide and allow myself to be carried along in a sea of sweaty bodies smelling of stale grappa and garlic. They are all jostling now for the best position from which to view the spectacle—for that is truly what it promises to be.

The scuffle has slowed our progress now as we make our way through the stench of offal rotting in gutters and the remains from chamber pots emptied during the night, their contents still steaming in the humid air. I struggle to control my rising nausea and to quell the persistent spasms of my sickened stomach. I fear I will collapse and be trampled.

Without thinking I reach for my coarse pilgrim's cloak that, in the excessive August heat, I have carelessly allowed to hang loosely from my shoulders. Now, however, I gather it tightly around my body as if I were suddenly seized by a chill, and draw the hood lower to cover as much of my face as I can. I tell myself that it is to block out the vile odors and hopefully mute the clamor of the crowd. But in my heart I know it is really to hide—to conceal my identity, for I am afraid!

In the noise and confusion, however, no one seems to notice me in my pilgrim's garb. "A penitent," I hear someone say. "Must be on his way to Rome." Another throws me a coin and calls out, "Godspeed you, penitent!"

That is good: Let them think so, for a pilgrim I am not, and though a pilgrim's pouch does indeed hang from the rope at my waist, it contains no scrip. Yet I am not without treasure. Mine lies safe in the recesses of my deep pocket and from time to time I reach in to reassure myself that it is still there.

It is difficult to see now, except through the small holes in the coarse weave of my hood, but I am aware of little boys romping excitedly under foot while workers manage to eat their coarse bread and drink their watered wine even as they fight for a place to stand. There is an aberrant air of festivity about the occasion that infuriates me and I want to cry out, "Do you not know what you are doing?"

Suddenly, through a slight opening in the crowd, I catch my first glimpse of the scaffold and I clutch at my stomach to keep from retching at the sight. They have hung it with bunting. They have decorated it—made it more stage than gibbet! The public execution of a woman, in this large and very important *piazza* is a statement—as if to say: "Disgruntled wives, heed the example you are about to witness. Yes, she was the wife of a prominent and successful Florentine silk merchant whose grand home stands in the Santa Croce quarter not far from the dyeing vats of his business. But she is not above the law: She must be taken to justice!"

"JUSTICE! What justice this? A travesty," I want to scream!

Over the months of her incarceration she has been trapped in a vortex of gossip and the list of indictments in her *libello* has multiplied as informants came forward seeking remuneration for their fabricated accusations. Her case was much talked of; whispered of in dark confessionals, discussed behind closed doors, debated in the marketplace and, above all, argued by doctors and lawyers in the court for seventy-five days. And now, heedless of whether she is innocent or guilty, a thousand prying eyes await the spectacle— like vultures circling over carrion! It is not justice but raw, callow curiosity that brings them here.

The crowd is becoming more restless now, eager for some action. For one brief moment the clouds part, allowing an oblique ray of sunlight to dance menacingly on the bright blade of the *mannaia*. That little personalized guillotine perfected in Florence has been carefully honed to a terrifying sharpness, and stands waiting to carry out its purpose with heartless and detached efficiency.

The clerk mounts the platform now and somberly reads the official sentence. In one brief statement he declares the lady's guilt. "To all here present, let it be known that on this tenth day of August in the year of our Lord, 1549, the Lady Prudenza, wife of Matteo Cecchi, is decapitated for the crime of murdering her husband. May God have mercy." The words sicken me and I can taste the bile of my anger like fire rising in my throat.

The reading of the sentence has distracted the mob momentarily. I notice a slight opening in the crowd and seize the opportunity to slip through it. Inching my way slowly I reach the foot of the *palco* just in time to hear the clerk launch into a bit of doggerel verse. He calls it an exhortation. I say it is a diatribe meant to strike fear into the hearts of unhappy wives, a reminder of the possible consequences of their discontent.

Now at midday, the sun is high and, in the intense heat, the crowd is almost uncontrollable as they await that moment when the condemned one emerges from the courtyard of the Bargello. She will be led by the *confortatori,* the comforters—those hooded, black-robed brothers of the Compagnia dei Neri who minister to the condemned. Although I myself have never seen it, I have heard of their ritual, and the crowd knows it well. Traditionally the brothers chant their psalms and litanies and murmur admonitions to the condemned as they slowly make their way through Via

Proconsolo, up Via dei Neri and finally along Via dei Malcontenti, which leads to the gallows at the Porta di Giustizia. But today is different. Because this is a public execution the procession is truncated, going but a short distance from the Bargello to the *palco* in Piazza Sant'Apollinare. Just as the prison gate finally swings open and the procession comes into view, the catcalls of the mob reach a deafening crescendo.

Now I see one of the hooded brothers (It is he, I am certain) walking backward, holding before her face the *tavoletta*, a tablet bearing some sacred image—likely John the Baptist. How appropriate! I have been told that beheading is a patrician privilege! At that thought my anger surges and I feel such a violent rush of blood to my head that my temples throb and I know that my ears must be turning red for, under my hood, I feel them burning feverishly.

I have secured my position so near the edge of the *palco* that I can almost reach out and touch the black bunting that drapes it—certainly near enough to observe how thin and pale she has become. I see that her beautiful hair, once the color of burnished bronze, is shot through with gray and is now crudely shorn so as not to impede the cruel blade's work. Her robe is of coarse homespun tied at the waist with an old piece of hemp. I can hear her labored breath as she struggles to climb the steps to the platform and, although I am near enough to detect an ongoing exchange between her and the brother who walks backward before her, I cannot really distinguish their words but can well imagine what they must be.

Still led by the brother holding the *tavoletta* she suddenly diverts her gaze from the sacred image and turns to survey the crowd briefly. They are shocked into sudden and absolute silence, straining to hear if she will speak some last words—perhaps in her own defense. I can see her lips move but even in this deathly silence her words are inaudible. I whisper to myself, "Dear God, does she see me? Does she know that I am here?"

No. Her gaze is directed far above my head and into the distance. She is searching, I am sure, searching for someone else. I understand. She makes no protestation of innocence. Instead, with one last determined step she bravely prostrates herself before the *mannaia* and just as the blade descends, I instinctively raise my cloak to cover my eyes and whisper a desperate prayer—"Merciful

God, Let it be done with but one blow." A dull thud and a roar of the crowd tell me—it is over.

It is over. It is done! In disbelief I repeat it as I flee into a quiet corner to escape the press of the unruly onlookers as they rush to leave the *piazza*, off to their day's work as if nothing happened. Their bellies now full and their curiosity sated, they seem utterly unmoved by the sight of the *palco* now crimsoned by her blood—holy blood, I believe. Only now as I cower in the shadows and attempt to dry my tears do I notice the crimson stain on my cloak—her last gift to me. I press it to my heart, a precious relic. Still half hidden in the shadows I watch as the brothers carry her to the burial place provided for criminals. I am comforted to see that he goes with them and I am grateful, too, that they take no notice of me as they respectfully tend to their sacred obligation while I am left to contemplate mine.

She, who had come to Florence from Ancona as a young bride, has paid her debt. And so it might seem, ends the tale of the Lady Prudenza!

THE LUTE

CHAPTER 1

Ancona, 1534

My name is Prudenza, but they call me a child of the sea. Some say it is because of the peculiar color of my eyes. But I believe it is because I was born on the shores of the Adriatic in Ancona, which very early on I reckoned must be one of the most magical places in the world. It was said that from here one could see both the sunrise and the sunset over its bay. Indeed it is true. Although the city lies on the country's eastern shore, the promontory upon which it is built juts into the sea like two gently curved arms that seem to embrace the harbor in a circle broken only where the waters of the lagoon meet the open sea. Here the color deepens to intense blue. Surely, I imagined, nowhere else in the world could I observe this complete cycle of the sun as it recreates the day with unfailing regularity.

It seems to me altogether appropriate that daybreak should begin high above the Conero promontory where the huge bulk of the cathedral dominates the blue of the sky and the sea. From here the first rosy tint signals the beginning of the sun's journey across the bay where it predictably comes to rest on the busy commercial side of the harbor. Tinting the skies with purple the sun dips out of sight behind the crowd of merchant galleys moored there. Their ensigns hang limp from masts that pierce the sky like so many spikes. Countless times I observed this phenomenon, and always my childish thoughts ventured far beyond what my eyes beheld. My mind conjured images of a magical shore on the far side of the sea that no one else could enter but me. It was my private world, my escape. Escape from what, I did not know then.

But I stray! My story really begins with my good parents, so I must tell you of them first. My mother, Caterina Castrucci, is a dignified woman, proud of her lineage, for the Castrucci were a respectable old Anconetane family. Their roots, she claimed, could be traced back to some of the earliest settlers from the East.

Being by nature a practical sort, Mother thought me too much of a dreamer and worried over the hours I spent lulled by the rhythmic lapping of the waves, lost in fantastic reveries that she could never have imagined. In fact, I believe that in some superstitious fashion she blamed my father for what she perceived to be my weakness, claiming that his very name—Beltramonto, beautiful sunset—somehow foreordained that any child of his would be a dreamer. I must admit that truly I was.

I loved both my parents dearly, but Father I adored. He dealt in fine dyes and mordants from the east, those very places to which my imagination transported me with such delight. Father's business often took him down to the *molo*, the wharf where he was obliged to go to the office of the *dogana* to pay the import tax on the exotic colors that he provided to the silk merchants who came to him from San Severino, Lucca, and especially Florence. He was a good, hardworking man who provided a fine home for my mother and me. Without brothers or sisters I had no companions to gambol about on the rocks of the seashore like a tomboy. But neither did I show any inclination to the more genteel domestic virtues of my mother who was so well known for her culinary skills and the delicacy of her fine needlecraft.

Even now as I write I still believe it annoyed her that Father seemed to encourage my reveries by allowing me to visit his *bottega* near Santa Maria della Piazza where I became intrigued by the many rows of strangely shaped vessels—jars, bottles, and amphorae, containing brightly colored dyes and powders. Each, I was certain, must hold the secret of a faraway world just ripe for imagining. I believe that Father loved explaining to me the sources and the properties of these colors. I can still remember how his eyes brightened and his voice became like music as he described the deep blues of indigo that came from India—the best, he claimed— the brilliant reds of cochineal from Spain and robbia from the East Indies. But most precious of all, he claimed, were the orechil and porpora from Tyre from which he created the deep purples that were so sought after both for high fashion and for liturgical regalia. He was especially proud of the rich palette of golden hues that he created with turmeric from the East Indies and saffron from near San Gimignano; a palette that ranged from the color of palest honey to a tawny burnished gold that was complimented so beautifully by the rich henna from Egypt.

I had heard that wealthy ladies sometimes used henna to color their hair, and I admit to a certain degree of vanity about my own auburn hair that needed no such artificial help to achieve that reddish-gold hue.

Alfonso Beltramonto, my father, was well known not only in Ancona, but his reputation was spread abroad as well. The fine quality of his dyes and his scrupulous business dealings caused him to be sought out by textile merchants from faraway places, especially the silk merchants of Florence. So famous were the deep, rich colors obtained from his dyes that finished cloth was sometimes sent from such distant markets as France and Flanders to be dyed in Florence.

Of all the intriguing things in Father's workshop though, there was one that puzzled me much for, although it was not beautiful in itself, without it, Father explained, it would not be possible to create the brilliant colors of the lovely brocades and velvets of ladies' gowns, and the elaborate vestments and rich trappings for the church. It was called alum. He explained to me that the quality of his alum was the secret of the rich colors that he could produce. I did not really understand it then. To me this was a strange alchemy, its magic enhanced by the very names of the exotic places from which it came—Aleppo, Smyrna, Constantinople and Alexandria.

This curiosity of mine caused Mother to worry that I was too idle a dreamer, and made her press Father to send me to be schooled in a convent where, she believed, the discipline and regular life might curb my unbridled imagination. So, after much discussion—to which I was not privy—it was decided that soon after my thirteenth birthday, I should enter the convent school of the Sisters at San Salvatore.

Although he dreaded the separation as much as I did, Father agreed. I foolishly harbored other fears as well. Perhaps the sisters might try to influence me, might force me to take the veil and become one of them. I had often heard the raucous songs of the rustics who gathered in *piazzas* and on street corners singing their lusty parodies. One of the most popular was the song of the young girl forced into a nunnery. Her pitiful refrain was the plea, *"Madre, non mi far monaca."* (Mother, don't make me become a nun.) Of this, as it turned out, I would not have needed to trouble my childish mind. I laugh now at the thought of it.

Next to staring out over the sea and dreaming of faraway romantic places, I enjoyed making up little rhymes and simple tunes that I loved to sing while strumming on an ancient bandura that someone left in Father's shop. I did have some modest talent, they say. Sometimes after our evening meal Father asked me to join him before the broad hearth in the great room where Mother prepared for him a draft of mulled wine. There, while his favorite hound dozed lazily before the fire, I sat enthroned on a high stool, proudly presenting my newest compositions. Typically Father nodded approvingly between drafts while Mother diligently plied her needle to her latest creation, a fine green mantle with a hood. I felt like a minstrel of old—indeed Father often called me his little troubadour. I wanted these precious moments never to end, but Alfonso Beltramonto was a man of his word, and he had not forgotten his promise to Mother. Indeed, I knew that the very cloak she was fashioning was for me to wear on the day I was to be presented at San Salvatore.

Recognizing that I had mixed feelings about my approaching thirteenth birthday, Father attempted to comfort me with the promise of a special surprise for that occasion. What it was he would not even hint—nor did Mother.

Early one day in April—before I was even awake—he left, claiming business that took him to Bologna. With only ten days until my birthday I could not believe that he would fail to return in time to celebrate with me. Every day I kept watch for sign of his arrival. One by one the days passed until finally, on the last, I watched downheartedly as the shadows lengthened and the tantalizing aromas coming from the kitchen signaled that it was nearly time for the celebratory meal to begin. Still no sign of Father!

Mother, in her thoughtful way, was preparing my favorite things, trying to lift my spirits with the promise of a banquet worthy of the troubadour I fancied myself to be. On the table stood an open bottle of Father's prized Rosso Conero, with which to wash down her famous *stocafisso*, my favorite dish of cod and roasted potatoes. Closing my eyes now, I can almost still smell the aroma of sausage, lentils, and glazed onions, as it mingled with the fragrance of saffron risotto and spicy stewed figs. There were delicate honey cakes with citron as well and, since this birthday marked an important turning point in my young life, I would be permitted to share with the adults in the mulled wine after dinner. Although I feigned enthusiasm over the feast that Mother so lovingly prepared, I truly was grateful.

Soon the guests began to arrive. I remember it well; first my godparents, Giulio and Lucia Ferretti, who smothered me with their embraces and usual chatter about how tall I had grown. Then came my grandmother, Nonna Teresa Castrucci. I loved her dearly but unfortunately my fussy maiden aunt, Luisa, always followed close behind like an unwanted appendage. *Zia* Luisa spoiled many a family gathering with her endless critical commentary upon everything and everyone in sight. Fortunately, before she could spread her gloom, my cousin Pippo arrived with his beautiful new wife, Bianca, and all attention was focused upon her.

Just as it appeared that the feast would proceed without Father, there was the unmistakable clatter of horses coming at a gallop, excited voices in the stable, and the sound of Father rushing up the stairs—still able to take two at a time like a young squire. He had ridden hard to get here on time and, though his boots were dusty and his tunic wet with perspiration, to my eager eyes he was a vision. After many embraces, proper greetings, and a hasty ablution he directed us all to sit before the fire for a moment before dinner. He beckoned to his stable boy who carried into the room a large box which Father placed on my lap. He ordered me to open the mysterious parcel, but I was so overcome with excitement and curiosity that my poor fingers fumbled with the fastenings and Mother had to help me.

Under the parchment wrappings was a beautiful wooden case, surely fine enough to contain the dowry of a young princess, I thought. The shiny brass closure yielded easily to my touch and a whole new wondrous world opened to me as I beheld there, in velvet wrappings, what seemed to me must surely be the most beautiful lute in all the world.

Father had gone all the way to Bologna to the workshop of the famous Laux Moler who produced fine instruments known for their slender design. Their size, he believed, was perfect for a young girl to play. Cautiously I lifted the instrument out of its case and ran my fingers gently over its sleek, glossy ribs of polished wood—reddish-gold maple alternated with strips of white ash—joined in seams as smooth as silk. I touched the rosewood pegs, glided my hand over the gracefully carved rose on the belly of the instrument and only then tentatively plucked the strings. It spoke— the instrument spoke! As the rich sound resonated throughout the room, I felt as if the vibrations came from deep within my own body. I dared to play a chord that seemed to linger in the air like a fine fragrance. I announced that if truly I must go away to the convent school to become a lady and a scholar, then my precious lute would go with me as my constant companion, and pledge of my parents' love and devotion.

Finally the dreaded day of departure arrived. As with all significant events in the Beltramonto family, God's blessing on this new endeavor had to be sought. So early in the morning on the eighth day of May, Father, Mother and I set off for the church of Santa Maria della Piazza, just past the Loggia dei Mercanti where Father so often conducted business. Accompanied by my grand-parents, friends, and a few neighbors, we sought the benediction of wise old *Padre* Barnaba who, sensing my apprehension, placed his hands gently on my head in a blessing that seemed to allay the feelings of my parents as well.

More than mere nostalgia drew our little society to this place. My parents were married here, and at its font I was baptized. As a child I often stood at the doors of the church, fascinated by the wonderful carvings that adorn the portal—especially the fig-ure of the knight on horseback and the minstrel with some musi-cal instrument that I could not identify. They had long ago joined the cast of characters that peopled the battlements of my dream castle.

The concluding blessing of the Mass signaled the moment for friends to depart as Father, Mother, and I began the steep climb to San Salvatore. On this spring morning of 1534, I left my home for the first time.

The convent in which the school was located was a nonde-script building on slopes just beneath the cathedral of San Ciriaco. I had passed here often in processions on feast days, paying no particular attention to it then. But now the uninviting gray exterior loomed like a fortress and the thick walls, pierced by only a few narrow windows, terrified me. I can still hear the tired grating sound as Father pushed open the ancient iron gate and reached for the bell cord. The portress appeared out of nowhere followed almost immediately by Suor Margherita, the *madre superiore* of the convent. She was an ample woman who looked as though she would be more at home in the kitchen with her hands in a mound of dough than seated on a throne with a crosier in hand, a mastiff at her feet.

At the thought of feet I suddenly felt self-conscious in my fine soft leather boots, and the hood on my stiff new green mantle rubbed uncomfortably where the skin on my neck still smarted from Mother's vigorous scrubbing that morning. I must have been a pitiful sight standing there frozen, clutching the case that held my precious lute.

Madre Margherita's warm voice broke the awkward silence. "Welcome, Prudenza: welcome to San Salvatore. It will be your new home for a time. I hope you will be happy here."

This was my cue to respond with the words Mother had prepared for me. Self-consciously I answered in a voice I hardly recognized myself as I mechanically parroted the speech accompanied by a much-practiced but awkward curtsy. "Venerable Madre Margherita, I thank you for your warm welcome and I promise to apply myself to my studies and to cause you no trouble."

Sensing my discomfort she placed her hand on my shoulder and quickly guided me into the large room where it was customary that a new student be introduced to her classmates. Outside in the convent garden, birds were chirping and wisteria hung languidly from the walls, giving off a wonderful fragrance that attracted swarms of bees; but inside the room felt cold and damp. Even through my fine shoes I could feel the numbing cold of the stone floor.

As the girls filed in, Madre Margherita reeled off their names; Ginevra, Beatrice, Coletta, Lucia, Gianetta, Arianna, and on. I attempted to smile but my head spun. I could think of one thing only, that Mother and Father must leave shortly, for it would soon be growing dark. Mercifully, Madre Margherita was well practiced in the art of shortened farewells, for she had presided over many such separations. A few quick embraces, tears, and once again the grating sound of the iron gate, and I was left clutching my lute like a life preserver. At that moment I decided to give her a name, *"Fedele."* I would call my lute, *"amica Fedele,"* my faithful friend.

The gate was hardly closed when the bell for Vespers rang and I heard the sound of felt-shod feet shuffling over the same stone floors that I found so cold even through my thick leather soles. From their white veils I could tell it was a procession of novices. They were on their way to Vespers.

Madre Margherita summoned one of the other students whose name I could not remember. She was a small girl with dark-brown eyes and a smile so welcoming that it seemed to warm even my chilled body. Her name was Coletta. She would in time become my best friend—my guardian angel, as Madre Margherita called her. But more immediately she would guide me through a confusing maze of corridors as well as the equally labyrinthine rules and customs of the school. Perhaps most important of all, it was her responsibility to introduce me to my tutors.

Coletta could not have been much older than I; but she had, I sensed, wisdom beyond her years. She had already learned the art of the *erborista,* and was skilled in the knowledge of the properties of herbs and spices. I soon discovered that she could create herbal remedies, unguents, essences, and elixirs for the treatment of any number of illnesses and humors. She learned this from her father who was a *speziale*—much as I had learned something (though far too little) of my father's trade. I felt an immediate bond with Coletta who, sensing my fear, at once took my hand and said with infectious enthusiasm, "Prudenza, do not be afraid. We were all frightened at first, but you will soon learn to love this place. And if you wish, I will share with you my garden. I tend it and I harvest the herbs, too, and if you like I will teach you the secrets of these wonderfully healing plants. One day you too will be able to prepare elixirs and ointments if you wish. You will see."

I felt obliged to reciprocate and impetuously promised the only thing I had to give: "I will teach you music!"

However, my services in that regard were not needed, for, as she explained, "We have a wonderful music teacher here, Prudenza. He is *Fra* Tommaso, a friar who comes regularly to instruct the novices in plainsong and teach them catechism."

Seeing my disappointment, she was quick to add, "He also teaches us music of a more secular nature, and he tutors us in language and literature."

She went on to extol his virtues. "They say he studied in Paris, and that he makes frequent visits to Florence, his hometown, where—so it is said—there are still venerable old men who once sat at the feet of the great scholars of that city in the days of Lorenzo the Magnificent."

This conversation did little to boost my waning self-confidence. With a sinking feeling I realized that, other than my fantasies, I really had nothing else to offer my new friend. Perhaps Mother was right about my dreaming. Fortunately, the bell for supper interrupted my ruminations on that sobering thought.

Coletta ushered me down a long dark corridor, past the novices' refectory where, from the corner of my eye, I saw young nuns seated on benches along the walls, eating with downcast eyes while someone read aloud at a high lectern. I had no taste for such austerity and breathed more freely when we had safely passed that door and entered the dining hall of the students. Here decorously modulated chatter was broken occasionally by girlish giggles that raised the eyebrow of the dour-looking mistress at a table on a dais in the front of the room. This was Suor Rufina, the disciplinarian—with whom I would have many an occasion to become acquainted. Her duty was to maintain the strict decorum of the school and, judging from her solemn demeanor, she took it very seriously. I soon learned that the goal of San Salvatore was to educate young girls from good families that could afford such schooling. Here they became cultivated ladies, knowledgeable not only in domestic skills but also comfortable in the fine art of conversation and manners that—along with a substantial dowry from their wealthy fathers—insured a good marriage. This was the first time I realized that I was from a privileged class.

My first meal in the convent was nothing like my mother's cooking, so I was grateful when it was over and Coletta showed me to my assigned little room. Here I collapsed, still fully clothed—my precious lute on the bed at my side, and soon drifted off.

—◆—

My first full day at San Salvatore began badly. In my exhaustion I had not heard the rising bell and, thanks to Coletta, just narrowly escaped being late for my first lesson.

"Come, hurry, Prudenza" she said, pressing into my hand a bread roll—for I had missed breakfast. "Eat this quickly or we will be late and *Fra* Tommaso is impatient with tardiness. You don't want to start out badly."

I choked down the bread, which was difficult without something to drink, smoothed my hair and attempted to straighten my dress, which was hopelessly wrinkled from having been slept in. Before I knew it Coletta guided me into a small room with a large desk behind which sat a sober-faced, surprisingly young man who greeted us rather formally.

Was this *Fra* Tommaso? From Coletta's description I pictured him to be an older man, with the look of a venerable scholar whose stooped shoulders betrayed a lifetime bent over musty old tomes in some monastic library. Instead, here was someone far too young to have achieved all the knowledge and wisdom Coletta had extolled—and, in my opinion, too young to possess such a stern countenance. I would have preferred a fatherly sort with a comforting smile. As I studied the figure before me, I could not help noticing that the whiteness of his Dominican habit only served to emphasize all the more his olive skin and the abundant black hair that framed his face. Moreover, I had the disquieting feeling that his jet-like eyes were looking right through me.

I shuffled my feet nervously, conscious of my wrinkled

clothes—for which Mother would have scolded me soundly—and struggled for something to say to cover my embarrassment. The awkward conversation that followed is forever engraved upon my memory.

Coletta came to the rescue as she would so many times in the future. "*Fra* Tommaso, this is Prudenza Beltramonto who will be joining your rhetoric class."

My fear and embarrassment momentarily vanished at the sound of the voice that I heard next. It was like music. "Beltramonto, *Bel-tra-mon-to*," he repeated slowly, drawing out each syllable. "What a beautiful poetic name. Tell me, Prudenza; do you like poetry?"

Still savoring the music of my own name as he pronounced it, I did not answer at once. With a nudge from Coletta I was jarred into consciousness and heard him repeat, "Do you like poetry, *Signorina* Beltramonto?"

I did not know what to say, for the only poems I knew were the childish rhymes I created to sing for my father's pleasure. I managed to stammer, "Yes, yes, Father," desperately hoping that he would not ask me to recite some.

Instead he continued his interrogation. "And what else do you know, Prudenza? Have you studied Latin?"

"Yes," I blurted out. Here, God forgive me, I stretched the truth considerably and, calling on my recollection of the Latin I knew from the Mass, I quickly illustrated with the first thing that came into my head. "*Ad Deum qui laetificat juventutem meam.*" A poor choice, I immediately recognized—speaking of "God who gives joy to my youth," for there was little joy in my young heart at this moment. Fleeing to what I thought would be safer ground I quickly offered, "I know something of the properties of colors, dyes, and the places from which they come…"

But his direct counter thwarted my hasty attempt at escape. "What literature do you read?"

"Read?" I stammered, stalling for time, "Well, sometimes in the evening Father helps me, and we read the holy scriptures together." There, I thought, that should impress him! But I quickly realized that this ploy had not satisfied either. This was becoming a contest—thrust and parry—only I was a defenseless peasant in combat with a well-armed knight.

I fled to my last resort. "I am good at numbers," I announced confidently. Father had taught me how to figure weights and measures and even sometimes to compute sums for the tax on his dyes. Clearly the friar remained unimpressed. At last I remembered my lute. Of course, why had I not thought of it sooner? I stiffened my spine resolutely and, with the desperation of one who knows she is about to expend her last currency, proudly declared, "I am a musician. I compose, I sing, and I play the lute."

At that I saw his face break into a warm smile and I knew I had at last reached safer ground. All was not lost—not yet at least. Perhaps this common interest salvaged my interview with my tutor.

"Good," he said. "Tomorrow we will begin to read." And after a moment added, "Bring your lute." I could hardly wait to show off my *amica Fedele*.

My classroom experience the following day was more successful. At least it began so. With my lute as my prop, and my appearance much improved since yesterday, I felt confident. A cheerier *Fra* Tommaso greeted me. "*Buon giorno, Signorina* Beltramonto. Today we are going to enter upon a new adventure—the world of literature, reading that opens the mind to a whole universe. Are you ready?"

A whole new universe! He has an imagination, I thought. Perhaps he was a dreamer, too, when he was my age. With a burst of self-confidence I began to remove my lute from its case, but he interrupted my movement. "Not yet!" he said, "First we must begin our language lesson. Music is language, yes—but words are music, too, you know. Now, in your own words, tell me something about yourself, your family, your life."

Was this a trap? I asked myself. What could I possibly tell him? That I spent too much time daydreaming? He would surely think that I am a dolt. I began tentatively. "I live with my mother and father near the seashore, not far from the church of Maria della Piazza"

Though the history of my thirteen years was indeed brief,

my progress in the telling of it was slow and laborious for, at every turn, he corrected my pronunciation or some point of grammar. With every sentence my already fragile self-confidence slipped another cog and I soon learned that we Anconetane have some peculiarities in our pronunciation.

"No, Prudenza! Not *zempre. Sempre,*" he said, making what I thought to be a truly ugly hissing sound on the "s." "And, yes, the sea is beautiful, *Il mare è bello. Bello, not belo.* Say *bello*!" He demonstrated, his tongue high behind his front teeth, exaggerating the length of the double *ll* to make his point. And so it went. Every word of dialect that I used was swiftly corrected. But what else could I expect from a native Florentine, so proud are they of the purity of the classical Tuscan language.

The litany of corrections went on until finally I burst into tears. As I look back now, I am sure that he took no pleasure in correcting me; after all, it was his job to teach me. His efforts to console me were so awkward that I almost felt sorrier for him than for myself.

"Do not be discouraged, Prudenza. You will learn quickly and when you do you will delight in the music of our beautiful language, for it truly is music." Staring off into space as if addressing some unknown presence, he mused aloud, "A long time ago, in Florence there was born something called the *dolce stil nuovo*, the sweet new style. He launched into a monologue praising great men whose names I had never before heard—Cavalcanti and Dante—who, he later explained, developed this sweet new style of writing.

I detected warmth in his demeanor. Although I did not really comprehend what these words, *dolce stil nuovo*, meant, I had to admit that when he said them, they truly did sound like music. Apparently they moved him, too, for after a long pause—as if suddenly remembering my presence—he added excitedly, "You must taste of the beauty of this poetry, Prudenza, and you will, for I will teach you to. In the meantime, enough of language for today. Let us see your lute."

As I opened the case, his expression changed. I believe he was surprised and, for the first time in the two days since I met him, I felt that I had a slight advantage. *Fedele* truly was proving to be my faithful friend.

He bade me play, which I did with some confidence, even surprising myself. I had learned to play solely by ear; so when he placed music before me I could not read it. He explained to me this strange system of writing music that he called tablature, and he proceeded to play and sing for me a beautiful *canzona*. By the time the bell for *pranzo* rang, my tears were long dried, and I was thrilled when he announced that besides language lessons he would instruct me in the finer points of the lute.

When I returned to my room I studied the scene from my window and was delighted to find that I had a panoramic view of the sea. This was a real turning point in my experience at San Salvatore. I could now say for the first time in days, "I am truly happy."

CHAPTER 2

The Friar, 1535

Three summers and two winters passed. I was two years older now and, like the changes in the sea, sky, and colors of the foliage that mark the passing seasons, my confidence—and my body—had changed. I had grown: I was becoming a young woman. Father and Mother noted these changes in me with satisfaction, too, as they visited me regularly. I was able to send home from time to time examples of my poetry and songs—now more polished. And true to her promise at our first meeting, Coletta unlocked for me the secrets of the many herbs in her garden. She was a good tutor and I soon learned the mysterious workings of such medicinal plants as laudanum, valeriana, pennyroyal, and bella donna. Under Coletta's supervision I even ventured to prepare an elixir to soothe the headaches from which Mother sometimes suffered.

Madre Margherita seemed pleased with my progress, and reported to my parents my improved decorum. Most of all I was thrilled with my progress in music. I had mastered that strange tablature and could with ease now play more difficult compositions. *Fra* Tommaso reported to Madre Margherita the progress I made with my language study and in literature—though I suspect she would not have approved of my reading Dante. I know Suor Rufina did not, for I had to hide my Dante under a pillow when she was around. Scripture and the lives of the saints, in her opinion, were the literature with which the young ladies at San Salvatore should nourish their minds.

Nonetheless, *Fra* Tommaso continued to expound the *dolce*

stil nuovo, which I slowly began to understand and appreciate. I believe it may have been my eagerness to learn that prompted him to give so generously of his time. With his help I was soon able to read Dante's *Vita Nuova* where I was introduced to Beatrice, who inspired the poems. Although he met her only twice, Dante adored her from afar and somehow this appealed greatly to the dreamer in me, which not even the strict training of San Salvatore managed to quell. I had simply become skilled in concealing it when prudent to do so. So it was a great day when *Fra* Tommaso gave me my very own copy of the *Divina Commedia.* He even encouraged me to begin to write in the peculiar rhyme scheme that Dante used. He called it *terza rima.* Interlocking rhymes connected the tercets, short stanzas of three verses that formed a kind of poetic chain.

Though I had often made simple rhymes for my father I was timid about attempting this for *Fra* Tommaso; but, like the good pedagogue that he was, he eased my fear by making a game of it. He called out a word and I was to answer immediately with two rhyming words. In the beginning they were easy. He said, *certo.*

It was not difficult to come up with *aperto,* and then *sofferto.* Then came *passo,* and I shot back, *grasso,* and after a moment's pause, *lasso.* That was too easy. I was quick to learn and he admired that. Soon he allowed me to call out the first word to challenge him. He responded with the second, and I completed with the third. The words became more and more difficult and he hurled them at me faster and faster. *Sciocchezze, aprezza, grandezza.* This was fun and we laughed as we made a game of it. Finally one day he declared it time for me to begin writing little poems with this type of rhyme. My first attempts were self-conscious and clumsy, but in time I began to manifest some modest literary talent. Even *Fra* Tommaso thought so.

By the third spring at San Salvatore he had guided me—as Virgil did Dante, I fantasized—as far as the second circle of the *Inferno.* Here I made the acquaintance of those whom Suor Rufina would certainly have regarded as most unsavory companions for a young lady of San Salvatore—the carnal sinners, gluttons, and misers. It was spring when I first met those ill-fated lovers, Paolo and Francesca.

I was seated on a bench in the garden reading Dante—my embroidery basket close at hand in case Suor Rufina should make her customary snooping rounds. Once again the bees swarmed around the clusters of purple wisteria that looked so like rich bunches of ripe grapes, and their buzzing created a comfortable background to my reading. I had grown to appreciate the tranquilizing effect of their humming, and over these two years the garden had become my retreat, a sanctuary where I could be alone with my thoughts. The day was lovely and I was lost in the story of Paolo and Francesca when I was interrupted by Coletta's hasty entrance. There was a sense of urgency in her voice. "Prudenza, Madre Margherita wishes to see you at once in her office. Hurry."

What was it? I asked myself, suddenly fearful that Suor Rufina may have reported some misconduct of mine. Collecting my embroidery basket I quickly slipped my volume of Dante under the linens that I was preparing as a surprise for Madre Margherita's nameday and went hurriedly to her office. To my surprise, I found Father with her. My heart leapt—partly with joy at seeing him—but just as quickly with fear that bad news brought him. His embrace was comforting but he offered no explanation, saying simply, "Prudenza, my dear, go and fetch your things for you must come home with me now. Do hurry."

Why? I asked myself and wanted to ask him as well—though I knew it not proper to question him; especially before Madre Margherita who offered no explanation either. Was Mother ill? Was something wrong at home? Had I committed some unforgivable infraction of the rule? I turned to Madre Margherita and dared to ask, "Am I being dismissed?"

"No, Prudenza, your father will explain."

But he did not. Instead he simply reiterated, "Please collect your things, Prudenza, since we must reach home before dark or Mother will be worried."

There was no time for farewells and in truth, I thought, I did not know what to say anyway, for I could not imagine why I was so abruptly being taken from this place I had grown to love as a second home, and where I had made so many friends. One person only, Suor Rufina, hinted at the possible reason—though I did not comprehend it at the time. As I passed her in the corridor on the way to my room she swept by me in her usual imperious manner, sniffing the air like a hound after the quarry, and muttered something about "money, business failing."

As always, Coletta was there for me. Since my first day at San Salvatore she appeared at those moments when I most needed her. She was like the sister I never had, and the thought of leaving her now was almost unbearable. Through our tears we gathered together my belongings and met Father standing near his coach. Madre Margherita spoke with him in a hushed voice and I could catch only an occasional word. It was difficult to say farewell to her, too. She had been unfailingly kind and understanding since that first day when I was so awkward and fearful. She never ceased to encourage me when I became homesick, or discouraged in my studies.

Most of all, I was heartbroken at the thought of leaving without saying goodbye to *Fra* Tommaso—and with no explanation. But how could I explain? I did not understand it myself so I determined I would write to him after I returned home and learned the reason for this hasty leave-taking.

Only after we were alone in the coach rumbling along noisily over the cobblestones did Father attempt to explain. Now that I am a parent I can appreciate how deeply it must have pained him as he confessed to me that he could no longer afford the high cost of educating me in the convent school. He alluded to some problem with business, but could explain no further. I would have to wait for that. For now he said only, "I'm very sorry, Prudenza. I am so sorry."

Clearly he was deeply distressed. I had never before seen my father in this state of anxiety. I was overwhelmed with a profound sense of love and respect for him. Alfonso Beltramonto should never need to speak so apologetically to his daughter. I loved him so, and in that moment of compassion I vowed never to do anything to displease or offend my dearest father. To conceal my own disappointment so as not to increase his feeling of failure, I attempted to smile and boldly offered, "But Babbo, think of it; it is nearly time for me to leave the security of San Salvatore anyway and find my place in the world. You yourself have said that in these two years since I have been gone, you have seen your little girl become a young woman." I nearly choked at the last words that came from my lips, "and...and it is perhaps time to think of making a good marriage." Of this he said nothing.

In the rarified shelter of the cloister I had given little consideration to marriage, though I assumed that someday I would be someone's wife; perhaps someone Father selected. Of one thing I was certain. He would be a man of whom Father approved—a good man, like himself. I comforted myself with the assurance that it was not yet time for such thoughts. Marriage lay somewhere in the future.

I had never been around boys of my own age and the only other male that I knew was *Fra* Tommaso for whom I felt great respect and admiration. But I recognized that there was growing within me a deep affection for him that caused confusion in my adolescent heart. These were troubling emotions that I could not understand or share with anyone except Coletta who, in her youthful but unfailing common sense, helped me to see that it was simply a case of adolescent hero worship. *Fra* Tommaso was a brilliant tutor, and I was just a student awed by his learning.

Despite my insecurities and the rocky beginning of our association he had invested a great deal of effort in my development and showed much satisfaction in my rapid progress. With the utmost sensitivity, he had gained my confidence; and I found it possible not only to be comfortable in his presence, but in turn to trust him completely.

Mother was waiting for us with a fine warm dinner, happy to have her daughter back, but there were no attempts at explanation that evening. I went to my room no more enlightened than before. However, I learned the reasons for this precipitous action as, little by little, my own observations served to piece together the missing bits of this puzzle.

I had always thought Father was somehow invincible, secure in the business for which he earned such renown. I noticed, however, that he made no trips to the *dogana* in the days after I returned. He spent many hours at his desk bent over ledgers, endlessly writing official-looking papers that he sealed with wax and passed to a courier to be dispatched. When I asked the reason for this departure from his usual routine, he dismissed it saying,

"There has been some trouble in obtaining the ingredients for my colors, Prudenza. Nothing more."

I knew enough not to probe.

I realize now how difficult it must have been for him to talk about it, for clearly he considered himself a failure. In the meantime, however, I was waging a battle of my own. Despite my efforts to conceal my emotions I felt a growing resentment over the disruption of my own life and, above all, the failure of my parents to communicate the reasons for this action. I found some comfort in long hours spent reading and quietly playing my lute in my room so as not to disturb Father at work in his study. But despite my best intentions, disappointment and resentment increasingly gave way to frustration and I found myself sometimes on the verge of hysteria, weeping uncontrollably.

Textile merchants often came to our home to meet with Father. On these occasions I had a responsibility as hostess while Mother provided delicacies from her kitchen. I knew the routine well. Father summoned me to bring refreshments for his guests— which at first I rather enjoyed. After a time I came to recognize some of these men who came regularly but this day three unfamiliar, grim-faced men appeared at our door. I could not help noting that their unexpected arrival seemed upsetting to Father.

My duty was to remain nearby in case Father required anything, perhaps parchment and pens for contracts. From my little alcove around the corner I could not help but hear bits of the conversation that ensued. Sometimes it began loudly enough for me to catch a word or two. Credit...interest...default...The voices faded and the remainder became completely inaudible. There were words I did not understand...liens...confiscation...and suddenly dead silence. At that moment I reached the chilling realization that these men were creditors from whom Father had borrowed money. I winced to think it must have been the expense of keeping me in a fine school that brought him to such a predicament. And now the creditors had come to collect. In an instant all my resentment dissolved into guilt.

Father's quiet hours at his desk began to multiply and I noticed that certain objects—family heirlooms most of them—began to disappear, I suspected rightly, to the pawnshop in Via Ciriaco. It was a tense time. I missed my friends at San Salvatore, but I was no longer a child. I sensed a growing responsibility to help my parents—just how I was not sure. But as I contemplated this I spent more and more time with *Fedele* and, as always, found solace in my music and the poetry I had come to love. God bless *Fra* Tommaso for introducing me to these sources of strength. How I longed to seek his counsel now!

Only a few days later another stranger appeared. He introduced himself as Matteo Cecchi, a silk merchant from Florence, though I would not have suspected it from his speech, which lacked the elegance of *Fra* Tommaso's.

When they were seated, Father as usual called for me to bring refreshments. On cue I fetched Mother's best silver ewer and, with all the propriety that I learned at San Salvatore, I began to fill their goblets with some of Father's diminishing supply of fine wine and to pass the gilded salver with an array of Mother's delicate sweetmeats. I had been taught well at San Salvatore and, as I moved to do the honors for Father, I was aware also that Father must be grateful for having given me those two precious years at school. Thank God, too, for Mother's determination to keep from the pawnbroker these last few silver pieces that were wedding presents.

Despite my self-assurance as I moved about fulfilling my serving obligations I felt a peculiar, indefinable discomfort with this particular stranger. Although I tried to keep my eyes modestly downcast as I was taught to do, I could not help noticing his penetrating black eyes assessing my every move, making me feel somehow like a brood mare at auction.

At San Salvatore young women were taught that grooming and deportment were the currency of womanhood, but that vanity was to be avoided for it led to the sin of pride. Certainly no one in the convent ever suggested that I was beautiful. I was aware of people's comments about the color of my eyes—like the sea they said—and my auburn hair. It had long been noted that Anconetane women were known for the whiteness of their skin—like alabaster it was often described. I did not think of myself as beautiful— perhaps blessed with unusual coloring—but that was an accident of birth. I had always perceived myself as rather plain of feature. Of one thing I was becoming ever more aware: My training at San Salvatore taught me that true beauty is in character. The maturity with which I faced the situation at home was a test of that.

I was relieved to absent myself when my services were completed, but I remained nearby as Father had instructed me to do. Their conversation was brief and their voices remained so low that I was unable to hear much of their exchange. Soon Father escorted him to the gate and as he departed I heard the stranger say something about returning in July for an answer—something about a proposal, a plan. It was clear to me from the bits I heard, the matter concerned the business of purchasing dyes—but that was not unusual. Why, then, did I feel so apprehensive? Father must have sensed my concern, and at last felt compelled to explain to me the gravity of our situation. Taking me by the hand he said, "Come, Prudenza, it is time we must talk."

Father's study had always been sacrosanct, so when he led me there and instructed me to sit in the large leather chair normally reserved for his clients, I realized that at last I was about to learn the cause of the upheaval in our lives.

There was a chill in the air and I watched impatiently as with slow and deliberate movements Father proceeded to add wood to the fire and light the candles on his desk. The sun was beginning to set over the bay by now and was casting long shadows on the tile floor. Finally he seated himself in the chair behind the great mahogany desk that reflected the flickering flame of the candles on its glossy surface. I realized that I was about to learn not only the nature of this family crisis, but even more importantly, the story of my Beltramonto ancestry.

Father had never before spoken of his family's involvement in the silk industry. But why would he? I was a girl and it was customary for the male members of a family to inherit the business and carry on the tradition. Since I had no brothers I wondered at the meaning of it all. He began, "The Beltramonto family has not always lived in Ancona, Prudenza. It was your grandfather, Luca, who established the business here that I inherited at his death. Since I have no son it may one day go to your husband."

Marriage and inheritance were the farthest things from my mind at this time, but I was eager to learn about my forebears on Father's side of the family. I urged him to go on. "Please, Babbo, tell me about them."

"The Beltramontos lived in Recanata just southwest of Ancona."

"I have heard of that town."

"Your grandmother, Costanza Torresi, lived in San Severino where there was at one time a thriving silk market. Luca frequently went there to do business for his family, for they were growers of the *gelso*—the mulberry trees that provide food for the silkworms and are so important to the production of raw silk."

"But, that was many years ago. What has that to do..."

He interrupted me, explaining the nature of the silk industry—sericulture—he called it. "It is a lucrative business, but a fragile one that depends greatly upon circumstances and events often beyond human control; the weather, the availability of mulberry branches, the quality of the local water, the health of the silkworms and, above all, the skillful drawing out of the filament."

I knew nothing of this and, pleased with the fact that Father was speaking to me as an adult, I was all the more eager to hear his story. He continued, "The majority of cultivators were women. Your grandmother, Costanza—my dear mother—was exceptionally skilled in the preparation of the raw silk."

"What was she like, Babbo? I wish I had known her. What was your mother like?"

"She was a very brave woman who actually lived in some danger."

"How is that?"

"Because the silk industry was a source of such great wealth, the secrets of successful cultivation were jealously guarded. So serious was it that a woman engaged in this work—like your grandmother—could never leave the town or marry anyone from outside the city, under pain of the *rogo*, the stake. A heavy fine was levied upon anyone who revealed these secrets or who sold mulberry branches outside the city."

"I don't understand, Babbo. If she could not leave the city how is it then that the family came to Ancona?"

"That is a wonderful story, Prudenza, a kind of fairytale romance. On his business trips to San Severino, Luca usually stayed with the Torresi family and, in time, he lost his heart to Costanza who was not only very intelligent and kind but was also exceptionally beautiful."

"But I thought she could not marry a foreigner!"

"That's right. But their love for each other was so great that they did a very dangerous thing; they planned an escape."

"They eloped?"

"You could call it that."

"How?"

"They waited until the dark of the moon. On a night when the cloud cover was especially dense Luca left town, his wagon loaded with produce to take back to Recanati, but hidden under the turnips and cabbages was Costanza. When they reached the River Potenza he paddled as far as Porto Recanati where friends were waiting with a fishing boat that carried them to Ancona where they were safe, and they were free. Luca began to work on the wharves there and in time became a customs officer. A short while later they were married—in the same church where you were baptized."

"What a romantic story, Babbo. But that is all about silk. Tell me how it is that you came to be in the dye business?"

"Ancona had at one time a thriving silk industry, but as you can see from what I have told you, it would have been very dangerous for your grandmother to practice her art here. Through his work at the *dogana,* Luca came to realize the potential of the business of importing—especially importing luxury goods. There was a heavy duty on them, yes, but there was also the possibility of considerable wealth. With Costanza's understanding and experience in the production of silk and Luca's familiarity with the complexities of international trade, they combined their knowledge and began a business. It was modest in the beginning, importing just a few dyes—mostly from Egypt and India. But the exceptional quality of their dyes soon attracted a wider clientele and Luca was able to increase the size of his import business to include colors from Greece, Turkey, Syria, and the East Indies; and their products came to be known simply as the Beltramonto colors."

He had never told me much about the process of dying textiles. Perhaps he meant to keep it secret, so I decided not to ask. Almost as if he had read my mind he began to explain. "To make the dye penetrate the fabric and hold without fading or running it needs something we call a mordant, a fixative. What we use is alum."

"Yes, I remember seeing it in your *bottega*."

"The secret of the Beltramonto colors is in the superior quality of our alum. In your great grandfather's time, rich deposits of alum were found in Tolfa, which belonged to the Holy See, and made the Papal States very wealthy—the richest province of Italy because it established a monopoly. To avoid the high tax levied upon it, much alum began to be imported from Spain, but the long voyage and the dangers of Barbary pirates in the Mediterranean eventually made that impossible. However, through your grandfather's work at the customs office he met merchants from the East who had knowledge of the purest sources of alum in that part of the world. Luca began traffic with the East and his reputation quickly spread abroad."

"And this is where you come into the story, Babbo?"

"Yes. When your grandfather died in 1510, I inherited the business. I had apprenticed with Father and learned a great deal from Mother, too; so, already as a young man I understood the industry very well."

After a pause, he continued. "Your mother and I married in 1514, but it was a long time until God blessed us with you, Prudenza. Only after your mother made a pilgrimage to the holy house of Loreto and begged the Virgin for a child did you come into our lives. So, you see, my dear, you are the answer to our prayers—a blessed child—our miracle child."

I was deeply moved, for I had heard nothing of this story before. As I sat absorbing these last words I was unable to speak.

Father went on slowly. "Of late, Prudenza, there have been problems. Between the cost of the long voyages of ships that must come from Livorno or Genoa, and the danger from piracy, that venue has become impractical for us. Routes from the Levant are shorter, but just now there is trouble from Venice, which looks upon the Adriatic as 'her gulf' and has decreed that all goods that enter the Adriatic must first call at Venice. As a result our supply of alum has been greatly affected. There is still a demand for Beltramonto dyes but, without quality alum, I must not sell my colors. I simply will not jeopardize the quality of our dyes or the good name of our enterprise by using inferior or diluted fixative. So that is why our income has decreased significantly. We have had to release some of the servants so your mother needs help here. It grieves me that you have had to give up so much to help us, my dear."

By the time Father finished his story, the fire was reduced to a few last glowing embers, and the candles on his desk guttered in their holders. I sat speechless with tears streaming down my cheeks, deeply ashamed that I had ever been angry or disappointed over leaving San Salvatore. I believe it was in that moment that I crossed into adulthood.

Without another word Father slowly extinguished the candles, kissed my forehead and, placing his arm about my waist, led me to my room. I detected a look of relief on his face such as I had not seen since I returned from San Salvatore. We said goodnight— nothing more—our silence cementing an unspoken but profoundly deepened relationship.

The next morning he appeared more relaxed as he, Mother, and I broke bread together. He began to speak, almost casually, about the stranger who came yesterday. Whoever he was, it was his visit that prompted Father to break his long silence. What was it about this Matteo Cecchi that caused Father at last to share his story with me?

CHAPTER 3

Florence, 1535

The sun was just rising over the hills to the east of the city and Zenobi Cecchi was already hard at work in his *bottega*, inspecting the account books his clerk checked just the day before. He had long since learned that figures could be tampered with, balances adjusted and funds cleverly siphoned from under the nose of an unwary employer. Not that he was suspicious, or parsimonious—just cautious—vigilant as a good Florentine merchant should be.

His habit was to rise early anyway and attend to business long before his workers arrived. This gave him some solitary peace before the pressing demands of the day. From where he sat he could see the Ponte alle Grazie and already hear the early morning commerce on the Arno with the raucous cries of the hucksters and fishwives hawking their wares.

It had been over a month now since he sent Matteo to Ancona to negotiate the purchase of dyes from his old friend Alfonso Beltramonto, and Zenobi was growing impatient to learn the results. The success of the deal was critical—indeed that was his motive for scrutinizing the accounts so attentively. His business was in trouble. The last dyes he received from his procurer in the north were inferior. The poor quality of the fixative used produced colors that were pale and streaked, and faded quickly in the sun. He was losing money and, if the situation were not rectified soon, the confidence of his patrons could be lost as well. He desperately needed the kind of deep rich colors that he used to purchase from his friend in Ancona. Surely Alfonso would come through for him now when he heard of his plight.

Over the years Zenobi had become a successful purveyor of silks and other luxury textiles, and was greatly respected both in Florence and abroad. But he was approaching sixty now; his eyesight was failing and he suffered the usual aches and pains that accompany aging. To complicate matters, his oldest son, Fabrizio—the responsible one—had shown no interest in the business and had instead entered the austere monastery of Vallombrosa whose rule of enclosure was so strict that monks might not go out even on an errand of mercy. It was up to Matteo now to carry on the business; but so far he had shown little aptitude for hard work.

While Matteo sought recognition and even praise for his slightest effort, he lacked responsibility and often dallied over long on the trips he made for his father. Besides, he was now thirty-three years old and showed no signs of being anxious to marry. That in itself was not unusual, for Zenobi was well aware that young Florentine men often remained single until their late thirties, or even forty, and continued to live at home. It was easier to take their pleasure with young boys and thus avoid the responsibilities of marriage and family.

Zenobi comforted himself, however, with the thought that Matteo never seemed to take any notice of the lissome bodies of the attractive young boys whose backs and shoulders glistened with sweat as they unloaded the heavy bales of fabric that came down from the north to be finished in Florence. He did wonder, however, if his son ever dallied in the whorehouses that abounded in Florence. He could not help remembering that the great Aneas Silvius Piccolomini had once called Florence "the city of whores."

Athough Zenobi never actually voiced these fears to his son, Matteo was well aware of his father's desire to see him settled in a good marriage, giving him grandsons and, above all, the security of knowing that the establishment he built so successfully would continue in the family. It is not that Matteo was without ambition; Zenobi knew his son aspired to be admitted one day to the powerful Silk Guild. As he pondered the thought, he began pacing the floor, turning over in his mind the possibility that this deal could not only resolve the problem of the dyes, but it might also be just the right opportunity for his son to prove himself worthy to take over the business.

The bells of the *duomo* were announcing the noonday Angelus just as Matteo reached the outskirts of the city. Knowing his father would be anxious, he wasted no time in changing out of his soiled travel costume but went straight to the *bottega* where he found Zenobi, as always, at his desk. There was no exchange of pleasantries—just business. Struggling to conceal his displeasure with Matteo's tardiness, Zenobi spoke first. "What is the news, son? Have you obtained the dyes, and how is my old friend Alfonso?"

"*Signore* Beltramonto is well, Father. He sends greetings— but no dyes—I am sorry to report."

Zenobi was visibly crestfallen. "How can that be? What has happened? We have always had such mutual trust. Is it that he cannot extend credit to us just now?"

"It is not that. He deeply regrets that he cannot meet our needs, Father. His supply of quality alum has been cut off by the increasing piracy in the Mediterranean so he can no longer obtain the fine quality mordants that have always given his colors such brilliance. He simply refuses to sell dyes that are of inferior quality."

"It is so like him—always a man of honor and scrupulous in his business. For this I cannot fault him, but I am at a loss as to how to solve our own problems. Without a quick solution we will lose the business of our valued buyers from France. The dyers of Rouen have already claimed much of the trade."

"There may be a way, Father. With your permission...may I make a suggestion?"

"By all means, speak up."

"What if we could obtain the alum for him?"

"How?"

Zenobi looked worn and weary, his eyes rheumy from long hours spent going over the account books in the dim light of a candle. He seemed puzzled by Matteo's words and a bit confused. But he had often found it difficult to read his son.

"All is not lost, Father. What we need is good alum."

"That is no revelation, Matteo. What we really need is a solution." Zenobi was losing patience with his son. This discussion was going nowhere. "Do you have a solution?"

"Yes. You may object at first, but hear me out. You know how you sometimes complain that I am gone too long when I attend to our business in Prato, Pistoia, Lucca, and other places. Well, one meets people along the way—interesting people on such occasions. Social exchanges in roadhouses, taverns, and inns, for example. I have made some acquaintances that might prove... well...useful."

"Are you saying what I think you are? What are you suggesting?"

"Surely you must be aware, Father, that there is a thriving commerce in contraband that bypasses Venice. Because Venice polices the sea with such efficiency, an overland route has developed, diverting goods as they come over the mountains from the north, before they reach Venice. With the cooperation of my contacts in the north we might be able to solve our problem."

Zenobi looked shocked. "You mean to say that you are consorting with brigands? This is illegal and immoral."

"No, not really...or not exactly! We would pay a fair price for the goods. Don't you see? With the alum I can obtain for Beltramonto, he can again give us the rich colors that made him famous. We can reclaim our losses, pay back our creditors and, at the same time, save your old friend's business." And though he did not say it, he was undoubtedly aware of what it could mean to him personally.

For what seemed an eternity, Zenobi sat motionless, in disbelief, turning over in his mind his son's proposition. He had to admit that the thought of solving three problems with one action was efficient, but it reeked of fraud and dishonesty. Slowly a flicker of a smile lighted his face as he thought of a tactical maneuver that could provide a way out of the dilemma. He would not have to be the one to say no to such an unsavory undertaking. Finally he broke the awkward silence. "Alfonso Beltramonto is a very honest man and I am sure that he would never agree to such corrupt dealings."

"Perhaps Beltramonto need not know the whole story.

Please let me try. When I left him I promised to return with a possible solution to his problem. He seemed encouraged but I could not reveal my plan to him without your permission, Father. Do please allow me to do this. You are always saying I need to prove myself and that it is time for me to assume responsibility for the enterprise."

"I do not like it, Son. It is dangerous and dishonest. We would be no better than the corsairs who roam the sea to rob and steal. The Cecchi family has a long-standing reputation for honesty and fair business dealings but…" After a long pause he drew a deep breath and added haltingly, "Perhaps God will forgive us if we can save the Cecchi business and at the same time help my old friend, Alfonso. See what you can do to negotiate with your—'friends'—but in God's name, let there be no bloodshed."

"Then as soon as I can make arrangements with my contacts I may return to Ancona?"

"Yes. Go with my blessing."

As Matteo turned to leave he paused and, looking back over his shoulder said, almost as an afterthought, "Beltramonto has a lovely daughter, Father!"

For a long time Zenobi sat rigid and still as death, his emotions running the gamut of confusion, anxiety, hope, and guilt. The reality that he had just consented to such blatant wrongdoing invaded his conscience with an overwhelming sense of shame and remorse. He had never been one to rationalize his behavior; but now he attempted to alleviate his guilt.

As he pondered Matteo's suggestion Zenobi reflected aloud, "Perhaps my own success as a silk merchant had more to do with luck—timing—and less with ability and hard work. Yes, perhaps I was just lucky, so how can I now deprive my son of this opportunity?"

Zenobi was just Matteo's age when, by God's grace, a Medici pope ascended the throne of Peter. He was Giovanni, son of Lorenzo the Magnificent, who took the name Leo X. For the elevation of a native son to this high office no expense was spared. Only a Florentine enterprise with the reputation of the House of Cecchi should be charged with the responsibility of clothing the new Pope and his court. It was Zenobi's good fortune to broker the purchase of endless bolts of the luxurious fabrics required for the Pope's regalia and that of his numerous attendants.

By the time the alum crisis threatened the Cecchi establishment it appeared that history might repeat itself. Once again the conclave was assembling in Rome to elect a new pope. Gossip grew from wirlwind proportions into a vortex of speculation that it might be another Medici. Hopes were high—in Florence especially—and nowhere more so than in the Cecchi *botegga*. The gossip proved right and Giulio, the bastard grandson of Lorenzo, became Clement VII.

Still, the new pope would need vestments and Zenobi hoped that Matteo might at least have procured a contract to provide these. But he had failed to do so—and failed also to find a wife and provide for his father some comfort and consolation in his old age. Zenobi shook his gray head and carefully closed the account books. As he snuffed out the candles the last curls of smoke ascended into the rafters and Zenobi shuffled slowly down the stairs muttering to himself, "*Dio mio!* Two failures! Two disappointments! Well, soon enough he will be off to Ancona again. Godspeed you, son of mine!"

CHAPTER 4

The Brigands

Matteo Cecchi did not often sing, but today he was up with the larks, humming lustily as he set about last minute preparations for this important trip. He had not been this happy in a long time. His father's acceptance of his plan—reluctant though it had been—was validation enough to raise his spirits as he spurred his horse onward past the lush vineyards of the Chianti country in the general direction of Arezzo. He knew the area well. At Pontessieve where the river Sieve flows into the Arno he planned to take the Passo della Consuma south to the Casentino district and on towards Poppi where there were contacts to be made, deals to be brokered before he could present his plan to Alfonso.

The task he was about to undertake was dangerous and complicated, and he was aware that this was only the beginning. But he was eager and ready. He chose the Pratomagno route above the east bank of the Arno despite the fact that it was hilly and progress would be slower than had he taken the Valdarno road. Perhaps it was some perverse impulse that directed him to do so, for the Pratomagno way would take him past the great Abbey of Vallombrosa where Fabrizio, his older, otherworldly brother, had chosen to live in silent monastic seclusion.

He had to admit that the view was breathtaking; but even the vast stretches of lush forest could not compensate for the luxury of his father's house, not to mention the pleasures of the flesh that Fabrizio had foolishly renounced only to live like a eunuch—wasted! Matteo shuddered at the mere thought of it and spurred his horse all the harder, eager to pass this holy place that made him so uncomfortable. Although he could not actually see the abbey hidden in the dense forest, he felt its austere presence like a weight on his chest that made his breath come in gasps. Was it possibly a twinge of conscience that caused this unwelcome reaction? No, he told himself, it was simply the air at this high elevation that made him lightheaded.

His horse was making good progress. He flaunted the tradition that men should ride stallions and chose instead his father's best chestnut mare for she was swift and sure-footed on the hills. Besides, she was beautiful, and it was important for him to make a good impression on Beltramonto and his daughter. Matteo had always been conscious of his image, aware that, with the fine clothes that his father's wealth provided, he could distract from what he was loath to admit were some imperfections in his looks. Thinking on that he shook his fist at the abbey and began to curse aloud, "Damn you, Fabrizio! Why did you have to be the one who is so tall and handsome? Why have you been blessed with such majestic bearing, a comely face, and a back straight as a reed, only to go bury yourself, to rot in a monastery? You fool. It isn't fair! And here I am, plain and swarthy—probably destined one day to be a *gobbo*, a hunchback. Ignorant, superstitious people will come and touch my ugly hump for good luck."

Matteo had of late noticed a slight curvature developing in his spine. Although he was able to conceal it by the way he wore his cloak, he imagined it to be much worse than it actually was. He quickly banished these unwelcome thoughts by conjuring up in their place a vision of the lovely face, the graceful body, and the lingering sweet fragrance of Beltramonto's modest daughter.

"By all that is holy I wager that the blush on her cheek did not come from a paint pot like that of the whores I have known in Florence. The skin of her long slender neck is like fine alabaster, and her softly rounded breasts were modestly covered." He had known plenty of other women but she was different. In his mind he relived her every move as she had waited on him and her father. It seemed to him that, although she possessed the polish and grace of a worldly lady brought up at court, there was an aura of innocence about her that radiated like a halo. It was curious. "Lustful thoughts had never before made me feel guilty. Why is this different? Is it because she seems so remote, so unattainable, that I want her?"

Such dreams helped to make the hours pass more quickly.

The mare was making good time, but she would soon need rest and water. As soon as he passed over the Pratomagno ridge and into the Casentino he planned to stop at the little village of Poppi. Here he would attempt to learn the whereabouts of his contact, a certain fellow known to him only as Lapo—the better to keep his identity secret, for this was risky business. He had never really met Lapo but knew from his reputation as the leader of the brigands, that he was the key to the success of this entire plan.

It had been many hours since the hearty breakfast his mother had prepared and Matteo was growing hungry. In her solicitude for her son, Maddalena stuffed his saddlebags with all sorts of provisions for the trip—bread, wine, cheeses, sausages, a change of clothing, and even some apples for the mare. He mused that his bulging saddlebags must make him look like a peddler, possibly a privateer for some city in the north.

"It is probably better that way. Except for my fine horse there is nothing to betray my station." Despite his envy of his brother's good looks, just this once he was grateful for his own unremarkable countenance. He could pass more or less unnoticed and hopefully avoid robbers who preyed on single horsemen, especially if they appeared too well dressed. He had deliberately chosen a simple riding costume and a plain, well-worn harness and saddle. No one would guess that buried deep under the food in his saddlebags was a small but precious gold goblet set with rubies, and a substantial cache of gold florins that he would need to grease Lapo's greedy palm.

Matteo was well aware that Arezzo controlled most of the passes through the forested mountains of the Casentino, so it was best to avoid going into the city itself. At the little village of Poppi he would call at the town tavern as he had often done on trips for his father's business. It was the hangout of older men who were quick to note a new face in town. They viewed with suspicion any stranger passing through, so it was good that they knew him— at least by sight—though beyond that, they had no idea who he was. They were a curious lot who spoke little but observed much, like sentinels, well practiced in the art of guarded but meaningful looks silently exchanged across the rims of their wine cups. Their gnarled brown hands and weathered faces were evidence of years of toil in the field that had earned for them the knowledge of every twist and turn of this terrain. Matteo knew that their collective knowledge of illicit trading in the area was vast. He needed to win their confidence if he was to succeed in this venture.

Having been here before, Matteo could name a few of them who in turn remembered him with a nod that indicated he was, if not actually welcome, at least tolerated in their midst. With a few coppers from the purse that hung from his waist Matteo was fairly confident that he could discover the whereabouts of Lapo, and that would be his entrée into the smugglers' trade route. But such information did not come cheap. It took two rounds of the wine flask on this warm day to loosen the tongue of this taciturn assembly, and three repetitions of the question: "Where can I find Lapo?"

Finally Bice, who appeared to be the elder spokesman, volunteered without even raising his eyes to Matteo. "Not here. Hut at the bend in the road above Bibbiena. About an hour away."

"But how will I know the place?"

With Bice's silent shrug Matteo understood that many more coppers would pass through his hands as he was forced to pay for each link in the chain that would lead him to the bandits' underground. He tossed another coin to Bice who bit it first and grudgingly muttered, "Big oak stump left of the hut—cross hatch marks—axe stuck in it. Go inside—say 'Bice is well!'"

Matteo tossed him an extra copper and was off on Mea. His horse was by now well rested, pawing the ground and eager to be on the road again. The mare's mane rippled in the air as she galloped southward, past the imposing Conti Guidi castle. It was a pleasant ride and in no time at all the hut came into view. With any luck he would find Lapo before sundown.

The stump with the axe was just as Bice described. At the sound of their arrival a grizzly man emerged through the door. Although he was probably little more than thirty he appeared much older. He scowled and said nothing until Matteo gave the password. "Bice is well."

With that the man's attitude changed and, with a quick jerk of his head, he gestured to Matteo to enter.

"I have come to seek your help, *Signore* Lapo."

The stranger snorted at being mistaken for Lapo and laughed derisively at the thought of being addressed as *"Signore."* He was quick to correct Matteo. "I am Nico," he said emphatically. "Lapo is not here."

"Where can I find him?" Another copper brought Nico's response. "You will find him in Bibbiena disguised as a beggar on the steps of the church of San Lorenzo. Give him a coin and say, 'Nico greets you.'"

With this latest morsel of information Matteo became acutely aware that this was going to be a long and complicated venture. These were experienced professionals he was dealing with and clearly they were going to reveal their plan only one bit at a time. "They are carefully testing me, leading me like a dumb animal from one contact to the next. In that way I am no risk, no danger to them." Although he resented being made to play the fool in their game, at the same time he was intrigued by their method and, despite himself, felt a certain admiration for their cunning. He was impatient and annoyed by these delays but found himself almost being seduced by the adventure, the danger of it all. Despite that fact, it angered him. "I may be green in the art of brigandry, but I can be devious, too. I will play their game—but very cautiously, careful not to reveal too much of my plan, either."

Dusk was descending by the time Matteo reached the church and, just as Nico said, there was Lapo begging at the door. He was a frightening specter. An ugly livid scar on his cheek and the stump of an ear that had been partially cut off were reminders of the dangerous game in which Matteo was now embroiled. So this was the elusive Lapo! For one brief moment Matteo's stomach sickened, but there was no turning back. He could not lose face with the smugglers nor did he want to admit failure to his father. In his distracted state he nearly forgot to give the password, but then came to his senses, handed Lapo a coin and said, "Nico greets you."

He was not surprised that Lapo said nothing: Apparently this was a silent brotherhood. He simply took Matteo by the arm, ushered him into the church, pushed him down on a *prie-dieu* in the semi-darkness of a side chapel that smelled of candle smoke and incense and knelt close beside him. Lapo had cleverly provided himself with a large and much-mended old rosary that he ostensibly fingered as he spoke with Matteo. Never were such illicit plans more deftly disguised. Even the sacristan suspected nothing as he made his rounds and respectfully passed the two men who appeared to be joined devoutly in prayer. The clever subterfuge enabled the two to negotiate undisturbed.

Matteo presented only the barest outlines of his plan, careful to reveal nothing of his motivation or identity. He was a good student and had already observed the usefulness of brevity in these clandestine dealings with the smugglers. Lapo assured him that for a price the alum could be procured, but he attached some conditions. "First, you must never reveal your source. You must promise to follow directions blindly from one step to the next without asking questions. Finally you must leave some security with your last contact in the chain."

He waited for Matteo to nod in agreement and continued, "Since the contraband comes into Italy at Bressanone in the Alto Adige region, we will need the help of a comrade who speaks German so you must meet Otto who works here in Bibbiena disguised as a blacksmith. His forge is just down the road a few yards from here: I will take you there."

The heat from the forge was extreme and the air reeked of sweat, scorched hair, and stale wine. A young man was working at the forge, while a squat, ruddy-faced older man in a leather apron was busy at work shoeing a horse. The noise was deafening and Lapo had to yell loudly several times to rouse Otto who paid no attention until he fixed the shoe securely to the foot of the animal. There was a look of satisfaction on his face and he actually smiled when he saw Lapo. Matteo found it hard to believe that such a jolly looking fellow was a part of a company of bandits.

Without saying a word Otto guided them into his room some distance away from the heat and the noise of the forge where the three men sat and shared a draft of local wine. Matteo was quickly learning the value of the silent gesture and observed that it was only after Otto nodded that Lapo began to speak. Giving a sketchy account of the plan as Matteo had described it to him in the church, Lapo explained: "The alum will come from the north, so we will need someone who speaks German—like you, Otto. My Florentine friend needs your help."

"So?" Looking squarely at Matteo, Otto announced in a

heavily accented dialect, "Our services require payment. *Ya!*"

"I am well prepared to make a partial payment now. As security I will leave with you a precious gold chalice set with rubies. It is worth a great deal. The remainder, upon delivery of the goods, the alum, I will pay you in gold florins."

Lapo shook his head in a gesture that meant no, and said, "Not yet! There are plans to lay and your security must be left only with the last of our comrades with whom you will seal the agreement. He will then give you the final directions. But for now it is enough that you show the goblet to us."

Meanwhile Otto seemed to be turning the plot over in his mind and muttered to himself. "Alum. Alum is heavy. The transport is expensive and dangerous. We will need burrows. They are smaller and better than mules in these narrow mountain passes, and for the overland part of the journey we will use barges on the rivers. There will be several points where the goods pass from one contact to the next and our men must be paid."

At this point Matteo cleverly drew the chalice from its hiding place, turning it in his hands in such a way that it glowed in the light of the fire. He noted with satisfaction that for once the smugglers made no attempt to conceal their reactions. Clearly they were impressed. For a brief moment he was in charge and would enjoy baiting them with just a glimpse before he slipped the chalice back into safekeeping.

The sight of the beautiful gold object loosed Otto's otherwise tied tongue and he began to outline the course to be followed. "First we will have to learn from our informants when the next shipment of alum is expected. Goods from across the mountains, destined for Venice, enter Italy through the Brenner Pass and are shipped south through Bressanone where the mountains provide good cover and the crags make fine hiding places. From there we will go through Passo di Castelunga, avoiding cities as much as possible, and then bypass Trent."

"To Lake Garda," Matteo interjected.

Otto just shook his head, marveling at Matteo's naiveté. "No, never, it is too dangerous—too many people there in summer. Instead we will take the Adige River that runs parallel to the lake."

Lapo shot a glance at Otto that indicated he should say no

more. Matteo would simply have to be patient and play their game if he was to learn the remainder of the route. Now, however, it was growing late and it had been a long and stressful day.

Otto assumed the role of host, and offered hospitality. "I will stable your horse tonight and you are welcome to our simple meal; some pasta, wine, and fruit, if it pleases you. Stay here tonight. No one will know. Early tomorrow morning you must ride to Monterchi where you will meet Picchino the town butcher. Ask him, 'Have you any fresh pork from the swineherds of Casentino?' He will advise you of your next step."

Although he was weary and his bones ached from the long ride, Matteo hesitated to accept Otto's invitation, turning over in his mind the possible consequences of accepting the offer of hospitality. "I do not know these men. Moreover they have now seen the treasure I am carrying. Suppose they have drugged my wine? What if they took my wonderful horse during the night? I saw how Lapo admired her."

Not knowing the whole picture made him nervous and when he was nervous he tended to stammer, so it was best that he said nothing. Realizing he was utterly dependent upon them to complete this operation, he could not afford to offend them. So as tactfully as possible he carried his belongings to the pallet of straw provided for him, drew the saddlebags as close to his body as possible and attempted to fall asleep. Anxiety and discomfort combined to make it a restless night, so he was happy to be up early in the morning, relieved to find the chalice where he had hidden it, and reassured too by the sound of Mea's soft neighing nearby. With a few more coppers given to his host and a symbolic florin to Lapo, without even taking time to break his fast, he was off in the direction of Monterchi in the upper Tiber Valley.

The morning air was stimulating and as Matteo rode through the Casentino with its patchwork of pasturelands and forests, friendly woodcutters and swineherds going about their morning business shouted greetings as he passed. After a while the terrain became more difficult. The climb was tiring, and he asked himself, "Why have the smugglers chosen this godforsaken place?" In the distance he could see the town of Anghiari perched high over the Valtiberina: "Would that not have been a better site?" Soon, however, he understood the smugglers' reasons for choosing this as the place of rendezvous. The streets of Monterchi were narrow; there were steep alleyways, and even small tunnels—perfect for concealing their loot.

It was not difficult to find the butcher shop with its rows of hares dangling from hooks in the rafters, and the chickens next to them, their necks abnormally distended from having been strangled. As he entered the butcher shop the stench of blood sickened his empty stomach, but he managed to inquire, "Do you have fresh pork from the swineherds of the Casentino?"

With a knowing look the butcher in his bloodied apron confirmed his identity as Picchino. "Yes. For you special pork, just slaughtered early this morning. Come." With that he led Matteo into another room where he disclosed the place at which Matteo would receive directions for the next part of this endeavor. "You must go to San Sepolcro and acquaint yourself thoroughly with the town since this is where you will pick up the contraband when the deal is completed. This must all be accomplished before winter. It is too easy to track our movements in the snow."

This was good news to Matteo for he wished to be done with this distasteful business as quickly as possible. But he questioned why Picchino insisted that this be done in the city, reminding him, "Otto believes it is best to bypass the cities. Would it not be safer to meet in some less public place?"

"No," he insisted, "the exchange must take place in San Sepolcro in September—on the second Sunday of the month when the town will be bustling with people from all over. They come to attend the Palio of the Balestra—the ancient contest of crossbowmen from Gubbio who come to challenge those of San Sepolcro. It is a colorful and noisy event. The spectacle of the *sbandieratori*, the flag wavers, will be a perfect distraction. There will be crowds of strangers, so you will not be noticed and the noise of the spectacle will provide the perfect cover for us to hand the contraband over to you. Only remember, you must provide a cart with flasks of wine stacked in straw."

"Who is my contact in San Sepolcro?"

"For now there is none. You must not remain there on this visit, just explore the city observing everything about it and noting the places that might be of use to you. You will dispatch this information to us as soon as possible. Now go!"

"No! Not yet." By this time, Matteo felt empowered to require some security from the brigands. He dared to ask, "What assurance have I that you will keep your part of the bargain? The gold chalice I leave with you is worth a great deal."

Taking it from his saddlebag he caressed it, holding it up to the bright morning sunlight where the rubies set in its base seemed to dance like liquid fire. Picchino's covetous hands instinctively reached out for it, but Matteo, with a gyration worthy of a dervish, deftly foiled his attempt to grasp it. There was some satisfaction in teasing this ignorant little butcher who at this time wielded so much control over him, and who had probably never set his eyes upon anything so beautiful and so valuable as this. Matteo had the temerity to ask, "How do I know I can trust you?

"We may smuggle and we may steal from others but we do not lie to each other. There is a smugglers' code of honor that we respect."

"But I am not one of you. I am not a smuggler. I have just come to ask your help."

"By your deal you have become one of us: You have made a covenant that must be honored. You are a part of our band."

"Prove it to me."

"Very well," he said, pulling a small dagger from under his apron. "We will make it a blood covenant. Give me your hand."

Matteo recoiled at the thought of it. Was it the same knife used to slaughter the pigs? It seemed barbaric but he dared not risk showing his feelings, allowing Picchino to see behind the façade that he had managed to maintain up to this point. So he closed his eyes tightly while, with a single deft motion, Picchino quickly scored an X on Matteo's wrist and upon his own. It smarted, but he dared not flinch as the two pressed their wrists together and their blood mingled, running down their forearms and dripping onto the floor, thus sealing the contract even as it mingled with pigs' blood. Whether he liked it or not, Matteo was now one of them.

With admission into the brotherhood of the brigands went

the rite of bestowing a name and by virtue of the covenant just completed it became Picchino's prerogative to name him. With great satisfaction he proudly announced, "Henceforth you will be known within our band as Cefo!"

"After you have visited San Sepolcro you must go on to Gola del Furlo where you will find Nafri. Say to him 'My horse is lame.' He will reveal to you the names of the smugglers from whom you are to pick up the contraband in September. Identify yourself as Cefo and he will give you a map and tell you the password. When you have done this you must return here and leave the chalice with me until you make the full payment in September. I am your last contact. But first you must acquaint yourself with San Sepolcro so you must leave at once."

The way to San Sepolcro was difficult terrain; the road turned back upon itself repeatedly until it rose higher and higher in the mountains, reaching above the mist and fog that moved like layers of clouds beneath him. It became clear to Matteo that he had not allowed sufficient time for this part of the adventure. But at least he found some relief in the knowledge that this was just reconnaissance—this time there would be no contacts to make with smugglers. He had never before seen San Sepolcro so he ambled about almost leisurely as he searched for the ideal spot to collect the contraband in September. He found it near the church of Santa Chiara, far enough away from the main square to escape notice and near enough to the city gate to ensure speedy exit. Satisfied with his choice he headed for his next assignment—to find the stonecutter, Nafri at Gola del Furlo.

Although the distance to Gola del Furlo was short, the landscape changed quickly and dramatically from gently rolling hills and pastures to a wild and rocky terrain. He had never been here before, though he had heard of this place. It was said that even before the time of Christ the Roman Consul Flaminius had a tunnel made through the rocks here when he built the Flaminian road. History was of little interest to Matteo at this point: All he knew was that the roughness of the landscape made passage slow. He was growing weary of this business and longed for a decent meal and a comfortable bed.

As he drew nearer he saw a small dark-skinned man standing at the approach to the bridge across the gorge. The sledgehammer in his hand suggested that this might be Nafri. So Matteo called out to him. Though the Condigliano stream that runs through the gorge is small the current is swift and noisy. He had to cup his hands around his mouth and yell three times. "My horse is lame."

The stonecutter finally motioned to follow him into the nearby shelter. Once inside he acknowledged his identity. "I am Nafri and you are safe here."

"I am Cefo. I have come from Picchino in Monterchi."

Apparently Nafri had few visitors in this godforsaken place carved into the rocks. At least his manner was more hospitable and he seemed pleased to invite his guest to share the simple fare that he placed on the rough wooden table, some coarse bread, cheese, and wine of non-descript vintage. Matteo was grateful and ate heartily for he had left early without breakfast and was hungry by now. There was little conversation but, after they had eaten, Nafri suddenly said, "Show me your right arm."

Matteo realized that the fresh wound on his wrist was Picchino's signature, signifying that the compact was ratified. He had staunched the flow of blood with a handkerchief and carefully pulled his sleeve down to conceal it. By now the sleeve was encrusted with dried blood so that when Nafri pulled it up roughly the blood again began to flow down his arm. Nafri surveyed the mark and, satisfied that all seemed in order, declared, "Good! Now we must complete our business." Quickly and without ceremony he handed over to Matteo a parchment rolled tightly enough to slide easily into the saddlebag. "Unroll it, Cefo."

Matteo did as he was told and Nafri traced his finger along the route that had been carefully drawn on the map, making sure that Matteo understood every point. Satisfied that he had, he quickly rolled the map and handed it to Cefo. For security purposes he completed the remainder of the directions verbally. "When you come to collect the contraband at San Sepolcro in September you will be met by two of our band, Renzo and Tonino. Identify yourself as Cefo and say, 'The oaks are losing their leaves early.'"

As if to impress it more surely on his memory Matteo repeated—parrot fashion, "The oaks are losing their leaves early."

"Do not write these instructions anywhere. Commit them to memory and guard the map with your life. Renzo and Tonino will assist you to load the alum on your cart, under the straw and the wine flasks that you will provide. You must do this quickly and leave. You are on your own after that. Now go back to Picchino in Monterchi and report that the contract is complete. He will send the message back to Lapo and your work is over until September."

—ɯ—

Matteo wasted no time in retracing his way to Monterchi all the while reviewing the happenings of these last days as he rode, and questioning why he must make this ridiculous trip back to Picchino. It dawned on him that the smugglers were simply ensuring that he could be trusted. "All the same it is degrading, insulting, that I, Matteo Cecchi, a Florentine, should be ordered around blindly by this scruffy, mangy lot."

At least this needless ride retracing his way back to Picchino gave him time to ponder all that had transpired. He wondered aloud, "Who are these men known only by strange nicknames—Lapo, Nico, Nafri? They are clever. No, they are more than clever, they are wily, devious, and dangerous. I must be extremely watchful. I saw their reaction to the gold goblet. They are covetous! Should I falter at any time I fear their retribution."

As he neared Monterchi again his thoughts turned to the crafty butcher he found so truly repugnant. And there he was, standing in the door of his butcher shop, squinting his beady little eyes against the setting sun, watching for Matteo's return. Matteo's eagerness to have this deed finally done was matched only by Picchino's avarice. Once again in the back room where Matteo had first received his instructions, Picchino gruffly demanded, "Give me the chalice."

As distasteful as it was, Matteo handed over the precious goblet into the butcher's grimy hands, all the while taking care not to touch them. He had not noticed before the filth and dried blood caked around Picchino's fingernails. It seemed to him almost a sacrilegious act to surrender this precious object to him, but not to do so now would negate all that had been accomplished up to this point. Besides, the retribution of the smugglers would be swift and bloody.

Picchino demanded to see the map and quizzed Matteo briefly on the verbal instructions that Nafri gave him. Satisfied that all was in order, he dismissed Matteo bluntly, clutched the chalice to his chest and began a half-crazed sort of dance, jumping madly about the shop in wild spins and pirouettes like a maniac, all the while whooping and yelling wildly. When finally he disappeared into the room at the back of the shop, Matteo bounded onto his horse and was gone.

For the first time since he left home three days before, he had no immediate orders, no cryptic passwords, and no one to report to. He was free! It was growing late, however, and he needed to find shelter for the night so he headed in the direction of Fossombrone. But finding a satisfactory inn at this hour was impossible for it was already very dark. Just outside the town he spied a barn, dismounted and quietly led his horse inside. Here he could sleep on hay one more night and Mea could have all the oats she wanted. He rose early before the farmer could find them and headed to Fano where the ancient Via Flaminia meets the Adriatic.

Fano was a larger city where he was sure he could find comfortable lodging and would rest before the last part of his journey. Once in the inn he realized how truly exhausting these last days had been. What remained to be accomplished now was strategic, and it would require clear thinking to negotiate with Alfonso Beltramonto without divulging the seamy side of this plot. Matteo could take no chances so he surrendered himself to a long, deep restorative sleep.

Feeling rested and sure of himself in the morning, he started off later than usual, riding at a leisurely pace down the Adriatic coast toward Ancona. The beauty of the sea, the sensuous music of waves lapping the shore, and the feel of the salt air were mesmerizing and a welcome respite after the events of these last days. His mind wandered lazily, but somehow always came to rest on the vision of Beltramonto's daughter.

At Senigallia, about halfway between Fano and Ancona, he stopped to investigate the harbor. He had heard it was the one Adriatic port that was duty free and, as such, handled a large volume of commerce. Familiarity with the city might be useful to him in the future—should anything go wrong in the course of transporting the alum in September. Matteo treated himself to a hearty local vintage and a fine meal at an inn overlooking the sea and was back on his way, but only after he raised his glass in a solitary toast and crowed, "To Ancona and victory!"

CHAPTER 5

The Bargain

The ancient Via Flaminia terminates at Fano. But the remainder of the old Roman road from there to Ancona follows the contour of the Adriatic coast like a gently unfurled ribbon. The paving stones, worn smooth by centuries of Roman military and mercantile traffic, were now bleached by a thousand years of sun and salt. By the time Ancona's crescent-shaped harbor came into view, Matteo's eyes burned, even as he instinctively shielded them with his left hand. The sun had completed nearly half its westward course across the bay, which meant that it must be midday. Soon the bells of Ancona's churches heralded the noon as they rang out the Angelus.

Matteo was almost startled to recognize his own voice as he involuntarily responded, *Angelus Domini nuntiavit Mariae.* He crossed himself automatically, a reflex he learned many years ago at the knees of his devout mother. For a moment he was shamed by the awareness that he was invoking the Virgin to come to his aid when he was so deeply involved in such an unlawful action—moreover, one motivated in no small measure by his lustful longing for an innocent young girl.

—◊◊◊—

Little by little Ancona's landmarks came into view. The skyline was dominated by the massive Cathedral of San Ciriaco, overlooking the city like a sentry. By this, his second visit to the city, Ancona was beginning to look familiar. He made his way through the narrow streets in search of a suitable inn where he could rest and prepare to meet Alfonso Beltramonto. Finding one near a fountain where he could water his horse, he dispatched a courier to Beltramonto with a request to meet on the morrow. This afternoon he must give to important preparations for this critical confrontation. He could not present himself to Beltramonto in his travel costume, nor did he want to be seen by the old man's daughter in such simple attire. And he needed to groom the mare whose fetlocks were encrusted with salt and sand from the old Roman road. The saddle and bridle he had brought were not fit for this occasion either, so at the inn he arranged for the mare's livery and contemplated what to do about her worn harness.

Matteo had used all the coppers he brought with him to pay the smugglers for their miserly handed-out bits of information, and he had even dipped into the gold florins. He knew his father had called in some loans in order to provide the money for this trip. Should he then use some of the gold to buy new reins, halter, and a good saddle? His desire to make a good impression was greater than the momentary twinge of conscience that such an indulgence would cost. So without weighing the matter further he sought out a good saddler and selected the most beautiful leather appointments in his shop.

He was fatigued from the ride in the glaring sunlight and a bit lightheaded in anticipation of his meeting with Beltramonto, but the smell of good, seasoned leather that filled the shop revived him. As he made his way through the maze of harnesses and other trappings, he stopped occasionally to stroke the leather. Finally he selected a harness of rusty sheen that would complement the mare's coppery color nicely. The horse nuzzled him gently, almost as if she understood. Yes, he and Mea would make a fine appearance. But for that he also needed proper clothes and was grateful that his ever-provident mother had packed his best doublet and hose. He would buy a cloak here in Ancona. Surely his father would overlook this extravagance when he learned that his son successfully completed this important transaction and secured the alum.

He spent the afternoon making preparations: To present his plan to Beltramonto without arousing his suspicion would re-

quire great tact. Satisfied that by evening Matteo had all his arguments in place, he relaxed, dined on Ancona's splendid seafood
and, after watching a spectacular sunset over the bay, retired for
the night. He arose early in order to groom his horse, bathe himself
and don his fine clothes, bristling with newfound self-confidence as
he observed his reflection in the looking glass.

At precisely three o'clock he presented himself at Beltramonto's door and was warmly received by the old gentleman himself. Matteo noted with satisfaction that Alfonso observed Mea.
His eyes scanned the mare and the look registered on his face suggested that he was indeed impressed. She did look beautiful in the
midday sun, her coat gleaming like silk. Not wanting to appear
unduly inquisitive though, Alfonso quickly turned his attention to
Matteo.

"*Signore* Cecchi, welcome. I trust your trip from Florence
was pleasant and you bring me good news."

"Thank you, *Signore* Beltramonto. I bring you first of all
good wishes and good health from my father. He speaks of you
often and with great affection. And I bring you good news, too."

The deep lines of Alfonso's face seemed visibly to relax
with that announcement and he wasted no time in further pleasantries. Leading Matteo into his study he motioned for him to sit
in the large leather chair near his desk and inquired, "Have you
obtained the alum we both need so desperately?"

"I have, sir."

"*Benissimo*! We must toast to your success." Without waiting for further comment Alfonso rang for Prudenza who entered
the room quietly, looking even lovlier than Matteo remembered.
She was wearing a silken gown of deepest azure trimmed with
silver embroidery. Her long hair was caught into a silver net at
the back of her neck, and her only ornament was a long string of
pearls twisted twice about her neck, with a third strand hanging
low, knotted just beneath her bosom. He took particular note, too,
that she was not wearing a ring.

Matteo had to suppress his enormous longing to reach out
and touch her—to embrace this lovely, unspoiled creature. Instead
he bowed low, somewhat stiffly, and said only, "Good day, *Signorina* Beltramonto, I wish you health."

Prudenza responded with a polite curtsy, but there was an

unmistakable rush of color to her cheeks that Matteo noticed. He asked himself, was it modesty, or did she find him attractive? Had she been impressed with the way he looked in his velvet doublet and silken hose that clung so flatteringly to his calves? He was glad he spent his father's money to buy the heavy turquoise cape that he had been careful to drape over his shoulder in such a way that it skillfully concealed the slight curvature of his back.

Just as she had done at his first visit, Prudenza filled their goblets, passed the pastries her mother provided and discreetly left the room. Even so, a faint fragrance of jasmine remained. Though it was ever so slight, to Matteo it was heady. He could not savor it long, however, for the time had come for him to present his plan to Alfonso—diplomatically avoiding the necessity of full disclosure.

"And so, young man, explain to me the plan."

Doing his best to appear calm and confident, Matteo began, "My sources have assured me that they can provide for us alum of the very best quality—even better than that from the mines of Tolfa."

"That is an extravagant promise! Have they their own deposits of the mineral?"

"No. Not exactly. They import it from mines in the north."

"Strange! I have never heard of mines in that part of Italy. Are you certain they can provide the quality we require?"

Then came the question Matteo most feared. In his very honest and direct way Alfonso looked squarely at him and queried, "Are these dealers—your sources—honest? Are they working within the law?"

Remembering the "law of the smugglers" that Picchino articulated to him just days ago, he stretched the truth beyond mental reservation, to deliberate deception and lied. "Yes."

He was becoming very nervous and in order to avoid the stammer that often overtook him in such moments, offered no detail.

"What is the name of your purveyor?"

Matteo was certainly not prepared for this one—though he chided himself for not anticipating such a reasonable question. Obviously he could not reel off the ridiculous monikers by which the smugglers identified themselves. What would Alfonso think?

Matteo was no stranger to mendacity when it was useful, but in this instance he was not quick enough to convince Alfonso. He swallowed hard and said the first name that came to mind. "The mine is owned by the Fratelli Bosi."

"In all my years of working in this profession I have never heard of the Bosi Brothers."

It was clear from Alfonso's expression that this artifice was less than convincing. Matteo noted at once that the lines seemed to return to the older man's troubled face, confirming that his well-planned argument was crumbling. Even as he frantically groped for words Alfonso slowly raised the goblet to his lips and, indicating that Matteo should do the same, said, "Do you swear to this? Can we drink to an honest solution?"

Lying was not a new experience to Cecchi, but never before had the consequences been of such import. He had always been able to wriggle his way out of trouble. It was not difficult to lie to the kind of people with whom he dealt, for they were not exactly scrupulous themselves. But this Beltramonto unnerved him with his honesty and the steady gaze of his clear gray eyes. Matteo was no match for his straightforward manner, his explicit questioning, and his directness. Like a trapped animal struggling to escape, Matteo made a last desperate attempt to salvage his story. Contrary to all he had been taught by his father, he raised the cup and drank to the deed. Yet he knew instinctively that Alfonso was not satisfied.

The old man continued his interrogation—prefaced by the disquieting statement, "I do not know of the Fratelli Bosi. Where are they located?"

In a moment there flashed through Matteo's mind the thought of the possible reprisal by the smugglers if he should not keep his part of the bargain. If they arrived in San Sepolcro with the contraband and he failed to meet them there, what would happen? Of course they did not know his identity any more than he knew theirs. But with their efficient underground he was certain they could find him. Visions of Lapo's mutilated ear sent a shudder down his spine. Although these images flashed through his mind in an instant, it seemed an eternity before he could pull himself together sufficiently to respond. "The Fratelli Bosi are located in a small city in the north, just west of Belfuno. And, yes, I have been assured of the purity the alum."

"When will they deliver it to us?"

"Before the end of September. I must collect it from them and I will then bring it to you."

"And what is the price of the alum?"

"One thousand florins."

Alfonso blanched noticeably. With the decline of his business in the past two years this was an impossible sum for him to raise in such a short time. Not wishing to expose the older man's embarrassment, Matteo pretended not to notice. Finally Alfonso spoke. "I must think about this. I cannot deny that I am doubtful about the arrangements you describe. A thousand florins is a large sum to risk on such a venture. I must have time to decide. Please allow me a day and I will give you my answer."

Politely, and with no further discussion, Alfonso ushered his guest to the gate where Mea stood awaiting her master. Matteo was shaken by the experience, fearful that Beltramonto might not agree, and at the same time he regretted that he had caught only a brief look at Prudenza. The self-confidence that he had felt only hours earlier gave way now to alarming doubts as he pondered the possible consequences of failure.

Meanwhile Alfonso had only twenty-four hours to decide on a course of action. Now more than ever he needed the good counsel of his devoted and ever-practical wife, but for that he would wait until tomorrow morning. He was too shaken to think clearly just now and sat motionless at his desk for a long time, not even lighting the candles when it became dark. Quietly, and without explanation, he simply retired.

Over the long years of their marriage Caterina had learned to read her husband's every mood with uncanny accuracy. She was well aware, too, that a good wife simply did not interfere with her husband's commerce. She respected his solitude, knowing it was his habit to be silent as he thought through problems and made important decisions concerning his business. She sensed it best not to intrude. It was clear to her, however, that whatever was troubling him just now was the result of this visit from Cecchi. She had not actually met Matteo, had caught only a glimpse of him as he left, and heard some reference to returning tomorrow for an answer. What could this mean? She suspected, rightly, that it was more than just routine business and determined that whatever was causing her husband this much anxiety, she must certainly find out. So without ado she confronted Alfonso early in the morning, careful to do so gently and before Prudenza had arisen.

He was sitting in a corner of the garden under an arbor where he often retreated in early morning when he wished to be alone. Not fearing to interrupt his solitude Caterina quietly approached, and placed her hand on his shoulder. "Husband, you are troubled. What is it?"

He was not prepared for Caterina's forthright approach, which went directly to his most vulnerable defense. With little provocation the words began to tumble out of his mouth as he shared some of the happenings of the previous day—but only some. She should know about the price of the alum, yes; but he would tactfully withhold from her his doubts about the honesty of the arrangement, rationalizing that it would only worry her needlessly.

"Together we will manage, Husband. Have faith. We will find a solution."

"You are a woman of such deep faith, Caterina, and you seem to see things in such simple terms."

"If you are uncertain about this plan, then when Cecchi comes in the morning you must tell him, 'no.' If, on the other hand, you agree to buy the alum, we will somehow find the money. I do still have some of my mother's jewels…"

"Never! I would not hear of it."

She was usually able to put him at ease, but this time her uncomplicated reasoning only increased his anxiety. "It is not that simple, Caterina. Think! A thousand florins is a great deal of money for us just now. The price of the alum is just about the amount that a husband should have a right to expect as a dowry for a young woman from a family of our station and reputation. Surely Cecchi must realize that, though he would never say so. To purchase the alum now we would have to use that money, Caterina—money that I have been saving ever since Prudenza was born. It would be a sacrilege to do so, especially now that she is of an age to be married. We must consider that."

"But she is still very young. There is time."

"I have tried—even during these difficult days—to leave her dowry money untouched. To use it now would be to deprive our daughter of the kind of life she deserves, and to which she is accustomed. No, I will not agree to the deal that young Cecchi has contrived. I cannot."

She sensed that there was more and knew that if she simply waited mutely, he would tell her. She was right. In the awkwardness of her silent strategy Alfonso's resolve to conceal his doubts about the honesty of the arrangement simply crumbled and finally he admitted, "It is not just the money!"

"What do you mean?"

"I fear that it is not a completely honest arrangement. It makes me uncomfortable."

"Why?"

"I sense he is not telling me all. But, Caterina, how can I doubt the son of such a dear and trusted friend as Zenobi Cecchi? It would be an insult."

"You must!"

"I will try, I promise. In the meantime, I must go now to speak with my friends at the *dogana*; perhaps they can advise if there is possibly some way to resume trade with the East?"

Taking both his hands in hers she said, "God go with you, Husband."

—◆◆◆—

Matteo was up early, eager to hear Alfonso's decision. It was a long and restless night for him as he lay awake scheming, trying to anticipate Beltramonto's answer and rehearsing his argument aloud: "Whatever the old man's answer, yea or nay, I will counter with a plan he cannot refuse. I am sure of it. Should Beltramonto continue doubting the legitimacy of my proposal, I will call upon my father's longstanding relationship with him, reminding him too of the unspotted reputation of the house of Cecchi to which I, Matteo, am the heir. Surely the son of his old friend can be trusted." But what if it was the money that caused Alfonso to withdraw? Oh! Here he had a daring suggestion—almost too bold to say aloud even to himself as he stared up at the ceiling. His face broke into a smile as he savored the almost sinful thought of it.

Promptly at nine o'clock Cecchi presented himself at Beltramonto's gate and announced himself with the sound of the old bell that hung there. His hopes were raised when he was greeted by a more-rested Alfonso. He must have come to some decision, Matteo thought.

Even before the conversation began Prudenza appeared with refreshments. She wore a simple gown of yellow silk, a diaphanous fabric that clung to her body in graceful folds as it fell softly from a neckline ornamented with garnets. For the moment Matteo was speechless, staring at her longer than he had dared on his last visits. How utterly desirable she looked as she modestly diverted her eyes.

The usual formalities dispensed with, Alfonso took charge by beginning the conversation. "I have given your proposal serious thought and…"

"Yes?" Matteo, alert and eagerly expecting good news interrupted.

"I regret to tell you that at this time I cannot agree to the arrangement you suggest."

This was not at all what Matteo expected. Just moments ago he had been so sure of himself, and now with these few words the old man whom he had thought so defenseless had brought his world crashing down about him. His heart raced and his temples throbbed at the thought that without Beltramonto's agreement he would incur the wrath of the smugglers, disappoint his father and be left to find the money to pay for the alum himself. The smugglers would certainly not take it back. After a moment of panic he regained his composure enough to ask, "Is it that you question the soundness of the agreement? Or the quality of the mineral? I beg you, in the name of my father, your good friend Zenobi Cecchi, to reconsider."

As the gravity of the situation increased, so did his boldness. In his desperation he was not too proud to grovel now, nor did he hesitate to make an oath on the Cecchi name. "On my family's name I solemnly swear to the truth."

Alfonso was silent for a moment, giving Matteo at least some fragile hope. Recognizing Alfonso's vulnerability on that score, Matteo shamelessly pursued the point. "Would you doubt the honesty of your old friend's son?" Buoyed by the thought that the consummation of the deal would resolve problems for both houses, he made bold to ask again, "Is it that you question the honesty of the agreement?"

This time Alfonso responded—half apologetically—nodding his head as he did so. "I do not wish to suggest that either you or your good father would ever deal in contraband, or would endanger both our names by doing so."

Matteo was not yet so deeply into deception that he could not feel some guilt as he pondered Alfonso's last statement. He was visibly relieved, however, and sensed that this was the moment to raise the delicate issue of the money. He must be cautious, sensitive to the fact that besides being an upright and honest man, Beltramonto was a proud man, and Matteo must respect his dignity. So he must move cautiously. Almost tentatively he queried, "Is it the thousand florins, sir? That is a large sum, I know. But this is only a temporary measure. Once you have the alum in September you will be back in business and you will quickly recover your losses. Think of it as an investment."

"That is possible, I suppose." But not knowing how to, or whether to, approach the matter of Prudenza's dowry, Alfonso skillfully talked around the issue saying, "I do have a sum of cash set aside for a specific purpose but I do not wish to use it for business—not even this."

Matteo was shrewd and surmised that Alfonso was referring to his daughter's dowry. Was this his opportunity? Did he dare to suggest something so audacious? He was emboldened by the vision of Prudenza again this morning—so silent, and so utterly desirable.

"*Signore* Beltramonto," he began formally, "I pray you not to find me discourteous or disrespectful. But I beg you to consider this." The gravity of this exchange was wearing on Alfonso. He was growing increasingly apprehensive and could not possibly guess what to expect next. He wished that Caterina were at his side as Matteo continued, "Good sir, I am a successful man, the son of a respected old friend of yours. My older brother has consecrated his life to God in a monastery. That means I will in time—when God calls my beloved father to himself—become the head of the Cecchi business. I am thirty-three years old and have not yet taken a wife, though I have had many opportunities.

"There are plenty of young women in Florence who have attempted to win my affections. But most are motivated by greed for wealth and their suit is represented by avaricious marriage brokers. My father is growing old and his health is fragile. I would, as a good son, like to brighten his old age with grandchildren. I want to marry but have found no one to satisfy my expectations and desires. Sir, forgive my boldness, but I confess to you that from the first time I saw your daughter, Prudenza, I have been smitten. Her modesty, her beauty! I desire her."

Alfonso was shocked by Matteo's openness—flattered, confused, unnerved and even angry, but at the same time deeply touched. In his honesty Alfonso was so transparent that Cecchi had been able to read him well. He recognized at once that the money Alfonso swore not to touch was undoubtedly Prudenza's dowry. He had been clever enough to direct his argument to the tender issue of Beltramonto's long friendship with his father, Zenobi—even daring to swear upon the reputation of his father.

Finally the old man managed to respond. "My daughter is indeed a treasure to her mother and me. The man who wins her hand will truly be rich."

With a sudden and uncharacteristic movement Matteo fell to one knee before Alfonso and declared, "I wish to be that man, Sir. I relinquish my right to a dowry for such a treasure. She is a pearl of great price and would be the joy of my life and a delight to my father."

Clearly Alfonso was taken by surprise—his large eyes opened wide as he took a deep breath and at last responded, "You must forgive me when I say your suggestion has stunned me. You have surmised correctly that the money I refer to is my daughter's dowry. I will not touch it." He began to pace the floor, muttering half audible thoughts—possible alternatives to the problem. "I am well aware that the Confraternity of the Holy Spirit supplies dowries for needy young girls. But I am not a poor man. Do not even suggest that. I have my pride. Nor can I simply give my daughter away."

"Sir, I do not wish to suggest that you appeal to the confraternity. Nor do I wish you to—as you say—'give' your daughter away. There is a simple solution. The dowry for a young woman of your daughter's station would easily equal the sum that the providers of the alum are asking. If you agree to use the money you have so caringly put aside for her, to pay for the alum I will consider it to be her dowry and gladly take her into our loving family. I beg you to consider."

After a long and awkward pause Alfonso replied, "What you suggest is unseemly—unbefitting such a one as Prudenza. I cannot barter my precious child for the sake of a business transaction no matter how important...Yet,...your plan does have some merit for her as well. Surely you must understand that I need time to ponder this unusual proposal."

"I do understand."

"Honor dictates that I cannot make such a decision without consulting my wife. And I must present it to Prudenza, too. To permit her to leave will be difficult, but I have always known that one day we must."

"Then you will consider it?"

"Yes. I will consider it, but I cannot promise..."

"When may I then expect an answer, sir? Would two days be sufficient time, sir?"

Half dazed Alfonso responded, "Yes, yes—two days."

"Then I shall return the day after tomorrow. Until then, good day, sir." He bowed deeply and left.

Alfonso watched as Matteo mounted his horse, and noted the lack of spirit that had been so evident when he arrived hardly an hour before. But then Alfonso, too, felt spent after this ordeal. His pulse pounded in time with the horse's hooves as he observed Matteo grow smaller and smaller until he finally disappeared into the misty distance. As he watched he asked himself, "Is this really the man destined to be my daughter's husband? I had not expected it to be so!"

A sudden pain behind his left eye made him reel momentarily and he grasped the iron bars of the gate to steady himself. For the moment he prayed it might all be a bad dream. He dared not face his wife in this state, so he sat quietly on the garden bench until the pain had passed and his strength began to return.

As difficult as this decision was, Alfonso was acutely aware of the reality that he must face Caterina with this latest development. How could he tell her that in this brief exchange with Matteo all of the carefully thought out considerations with which she had calmed him so gently the night before, lay shattered like so much broken glass? "It had all seemed clear then, so easily resolved. How can I explain this change of heart to my practical wife who tends to see things in simple, precise terms? And if I use Prudenza's dowry to accomplish the deal, how can I face my daughter who will surely look upon herself now as a marriage pawn?"

As the sun disappeared behind a cloud the hard stone bench upon which he sat became cold, and overhead the gulls screeched loudly. He rehearsed mentally all the possible arguments he would present to Caterina but, before he had a chance to, she appeared. Suspecting from Matteo's hasty departure, that things had not gone as planned the night before, she fabricated a reason to go into the courtyard where Alfonso sat, his head inclined and shoulders uncharacteristicaly bent.

"Husband, are you all right? Young Cecchi has been gone for some time now and still you remain here. How did he…"

Before she could finish Alfonso interrupted, "Caterina…" Large tears formed in his eyes as he reached out to her, unable for a moment to speak. Silently they walked to his study where Caterina noted that Alfonso did not sit behind his desk in a position of authority that always gave him the upper hand in control of business. Instead he pulled two small chairs before the fire where they could sit face to face, equal partners in this most significant decision.

Slowly he related the conversation with Matteo. It became painfully clear to Caterina that her husband's mind was not yet truly made up. Methodically, like the astute businessman that he was, he laid out the pros and cons of the situation and, just as systematically, Caterina responded, sometimes agreeing, but more often countering. On the prospect of Matteo's marrying Prudenza she had serious misgivings. Although she had not actually met him she announced emphatically, "I do not trust him."

"You do not know him, Caterina."

"No. But neither do you, really."

"I know his father who is a dear and trusted friend. Matteo is of a good family."

"He seems much older than Prudenza—and she is so innocent."

"He is thirty-three years old."

"And Prudenza is fifteen! Young enough to be his daughter."

"All the better for her to have an older man who can be a protector to her—one who can provide for her. Have you forgotten, Caterina, that I am ten years older than you? You were eighteen and I was twenty-eight when we were wed."

She could not argue that point and had to admit, "Yes, but do not forget, we knew each other. Prudenza has never even met him. Ours was a real love relationship, not an arranged marriage."

Alfonso sensed that his wife was softening in her resolve and cautiously moved on to some practical considerations. "We would be giving our daughter to a respectable, wealthy family. She will have a good home in Florence."

"But Florence is so far away. And she is our only child."

"We must think of her future, my dear. Florence would be a very stimulating place for Prudenza to live."

After a long, deep sigh Caterina admitted, "It is true that Prudenza has a fine mind. Think how much she has developed in just the two years of schooling at San Salvatore."

"Yes, she is gifted, and in Florence she will have cultural opportunities we could not provide here in Ancona. Remember how you always complained that she was a daydreamer? Now, you have to admit that under her tutors at San Salvatore she has become much more disciplined. Her reading...her music...these are so important to her and she could continue them under the guidance of scholars in Florence." Finally, and cautiously, Alfonso introduced the issue of the dowry bargain that he had carefully avoided mentioning up to now. All the ground that he had gained in the previous discussion now thundered down on him like an avalanche with Caterina's uncharacteristic outburst.

"How could you ever consider that, Alfonso?"

Only in a state of heightened emotion did Caterina ever address her husband by his Christian name. He made no response, but stared glassy-eyed into the fire for a time. Then slowly he reviewed for her all the reasons that Cecchi outlined only an hour before. Half dazed, his words came out almost mechanically. "Temporary measure...business stabilized...both families benefit..."

Finally, her resistance flagging, Caterina's attributes as a dutiful wife outweighed her misgivings and she accepted the scenario that her husband laid out before her, but with one important proviso: "It must be Prudenza's decision. We must not force her."

"Yes, it must be Prudenza's will."

But for Alfonso the most painful battle still lay ahead. How could he convince his daughter that this was an act of their love for her and not just a business transaction, a solution to a financial crisis. Before his courage failed him he rang for her.

—⁂—

She had not meant to listen! She had never done such a thing before. For just a moment she left her usual post in the alcove near her father's office, so she did not see Cecchi leave. Soon, however, she recognized that her father's conversation was not with Cecchi but with her mother. A certain terror overcame her as she caught fragments of their conversation, enough to realize that it concerned her. Feeling guilty that she overheard as much as she did, she quietly slipped away to her room, knowing that all too soon she would be summoned and learn the whole story.

She did not have to wait long. The familiar sound of the bell from her father's study usually summoned her to appear as hostess to serve up cakes or contracts. This time, however, she could not suppress the ominous feeling that it was she herself being served up. When she reached the door she was met with a different picture than ever before. Father was not at his desk. This was the first time that she ever saw her mother with him in the study. They were seated on either side of the hearth. Alfonso pulled up a third chair for Prudenza and motioned for her to sit between them.

Gently he revealed the situation to her. As the scenario unfolded, Prudenza said little and did not divulge that she overheard any of their private conversation. After all, she had not meant to. Almost as if in another world her thoughts returned to that day when her father came to take her home from San Salvatore—how he attempted to apologize to her. And she, so overwhelmed with love and respect for him, vowed in that moment that she would never do anything to displease or offend him. Although she had not said it aloud at the time, she had vowed it to herself. And a vow was a solemn thing. How could she refuse now?

Her father's voice seemed to be coming from a distance as she heard him ask, "What is your desire, Prudenza? Do not answer now. You must ponder the matter."

"You know, Father, that I will always do as you and Mother wish."

"No. No! What your mother and I wish is that this be your decision. Whatever you decide, we will accept as a family and support you. But tomorrow we must have an answer for young Cecchi. We will speak no more of it now, Prudenza. Go, weigh the matter well, pray to know God's will and believe that we love you and want only your happiness."

As she climbed the stairs to her room, her mind was dazed, her heart as cold and heavy as the gray stone under her feet. This was too much to absorb in one encounter. Her lute and her much-fingered volume of Dante did not lift her spirits now. She lay on her bed too weary to cry. In her emotionally exhausted state even sleep failed her. Instead, in her head there raged an intense debate that grew more vehement as the options seemed fewer and fewer. At times she murmured aloud, attempting to reason as if arguing with an adversary. "Was not all of my training at San Salvatore to prepare me for marriage and motherhood? Have not my parents sacrificed to provide this for me?" Clearly the answer was yes, but her other self countered, "You would be sacrificing yourself for the sake of a business deal, keeping a vow that you made in a moment of emotion. That was no vow at all, and surely no one would hold you to it."

"But not to do so would ruin my father's business, and I

would be disappointing my parents. My parents…my parents…"

The words trailed off as finally she succumbed to a fitful sleep as thick as the darkness that now shrouded Ancona.

CHAPTER 6

The Contract

It was still dark when Prudenza awakened, but her troubled sleep had not dispelled the anxiety of last night. She felt a tightness in her throat and chest like a crushing weight whose gravity pinned her to her bed while she struggled to free herself. She was not physically trapped, but the feverish emotion that she grappled with was paralyzing. Within her there raged a veritable war between her desire to please her parents and the urge to flee to the security of her friends at San Salvatore. If only she could talk with Coletta who always seemed so wise. And *Fra* Tommaso, he would surely counsel her if he were here.

By the time the first faint rays of light were visible behind San Ciriaco she could no longer suppress her desire to see these friends who knew her so well. If they could not come to her, she must go to them: She would have to run away. She was momentarily shocked by the sudden emergence of this rebellious side of her nature. It was like a vehement debate between the voice of her conscience and this new defiant person within, as she began waging a war of words. Somehow speaking aloud gave her greater resolve. The docile Prudenza argued, "This would be disobedient: My parents would never allow me to go out in the streets alone, especially at this hour. They will worry."

But her newly emerged defiant self reminded, "You've already committed one transgression you have eavesdropped! One more would not matter."

"But that was different; I didn't mean to. This would be disobedient." Her adversarial self grew more forceful and cunningly struck where she was most vulnerable. "You cannot do this alone, you need help; you must go to *Fra* Tommaso. He will understand."

She felt her resolve weakening. "No proper young woman should go out into the streets unattended. I might be taken for a prostitute." Her demon laughed at her now. "Prudenza, have you never seen a *puttana* in the streets? Surely you know you do not look like one of them. Now hurry! You must go before full daylight."

"What will I wear to disguise myself? A proper lady of Ancona when she goes outside the home must wear a cloak that covers her gown and a hood that hides her face. I have no such mantle except the one Mother made for me when I entered San Salvatore."

The immediate problem of trying to devise a disguise confirmed that her rebellious side won the debate. Thinking quickly she crept down the stairs to the closet where the gardener's clothes were kept and took a large gray canvas tarpaulin that was used to collect leaves in in the fall. She struggled with the stiff material and finally managed to wrap it tightly enough to cover her dress and conceal her auburn hair. It was fortunate that she had fallen asleep the night before still fully dressed for it saved time now that the sky was beginning to grow light.

With that problem solved she now faced the dilemma of how to escape from the house without rousing anyone. She crept past her parents' room comforted by the sound of their heavy, regular breathing. Her greatest challenge was to escape without Lupo awakening the whole household with his barking. Just this once she wished he were not such a faithful watchdog. Thinking it best to take the initiative she called softly, "Lupo, good boy, Lupo," and was rewarded with a soft wet muzzle against her hand and a vigorous wag of his tail that signaled he would not give away her secret.

She needed all the strength she could muster to lift the heavy beam that secured the latch on the door to the garden. The scraping noise it made seemed magnified in the stillness of the night. She waited—barely breathing. No one stirred. She felt a rush of the chill night air as she opened the great door just wide enough to slip her slender body through. In a moment it closed behind her and she was safely on the other side. But she did not feel safe! On the contrary, she trembled as she realized where she was, alone in the darkness.

"Why did I not take Lupo with me? He might not be fierce but at least his lusty barking might frighten away an attacker. Well, it is too late to worry about that now: I cannot turn back."

She realized suddenly that there was the added problem of how to return without being found out. There was nothing to do now but follow her plan and deal with that when the time came. As darkness gradually gave way to light, she realized, "San Salvatore is too far. I cannot reach there before daylight. I will go to San Domenico where *Fra* Tommaso lives—all will be well if only I can speak to him. He will know what to do"

She was well acquainted with that area for it was not far from her father's shop and she felt she could manage to be inconspicuous if only she remained in the shadows as much as possible. Just before turning into Via Catena she stumbled and fell, letting out a small cry—just startled, not hurt. She merely tripped over a beggar curled up in a corner of the stairs. Smelling of sour wine and vomit he cursed her loudly as he turned over again and, in a moment, fell back into his drunken stupor.

She decided to make her way up Via Bernabei. It was narrow and still in deep shadows from the steep overhanging roofs. She knew it well.

"Courage, keep going, just a few more steps." At the top she had only to turn to the right a few paces and she would be at the church of San Domenico. The sun was beginning to shine through the clouds as she pounded on the great door of the friary with the large iron knocker that hung there. She knew that by this hour the friars must certainly be awake. Up to now she was so preoccupied with the business of escaping that she had not considered her appearance. What would the porter think? She wanted to turn and run but it was too late. The door opened and in a moment she found herself face to face with the old friar. He was bent and lame, but had a kindly face that seemed to betray no annoyance at being summoned so early. He had undoubtedly seen many a sight in his long service as porter and betrayed no sign of surprise at the spectacle of this peculiarly clad young girl. Instead he smiled benignly and simply inquired, "What is it that brings you out at this untimely hour, child?"

"Father, I am sorry to trouble you so early but I must speak with *Fra* Tommaso."

"*Fra* Tommaso is at prayer just now…"

"Please, Father, it is important. I must return home before my parents miss me."

"Oh, a runaway?"

"No. Well, yes. I can't explain…I must speak with him"

"Very well, I will call him."

Already she felt better. In the distance she could hear the faint sound of the friars chanting their morning office, and she felt comforted too by rich fragrance of warm candlewax mingled with the unmistakable aroma of fresh bread.

The large rosary beads that hung from *Fra* Tommaso's waist always made a muted rattling sound as he walked. She had often teased him about never being able to surprise anyone. Now however the sound was comforting as it announced his arrival. He did not recognize this strangely attired waif until she dropped the dingy canvas wrap and ran to him.

"Prudenza!" He seemed genuinely alarmed at her disheveled appearance. "What is it?" Clearly something was very wrong. "What brings you here at this hour?"

His strong presence and the sound of his voice released her pent-up emotion and fear as through convulsed sobs she relayed the events of the last two days. He tried not to allow her to see his alarm at what he heard. It was clear that she needed him now.

"Oh, what shall I do, Father?"

"For now it is important to be calm, Prudenza. I know it is difficult, but you must realize that you have just been through a very emotional experience. You need time."

"But there is no time. I must give my answer by tomorrow. Cecchi will return then."

"Your parents love you very much, Prudenza, and you know that they want only the best for you, your happiness. This *Signore* Cecchi—if your father thinks so highly of him he must surely be a good man. You have met him?"

"No. I have only seen him, served him when he came on business, but I have never been presented to him. He is polite enough, but…but he looks at me like…It makes me uncomfortable, Father."

Tommaso wished she had more experience, was better prepared to deal with life outside convent walls. She was so innocent and looked to him now to advise her. It was a grave responsibility.

"Prudenza, you are a lovely young woman. Perhaps Cecchi is just admiring your beauty. After you have been introduced and you have time to come to know each other, you will undoubtedly find him desirable, too."

"Do you think so?"

"Yes, I believe you will grow to like him. Besides, there is always a proper period of time between betrothal and marriage."

She was silent for a moment. "I know he has money and he dresses well, but that is not important to me, Father."

The friar detected a slightly playful attitude in her gesture as she continued, "You know, Father, Cecchi is from Florence, like you," and then added a bit mischievously, "but I'll wager he has never even heard of Dante!"

"No? You don't think so?"

"No! And I'm sure he cannot play the lute. He probably would not know a lute from a cornamuse."

Fra Tommaso laughed. "That's better, Prudenza. More like my old student."

Suddenly becoming serious again, she looked squarely into his sympathetic face and declared, "Father, I want to do the right thing. Maybe I'm just frightened. I've never been around men before."

"Of course you are frightened. That is natural. But you are a good, devoted daughter, Prudenza. Tell me something; do you remember what is the fourth commandment?"

"Yes, of course. 'Honor thy father and thy mother.' So you are saying that I should agree to marry this man?"

"No, that must be your decision. But remember, obedience never fails to elicit God's blessing. I believe you will see. In the meantime I will be here for you whenever you need me." Lightening the conversation he said, "You know I really miss our little rhyming games. How about one for good measure before you go?" He challenged, *godevo*.

Even in her distraught state she shot back without hesitation, "*fondevo, giungevo*."

"My turn! A hard one for the professor!" She wrinkled her brow thoughtfully and then challenged, *imperscrutabile.*

He countered *inalterabile, inapplicabile.* "Prudenza, above all, remember *obedienza!*"

Ah, about that one she could not jest nor make a rhyme— not right now at least. "Tell me, *Fra* Tommaso, if I must marry this man, will you bless our nuptials?"

"Of course. I would be honored, Prudenza, to do so for my brightest and best student," and after a thoughtful pause added, "for my friend. Now you must return home. Do not creep back in disguise as if you had done something wrong."

"But I have, Father."

"Your parents will understand. Leave that dingy wrap and do not be afraid. Wait here for a moment." He returned shortly wearing a black mantle, his outdoor attire. "I will go with you and explain."

"Oh, would you?"

"I offered, did I not?"

With that they were off. Prudenza held her head high now, walking confidently behind her friend. Yes, she thought, he called me his friend!

When they reached home everything was as he said it would be. Her parents had not even realized she was gone. Lupo met them at the gate, panting and jumping with delight and they entered by the main door. She introduced *Fra* Tommaso and allowed him to explain.

Alfonso responded first. "My dear, you know we would have allowed you to go to seek *Fra* Tommaso's advice if you had asked." He was not angry. In fact he seemed relieved and was obviously pleased to have the opportunity to meet this priest who had done so much for Prudenza during her days at San Salvatore.

Ever the gracious hostess, Caterina would not hear of their guest leaving without refreshments. With a sign from her mother, Prudenza assumed her usual duties. Never had she been so pleased to serve anyone.

It was settled then. Or was it? Alfonso and Caterina were relieved that the priest had calmed Prudenza, but there remained a lingering doubt in their own minds. Was this really the right thing to do?

As he climbed back to his friary, *Fra* Tommaso, too, had misgivings about this extraordinary arrangement. "I would feel so much better if I could meet this Cecchi. But Alfonso Beltramonto is a good father, and I must trust that he would do what is right."

While the three most important people in her life wrestled with doubts, Prudenza was alone now to contend with her own demons. Surely *Fra* Tommaso would not have counseled her to go through with this marriage if it were wrong for her. Despite the comfort she gained from his words, her anxiety would not go away but remained like a harpy sitting on her shoulder.

Even her beloved Dante could not quell her fears, as she turned to her favorite episode in the *Inferno, Canto* V. It was a poor choice for she had begun to identify with the doomed Francesca da Rimini who, for political reasons, was married to a husband she did not love.

She put down the book suddenly, knowing that she dared not follow Francesca's story to its sad ending. "I know her fate. Francsca loved the wrong man, Paolo, the brother of her husband. And, for that, her soul and that of her lover were doomed eternally to be driven about hell by a never-ceasing wind, the symbol of their passion. It would give them no rest."

Her common sense reminded her that this was not the same. "For one thing there is no other man in my life, no brother with whom I have fallen in love. There is, in fact, no love at all in my story—certainly not from the man I seem destined to marry. I do not even know him."

For Matteo this endless waiting was difficult, too. While Prudenza sought solace in music and poetry, he attempted to quiet his nerves in Ancona's taverns, drinking heartily and at the same time attempting to scavenge as much information about Beltramonto as he could. He was growing weary of being scrutinized, first by the smugglers and now by Beltramonto. "Now it is my turn. Is this friend of my father's really such a paragon of honesty and integrity? The locals will know. If I was able to wrest information from those crafty smugglers surely I can tap into the local gossip for a realistic look at the man who will soon, I hope, be my father-in-law."

But not even an abundance of grappa and many rounds of the flask turned up one scintilla of wrongdoing on the part of

Alfonso. "What bad luck! Somehow I would feel better if Beltramonto were not so perfect."

—⁓—

At the appointed time, he groomed his horse, donned his best clothes and appeared at Beltramonto's door, this time armed with a gift for Caterina, a fine Florentine silk handkerchief embroidered in gold with her initials—a product of the Cecchi *botegga*. This would be his first meeting with his prospective mother-in-law and he was understandably nervous. He suspected that she might be a formidable obstacle to this union. This time Alfonso ushered Matteo into the salon instead of their usual place in his office.

To Matteo this seemed a good omen for, though it was still very formal, at least this gesture lifted the meeting above the level of business. In a departure from the previous routine Prudenza did not serve the refreshments. Instead, Alfonso introduced Matteo to Caterina who graciously accepted the beautiful gift he brought her and then assumed the role of hostess. She appeared to be all that the prospective mother-in-law was expected to be. Although exceedingly polite, there remained a slight coolness as she tended to her duties.

Matteo was impressed with her appearance, though. He noted that she showed no signs of her age other than a few wisps of gray in her carefully arranged dark-brown hair. Her carriage was regal and gave her the appearance of being taller than she actually was. She looked dignified in her simple morning dress of deep, rich burgundy color, modest in design, with high neck and long sleeves trimmed with delicate lace. She wore no ostentatious jewelry—only a simple gold wedding band. As she served the two men she engaged Matteo in benign conversation, inquiring of his family, his father's business, and the climate in Florence. After what seemed to him a very long time, Alfonso finally got around to the reason for this meeting.

"*Signore* Cecchi."

Matteo's heart was pounding so violently now that he felt certain they must surely be able to hear it. This Beltramonto was not as malleable as he originally seemed, and he had made Matteo wait for his answer.

"My wife and I have given much thought to the arrangement we discussed at your last visit and I am pleased to tell you that we agree to the plan. I will provide the one thousand florins that you need to buy the alum and, if all of the details are carried out satisfactorily, we will agree to our daughter's marriage."

"Oh, *Signore* Beltramonto, this is good news indeed. You make me very happy and you will bring much joy to my dear father, as well. I thank you." Turning to Caterina he bowed deeply and said, "I give you my word, *Signora* Beltramonto, that I will abide by the letter of our agreement; I will cherish your daughter and make a good home for her."

Caterina managed to produce a polite smile, excused herself momentarily, and returned shortly with Prudenza.

For Matteo this moment was worth all the waiting. All thought of contracts, deadlines, and unpleasant encounters with the smugglers dissolved into euphoria at the vision of this young woman who had captured his heart without ever speaking a word.

Prudenza's confident appearance on her mother's arm actually belied her fears, for inside she was trembling, frightened that her legs would collapse beneath her as she walked into the salon. Caterina's support was more than symbolic: She needed the physical assistance as she faced this ordeal.

For the occasion Caterina had suggested her daughter wear the same green brocade gown that she wore the first time Cecchi saw her. He relived that moment and even detected the same delicate fragrance as before. What was different about this encounter, however, was her steady gaze at him. On all of their previous meetings she had fulfilled her tasks with eyes demurely downcast as she had been taught at San Salvatore. Matteo was surprised at his own reaction—for a moment unnerved by that look. This bride he chose had something of her father's disquieting, direct gaze. Hers was a sort of emerald-eyed version of her father's steady gray stare.

Alfonso stepped forward and, taking Prudenza's hand, presented her saying, "*Signore* Cecchi, this is my beloved daughter Prudenza Maria Cecilia Beltramonto."

With his hat in his left hand and his right over his heart

Matteo managed to execute a perfect deep bow before his prospective bride and said, "I am deeply honored, *Signorina* Beltramonto." Then turning to Caterina and Alfonso he repeated his thanks. "I promise you will not regret your decision."

It was then Prudenza's turn. With the graceful curtsy she had perfected at San Salvatore she spoke the very first words Matteo heard from her, her formal acceptance. "*Signore* Cecchi, I am honored to meet you. I accept your proposal of marriage and will strive to be a faithful wife."

He was mesmerized at the sweet sound of her voice and her fine Tuscan diction. He had not expected that from an Anconetana, and would have to polish his own language if he were ever to be a proper husband to this fine specimen of a woman.

Caterina stood by silently while Alfonso shook Matteo's hand and gave him a fatherly embrace. The formalities thus properly dispensed with, Alfonso moved to the business at hand. "We must have a contract with all of the provisions laid out."

"Yes, of course. My father would certainly wish it so."

"I have asked a notary to draft the contract and he is waiting in my study now with the document. Allow me to call him."

Prudenza moved into the background now and for a brief moment Matteo felt he was alone with Caterina. She managed a wan smile and attempted to sound sincere when she assured him, "My husband and I welcome you into our family. We pray that you will treasure our daughter as we do, and that you will give us many happy grandchildren."

This was the first mention of such a thought and Prudenza hoped he did not notice her blush at her mother's remark.

"I assure you, *Signora*, that..." Before he could finish Alfonso entered escorting the notary, *Ser* Bernardino Spinelli, who wore the long robes and peculiar hat of his office. Under his arm he carried a parchment roll that he unfurled with a practiced flourish. Alfonso had attended to every detail of the agreement and insisted that the notary read the entire statement aloud for all to hear.

Prudenza found herself relegated to the role of observer, a witness at the very auction block where her life was about to be bartered. Usually what was sold in her father's study was lifeless merchandise. It was her duty to carry in the parchments, the ink, the pens, and the sealing wax. Now however, she was no longer the secretary. She was a part of the bargain, an item in a legal agreement. She was being sold! With the realization of what was happening, a chill gripped her entire body and suddenly she questioned if *Fra* Tommaso could have been wrong. If only he were here now!

To Prudenza the notary looked like a plump owl. His eyes were like small orbs of dull black obsidian as he peered through the thick eyeglasses perched on his nose and began to wheeze in a thin, nasal, high-pitched voice:

"With this document:

I, Alfonso Eduardo Beltramonto, Anconetano and

I, Matteo Benedetto Cecchi, Fiorentino, enter into the following solemn agreement:

Item: *Signore* Beltramonto will pay the sum of one thousand gold florins to *Signore* Cecchi for the purchase of alum from the mines of the Fratelli Bosi;

Item: The said *Signore* Cecchi agrees to waive the usual dowry due him at this time, the one thousand florins being payment for the alum in lieu of the dowry for *Signore* Beltramonto's daughter, Prudenza Maria Cecilia;

Item: The said alum is to be delivered to *Signore* Beltramonto by *Signore* Cecchi before the end of September 1536;

Item: At the time the alum is delivered the document of betrothal will be signed, and the ceremony will take place in Ancona at the church of Maria della Piazza;

Item: The bride's parents shall provide the ring at the time of this ceremony;

Item: *Signore* Beltramonto will process the alum and the dyes by April 1537 when *Signore* Cecchi will come to collect them. At that time *Signore* Cecchi will return to Florence with his bride, taking also the wedding chest of linens and plate provided by the bride's parents. The wedding ceremony will be solemnized at the church of Santa Croce in the city of Florence.

Given on this 26th day of June, 1536."

Satisfied that all was in order, Alfonso stepped forward and signed in his usual round, carefully formed letters. Matteo followed and affixed a wildly florid signature.

Suddenly it was done. "At least for them," Prudenza reflected. "This document that determines my future does not even require my signature!" With the sterile formality of the contract, any illusion of love or romance plummeted to the level of a business transaction as she stood silently by.

While the notary was droning away in his pinched, reedy voice, Prudenza's eyes scrutinized the man destined to be her husband. He was distracted with the business of the contract and the signatures and was unaware of her critical assessment.

Despite his fine clothes and careful grooming for the occasion, she found him wanting in some respects. As he bent to fix his signature to the contract his cloak had slipped from its place to reveal the curvature that he had been so careful to conceal before. Prudenza felt a slight revulsion at the sight and could not help thinking of Francesca da Rimini's husband who, it was said, was ugly and deformed.

The elegant rings that Cecchi wore on his carefully manicured hands seemed ostentatious, even garish compared to the understated elegance of her parents. And his speech certainly did not establish his Florentine origin. She reminded herself, "It is not fair to compare him with *Fra* Tommaso who is a scholar. Cecchi is a merchant."

The business of the contract over, Matteo directed his entire attention to Prudenza. All of the bravura he managed in dealing with the smugglers was as nothing compared to the courage it required for him to face his prospective bride and address her in language befitting her station, her innocence. It was appropriate now for him to make some more or less conventional remarks.

He moved hesitantly toward her, knelt on one knee and, taking her right hand in his pressed his lips to her hand. In that moment Prudenza felt an unfamiliar rush of warmth, of emotion, a sensation she could not explain. He, too, seemed moved and was about to address her when that cursed stammering that always affected him in times of emotion and tension returned. "*Signorina* Be-bel-tr- tra tra tr…"

Prudenza felt his discomfort. How humiliating for him to stammer at this solemn moment. With the utmost delicacy, she accepted his hand and said, "I bring my heart and my mind to this sacred promise, sir."

"You will b-b-be m-my…"

"Faithful wife." Prudenza gracefully finished for him.

He was embarrassed but visibly relieved and at the same time impressed at her sensitivity and quick thinking.

Eager to escape he made his obeisance to Caterina and bowed to Alfonso who, in his efficiency, provided duplicate copies of the contract. Prudenza noted how Cecchi clutched it in his hand—like the spoils of a well-fought battle she thought. He again proffered his hand to Prudenza without attempting to speak this time. He continued bowing as he backed through the door of the salon and finally disappeared into the stable where Mea awaited him.

He spurred the mare to a gallop, brandishing the parchment roll like a weapon, crying aloud, "Father, I bring you my trophy!"

CHAPTER 7

The Contraband

The sliver of light that shone under Zenobi's door meant he was still awake, so Matteo knocked impatiently and, without waiting for an answer, bolted in to find the old man still at his desk, scrutinizing his accounts as always—much as when Matteo had left him.

Tired from a hard four-day ride, but strangely energized by his success, he related the events in as much detail as he thought prudent to share, carefully avoiding the subject of the dowry he had renounced or his experiences with the smugglers. After all, he told himself, there was no need to worry the old man. He may be a bit of a pious old fool but I need his approval. So I will keep the good news about Beltramonto's daughter until last and that will leave him happy.

It was a great deal for Zenobi to absorb in such a speedy report. Twice he interrupted his son saying, *"piano, piano,"* as though choking down too much food in one gulp. Finally he raised his hands, turning his palms toward Matteo in a gesture that said, "Enough. Have mercy on my tired old brain. Now please tell me again, slowly."

"Forgive me, Father. I am so happy. I could not wait to share this good news with you."

"And it is good news, Son. You have done well for us and for my friend Alfonso."

"There is more, Father, more that I believe will bring you greater joy than you can imagine. I have asked Beltramonto for his daughter's hand in marriage, and he has agreed."

Zenobi's mouth fell open and his eyes were wide with disbelief. "Please, Son, the hour is late and I am weary. Tell me that I have not misunderstood."

"No, you have not, Father. It is true. The formal betrothal will take place when I return to Ancona in September to deliver the alum to Beltramonto. Oh, Father, you will love her. She is a treasure—modest and beautiful and will bring honor to the Cecchi family."

Zenobi's face had become radiant now, and the worry lines around his eyes began to relax as he mused aloud, "My old friend Alfonso's daughter—to become my daughter-in-law. It is more than I could ever have hoped for, Matteo. She will be the daughter I never had."

"*Signore* Beltramonto expects to have the alum processed by spring when I will go to collect it along with the dyes, and at that time I will bring my bride back with me to Florence. I would like the wedding to be at Santa Croce."

"Matteo, in all your excitement you have not told me the name of your bride."

"She is called Prudenza, Father." Like a bee savoring the nectar from each blossom he dwelt long on every syllable as he announced her full name. "She is called *Pru-den-za Ma-ri-a Ce-ci-li-a Bel-tra-mon-to.* Is it not a beautiful name, Father, for a beautiful young woman?"

"Yes, yes indeed." With difficulty Zenobi rose from his place and warmly embraced his son. Even as the tears welled up in his tired eyes, he showed no embarrassment at this uncharacteristic display of emotion. "You have pleased me, Son, and I am proud of you. Your mother, too, will be so happy. But it is late now: You must wait until tomorrow to tell her the good news."

For now all thoughts of finance and bookkeeping vanished and Zenobi was a happy man. This was more than commerce; it was the union of two families, a union that transcended the commercial.

—ॐ—

Maddalena was rarely in the kitchen—especially at this early hour. Anna, that irresponsible kitchen maid, had failed to show up again and Maddalena made no secret of her annoyance. She was standing at the hearth: With her left hand she poked the fire beneath a huge iron cauldron of polenta while, with her right, she stirred the contents with a vigor that betrayed the degree of her irritation. Her back was turned toward the door so she did not see her son enter. For that matter Matteo seldom ventured into the cook's domain, but this morning was different. He must tell his mother the good news as soon as possible. Even so, he stood quietly for a moment, mildly amused to hear his genteel mother muttering, "Lazy thing! She must go."

Finally he called to her from the doorway, *"Mamma…
Mamma*, may I speak with you?"

She was surprised. What could he possibly want to speak to her about at this hour and in the kitchen of all places? Without turning to him she responded—a bit impatiently—"Yes, speak up. I am listening." Still she did not turn around and despite the urgency in his voice continued to stir the polenta, explaining, "It will become lumpy if I do not continue to stir. Come, stand beside me and tell me what it is that you want."

"What I want, *Mamma,* is to share with you the greatest happiness of my life." Almost without pausing to breathe between sentences, Matteo delivered the good news. And, just as Zenobi had predicted, Maddalena was ecstatic at the thought of acquiring a daughter-in-law; it would be so good to have another female member of the family.

Immediately, but without losing the rhythm of her stirring, she began a mental catalogue of all the preparations she would need to make for the wedding which was already less than a year away. Her mind raced as she tabulated aloud all of the matters that would be her responsibility.

"The wedding of the son of such a prominent merchant as Zenobi Cecchi must be elegant. Perhaps with your father's influence he could obtain some exception from those foolish sumptuary laws that control ridiculous things like the number of candles on the altar and the width of a woman's sleeves."

"Mamma, there is time for all that later."

"Of course there will be the usual notary to preside, but

your father must obtain permission from the prior for a clergyman to be present, too, as you exchange your vows—and not just in some dark, side chapel."

Nothing was too extravagant now for Maddalena's imagination as she envisioned the marriage ceremony to be held in no less a place of honor than the high altar. "The wedding will be in early summer so flowers will be abundant—lilies, irises, oxalis, orange blossoms. Oh, I can see it now. Beneath Giotto's great crucifix the whole sanctuary should be banked with all manner of roses and ginestra the color of gold."

With the mention of flowers, her stirring grew more vigorous and the polenta actually seemed to be bubbling in time with Maddalena's chatter. As her catalogue grew, her stirring of the polenta became so animated that bits of the golden porridge in the kettle began to fly about leaving traces of cornmeal on the hearth, the floor, and even on Maddalena's bodice. She did not even seem to mind.

Matteo was pleased to make her so happy. Soon the two of them began to laugh like delighted children and, absolutely uninhibited now, together did a quick pirouette like youthful lovers. Without warning Maddalena stopped. She picked up the large spoon she had abandoned to do her dance and suddenly looked very serious as she resumed her stirring of the polenta, her thoughts moving on quickly to the important matter of costume. "Surely the son of a silk merchant would be expected to represent the highest in standard of dress and the most current styles. I must contact a fine tailor; someone in the *oltr'arno*, perhaps. I have heard that Biagio Poro, the *sarto* whose shop is in Borgo San Frediano, is excellent. And my friends tell me he knows the latest fashions. It will be my responsibility."

"You will attend to that, Mother dear, I am sure."

Ignoring Matteo's words, her thoughts sped on down the same course. "Not only will I have to attend to your costume and to my own clothes for the festivities, but for your father's as well. Although he deals in textiles he seems not to care at all about the latest fashions."

"All will be well, Mother, I know. You must not worry about it. This will be a happy occasion."

Without seeming to hear her son she carried on, "Yes,

and there will be fêtes! The wedding festivities are never complete without a sumptuous meal and entertainment. We will have music, dancing and singing, and maybe even jugglers." She clapped her hands like an excited child as she spoke. "Oh, Matteo it will be beautiful—so beautiful."

With this last announcement Matteo excused himself and attempted to leave but she stopped him abruptly, "Wait, Son. You have not told me what she looks like."

"She is comely, *Mamma*, with hair the color of burnished bronze, like the sun on coral; and her eyes are the color of the sea—like two beautiful aquamarines set in a face with skin like fine porcelain."

"Indeed, you must be in love, Matteo! I have never heard you speak so poetically."

Without another thought of the porridge steadily thickening in the pot, Maddalena abandoned the polenta to become one huge sodden lump, and went scurrying out of the room, still muttering—this time delightedly, "It is going to be a busy year."

"Yes, Mother. It is going to be a busy year. If only you knew!"

Zenobi gave Matteo a small room—an annex next to his own office, in hope that he would apply himself like a proper apprentice to the Cecchi business. It was a good thing for, now more than ever, Matteo needed a place of his own where he could contemplate his next move.

He began to chart in his mind the sequence of events. The most immediate problem was how to obtain the things necessary for transport of the alum without arousing his father's suspicions. The situation was further complicated by the need to attend to every detail precisely as dictated by the smugglers. The wagon, the straw, and the flasks that they demand—these he dare not collect while still in Forence where he was so well-known. Besides, Zenobi would certainly ask questions.

In order not to arouse Father's curiosity I will ride out of the city on Mea just like the last time. But after I reach Monterchi, I will hire burrows to haul the wagon. I cannot use this fine horse to pull a dray. That is a donkey's work. And I will certainly not ride a donkey myself—damned stubborn, stupid animals! I will simply ride ahead on my beautiful horse, with the donkey cart following. After all, I have my pride!

This was the time to call in some favors from his drinking partners and gambling cronies on the outskirts of Arezzo. He had rendered favors for some and many owed him money. They need not know the real reason for his strange needs at this time. Surely it should not be difficult to rent a cart full of straw, and in *chianti* country there would be no dearth of wine flasks to complete the camouflage.

Matteo had a reputation for being lucky at dice—some even accused him of using loaded dice. It would be simple for him to call in some gambling debts owed him from the many trips he made for his father's business. By this means he could finance the trip without arousing Zenobi's suspicions.

His biggest debtor was Cinghi—so called for his broad, ugly features half covered with an immense mustache that resembled the tusks of a wild boar, a *cinghialo*. And there was Spina, whose vicious tongue could skewer an adversary as effectively as the spines of the *porcospina*. But the kindest and best of them was Moro, a rather sweet fellow whose round face and bulging eyes that never seemed to blink made him resemble an owl, a *gufo*. Indeed, among his gambling cronies, that is how he was affectionately known.

Matteo never before questioned why so many of his shady friends were known by animal names. "Oh, well. It doesn't really seem to bother them." He mused, "I wonder what they call me. Maybe I should adopt an animal name, too, but what should it be? Something clever, of course; better than pig or porcupine! Yes, I should be *volpe*, for am I not cunning like a fox? Surely my name must be written in the stars, for I am not only Matteo, from Matthew, the tax collector of the gospels, but also Cefo the smuggler and now Volpe the clever fox." He laughed as he repeated it aloud several times, "Cefo Volpe, Cefo Volpe shall surpass Matteo!"

Alone in his little cubicle Matteo penned urgent notes to these denizens of the gaming table as well as to the numerous acquaintances with whom he had shared many a generous round of grappa. He had always been liberal when it came to sharing the fruit of the vine. It made him feel superior. Now was their time to be benevolent. To all of them the message was the same. He would be leaving Florence on an important business trip of undisclosed nature and was requesting payment of whatever they owed him. To each he specified the meeting place and reminded them of the amount of their debt.

Cinghi, the largest debtor, was ordered to meet him on Saturday, the first day of September at the inn called the Cinque Corvi, the Five Crows, just north of Terranuovo. He had planned to stop here overnight, long enough to collect the 137 florins that Cinghi owed him and to rest for the next day's journey, which would take him to some of the villages in the environs of Arezzo to collect from debtors there. Just before the little town of LeVille he would turn off to Monterchi where Gufo was ordered to await him. Not only would Matteo exact money from his owl-faced friend but he had ordered Gufo to obtain for him the wagon and the burrows needed to pull it.

He was satisfied that all seemed to be in order until gradually his debtors began to respond—all of them imploring patience, and most of them entreating him to accept only partial payment. There were all the usual excuses. A sick wife, a poor crop, a flood that had carried off half the livestock, lightning had struck the barn, and on and on. He had expected as much and even allowed for it in his plans without letting his debtors know. He comforted himself with the realization that if he could collect even half, he would have a comfortable sum. He needed to realize 500 florins in order to pay half of the agreed 1,000 to the smugglers when he picked up the alum. When he delivered the alum to Beltramonto he would receive his payment of 1,000 from which Matteo could then take 500 to ransom the gold chalice from the butcher Picchino. With the money he had received from his father he could make it work. All seemed clear.

August was drawing to a close and, despite the fact that his plans seemed secure, Matteo was becoming tense and uneasy; but he dared not allow his feelings to show. The weather was hot and humid and his little cubicle had become stifling. From its small window he saw that the Arno was so low, one could nearly cross it on foot, from stone to exposed stone, without even becoming wet.

But that was to be expected, for the rivers of Tuscany were generally not navigable in summer. He hoped that those of the north were, for he remembered that Otto planned to transport the alum part of the way down from Bressanone by means of barges on the Adige. Hopefully it would be passable.

For all his apparent bravado and posturing, Matteo was experiencing some doubts. Despite his success so far with the smugglers he realized that the more difficult part of the plot still lay ahead. If he had learned anything from his previous experience, it was to attack one problem at a time.

For the sake of his devout parents he maintained at least the appearance of fidelity to the religion of his childhood. Although now he was a man and had long ago sloughed off the appurtenances of childhood, he was beginning to be troubled with guilt and had to admit to the need for some assistance from a higher power of some sort. But how did he dare to expect divine intervention in such an illegal act? Moreover, by concealing the truth from his honest father, he was betraying his own flesh and blood and possibly endangering the Cecchi business. If found out, he might even spend his days in the Stinche, Florence's notorious debtor's prison. But there was no turning back now.

As the time for his departure drew nearer, Matteo's fretting became more intense and more difficult to conceal. He recognized that some of the piety his mother attempted to instill in her boys had left more of an impression upon him than he wished to admit. To be sure, it had infected his pious older brother now locked away in a monastery. But Matteo boasted, "I have put off these childish beliefs. I have no need of them. Besides, religion is for women."

Nonetheless, some remnants of his conscience refused to be silenced and asserted themselves in a curious and surprising incident. Superstition, never very remote from his concept of religion, became a factor determining the date for his departure from Florence. He had thought to leave on August twenty-fourth. It was a Friday that year, which meant he could spend the weekend in Terranuovo settling affairs with Cinghi if necessary. Caution suggested he consider the alignment of the planets and the phase of the moon: They would be his oracle. But to satisfy his mother he also consulted the calendar of saints. That day was the feast of the Apostle Bartholomew who, she reminded him, had been martyred by being flayed alive! The thought of Lapo's mutilated ear and Picchino's skill with the dagger were all too fresh in his memory to allow him to ignore this frightening omen.

He considered Wednesday the twenty-ninth day of August. The moon would be favorable, in its first quarter. He could still reach San Sepolcro by the second Sunday of September as agreed with the smugglers. Again he consulted the church calendar to determine if this was a more auspicious day. He let out a horrified yelp as he read aloud, "The Solemnity of the beheading of John the Baptist!"

This was awful! He knew, like everyone in Florence, that the Baptist was the great patron saint of the city and all Florence celebrated June twenty-fourth, the day of his birth, with processions, parades, bonfires, banquets, fireworks, and, of course, the great game of the *calcio*. But beheading! This cannot be. He must find another day.

Still brooding over this apparent evil omen he ventured one more time to consult the liturgical calendar that had so upset him thus far. He noted that the day before the feast commemorating the Baptist's loss of his head was dedicated to Augustine, the great sinner who became a saint—so it is believed—through the intercession of his Holy Mother Monica. With Augustine the sinner, Matteo could identify. Besides, did he not also have a pious mother in Maddalena? Like his luck with the toss of the dice Matteo felt he won yet another round in this gambit. So on the twenty-eighth day of August—assuming the protection of St. Augustine—he once more rode out of Florence on his beautiful horse with confidence, and with his saddlebags again provisioned by his loving mother.

Although the weather was still warm, the summer was waning and soon it would be vintage time—the *vendemmia*. The grape harvest and the olive gathering were autumnal work that brought with it good fellowship and wholesome celebration of the land's bounty. As he rode through the countryside, Matteo saw the unmistakable signs of approaching fall. Braids of garlic and onions were hung to dry outside the doors of farmhouses and festoons of golden maize decorated many a modest cowshed. There was something good and wholesome about it that calmed his anxieties. This time of the year the slant of the sun's rays was different and the tawny haystacks that dotted the land reflected the intense gold of the setting sun like so many jewels. It was a bit too early for hunters, or for trufflers to be out with their pigs; but the chestnuts were always at their peak during the grape harvest. He suddenly felt thirsty at the thought of these roasted savories so rewarding with a mug of red wine after a long ride.

Shortly after leaving Florence he passed a group of pilgrims singing their simple hymns as they made their way on foot to Impruneta to worship at the shrine of Our Lady. They seemed so happy and full of expectation that their prayers would be answered. Simple folks, these, he thought. Though his attitude was one of condescension, the very simplicity of their faith left him with a momentary feeling of envy. He had long ago lost his innocence, but this was no time for regret. He forced the sound of the pilgrims' hymns to fade in the distance as he spurred his horse on toward Terranuovo where he hoped Cinghi was waiting.

Partly in the interest of time, he took the Valdarno route instead of the more scenic Pratomagno that would have again taken him past Vallombrosa. By avoiding the sight of the great abbey he would also spare himself any feeling of guilt when he thought of his pious brother Fabrizio. Matteo was much too far into his devious plot to allow any doubts to enter his mind now.

Soon the walls of the old Aretine fortress at Terranuovo came into view and in minutes he spied the sign. It was unmistakable. The flurry of ten black wings against a blue sky confirmed that this was indeed the Inn of the Five Crows.

Although it was still early in the day to be drinking, Cinghi was already inebriated. He brandished a bottle so tightly clenched in his left hand that his knuckles appeared white, while his right arm flailed about in the air as if thrashing an imaginary sparring partner. He had obviously attempted to numb himself to lessen the pain of parting with the large sum he owed. But his eyes were not yet so completely dulled by the liquor that he did not recognize Matteo, who was in no mood to argue with this drunken fool.

Matteo went straight to the point. "I am here, Cinghi, to

collect the gambling debt you owe me." He then pulled from under his shirt a formal-looking document that he had drawn up and read it aloud, stressing the sum, "one hundred thirty-seven florins owed to Matteo Cecchi."

From beneath heavy eyelids the "wild boar" glowered at Matteo but said nothing.

Matteo repeated more forcefully, "I have come to collect. Hurry! I must be on my way quickly for I have a long way to go before nightfall." It was not true, of course, for he had planned to remain overnight.

Blurry-eyed and reeling unsteadily from side to side, Cinghi managed to pull from a dingy bag at his side a small purse of worn leather and defiantly dumped its contents on the floor at Matteo's feet. "Here. Take it you thief! It is all I have." Even under the thatch of his heavy mustache Matteo could see the sneer and the contemptuous curl of Cinghi's lip as he snarled, "But what do you care—you pretty rich boy from Florence, with your fine horse. Now my children will go hungry and my wife will beat me, too."

"You should have thought of that sooner. A debt is a debt." Without actually touching the money, Matteo pointed to the coins with the toe of his right boot and commanded in a cold and calculated tone, "Pick it up, you swine! Give it to me! Now. Or I will beat you."

Cinghi had never seen Matteo angry and it frightened him so much that when he stooped to collect the money from the floor he fell backward and like a huge thrashing animal spewed forth a geyser, vomiting not only on the money but also on Matteo's fine leather boots.

His anger almost uncontrollable, Matteo kicked Cinghi so vehemently that the tavern keeper intervened, pushing the drunken man onto a bench out of Matteo's reach. He dumped a pail of water over the filthy floor and the money and ordered the young barmaid to wash the coins and give them to Matteo. In an attempt to forestall an all-out brawl he ordered both men out of the tavern.

Still seething, Matteo attempted to clean his befouled boots in the tall grass at the side of the road, while he sat on a nearby stump and counted the still-wet coins. "Ninety-three in all! That filthy scoundrel! He still owes me forty-four more florins."

Realizing that nothing more was to be gained here just

now, he bounded into the saddle and looking down at Cinghi, lying there on the ground in a drunken stupor, he brandished his fist angrily and screamed, "You will pay, you swine." Almost as an afterthought he laughed derisively and declared, "You are well named, Pig." With that he was off in the direction of Monterchi.

—m—

As he followed the bend in the Arno, passing above Arezzo, the scenery and the cool air began to calm his anger and clear the awful stench of the tavern from his nostrils. Just beyond LeVille he turned off to the right on the road to Monterchi where Gufo was waiting. He comforted himself with the knowledge that his little owl-faced friend was a good-natured sort and this would not be a difficult encounter. Besides, he genuinely liked Gufo. As expected, there he was—standing in the shade, his beady little owl eyes fixed upon the road as he awaited Matteo in the designated place.

With good reason Gufo had suggested this little town for he was well acquainted here. More importantly, he knew of the strange subterranean passageway around the apse of the church where he had been able to stow the straw, the flasks, and the other provisions Matteo needed in order to conceal the alum after he collected it in San Sepolcro. In the meantime, he had been able to arrange for the rental of the wagon and the beasts to pull it. Matteo was greatly relieved to see his smiling friend waiting on the steps of the little church near the gate of the cemetery.

In his plans Matteo had allowed for a longer time in Monterchi to permit him to make excursions into some nearby villages to collect other small sums owed him. Besides, there was much to do here, and he enjoyed Gufo's company. But first he needed to rest and keep his promise to Gufo of a good meal and the best wine of the region.

First thing the next day he arranged the hire of the donkeys. He had never ridden a donkey and had no intention of doing so now—nor had he driven a muleteam though he knew of the animals' stubborn nature. Perhaps it was simply a dogged childhood memory that caused him to insist upon donkeys rather than mules.

Once, when he was a young boy his father took him to see the *palio* of the Somari, a donkey race held annually in Montepulciano, where friendly looking little beasts—upon whom it was said Christ himself once rode—butted and reared and bolted and seemed to delight in dumping their riders in the muck.

By the third day all appeared to be in order. Matteo successfully collected the money from many of his debtors in the environs, and the flasks, the straw, and the wagon were procured. All that remained was to fetch the donkeys.

Early in the afternoon Matteo and Gufo met with the farmer who owned them. The mild-looking little black creatures with a pool of white circling their eyes were peacefully grazing in the meadow. The farmer explained that Matteo could not expect the animals to pull the wagon without a driver or a rider on the lead donkey. He would have to do that.

Disregarding the farmer's suggestion, Matteo stubbornly refused. "I will not ride a donkey; I will simply ride ahead on Mea and expect the donkeys to follow."

The farmer was almost amused at the stupidity of the suggestion and warned him, "This will never work. You must ride the donkey."

It would be a challenge to control the animals this way but he was confident that with his skill as a horseman he could certainly learn to manage these little beasts with no trouble. After all, in Florence, Matteo Cecchi was well known as an able equestrian.

Finally, and after much argument, Matteo reluctantly mounted the donkey designated to lead, a sweet-looking little fellow who certainly posed no threat. He reminded himself that the riders he had seen in the donkey race rode bareback, with only a bit and bridle to control the animals. He was not worried. But no sooner had he sat on the beast's back than it began to kick, buck and—even more embarrassingly—to bray loudly. In a moment it dumped Matteo on the ground and stood looking triumphantly down on him. The pain in his rump was nothing compared to the injury to his pride as he lay there on the grass, dazed.

After a moment he rose, brushed off the dirt and announced emphatically, "I will not ride this wicked animal!"

Following some animated haggling with the farmer it was agreed that Gufo would ride with Matteo for the remainder of the trip and be responsible for the care of the donkeys. The recalcitrant one that deposited Matteo on the ground was now nuzzling Gufo and munching on a carrot that he wisely provided, anticipating what might happen. For his assistance, Matteo gladly forgave Gufo the debt he owed. Thus arranged, it was agreed that the wagon would be loaded before dawn and the little team would leave Monterchi for San Sepolcro before sunrise.

The wagon was modest-sized, well constructed and capable of bearing the weight of the alum. Since the sides could be lowered it made the loading easier and in only a short time the two men quietly stowed all of the straw and began to secure the flasks in place. Gufo had cleverly collected some demijons so it required only a few of them nestling in the straw to conceal the space inside where the alum would later be hidden.

All was proceeding smoothly until the donkeys were to be hitched to the wagon. Mindful that their braying at this untimely hour was bound to draw attention, the quick-thinking Gufo provided more carrots and apples to quiet them. Matteo watched admiringly as his friend spoke softly to the animals and patted their velvety noses while he went about hitching them. Though the wagon did not weigh a great deal now, once the alum was loaded it would be extremely heavy so it required a team of eight donkeys. As he stood back and surveyed their work, Matteo uttered a quiet, "Thank God for Gufo."

Mea stood apart snorting and pawing the ground from time to time as she observed this strange early-morning exercise. Almost as if reflecting the attitude of her master she seemed to assume an air of disdain for the lowly dray animals that might be her distant cousins.

Matteo mounted the mare and rode ahead as Gufo took his place on the lead donkey and cracked his whip. The wagon creaked slightly and the donkeys' hooves resounded against the stone pavement. Dawn was just breaking and there was still a heavy dew on the tall grass alongside the road.

As they passed through the city gates Matteo breathed more freely, confident that with Gufo everything was under control. Progress was slow, however, with the donkeys and the wagon lumbering along behind. Mea seemed to reflect Matteo's impatience with the pace of things as, from time to time, he paused for the pack animals to catch up. Even so, the little caravan made it to the walls of San Sepolcro before noon.

Along the way they passed large numbers of noisy people headed for the festivities. Most were happily chatting and even singing as they went, feasting on panini, figs, and new wine. Matteo could not help reflecting how correct Picchino had been when he predicted that no one would take much note of him and his wagon train of donkeys amid all the distractions. He appeared to be just another vendor taking his wares to the festival. All about him hucksters were loudly hawking their goods and the aroma of roasted chestnuts and sausages mingling in the morning air prompted some thirsty young men to attempt to buy wine from Gufo, who cleverly put them off with some excuse about having promised his cargo to the managers of the *palio*. He truly was proving to be as wise as the owl for whom he was named.

As the caravan approached the city gate, the keeper attempted to collect the *gabella*, the duty upon materials brought into the city. To Matteo this seemed utterly inappropriate and he argued with the man, calling on his distant knowledge of scripture. "Is this venerable old city not the repository of some actual stones taken from the tomb of Christ? Had not Christ driven the moneychangers from the temple? This was sacriligious!"

As the gatekeeper persisted, their bickering became louder and finally Matteo capitulated, fearing that his arguing would draw unwanted attention.

Trying to appear as inconspicuous as possible they continued along the way that Matteo decided upon when he investigated the city in June. It was becoming more difficult to progress through the narrow streets, now made nearly impassable by crowds of children waving little flags, young lovers wandering arm in arm, vendors selling toy crossbows, and garrulous young men wagering over the outcome of the contest.

A large contingent of young men from Gubbio were rumored to be coming to San Sepolcro bent on revenge. The longstanding rivalry between the two cities always surfaced in demonstrations at the time of the *palio*, which was a two-part event. This year Gubbio lost to San Sepolcro in the first match in May, and now the Gubbians were here seeking vindication, claiming the contest was unfair. From the open doors of crowded taverns came the loud and sometimes angry-sounding arguments that spilled into the streets. Inebriated young men became combative, their language abusive, and their behavior churlish as they spit and urinated in the fountains, hoping to initiate an outright fight before the archery match even began.

Matteo tried to guide his little convoy away from the demonstrations but even so some of the offenders came near the wagon and attempted to snatch the flasks from the straw. The donkeys seemed to understand the danger and accommodated by braying in an ear-splitting unison that drew attention to the would-be thieves who quickly took cover. Once again Gufo had everything under control. Surely he had more than repaid his gambling debt to Matteo.

As they came nearer to the center of the city where the contest would take place, Matteo was surprised to hear the familiar sound of the *pifferi* and *zampogne*. Even Mea pricked up her ears. The sight of the rustics and the sound of the wheezy out-of-tune droning of their primitive bagpipes brought back cheerful thoughts of his childhood when Maddalena took him and Fabrizio to hear the revelers. She always gave them a few coppers to toss to the musicians who usually came down into the towns only at Christmas. The sound of the festivities of the *palio* must have brought them down from the hills in hopes of collecting a few coins.

The site Matteo selected back in June to pick up the contraband was an old shed behind the church of Santa Chiara. Here they would be far away from the crowd in the town's center and could load the alum without attracting attention. The church was next to the south wall of the city and close to a gate that allowed swift and easy exit. It led directly to Borgo Pace on the road leading to Fossombrone and finally to Fano on the coast. The site suited the smugglers, too, for they could stay in the seedy inn close by the church, near enough to the shed to keep watch on the contraband. Matteo knew the way and had carefully rehearsed the route in his mind many times and traced it over and over with his finger on the map that Nafri gave him.

Meandering slowly through the crowd, Matteo had an opportunity to catch a bit of the show of the famous flag throwers, the *sbandieratori* who demonstrated their skill by tossing colorful silken banners about in the air. As the little caravan approached the *duomo*, near Piazza Torre di Berta where the show was about to begin, the crowd was too dense to permit wagons to enter, so Gufo remained patiently behind with the donkeys and Matteo stayed a short distance apart, seated up high on Mea so that he could watch the show. He surveyed the crowd, studying faces and imagining what his contacts, Renzo and Tonino—whom he had never met— might look like. Could they be here in the crowd somewhere, per- haps looking for him as well? All the while he silently reviewed the password. "The oaks are losing their leaves early this year."

Matteo had often attended the *palio* in Siena and was eager to compare San Sepolcro's display with it. The demonstration of the San Sepolcrans did not disappoint him. The performers prac- ticed all year long in preparation for the event. In their hands the delicate silk flags seemed almost weightless as the air was filled with a blaze of brilliant colors. His eye caught the rapidly chang- ing medley of symbols representing various parts of the city. Here a castle on a field of blue, quickly gave way to a gold crown against a background of scarlet. There were towers, scales, the moon and stars, and rainbows all in their turn creating a dizzying jumble that delighted the eye.

Reluctantly, however, he turned his horse away from the spectacle for it was nearly time to meet his contacts. He instructed Gufo to take the donkeys and the cart to the inn and wait inside, out of sight, but near a window where he could keep watch on the wagon and the animals. Matteo's plan was to leave Mea at a near- by livery stable and walk on foot to the meeting place, which was near the old Palazzo Pretorio where he paused briefly to examine the façade of the building with its impressive display of *terra cotta* arms representing the various rulers of the city. He did not tarry long, however, for he was eager to make contact with the smug- glers who by now would be waiting for him at the church of Santa Maria delle Grazie, the spot he had chosen for the meeting because its double *loggia* provided shelter and offered some privacy. As he made his way toward the church he observed some movement un- der the *loggia* and realized that it might be his contacts, Renzo and Tonino, waiting for him.

He watched for a few minutes as the two shadowy figures moved about under the *loggia*. Cautiously he crossed the *piazza* and approached the church, trying to appear casual as he did so. Despite the fact that it was midday and the sun was high, the *loggia* was shaded so even as he came closer to the two men, he could not distinguish their features. He greeted them, "*Buon giorno.*" They merely grunted in response.

Now it was time for the test. With his heart beating wildly he uttered the password that he had rehearsed mentally so many times since June. "The oaks are losing their leaves early this year." In unison *sotto voce*, the two unshaven and darkly clad men acknowledged their identity with one word: "Cefo." Matteo had successfully made his contact.

Only a few words were exchanged before the three began to make their way down Via Pacioli toward their treasure. As the church of Santa Chiara came into view Matteo was relieved to see that the donkeys were quiet, their heads in their feedbags. He felt a great sense of relief at the sight of Gufo inside the tavern seated near a window where he was discreetly keeping watch.

Satisfied that all was in order Renzo and Tonino opened the abandoned old shed behind the church and Matteo viewed for the first time, the alum in its crude state, the mineral trapped in stone. Was this the treasure for which he had risked so much? This plain dull-looking mess! Had all this been a futile exercise—all for a pile of rocks? There was a momentary feeling of disappointment but he dared not allow the smugglers to see his disillusionment. He had been so ignorant, not realizing that the alum would have to be extracted from the stone by smelting. Now he understood why Alfonso Beltramonto would need several months to prepare it.

There was no time to waste, so the three men set to work loading the rock. It was heavier work than Matteo was accustomed to, and he had to drive himself to keep up with the smugglers. After a little while his soft white hands were badly scratched and bleeding. He attempted to conceal this by brushing the blood onto the straw. Meanwhile Gufo unhitched the donkeys from the wagon so they were reasonably quiet, still content with their oats.

The stone containing the mineral was heavy and, to the uninitiated, Matteo's cargo might simply appear to be a load of rocks for some farmer's fence or shed. When the last of it was loaded Matteo moved to complete his part of the bargain. From inside his simple shirt he pulled a leather pouch containing the promised 500 florins that he had carefully counted and re-counted the night before. He handed it to Tonino who watched as Renzo counted it and announced, "Five hundred florins, exactly!"

They exchanged looks that indicated all was in order and in that predictably taciturn manner of the smugglers he had encountered earlier, they departed quickly, blending into the noisy anonymity of the crowd as the shooting contest was about to begin. It was a bit of theater safely concluded.

The combination of fatigue from unaccustomed hard work and sheer relief that this all-important move was completed left Matteo feeling drained. Entering the inn he collapsed on a stool next to Gufo and near the window in clear view of the treasure that he now had in his possession. One more small success! He motioned to the innkeeper who filled their cups with a generous draft of hearty local vintage and the two felt a strong bond as they toasted their success.

CHAPTER 8

"A Certain Delicate Indulgence"

There was little time to savor this latest achievement. The distant roar of the crowd assured Matteo that the archery match was still in progress and would provide safe cover for their escape from the city, but they must hurry. Besides, he was eager to have it over with. He had not, however, taken into account the difficulty of navigating the donkey train on the extremely narrow and winding roads just outside the city. The straining of the animals and the creaking of the wagon under its heavy load made Matteo impatient, irascible and, above all, fearful. So far everything had gone as planned; how awful it would be to fail now when his goal seemed in sight. He began to curse the animals and the cart and even hurled abusive expletives at the ever good-natured Gufo who was too absorbed in the immediate challenge of managing the donkey train to take notice.

Little by little the serpentine road gently unfolded to undulating curves that simply mirrored the contour of the river and made progress less labored. Indeed the ride became almost enjoyable and Matteo relaxed sufficiently to notice the colors of the vegetation that lined the roadside. Some of the lupines still bloomed, though their rose-and-blue hues were beginning to fade. Others were already heavy with seedpods, their bent stems evidence of the traffic of provident birds that fed on the kernels nestled inside—an affirmation that winter was not far off.

As they passed Borgo Pace they followed the Metauro waterway and pressed on to Fossombrone without incident. Here

Matteo planned to spend a quiet night in preparation for the last leg of the trip. He was by now bone weary and hungry and willingly stopped at the first inn they encountered on the outskirts of the city. He could not relax, however, until he had secured a safe spot in the stable where Mea, the donkeys, and their precious burden were in sight at all times. That done, the two men celebrated their safe progress thus far with the best meal the inn could offer. They drank liberally and turned in for the night.

In the morning the little caravan turned out onto the road toward Fano where the Arch of Augustus marked the end of the Flaminian Way from Rome. The city boasted a Temple of the goddess Fortuna as well as a fountain bearing her name where the superstitious Matteo was quick to water the animals, believing that Fortuna would bless and guide.

They went on confidently, enjoying the salt sea air and the beautiful beach as they passed through Senigallia and pressed on to Ancona. The final stretch of the trip over the same old Roman road that he had traversed just last June when he pressed his deal with Alfonso was now pleasantly familiar to Matteo. He reflected how much more confident he felt now. Undoubtedly his high spirits had to do not only with the promise of seeing his trophy bride but also of ridding himself of this burdensome load of rocks and those noisy donkeys.

As they entered the city from the north, the dandy on his beautiful horse betrayed his obvious sense of superiority over the peasant driving the donkeys. Though Matteo had been here only twice-he was able to point out certain landmarks to Gufo, who had undoubtedly never seen such a large city. He was duly impressed, not only with Matteo's knowledge of the place but also with the bustling commerce evident on its shore.

Matteo went directly to the same paddock where he had stabled Mea before, and was pleased that the friendly stable boy remembered him. After settling Gufo and the animals there Matteo send word of his arrival to Alfonso and requested to meet him to deliver the alum the following day. Only after that did he treat his trusted helper to a richly deserved feast on Ancona's famous seafood and best vintage. They sat a long time, quietly watching the rosy hues of the sky turn to purple as the sun set behind the merchant galleys moored in the bay. In a strangely wordless communication the two men shared a perceived satisfaction at a difficult mission safely accomplished, and sat now savoring the rich Rosso Conero, as they silently drained their cups of the very last ruby drops.

Alfonso was delighted to hear of Matteo's arrival and agreed to meet him the next day at his *bottega*. Matteo knew the place well by now, for he had, out of curiosity, ridden past it numerous times on his previous visit but he had never ventured inside the workshop. It was a practical arrangement that Alfonso suggested, but Matteo realized that it meant he would not see Prudenza today.

At the appointed hour of three, Matteo and his cargo met a smiling Alfonso standing in the doorway of his shop. Alfonso watched intently as Gufo quietly burrowed through the wall of straw and flasks to retrieve the alum. Fortunately he did not question the need of this strange camouflage—thinking perhaps it was simply evidence of Matteo's extra care to protect his precious load from robbers along the way. For that he was grateful. It was obvious that Alfonso was impressed with the hoard and as he examined it he ran his fingers lightly over the stone, caressing it as if it were made of silk. "You have done well, young man. Now we must discuss the payment."

Noting that Matteo looked slightly alarmed at this, Alfonso quickly assured him, "Oh, do not worry, my son. I mean to keep my sworn word to you; you will have the thousand florins just as we agreed."

"I have never doubted your honesty, sir."

Motioning for him to go inside, out of Gufo's hearing, Alfonso explained. "I must ask of you a certain delicate indulgence."

"Do please speak, *Signore* Beltramonto."

"Would you agree to allow me to present the money to you at the door of the church where the dowry customarily is given?"

He realized that the older man was trying to avoid the embarrassment that would be certain to result if those in attendance at the betrothal ceremony did not observe the traditional handing over of the dowry to the prospective groom at that time. Matteo was not without sensitivity and besides, he liked and respected Alfonso. Of course he would spare Alfonso the embarrassment.

"After all, *Signore* Beltramonto, this money was meant to be Prudenza's dowry in the first place. No one else need know that it was part of an arrangement."

Alfonso was relieved and grateful and suggested that Matteo come to the Beltramonto home the following evening to seal the arrangement with a drink, to break bread and discuss plans for the betrothal ceremony. Matteo had to restrain himself in order not to appear overly eager at the thought of seeing his bride.

For months now the Beltramonto household had been a flurry of preparations for the betrothal celebration. However, the more Caterina scurried and fussed over details of the trousseau, the marriage chest and other domestic matters, the more Prudenza appeared to withdraw into the solitude of her room with her books and her music. Caterina was finding it difficult to deal with her daughter's rapidly changing moods. At times she seemed almost euphoric as she perceived herself to be the star of this event. The prospect of becoming the wife of a rich and successful merchant and of living in such a cultural center as Florence aroused in her an almost adolescent excitement. Though she had never been there— indeed she had never been beyond the confines of Ancona—she created a fantasy city of her prospective home, a place of flawless beauty and endless delights.

Intermittently, and with equal intensity, that same thought of living in Florence sent her spiraling into wordless melancholy since it confirmed that she must soon leave her loving parents, the city, and the sea to which she was so attached. She trembled, too, at the thought of fulfilling what her mother had only gingerly referred to as her "wifely duties." Even in her naiveté Prudenza recognized that these discreetly couched intimations undoubtedly referred to the matter of sex, and she began to ply her mother with questions. Caterina recoiled from the delicate subject, offering only guarded references to "grandchildren," and "the duty of procreation."

Prudenza was well aware that the sheltered existence she led up to now had not prepared her for this important step. There were no young men in her acquaintance and, for that matter, she had never been alone with Matteo even for a moment. The prospect of intimacy with a man terrified her. The only naked bodies she had ever seen were cold monuments sculpted in stone. Her ignorance of the physical aspects of marriage and her mother's avoidance of the subject only contributed to her often-introverted behavior.

After a time Prudenza's emotional seesaw began to be punctuated by seemingly unexplained but welcome periods of calm. Embarrassed by her own behavior she was determined to control the radical changes of mood she knew were alarming to her parents. She resolved—by sheer dint of self control—to focus on a comforting lesson that *Fra* Tommaso taught her back at San Salvatore when he explained the significance of her name. She remembered it well—almost word for word.

"*Prudentia*" he had said, "is the Latin word for the virtue that enables a human being to distinguish good from evil, to take counsel, to judge correctly and act on prudent judgment, choosing the good and avoiding evil."

"I can do this. I must do it," she told herself. It was a praiseworthy but not altogether successful solution; so when her determination flagged, as it did from time to time, she turned to her beloved Dante. But that solace became a near obsession as she identified more and more with the ill-fated Francesca da Rimini. In her utterly mixed-up emotional state this dichotomy between pious contemplation of virtue and identification with the adulterous Francesca only deepened her depression.

The one consolation that never failed her was *Fedele*. As Prudenza's silence became more profound, and words failed her completely, she seemed to be able to release her emotions only through music. *Fedele* was becoming her voice: Through the lute she could safely express all her disparate thoughts and emotions without fear of hurting those she loved.

Blessed relief arrived in the person of *Fra* Tommaso to whom Alfonso and Caterina turned for help. Despairing of their inability to comfort their daughter, and undoubtedly feeling a good deal of guilt over the whole matter, Alfonso asked him to intervene. The friar's periodic visits to their home not only roused Prudenza from her depression but also benefited her worried parents. Hers was an added joy when he brought news of Coletta who even sent an elixir that she had made especially for Prudenza from the herbs in her garden at San Salvatore. Vanity likely played a part in Prudenza's recovery also as she realized the possible consequences if the groom should find his bride in such a state of mind and body.

By the time Cecchi arrived to deliver the alum, the bustle of preparations had reached new heights. Alfonso had already engaged the notary to draw up the betrothal document and conduct the civil ceremony by which Prudenza would legally become Matteo Cecchi's wife. To please his daughter, and in gratitude to *Fra* Tommaso who had done so much for the Beltramonto family, Alfonso ensured that the priest would be there as well, standing in a place of honor next to the notary and near the bride's mother and father at the door of the church where the ceremony would take place. By tradition it was here that the groom and the bride's father accepted the terms of the contract redacted by the notary and signed the document before entering the church.

Caterina had been busy for months managing more immediate domestic matters: the trousseau, the wedding gown, the properly appointed and generously provisioned marriage chest, and planning the celebration to follow the ritual. There was also the sensitive matter of who should supply the ring. Alfonso settled the question by insisting that the wedding ring be his gift—the ring of his mother, Costanza, which at the appropriate moment he would give to Matteo who would then place it on Prudenza's finger.

In some cases the bride's wedding gown and her marriage chest could be considered a part of her dowry, but Caterina was insistent that it not be so for her daughter. She was extremely sensitive to the very unusual conditions of the transaction with Cecchi, which she perceived as sacrificing Prudenza's rightful dowry to save Alfonso's business. Prudently she kept these thoughts to herself now that the deed was done, and attempted to conceal from Alfonso the resentment that she still quietly harbored about this unsavory arrangement.

Caterina worked, often by candlelight and late into the night, until her head nodded over her embroidery hoop and her eyes burned. But the satisfaction she felt as she observed the pile of linens accumulate was more than ample reward for her hard work. She was determined to provide Prudenza with a marriage chest she could be proud of.

Her greatest challenge of course was the wedding gown itself. For her treasured child it must be perfect. Fortunately one of Alfonzo's clients from the north had never come to collect a bolt of lustrous silk brocade he brought from Florence. The muted shade of aquamarine appeared iridescent in the changing light and would beautifully complement the golden highlights of her hair. Yes, Caterina was determined to fashion as fine and rich a wedding gown as she possibly could within the strictures of the sumptuary laws.

Jewelry and plate were a more difficult matter. A good deal of it had found its way to the pawnshop during the difficult days when Alfonso's business faltered. However he had scraped together enough money to redeem a respectable amount of it now, and added to it the silver serving pieces that Caterina had kept. A few of her mother's jewels remained, too, and she was pleased to be able to contribute these to the marriage chest, which was by now more than merely respectable. Grateful to Caterina and proud of his wife's work, Alfonso pronounced the *cassone* admirable—worthy of a princess.

Of more immediate concern was the meal to which Alfonso invited Matteo in order to celebrate the delivery of the alum and to discuss some of the formalities of the betrothal. Prudenza was anxious, at once excited at the prospect of seeing her bridegroom again, yet fearful. What will I say to him now? Up to this time we have exchanged only a few formal words and in the presence of my parents. Will he still find me attractive, or might he have changed his mind? Then her thoughts took a different turn. What if I find him now to be repulsive? Perhaps the scoliosis that he took such pains to conceal might have by now grown larger. What if he now has a hump? What if...?

They were needless worries as she would soon see. Matteo appeared truly jubilant when he arrived impeccably turned out in his best. The reception was different, too. Prudenza was not the serving girl now. She was the center of attention, beautifully gowned in embroidered ivory silk, her auburn hair hanging loose over her shoulders.

They met in the salon, without the trappings of business. Matteo seemed relaxed, not stammering as when she last saw him. Prudenza, too, remained calm even when he bowed low, took both her hands in his and pressed his lips firmly against them for what seemed to her an inordinately long time. His hands were perfumed, his touch soft but firm, his lips warm and moist. She felt a sudden and uncontrollable rush of warmth to her own cheeks and was momentarily embarrassed by it. Her body was behaving in a manner unfamiliar to her and she felt almost guilty to be enjoying this new sensation. Did this have anything to do with the "womanly matters" that her mother so deftly avoided discussing? She felt like a young sapling bending in an uncontrollable gale, not resisting but surrendering herself to the wild danger of it all and happily shedding the guilt that so easily overtook her delicate conscience. Was this some recognition of her official entry into womanhood?

All this was very foggy and she felt strangely outside herself, almost a spectator. She was aware of her father's voice as if coming from a great distance, filtered through some long hollow passageway in which it bounced from side to side and echoed strangely in her ears. He was raising a welcoming glass to toast Matteo's acceptance into the family. The tinkling of crystal like tiny bells called to her to join in so, finally, and reluctantly, she emerged from her trance-like state to raise her glass with the others.

Caterina looked refined and proud as she took her place at the table. From the tasteful and understated elegance of her gown to her always-striking posture, no one would guess that much of the preparation of the food had been her work, accomplished in countless hours of cutting and chopping, braising, basting and stirring the contents of huge pots that hung in the kitchen fireplace. It would not be proper for her to serve at table for such a formal occasion. For that she called upon several of her nieces—cousins of Prudenza who were about her age. She carefully instructed them in the refinements of serving and promised that as their reward they could partake of all the delicacies that the family enjoyed, as long as the girls confined their laughter to the kitchen and waited to take their meal only after the family and honored guest had risen from the table. In the best tradition of a celebratory Italian meal, the banquet stretched on through many courses, each with its proper wine that Alfonso had prudently stowed in the recesses of his cellar, keeping it for just such an occasion.

When the last delicate *dolce* was consumed the *vin santo* was decanted and now it was Matteo's turn to toast. Looking squarely at Alfonso and Caterina he raised his glass and began. "To you, *Signore* Beltramonto, beloved friend of my own father, and to you *Signora* Beltramonto, revered mother of my bride, I give my heartfelt thanks for so graciously accepting me into your family and entrusting to me your dearest treasure." Fixing his eyes on Prudenza he continued, "And to you, my bride, I proffer my love and swear to respect, protect and reverence you as long as I live."

The tinkle of glass touching glass had hardly faded when events took an abrupt but familiar turn and the two men became the focus of attention. Alfonso surprised both wife and daughter by announcing, "I must begin the time-consuming processing of the alum immediately, so I have arranged for the betrothal to take place on September ninth, four days hence."

Seeing the alarm registered on the faces of the two women, he attempted to soften their apparent shock with a further explanation. "You know, that is the feast of St. Nicholas of Tolentino, a native son of Ancona who, like you, Prudenza, was the child of his parents' mature years. As your father I wish to invoke his protection of you."

His sincere but feeble explanation was small comfort, however, as once again business considerations appeared to take precedence over finer sentiments. Alfonso had thought the matter through and it would have been improper to argue the point, especially in the presence of Cecchi who seemed to have no objections. He readily agreed—not out of any pious considerations, to be sure—but from sheer eagerness to make Prudenza his own.

Both men rose from the table and moved to a place near the fire where they examined the document the notary prepared. Matteo agreed, believing that all was happily resolved—at least for the two of them. Caterina had been caught by surprise but at this point she could hardly demur.

Satisfied that all was in order Matteo prepared to leave. He bowed to Caterina and Alfonso and again kissed Prudenza's hands, which, had he been more sensitive, he would have realized were now cold and trembling slightly. As she watched him disappear she realized that the next time they would see each other would be at the church door when she would irrevocably become his.

Prudenza awoke before dawn on her betrothal day, partly

because her jangled nerves would not allow her to sleep but also because she longed for a quiet moment alone to watch once again the first rays of sunlight silently creep up from behind the massive cathedral. She took little comfort in what she saw, however. Before her disbelieving eyes the sky took on a strangely greenish, opalescent appearance, as if some gigantic brush had swept across it with a spray of absinthe. The sight was at once strangely beautiful but unnerving. Convinced that it was an evil omen she ran from her room, her bare feet hardly touching the cold stone floor, and bolted into the arms of her mother who had been awakened by her cry.

Caterina attempted to calm her, suggesting that it was merely the dense fog over the bay that caused the light to refract this strange hue. It was surely not a portent and, anyway, the fog would certainly burn off by midday when the betrothal ritual was to commence. In the meantime her mother and father did their best to distract her by liesurely breaking their fast with some of the fine honeyed rolls that her mother had prepared for the celebration later.

While Caterina brushed her daughter's hair and gently anointed the long strands with fragrant pomade, the early-morning green of the sky gradually evolved to a faded sepia that finally gave way to grayish-blue. Just as Caterina predicted, by the time the Beltramontos departed for the church, the sky was like sapphire.

Tradition dictated that the bride and groom arrive at the church separately, each accompanied by family and friends. Since Zenobi Cecchi was not strong enough to make the trip from Florence he sent a notary, *Ser* Ugo Crisofano, to be his proxy at the betrothal.

Matteo cut a fine figure as he arrived impeccably dressed in a handsome doublet of velvet the color of claret, with amber satin visible through the fashionable slashes of his sleeves. Seated high upon a richly caparisoned Mea, whose coat had been brushed to a satiny luster, he made an impressive entry. From the mare's spirited gait it almost seemed that she sensed the importance of the occasion. Matteo dismounted, stood erect—almost handsome—as he watched his bride alight from the coach. He was suddenly struck with the realization that her beauty was not merely perfection of form and face; it seemed to come from a much deeper source that radiated from inside her. Momentarily it almost frightened him.

Caterina was right about the color of Prudenza's bridal gown. It was perfect. As she walked the dazzling sunlight sent fleeting glimpses of iridescent blues, greens, and golds through the folds of her skirt. Caterina had good reason to be proud of her handiwork. As for her own attire she insisted that she and Alfonso should be sedately dressed so as not to detract attention from their daughter. With Prudenza between them they walked solemnly toward the notary who read aloud the document. As agreed, Alfonso handed the dowry/alum money to Matteo and afixed his signature to the document, as did his son-in-law. Zenobi's proxy looked on with obvious satisfaction. Caterina's emotions, however, were not so easy to interpret.

The moment had come for the couple to exchange vows. Holding Prudenza's hand in his, a smiling Alfonso stepped forward and placed her hand in Matteo's. Just as Alfonso had promised his daughter, there was *Fra* Tommaso standing next to the notary. His reassuring smile had a calming effect on her as she felt her hand in Matteo's and pressed it, hoping that in this moment of emotion he would not sucumb to that embarrassing stammer.

Their eyes locked in an unfaltering gaze as he began the solemn ritual promise: "I, Matteo Benedetto Cecchi, son of Zenobi Eduardo Cecchi of Florence, do receive you, Prudenza Maria Cecilia Beltramonto, into my life to be henceforth my companion and wife, to honor and protect as my very self."

With a clear strong voice Prudenza pronounced her vow "to serve and obey." Alfonso handed the ring to Matteo who slipped it on her finger. The notary pronounced the contract valid and binding, and *Fra* Tommaso stepped forward to bestow a blessing on the couple. With that the entire party moved inside the little church, now filled with Prudenza's relatives and friends. *Fra* Tomasso walked to the chancel and spoke some eloquent words on the beauty of human love and the gravity of the promise the couple just made.

After the ceremony the bridal party and guests moved to the Beltramonto home to celebrate with feasting, dancing, and singing. Considering the short time Caterina had to prepare, she had truly outdone herself. Every room of the house was adorned with large fragrant sprays of juniper, and garlands of wild aster braided with pungent sprigs of rosemary draped every doorframe and adorned the banquet table lavishly spread with all manner of delights.

As the wine flowed bountifully so did the conversation and song grow in volume and tempo. A crowd of young people gathered in one corner of the great room and began spontaneously to sing popular *canzone* only to be interrupted by a particularly boisterous gaggle of young men who had gathered on the opposite side of the salon. Their raucous singing of lusty songs, punctuated with the most ribald jokes, grew increasingly offensive as the afternoon wore on until, incensed by their bad behavior, Alfonso commanded them to leave. Through it all Prudenza was happy to stay close to Matteo's side, grateful for his protection, for he had not allowed her out of his sight. For his part, Alfonso was grateful that his daughter would probably not have understood the vulgar jokes of the unwanted guests.

With the setting of the sun the guests gradually departed, leaving only the bridal couple, the notary, *Fra* Tommaso, and the family. Prudenza realized that soon Matteo must also leave, for although she was now legally his wife, their union could not be consummated until after the marriage rite that would take place in Florence in spring. Matteo appeared reluctant to go but knew that he must overcome his intense desire to make Prudenza his own this night. He delayed his departure as long as possible but finally, taking her hands in his, he again pressed his lips, this time more ardently, upon first her left and then her right hand, where Costanza's ring—now her ring—reminded them of the solemn union into which they had just entered. Bowing deeply to Alfonso and Caterina he left quickly, not daring to look back lest he could not bear to separate himself from his bride.

As she watched his figure recede Prudenza realized that she would not see him again until he came in spring to collect the dyes and to take her back to Florence with him. She had not expected him to leave so soon and had hoped for time to become better acquainted with her new husband, but the notary Zenobi sent urged Matteo to return home promptly the next day since his father had need of him.

As the darkness enveloped the last glimpse of her husband, Prudenza contemplated the gold band on her finger, remembering the story that her father told her about her grandmother, Costanza, the courageous woman who risked her life for the love of her husband by running away under cover of night. Prudenza took comfort now in the realization that the blood of that fearless woman flowed in her veins as well.

She carefully placed her beautiful dress where she could see it as she fell asleep. Lying there alone on her bed, she watched the colors cease to shimmer as the dying candles guttered in their holders, their flickering light no longer able to work their magic on the silken folds. The same darkness that extinguished the radiance of her gown now enfolded her as well. Exhausted from the emotion of the day she surrendered to sleep caressing the ring on her finger and uttered a simple prayer, "O, Nonna Costanza, be my strength."

CHAPTER 9

Farewell, Ancona, 1537

The festive betrothal celebration was but a memory now. The china was washed and stacked neatly back in place; the fine damask tablecloths hung out to bleach in the sun, and the Beltramonto household settled into a numbing routine. Alfonso rose early each morning and spent long hours at his *botegga*, often returning only after dark, while Caterina continued to fuss over the marriage chest. The piles of linen and clothing had reached the top. There was room for no more, so she busied herself with adding refinements to the contents of the chest—here a bit of lace, there a ribbon or some more florid embroidery. But above all, she concentrated on the wedding gown, contemplating what she might add to its splendor without breaking the law. She was not sure what the sumptuary laws of Florence would prohibit, but she guessed that such a rich and noble city might be a bit more permissive. No hesitation was going to stop her now. Although she was driven partly by the need to keep herself occupied, she was animated even more by the desire to show the Florentines that a young bride from Ancona could certainly hold her own in their society.

This last autumn at home was difficult for Prudenza; she felt somehow caught in a vacuum where time stood still and the sameness of the days was broken only by the progressive change in the colors of the trees and the sea. At the same time, however, the incessant ticking of the great clock that stood at the foot of the stairs reminded her that the days were indeed passing, with each stroke of the hour bringing closer the dreaded day of departure.

Even Lupo seemed to sense the inevitable. He stayed close at all times, followed her from room to room and even sat at her feet curled up like a fuzzy black ball, wagging his tail in time with the music as she poured out her feelings through her lute. Prudenza felt a special bond with the dog. She would never forget that he had been her accomplice the night she made her escape to find *Fra* Tommaso. She would miss Lupo very much: He had always been able to make her laugh even when she was most troubled. Sometimes as he ran in circles chasing his tail the funny little white plume on the very tip became a snowy blur in the otherwise unrelieved blackness of his glossy coat. Some might see this mark as a flaw, but for Prudenza it was what made him unique. Moreover, when he ceased the dizzying antics in pursuit of his tail, the effort usually left him with his left ear somehow falling forward on his face almost covering his eye. That never failed to cheer her. To Prudenza, Lupo's tricks were every bit as entertaining as those performed for dukes and duchesses by their fools. Lupo was her clown.

As autumn progressed to winter, the cold winds off the bay were a reminder that this was her last Christmas at home with her parents and she pondered what gifts she might give them. They must be special. For her father she determined to write a poem and a new song, one that she could sing to him as she accompanied herself on the lute. It would be just like the days before she went to San Salvatore, only she was more accomplished now. A proper gift for her mother was a more difficult matter. She contemplated surprising her with some needlework. That would certainly be a surprise since she had never revealed to her mother that fine sewing had been a part of her training at San Salvatore. Sheer pride prevented her from showing off her own limited skills to her accomplished mother.

Once again Coletta provided a solution. Her weekly visits to Prudenza were the only diversion in the gray days of early winter and, on one of these, she suggested that Prudenza (or "Pru" as she called her now that they were no longer prohibited from using nicknames) should prepare some fragrant sachets for her mother. It seemed a wonderful idea so with each visit Coletta brought more of the aromatic herbs and sweet-smelling flower petals from her garden. The two of them became like schoolgirls again, chattering and laughing, recalling their secret exploits that escaped even the prying eyes of Suor Rufina, as they fabricated dreams of their futures. By Christmas the number of sachets had grown to nearly a dozen and Prudenza's room was sweet with the mingled scents of lavender, rose, jasmine—a fantasy of flower petals the two of them packed tightly into the little pouches Prudenza had sewn. It was a perfect gift for Caterina. She could place the little packets, each now tied securely with a bright ribbon, within the folds of her mother's clothing and between layers of linens. In this way Prudenza's presence would linger in the fragrance long after she was gone.

Caterina continued to avoid the delicate subject of wifely duties, and when queried only said, "When the time comes you will know what to do."

Making no progress on that front Prudenza turned to Coletta who had always been wise beyond her years. And now that she was no longer at San Salvatore she was even more insightful—perhaps even a bit worldly. Coletta was pleased to be asked and willingly became Pru's tutor, sharing her admittedly meager knowledge on the subject. Although she was now betrothed, the wedding would not take place until February. In any case, it was easier for Prudenza to discuss such intimate matters with Coletta than with her mother.

Coletta assured her, "Dearest Pru, your anxiety simply comes from your lack of knowledge, of experience. Think for a moment, your husband has undoubtedly had women before, and he can guide you the first time he takes you. It is a beautiful thing when you become one flesh."

Prudenza had not even heard the last sentence. She was still processing Coletta's almost nonchalant pronouncement about "other women" in Matteo's life. The thought so startled her that she pricked her finger sharply and was alarmed to see that she bloodied the little linen sachet she was stitching. She chided herself for being so naive and after a moment admitted to Coletta, "After all he is more than twice my age, and he is a worldly man—experienced…"

Coletta interrupted, "Do not worry, Pru. I will prepare for you an elixir that will calm you on your wedding night, take away your fears and increase your pleasure. It will make you utterly desirable to your husband."

"Oh, Coletta, how can I ever thank you?"

"No need, Pru. Your friendship is all the thanks I could ever want. As a constant reminder of that, I promise to give you my little porcelain locket. Not yet, but one day. You will see." As she retrieved it from inside her blouse she held it up for Prudenza to admire. It was painted with the most delicate violets and tendrils of ivy that twined about the blossoms, and shimmered in the sunlight. "One day it will be yours, Pru."

"Oh, it is beautiful, Coletta. But are you sure you want to part with it?"

"This will be my parting gift to you when you leave Ancona. Until then I will wear it next to my heart as a symbol of our friendship—from my heart to yours, Prudenza. You must promise to wear it always, but especially on your wedding night. Promise me!"

"I promise, Coletta." Laughing she asked, "And must I sing an incantation over it before I place it on my bosom?"

"No!" With that she tucked the locket safely inside her blouse. "It is not merely a talisman, Pru: It is a blessed thing." More than that she could not say.

***

Christmas was a bittersweet festivity with all concerned making every effort to be cheerful and avoid talk of this being their last together. Prudenza was happy that her mother and father were so pleased with their gifts, pleased and surprised. It helped that so many relatives and friends came by—especially *Fra* Tommaso, and Coletta, who brought along Giampaolo, her betrothed. He was a charming young man, bright and jovial, and seemed delighted to meet Coletta's friends about whom she had talked so much. He appeared calm and at ease in their company in a way that Prudenza had never observed in Matteo but she dared not make such comparisons now. It was too late.

The great room was fragrant with the aroma of laurel and juniper, and as they all sat around the fire with their goblets of spiced wine and sweetmeats, Prudenza became strangely aware of something she had never before noticed. The walls had long been adorned with huge majolica plates and platters that her mother had collected over the years. This evening the flicker of the flames danced on their highly glazed surfaces and seemed to bring to life the images painted on them. Surrounded by borders filled with all manner of fruits and flowers, from their centers fierce-looking helmeted warriors and bland-faced virgins stared down expressionless at the assembly. No one else appeared to take note of them—nor had Prudenza before this time.

She was grateful when Alfonso suggested that she sing for their company the Christmas gift she had given him. Seated on a stool near the fire, she could now turn her back to the glassy stare of those majolica images. She took her lute carefully from its case and began softly to tune it. That was Lupo's cue. Up to now he had been totally absorbed, contentedly gnawing on a huge marrow bone, but at the first sound of the lute he took up his position at her feet like a sentry, ready to beat a tattoo to the rhythm of her song. Fortunately the drumming of his tail was muted by the thick carpet upon which he was now curled. It brought back sweet memories of the days before she went to San Salvatore, only now she was much more skilled.

As she held the instrument it seemed almost alive, in some way an extension of herself. Her soul and the vibrating strings seemed to resonate almost as one. *Fedele* had long been her consolation and now became her voice. With her lute she could safely pour out the emotions that she had been trying so valiantly to keep to herself during this precious time. But like all good things, this too must end. As the last notes reverberated softly in the air, darkness had descended. Gradually the guests departed, and this Christmas day was nearly spent. Tomorrow it would be only a memory!

With the new year Alfonso began communicating regularly with Matteo, reporting on his progress with the alum. The smelting of the mineral from the rocks was nearly completed and he began to experiment with it, treating lengths of cloth with the extracted alum solution and submerging them in large vats of pigment. So far he was delighted with the results, especially thrilled with the quality of the ultramarines and porpora that he was able to produce.

The wisteria buds were about to bloom again when Alfonso completed his work and sent word to Matteo that it was time to come. By return dispatch Matteo announced that he would leave Florence on the twenty-second day of April and, as expected, he rode into Ancona on the twenty-sixth. He stopped first to pay his respects to his new in-laws and once again to see his bride— greeting her as before, but this time making bold to embrace her as well—even with Alfonso and Caterina looking on. This was a new experience for Prudenza.

After a simple repast the two men went off to the *bottega* where Alfonso was eager to display the results of his experiments. Matteo was delighted and announced with great bravado that once again the unmistakable Beltramonto colors would make their appearance in Florence's silk market. Everyone was certain to take note. Carefully holding the containers up to the light to examine the colors, they began to pack the amphorae, jars, and bottles containing the dyes, wrapping each carefully in cotton wool before placing them gently in baskets filled with straw. The alum extract they put in larger boxes and stowed all of the packed items in sturdy metal chests that would be loaded onto the boat.

Matteo arranged for their departure to take place on Mayday. They would sail up the coast as far as Rimini where Zenobi had arranged to have a coach waiting to carry them and a wagon to transport their treasure overland to Florence.

Prudenza appeared to settle into a kind of silent resignation and went about her preparations for the departure almost stoically. It seemed appropriate that the dreaded day should be overcast. The sky was heavy with slate-colored clouds. Moreover it was a great disappointment that Coletta was unable to be there to bid her farewell. She was now married and with her new husband had moved to Rignano sul Arno. The only consolation was that Rignano was not far from Florence and it meant that perhaps they could visit one another.

Before the Beltramontos left the house, Prudenza wandered from room to room, looking about as if to imprint indelibly on her mind the memories they held. Last of all she embraced Lupo who nussled her face affectionately. Turning quickly she picked up her lute and without saying a word left, never looking back.

The vessel awaiting them at the dock was unimpressive, quite ordinary compared to the caravals moored on the western side of the bay. It was utterly dwarfed by a handsome square-masted galleon—a Spanish merchantman. The mizzenmast had, in fact, been lowered turning it into a modest single-masted sloop. It was quite adequate however, for the trip to Rimini was not long.

Alfonso, Caterina, Prudenza, and Matteo watched apprehensively from the quay as sailors hoisted the metal chests containing the precious alum and the dyes, aware that in one instant all could be lost if the hoisting apparatus should fail. With every creak of the cable Matteo's throat felt more constricted and he finally breathed easily only after the last chest was safely stowed below deck. But for Prudenza, wrapped inside the huge shawl that covered her and the lute, it meant that the dreaded moment of farewell had come.

Fra Tommaso arrived in time to give his blessing to the couple and wish them a *buon viaggio*. The ever-practical Caterina, who believed that such things are best done quickly, did her utmost to hide her tears as she embraced her daughter, whispered something in her ear, and passed her quickly to Alfonso who made no effort to hide his tears as he kissed her forehead tenderly and pressed something small and smooth into her hand. She did not dare to look at it yet for she knew Matteo was waiting to escort her on board and he seemed impatient. Offering her his arm he guided her slowly up the gangplank and safely onto the ship, where they stood leaning on the rail on the leeward side.

The wind from starboard was blowing Prudenza's hair causing it to fan up from behind and frame her face like a golden/bronze halo. Matteo had taken care to arrange for her comfort, providing a small cabin near the forecastle, but she preferred to remain on deck as long as the shoreline was visible. Already the capstan was winding the hawser and the top of the anchor was visible. The helmsman was at the tiller, eager to set sail while the wind was favorable.

Matteo surprised her by asking almost curtly, "Who is this priest who seems to mean so much to you?" Something in his voice caused Prudenza to shiver. She hoped he would think it was from the coolness of the sea air. She was silent, all her words spent.

—⁓—

Gulls wheeling overhead screeched loudly and the boat began to creak as it heaved away from the dock. But soon it took on the familiar rhythm of the waves, those same waves that Prudenza so often contemplated in her childish reveries. She saw *Fra* Tommaso raise his hand in a blessing and she crossed herself as she watched the figures of the three people whom she loved most in life gradually recede from view. As the vessel veered to the north and moved out into the open sea she ran to the stern to catch these last precious glimpses before they disappeared from view. Remembering the cool, small object that her father handed to her, she opened her palm and saw tiny violets entwined in ivy tendrils—the symbol of fertility Coletta had said. Although she began to weep, she smiled to think that a little of Coletta went with her to her new life. She was quiet, in a strange way detached from the man who stood at her side. A kind of numbness overtook her as she realized, "I do not know him."

In that moment as she stared into the spume left in the wake of the ship she identified with the words of Francesca da Rimini

> *Nessun maggior dolore,*
> *che ricordarsi del tempo felice*
> *nella miseria.*

> In all adversity of fortune
> it is the most unhappy kind of misfortune
> to have been happy.

"*Addio,* Ancona!"

CHAPTER 10

Benvenuto, Firenze, 1537

She stood fixed, chilled to the bone and, except for a slight pain in her left hand where she clutched the locket so tightly, unaware of the passage of time. She warmed her hands with her breath and pried her cold fingers open to look once again at the reassuring oval imprint on her palm. Not wishing to share this precious moment she pulled her shawl to hide her face, lest Matteo see her tears. She feared the unwelcome questions he might ask.

He had been watching from a distance, contemplating if he should leave her alone with her thoughts. He was not so insensitive as to disdain a young woman's sadness at leaving home and family. But the realization of her vulnerability determined his actions. "No, I have seen the lust in the eyes of the sailors as they follow her every move; I've heard their vulgar remarks and watched their obscene gestures. I cannot leave her unattended. She would not be safe."

Emboldened by concern for her—though not without a measure of jealousy—he moved quietly to her side and as gently as he knew how, drew her close to him. All too soon, however, he became aware of some large and unforgiving object between them, bearing down unpleasantly on his ribs. It was the lute that she still held under her shawl, close to her body. As the lock on its case dug more deeply into his flesh his first reaction was to curse at this damnable object that robbed him of a stolen moment of intimacy.

For all her naïveté Prudenza was not above dissembling and deftly turned the situation to her advantage, pretending that her trembling response to his advances was from the cold wind that sent sea spray gradually soaking through her shawl. Aware of her discomfort Matteo led her to the door of her little cabin and said, "Dry yourself, *cara mia*, and I will return with wine to warm you."

"*Grazie!* You are very kind, *Signore* Cecchi."

Even though he was soon to become her husband she had never called him by his baptismal name. They stood for a moment in silence as he took both her hands in his and rubbed them gently as if to warm them. After what seemed to Prudenza a very long time he kissed them lightly and moved to open the cabin door for her. What he saw there startled him. Inside was an elderly woman seated near the *cassone*. She had the bearing of a distinguished person as she sat there ramrod erect, her posture giving her the appearance of a sentinel guarding not only the marriage chest but also her young charge.

Though an awkward moment, Matteo did his best to conceal his surprise at the sight of this dignified being whose regal bearing momentarily threw him off guard. Only as the book she had been reading fell softly to the floor did she look up. He was relieved to see her countenance softened by a kindly smile. Neither of them said anything, waiting for Prudenza to make the appropriate introductions. For once her proper training failed her. There was an awkward silence and Matteo simply closed the door, shutting himself out. "Perhaps she is just embarrassed," he told himself.

Prudenza was both surprised and relieved when, at the moment of farewell, her mother whispered in her ear that with Alfonso's permission she had arranged for an older woman to be Prudenza's companion until the day of her marriage when the affable dowager would also attend the wedding in her parents' place. It was right and proper to provide a respectable and loving attendant for their daughter and, although Alfonso felt certain that Zenobi would agree, he did the proper thing, asking his old friend's permission. Obviously Zenobi had neglected to communicate this information to his son.

After his polite but hasty retreat Matteo found himself alone, his hopes for a stolen moment of intimacy with his bride foiled again. Shut out of his *fidanzata*'s cabin, cold and frustrated, he began muttering angrily to himself, "Who is this woman? How did she manage to board the vessel in plain sight? I must have been distracted overseeing the loading of the cargo. *Che malaugurato!"*

Prudenza was relieved, grateful for the presence of her aunt Teresina. She was a wise and kindly woman and, though she was old now, her sparkling eyes and fine features were remnants of the great beauty she had been in her youth. Long ago widowed by the death of Caterina's older brother, Guidobaldo, Teresina had enjoyed a happy marriage and a good life with her successful merchant husband. Best of all, she loved Prudenza very much and wished the same for her.

"Olà!" One of the sailors was calling to Matteo, *"Eh!* She turned you out already?" With one eyebrow knowingly raised and his thin lips curled into a sarcastic smile, he began taunting Matteo and soon the others joined in, laughing and making obscene jokes. Although in the past Matteo had been serviced by many a *puttana,* he deeply resented their implication that Prudenza was a *sciattona*—a slattern. Could they not see what a fair and unspoiled creature she was? He felt his anger rising and, as much as he wanted to curse them, he knew better than to start a fight now while he was so dependent upon their services.

Finally one of them yelled, *"Ey!* Come drink with us." Holding up a rusty flagon, another chimed in, "A couple of hearty drafts of our brew will warm you more and cost you less than a night with a *puttana."* He hated the implication but there was little else to pass the time so he joined them as they shared a flask of grappa— grappa so vile that it seared his throat and his first impulse was to spit it out immediately. For a moment he considered suggesting a game of dice instead, but thought better of it. He could not risk their anger if he defeated them—as he was sure he could. After all, he had already insulted them with his reaction to their grappa, so he did the only sensible thing; he found a bunk in the seamen's quarters in the forecastle and surrendered himself to sleep. It was just as well, for by morning they would be approaching Rimini and he would need to be wide-awake to oversee the unloading. These fellows were probably not above filching the odd bit of cargo if not supervised, and he could not afford to lose anything.

The sun was just rising when he went on deck and, to his surprise, found Prudenza already there. She was standing alone and motionless at the extreme point of the prow, her eyes fixed on the horizon. The wind was blowing her long hair back from her face setting her profile in relief against the crimson and gold of the sky. To Matteo she looked like one of those beautifully carved figureheads that grace the prow of great vessels.

"How lovely she is! And how lucky I am!" He didn't realize he had spoken aloud until she turned and smiled at him. He was grateful to see that she was alone; her elderly companion had apparently elected to stay inside to spare her joints the early morning dampness. The sight of Prudenza's smile gave him courage to ask, "You have slept well, my *fidanzata*? Your quarters were comfortable?"

"Oh yes. I feel wonderfully rested and eager to see Rimini."

"And soon you shall, my dear one. And your lady companion—she is well I trust?"

"Yes, quite." Recalling that she had failed to make the proper introductions the night before, she apologized and explained *Zia* Teresina's presence. He could not help wondering if this elderly companion might have something to do with the striking change in Prudenza's attitude this morning. She seemed so relaxed and her animated response to his questions encouraged him to pursue his quest yet again. But just as he moved closer to her side and placed his arm about her shoulders she pointed excitedly to what appeared to be a city just faintly visible on the distant shore and asked, "What is that, Matteo?"

Suddenly she realized that this was the first time she had addressed him so familiarly by his baptismal name. It seemed natural and spontaneous. He noted it, too, and was encouraged to continue his pursuit.

"That, my *fidanzata,* is Pesaro. If you look closely you can just begin to make out the shape of the great fortress there. It is called the Rocca Costanza."

She laughed delightedly—the first time he had heard her do so. It was a free and musical sound like that of a delighted child. She explained, "Costanza! That was the name of my grandmother, my father's mother, and this"—pointing to her ring—"this was her wedding ring."

He seized the moment, not about to let another opportunity escape. Such restraint as he had shown up to now was not characteristic of Matteo Cecchi when he was in pursuit of his quarry.

It was time to assert himself. Before she could object, he gathered her into his arms and held her so close that it seemed he could feel the pulsating of her heart against his own. This time she did not resist. He wondered what magic *Zia* Teresina had worked on her.

They remained there a long time in silence, together physically, though their thoughts could not have been farther apart. Hers were of Pesaro and the Castle Gadera where, so she had read, Paolo and Francesca met their fate. There was no point in speaking of it with Matteo for, even though he was from Florence, he probably knew nothing of Dante.

Matteo's thoughts were of conquest—past and future—satisfaction at having dealt successfully with the crafty smugglers and assurance that the spoils of that conquest would soon grace his marriage bed as well. He savored the thought for a long time but finally and reluctantly broke the spell. With his nose in the air like a hound picking up a scent, he announced, "The winds are favorable, *cara*. We should reach Rimini before noon."

Longing to see the city that was home to Francesca, she dared to ask, "Oh, Matteo, when we arrive there may we explore the city a bit?"

"I'm sorry to disappoint you, Prudenza, but there is no time for that. You see my father has sent some of his workers with a wagon to transport the alum and the dyes to his *bottega* in Florence, and the *scaricatore* will be impatient to transfer the cargo and begin the trip home. You understand that I must be here to supervise them."

"Then could I, with my *Zia* Teresina, not at least explore the quayside?"

"Oh, no, *cara*!" He seemed almost shocked at the suggestion that signaled how utterly naïve she was. "It would be unseemly for you to do it without a male companion—without me. Besides, this is your introduction into the family. You must understand that because my father is old and not too well, he could not make the trip from Florence to Rimini himself, but he has sent representatives to welcome you. They will be waiting for you when we reach the port and will accompany you to the safety of the coach he has provided for your comfort. You see, Zenobi Cecchi is a very proper man, and we must comply."

She had to agree, albeit reluctantly. "Of course. You are

right; I would not want to offend my future father-in-law."

They stood a long time and watched in silence as the shoreline seemed to emerge gradually from the haze and the outlines of buildings became more and more distinct. Matteo's thoughts were for the safe delivery of the treasure he had so cleverly obtained. After such a long and dangerous expedition, he was not about to allow anything to go wrong now.

Prudenza's thoughts however, were of Ravenna, less than a day's journey up the coast. She sighed audibly as she considered how much she would love to visit the tomb of the poet she so venerated. "But it is useless..."

"What is useless?"

"Oh, nothing, Matteo. Really. I was just daydreaming, I guess."

"You're sure?"

"Yes, I am sure." Breaking free of his embrace she excused herself on pretext of checking to see if *Zia* Teresina needed her.

As she turned to walk toward her cabin Matteo stood there a long time completely absorbed with the thought of her. Suddenly he was jolted from his reverie by one of the sailors who was calling to him. "*Eh, attentione!* We are approaching Rimini. The pilot will soon board the ship to take her into port and the *scaricatore* will want to unload the cargo at once. Your ladies should be ready to leave the ship first. *Capisci?*"

"*Capisco. Grazie!* I will tell them."

He was concerned that Prudenza should make the very best impression possible, so she must have ample time to dress for the occasion. He had not told her in advance that Zenobi was sending a small contingent to welcome her. Representing him and Maddalena would be Zenobi's notary *Ser* Ugo da Cristofano and his trusted friend *Fra* Filippo.

The ship was already nearing the quay by the time Prudenza and *Zia* Teresina emerged from their cabin and had their first glimpse of Rimini. Matteo looked on with unmistakable pride as he scrutinized her appearance from her burnished hair down to the very tip of her new slippers. Her first real glimpse of Rimini set her heart racing and brought color to her cheeks. It did not go unnoticed by Matteo—or the sailors.

Having grown up in a seaport, the noises of commerce on

the shore were familiar sounds to Prudenza but here the look was different—as was the language. In Ancona she had never wandered close enough to hear the profanity of the sailors as they worked the yardarms and hoisted cargo. She seemed not to notice the clamor now, being instead preoccupied with the extreme and puzzling changes she had seen in Matteo's behavior and his speech over the course of these few days.

While she was still inside her cabin she had heard him barking commands at the sailors with a fierceness in his voice that frightened her. His orders were punctuated with curses the likes of which she had never before heard. Yet when she opened the door and stepped on the deck he seemed a different person. Perhaps men were given to these mercurial changes in personality. She had no experience to compare it with. Yet she never observed such behavior in her own father—and surely never in *Fra* Tommaso.

By now Matteo again assumed his more respectful behavior as he escorted her to the rail where they awaited the lowering of the gangplank. She was about to be presented like a trophy—his laurel wreath! *Zia* Teresina followed a few paces behind, walking with reserve, yet never taking her eyes off her charge, who she obviously adored. Following after her was a boy—too young to be a seaman, perhaps a stowaway— called into service to carry the precious lute.

On the quay stood two elderly gentlemen. One appeared to be a cleric, the other, judging from his costume, a notary she recognized immediately as the same who attended their betrothal. Her heart skipped a beat when the breeze blew open the priest's black mantle, revealing beneath the unmistakable white robe of a Dominican. She could not help thinking this was a good omen, for just as *Fra* Tommaso blessed them at their departure, so here was another Dominican friar welcoming them, his hand already raised in benediction.

Almost as if he read her mind Matteo volunteered, "That is Father's old friend *Fra* Filippo from the monastery of San Marco, and the notary is…"

"Yes, I recognize him. He came to Ancona for our betrothal. He is *Ser* Ugo da Cristofano."

"The same. *Brava, cara!* Not only are you beautiful, but you have an excellent memory as well." He had never before told her she was beautiful, but there was no time now to savor the compliment, for the gangplank ceased jerking and twitching and finally settled into place. Holding her hand tightly Matteo steadied her and, with an almost gallant gesture, led her proudly to the quay where, bowing first to one and then to the other, he introduced his bride. "*Fra* Filippo, *Ser* Ugo da Cristofano, I present to you my *fidanzata*, Prudenza Maria Cecilia Beltramonto from Ancona."

Ser Ugo stepped forward and spoke first. "In the name of my client and dear friend, Zenobi Benedetto Cecchi, I welcome you to the Cecchi family and to the city of Florence, which will, *Deo volente*, shortly be your new and happy home." With a deep bow he presented to her a small but ornate wooden box inlaid with ivory in the shape of the Florentine lily.

Then it was *Fra* Filippo's turn. "My gift to you, my child, is simple. It is a prayer that God will bless you with a long and happy life together, with many children to grace your table, and with prosperity."

She curtsied graciously and said simply, "*Grazie. Molto grazie Padre!*"

Matteo looked on with obvious pride while Prudenza contemplated the kindly face and manner of the old friar who appeared to wear his years so well. Under a shock of white hair his blue eyes still shone with a youthful twinkle.

When the brief introductions were over, Matteo hurriedly ushered the party into the waiting coach and returned on deck, again shouting commands to the *scaricatore* to be especially careful of the precious metal boxes containing the dyes and the alum. Knowing how important it was to his bride, he had already taken care to stow the marriage *cassone* and her lute in the carriage while Prudenza was being welcomed by Zenobi's proxies. His action did not escape the watchful eye of *Zia* Teresina. "How very kind and thoughtful your young man is, Prudenza, to tend to your belongings first."

"Yes, *Zia*. I am fortunate." She felt something inside relaxing a bit and ventured, "He will be a good husband, I believe."

However, wise old woman that she was, *Zia* Teresina noted something tentative in her charge's voice that made Prudenza's statement seem more a question than an assertion. Or was it hope?

Once the cargo was safely stashed in the waiting cart and the seamen paid, Matteo joined the party in the coach, looking very proud and happier than Prudenza could ever remember—prouder even than at the festivities after the betrothal ceremony when he had not left her side for a moment. He longed now to sit next to her where he could feel the warmth of her fragrant presence, press his body close to hers and perhaps surreptitiously hold her hand beneath the folds of her abundant skirt during the long ride ahead. He realized however that propriety dictated he should surrender that place to *Zia* Teresina, who, for some unexplainable reason he sensed was an ally in his cause. So he politely gave up his seat to her and at the same time placed a small stool beneath her feet.

Settling into his own place opposite Prudenza he soon realized that from this vantage he could study her every feature in a way he had never dared during his visits to Ancona with Alfonso always looking on protectively. This was good! He could now pass the time admiring her grace, contemplating those eyes that had so completely captivated him since the very first time he saw her in her father's study.

Fortunately, no one could read his thoughts as he gave himself over completely to the delicious mental exercise of peeling away her clothing to reveal the ripe fruit beneath. Though her gown was as suitably chaste as was her demeanor, and her bodice was appropriately modest for a young virgin, he became mesmerized as he watched the steady, rhythmic rise and fall of her breast with every breath, until he imagined the delight of caressing the warm softness of that delectable forbidden prize now hidden from sight.

There was nothing to stop him now from even more daring exploration until he reached the ultimate satisfaction of his desire, lost inside her chaste flesh. Surely he must be the first to explore that prize, for he was certain that she was untouched by any other. Although the thought of divesting her of her virginity was all the more titillating, it also prompted a thought quite uncharacteristic of Matteo Cecchi. Guilt!

Just then the wheels caught a rut in the road and pitched

the carriage sharply to the side, causing Matteo to be thrown momentarily against *Fra* Filippo on his right. Not only did this untimely jolt interrupt his forbidden fantasy, it shocked him with the realization that perhaps the venerable old friar seated next to him with his head bent low over the open breviary in his lap might actually have the power to read his sinful thoughts. The sense of shame and embarrassment was short-lived however, and he was relieved to see that *Fra* Filippo had simply dozed off. He was free to resume his forbidden explorations.

From time to time Prudenza stole a furtive glance at him, too. He wondered, is it embarrassment that causes her cheeks to flush when our eyes meet ever so briefly? Could she possibly know what I am thinking? I hope it means that with her eyes she is saying, "I wish we were alone."

As the carriage clattered along over the rough roads the sun was beginning to set, casting long slanted shadows now. Matteo had arranged that they should stop to rest overnight at an inn in Bagno di Romagna, rise early and resume their journey before dawn, stopping at Bibbiena to rest the horses and find food before crossing the Pratomagno for the last part of their journey to Florence.

Zenobi sent explicit directions to his son regarding their entry into the city. He was very proud of Florence and wanted the arrival of his daughter-in-law not only to impress her, but also to show her off to the best advantage. He had waited a long time for this day.

The bridal party was instructed to enter Florence crossing the Arno at the Ponte alle Grazie, the old Rubaconte bridge, but not before stopping at the little church of San Niccolò to give thanks for a safe journey. The movement of the carriage as it pitched from side to side over the cobblestones of the Lungarno, combined with the stench of the river fouled by rotting garbage and raw sewage, began to make Prudenza nauseated. Noting how pale she had become in the last hour Matteo attempted to distract her by pointing out various landmarks as they neared the city. He could not, of course, calm the disparate emotions of these last days any more than he could staunch the fetid odors.

Not wishing to offend *Fra* Filippo and *Ser* Ugo by her reactions to their city, Prudenza pretended to use her handkerchief to wipe perspiration from her brow. Actually *Zia* Teresina had deftly hidden a small pomander inside it so that Prudenza could stave off the offending odors by holding it close to her face. She attempted to show her gratitude to Matteo for his obvious concern by making casual conversation, and was noticeably relieved when he pointed out the bridge of San Niccolò on their right. That must mean that they were nearing the church and could leave the stuffy coach for a bit.

Shortly she noticed a low diagonal stone wall, a sort of dam in the river and asked, "What is that, Matteo?"

"That is the *pescaia* of San Niccolò, a fish weir, a kind of dam to trap the fish."

She was surprised to see fishermen there hauling in their catch while at the same time women were beating clothing against the stone, scrubbing their laundry in the same murky waters. Recalling the fine seafood for which Ancona was famous she muttered words that she had not intended to speak aloud. "I cannot imagine eating fish from this putrid smelling stream!"

The notary winced visibly at her pronouncement, clearly taking umbrage at the remark; but Matteo was quick to the rescue. "In spring and summer, Prudenza, the Arno is often very low, but it will swell in fall and winter and sometimes even flood. You will see."

Just then the coach made a quick left turn through a delightful little garden of brightly blooming geraniums and blossoming vines that she did not recognize, but which gave off a welcome fragrance. They stopped short in front of the church of San Niccolò just as Zenobi had instructed them to do. Telltale puddles suggested that it had rained during the night but by now the sun was high and shone so brightly on the simple white façade of the little church that it nearly blinded Matteo as he helped Prudenza down from the coach.

Centuries of pilgrim's feet had worn small hollows in the gray stone pavement where rainwater now collected in little pools. Remembering her mother's admonition that she should don her best clothes on the day she was to meet her new family, she carefully lifted her skirts as she picked her way between errant trickles that formed small rivulets in the grooves between the stones.

It was very warm for May and the carriage had become

unbearably hot so the damp coolness that greeted her inside the church was welcome. As her eyes gradually adjusted to the relative darkness she meandered from one shrine to the next and, like a delighted child who had made a discovery, she ran her fingers along the cool gray stone of plinths and pilasters, her first sight of the *pietra serena* so common in the grand buildings of Florence.

Entering the sacristy her eyes were drawn to a particular painting before which she spontaneously fell to her knees. She stared for a long time in silence, unaware that Matteo had knelt down next to her—a bit awkwardly. He had not been on his knees since he knelt next to Lapo back in the church of San Lorenzo in Bibbiena where they plotted his next move with the brigands. Clearly this was not a posture familiar to him: He would have felt more comfortable on his horse but he knew it was the right thing to do. Besides, he was aware of *Zia* Teresina standing discreetly in the shadows.

After what seemed to Matteo a very long time Prudenza pointed to the painting. "Look, Matteo. The Madonna! Isn't she lovely?"

Clearly less enchanted than Prudenza he managed a feeble response. "Yes. But what is she doing? I don't understand. It is a strange picture, *cara*. And who is that man kneeling there?"

"That is Thomas the apostle."

"Why is he there? What is he doing? She seems to be giving something to him."

"She is."

For once Prudenza was grateful to Suor Rufina who had so often subjected the students at San Salvatore to her reading aloud from the *Golden Legend* of *Voragine*. This was one of the old nun's favorite stories and Prudenza had heard it so many times she could repeat it almost verbatim.

"You remember, Matteo, that Thomas was the apostle who was always late so he was not there when Mary was taken up into heaven. He was very sad when he found her tomb empty, but Mary was so touched by his sorrow that she removed the belt she was wearing and dropped it down to him."

Almost sorry that he had asked, Matteo managed to say blandly, "Oh. I see." Though he did not, of course. It seemed to him a silly story but he knew better than to express his opinion aloud. Before Prudenza could tutor him further with any more of her saintly fairy tales he announced, "Come, we must go now. Father and Mother will be waiting for us at Santa Croce."

The short ride across the Ponte alle Grazie was filled with myriad sights, sounds, and even smells that merged dizzingly into a whirling mass like a giant kaleidoscope in her brain.

Once across the bridge—the oldest and the longest in the city, Matteo was proud to point out—he instructed the driver to turn right immediately. Doing so, they retraced briefly the direction from which they had just come, but now on the opposite bank. A sharp left turn and they were on Corso dei Tintori, the street of the dyers. Matteo was eager to point out the area where much of the Cecchi business was conducted.

"See there, Prudenza, the *travi*." He pointed to the large drying racks of their trade festooned with long limp swaths of silk. The air was so still that the fabric hung there like the drooping heads of wilted half-dead flowers, their colors not brilliant but faded in the sun.

"Soon the *travi* will again be filled with the famous Beltramonto colors, *cara*, and merchants will come from far away places to purchase fine Cecchi silks and brocades to take to markets in the north."

Prudenza did not want to dampen his enthusiasm so she hid her disappointment at the squalid conditions she observed in the shabby run-down sheds that lined the street and the river's edge. This was not at all the Florence she had dreamed of, the Florence of famous scholars and great art works of which *Fra* Tommaso had spoken so often.

Another unexpected sharp turn, this time to the right, as the carriage traced a backward Z that caused her to go careening forward from her place, saved only by the quick reaction of Matteo who willingly caught her in his arms. "We are nearly there, *cara*. No more sharp turns, I promise. This is Borgo Santa Croce."

At that the coach came to a sudden halt and Prudenza realized for the first time that this bridegroom of hers had a sense of the dramatic. After lurching through narrow streets where laundry flapped against walls thick with decades of grime, there suddenly appeared before her a vast open space where she beheld a vision on the far side. Facing her was a large church, larger than any she had seen in Ancona—larger even than the cathedral of San Ciriaco. And although its vast façade of ochre-colored stone was unadorned, in the noonday sun it shone almost golden. There was pride in Matteo's voice as he announced, *"Ecco Santa Croce, cara. This is where our wedding will take place."*

She wished with all her might that her parents could be here for this moment to share the multitude of images. She determined that she would do her best to share the experience with her parents in detailed letters home.

In the brief moments before they alighted from the carriage Prudenza noted that Matteo suddenly seemed quite concerned with his appearance. Very carefully he arranged his cloak, smoothed the wrinkles of his doublet and pushed an errant strand of black hair back from his forehead before he stepped down from the carriage and offered his hand to Prudenza. "We are here at last, Prudenza. This is the end of our journey. Come, *cara mia.*"

Protocol would have dictated that he assist *Zia* Teresina first, but she thoughtfully held back and motioned for Prudenza to go before her. She would not want the assembled onlookers— many of them Zenobi's employees who had been told that Matteo and his bride were to arrive at midday—to think that this elderly lady was the bride.

It soon became obvious to Prudenza that Matteo staged this entrance to provide an opportunity to show off his *fidanzata*, promenading the length of the *piazza*, up to the church steps where his parents awaited them. *Zia* Teresina followed close behind carefully arranging Prudenza's skirt.

—◊◊◊—

There were no trees in the *piazza* to protect from the unrelieved sun beating down on the cobblestones, and Prudenza felt as if a thousand prying eyes were turned upon her, passing judgment on her every move. She was conscious that in the heat small beads of perspiration were beginning to form on her forehead, making of her hair a halo of tight little tendrils that framed her face like the curls of a little plaster *putto*. She whispered to Matteo, "Who are these people? And why are they looking at us so intently?"

"Most of them are textile workers, *tintori* and *tiratoi,* the dyers and stretchers of cloth employed by my father." Indeed their stained and weathered hands revealed telltale remnants of their trade.

Prudenza could not have known that what sustained the crowd through the long wait in the heat of the day was their curiosity to see what sort of bride Matteo Cecchi would bring home. They realized that their presence would make Zenobi happy and they were loyal to him. Matteo was also eager to please his old father who had waited so long for this day, but his thoughts on the crowd that had gathered were far from friendly. He was acutely aware of their opinion of him and his contemptuous looks in their direction warned, "Keep your thoughts to yourself or you shall pay!"

They knew him as the erratic son of their employer and had long wondered how such a good man as Zenobi Cecchi could produce such bad seed. Some had experienced the son's ill-tempered outbursts and a few had even suffered the physical consequences, so they were careful to keep their remarks *sotto voce,* fearful of retribution later. For now they entertained themselves by speculating what sort of wife Matteo would bring home. By the time the coach entered the *piazza* speculation had turned to wagering.

A stifled exclamation of surprise rippled through the crowd as Prudenza stepped out of the coach.

"*Dio, mio!* Where did he find this one?"

"She's a fair one, all right!"

"And modest, too."

"He must have raided a nunnery!"

Cynical old Enzo spoke up. "Oh, she has to be a *puttana* to go with the likes of him."

"But she is not his type. Look at her! She is young and so innocent-looking."

"You think so?" From the ranks came another voice.

"*Eh!* She's a ripe one, for sure."

And from yet another, "Ripe fruit, maybe, but I'll wager she's already been plucked."

For now Matteo was again on his good behavior, acting as if he had not heard their suppressed laughter. He was too busy looking extremely pleased with himself, showing off his *fidanzata* while she tried with all her might to recall her mother's admonitions about making a good impression. She could almost hear her mother say, "Watch your posture! Hold your head high, but not so high that you appear proud."

Prudenza dutifully made mental inventory of every aspect of her appearance, as they walked slowly down this seemingly interminable path toward the church. It tested her self-control to look from side to side and smile kindly at the curious crowd. By now the heat and her nervousness made her mouth dry: She longed for a drink of water. At the same time her palms were moist and she recalled Suor Rufina's declaration that "moist palms are the sign of a wanton woman." She was momentarily amused, wondering how Suor Rufina came to that bit of knowledge.

She was grateful now for Matteo's strong arm where she felt secure from the stares of gimlet-eyed bystanders and was relieved when they were close enough that she could see the reassuring smiles on the faces of Zenobi and Maddalena. This was for them, as well as for their son, a very happy moment. By the time they finally reached the foot of the steps Zenobi could no longer contain himself. He left his wife's side and with difficulty stepped down to embrace his new daughter-in-law.

Prudenza was acutely aware that, although it had been only a few days since she left home, in some ways it was a lifetime ago. The close confinement of the voyage had compressed both time and experience into a new reality. She saw a new side of her *fidanzato*—at once thoughtful and ardent, solicitous for her comfort and attentive to the needs of *Zia* Teresina. What more could she ask? Yet this soon-to-be husband of hers was an enigma.

She was mystified at the changes she had experienced in herself as well, mindful that it was largely through *Zia* Teresina's gentle, calming influence that she was no longer terrified at Matteo's advances.

All of these disparate thoughts racing through her consciousness seemed to vanish now as Zenobi reached out to her. In the warmth of the old man's welcome embrace she knew she had a protector and an advocate in her father's old friend. There was at once a silent but comforting understanding that passed between them almost as if they had known each other in a previous life.

Within a few minutes she and her new family passed

through the portals of Santa Croce, safe from the prying eyes of the crowd and into the welcome coolness and security of this sacred space. She heard the creaking of the hinges of the ancient doors as they closed behind her and tried to believe that they were not shutting out the past; they were simply marking the end of a chapter, the beginning of a new life. The very stones of Santa Croce were welcoming her, "*Benvenuto a Firenze.*"

CHAPTER 11

Trophy Bride

Inside the cavernous church—the burial place of famous Florentines of whom Prudenza knew nothing—the little party made its way through the nave. Her eyes were drawn gradually to the soaring vault above the high altar where light streaming through the stained glass splashed pools of vibrant color on the stone pavement. Sumptuous frescoes covered every inch of the walls, defining the portraits of saints rising above one another like tall columns. She stood transfixed, longing to know more of the stories depicted in these marvelous paintings. She had never seen anything like this place.

Zenobi was eager to explain some of the beauties of this church that he lovead so much, and share its rich history. But Maddalena intervened. "Husband, be merciful. It has been a long journey for our children and they must surely be tired and hungry. Another day you can bring Lady Prudenza here to study the treasures of the church."

Chastened and disappointed, Zenobi reluctantly agreed. "Of course, you are right, *Madama*. I will do it another time."

Prudenza's enthusiastic reaction to the suggestion pleased him. "Oh, yes. Please do. I would like that very much, *Signore* Cecchi."

To prove to his wife that he was not completely oblivious to their physical needs Zenobi quickly guided the group to a private exit where they easily escaped unnoticed into the street leading to their home without passing through the crowd again—for which

Prudenza was grateful. The stalls of the vendors were now closed during the heat of the day, which made it possible to proceed without attracting attention. They came to a halt before an unremarkable and somewhat dingy wall whose only adornment was an impressive entrance framed with hewn stone. Realizing the door was too heavy for his father, Matteo stepped forward and pushed it open to reveal a lovely garden of luxuriously colorful blooming things and rows of huge *terra cotta* pots containing orange and lemon trees in full blossom, filling the air with a heady fragrance.

Swarms of bees were so attentive to the business of extracting the delicate nectar that they were undisturbed by the intrusion of these humans into their enterprise. For one brief moment Prudenza was overtaken by a distinct longing for the familiar surroundings of San Salvatore where she had so often been lulled by the hum of bees as they visited the lush wisteria at this time of year.

Matteo was proud to act as host now, taking over for his father who was obviously tired from the heat and excitement of the day. He was pleased to make the formal introduction into the home. "Welcome to *casa* Cecchi, Prudenza. You like the garden?"

"Oh, thank you, Matteo. I do like it. It is lovely."

"It is my mother's pride. She has a magical way with such things."

Maddalena was noticeably pleased with her son's recognition; but mindful of the hour, she urged the party on into the coolness of the house and up the broad stone staircase to the great room where she had directed the servants to lay the table for the occasion.

Prudenza was struck by the high vaulted ceilings of the room and the beauty of the large fireplace with its intricately carved mantel. Though there was no need to call it into service now in this warm spring weather, the bellows, andirons, and the tongs that hung there gave evidence of serious use in another season.

The beautifully appointed table was evidence that Maddalena was intent upon impressing her new daughter-in-law with the refinements of her best linens, china, and cutlery. But the food, of course, was the centerpiece, a satisfying and suitably light repast for such a warm day as this. There were large carafes of cool white wines of Tuscany, cold roast capon, leafy bitter greens with morels and early asparagus. Fruit, cheese, and small honey cakes flecked with tiny bits of preserved ginger completed the feast.

Despite her fatigue and nervousness, Prudenza made polite conversation, answering Zenobi's barrage of questions concerning the state of his dear friend Alfonso. Maddalena, too, appeared happy at the prospect of having a daughter after all these years—especially such a lovely one.

Matteo bristled with pride like a peacock preening for his audience until the conversation seemed to turn completely upon Prudenza. After a time—and a bit too much wine—he became visibly sullen and no longer joined in the conversation. He seemed to sink into some remote dark place where he nursed thoughts of self-pity. *Of course she is lovely and good, and of course my parents are happy. But have they forgotten that it was I who won her, and at such great effort? Could not my father at least say thank you for giving him a daughter at long last?*

By this time Prudenza was very tired and was increasingly uncomfortable with this change in Matteo's behavior. It was like the volatile shifts of mood that she observed on board the ship. But she reminded herself that he had been charming and attentive, too.

Zenobi apparently did not notice his son's sulking and turned the conversation to the practical matter of Prudenza's lodgings in Florence. "You know that Matteo still lives here at home with his mother and me. So it would not be proper for you to stay under the same roof before you two are actually married. I have made other arrangements for you and your *Zia* Teresina to lodge at the nearby convent of Santa Maria degli Angeli. It is not far from here. The sisters are very kind and you will have comfortable accommodations there until your nuptials."

"*Grazie, Signore* Cecchi. You are very thoughtful. I am most grateful, and I know that my father and mother would be pleased with this arrangement as well."

To this *Zia* Teresina acquiesced heartily. The time alone there would provide a welcome opportunity for Prudenza to process the bewildering mix of emotions she experienced all compressed into these last few days since leaving Ancona. While she pondered the thought Zenobi continued, "The shadows that lace the floor tell me that it is growing late so you must go soon—before it is dark. Matteo will escort you to the convent where you can rest. You will find your *cassone* and all your belongings already there for you."

"You are very kind and thoughtful, sir."

The weary little procession made its way back through the garden—where even the bees were quiet for the night—and out into the street leading to the convent that was to be Prudenza's temporary home. How long she might remain there she did not know, for the wedding date had not yet been set.

Once inside the gates of the monastery she felt very much at home for it was so like San Salvatore with its cloister full of flowers and vines, and even an old well in the center. Only as her body relaxed in the familiar setting did she realize fully the toll taken by the tension of these last days.

The *madre superiore* welcomed them and promptly showed them to their respective rooms. The modest little monastic cell, unadorned except for a simple crucifix above the bed, was comfortingly familiar. She took note of the desk where she promised herself to write long letters home relating the events of these days. And there, just as Zenobi had promised, was her precious *cassone*. She deposited the lute safely in the corner where she could see it from her bed, then collapsed—still fully clothed—and fell at once into a welcome sleep.

Finch and thrush were already singing their lusty morning songs by the time she awakened. Momentarily disoriented by the new surroundings she shut her eyes tightly, hoping that when she opened them again she would find it was all a dream. But alas, no! *Zia* Teresina was awake and dressed, exploring the cloister. A young novice (about Prudenza's age) brought her warm water to wash in, and tea and bread to break her fast. She had not yet finished her ablutions when Maddalena appeared and found her still in her shift.

Zia Teresina eased Prudenza's embarrassment by engaging Maddalena in conversation until Prudenza completed her toilette. Her prospective mother-in-law was energized and full of plans. In her eagerness to make this wedding a social event Maddalena simply had to know if Prudenza was adequately provisioned for the occasion. "I must see your wedding gown, my dear."

"Of course, *Signora*, I am happy to show you. Allow me to get it." She returned quickly holding it up proudly but excusing the wrinkles. "I fear it is wrinkled from being in the *cassone* but it will be fine when it has hung out for a time."

A cloud suddenly darkened Maddalena's face. Though she attempted to conceal her reaction, it was clear that she found the gown wanting. She realized the delicacy of the situation when Prudenza proudly announced, "My mother made it for me. Every stitch an act of love."

"It is beautiful work, Prudenza. Your mother is truly a fine seamstress, but…"

"You do not like it, do you?"

"I do. Yes, yes, I do. But I find it just a bit…a bit plain." Seeing that Prudenza was offended by this last remark she was quick to add, "The fabric is truly exquisite. Perhaps we can make some simple alterations to adapt it to the current Florentine fashion."

"But what will you do to it? What is the Florentine style?"

"The fashion here is to wear an outer garment opened in the front to expose the petticoat of some rich fabric. Your gown will serve beautifully as the petticoat."

At the thought of her precious wedding garment relegated to the function of petticoat, Prudenza fought back tears. She hoped with all her heart that her mother would never hear of this desecration of her handiwork. She would make *Zia* Teresina promise never to tell her.

Meanwhile Maddalena carried on. "The elegant fabric of your gown would be beautifully complimented by an overskirt of some rich satin or perhaps velvet. Yes. Yes, velvet. of some shade of blue—azure or aquamarine to pick up the lights from your petticoat."

Prudenza had retreated into her own thoughts, dimly aware of Maddalena's ongoing monologue. "I must make an appointment at once with a fine *sarta,* a seamstress who will make of it a splendid bridal gown worthy of your beauty."

"As you wish, *Signora.*"

"The bodice should be tight so you will need one of those stiff linen corsets. And the neckline must be a bit lower."

At that Prudenza blushed, so she quickly added, "If you feel uncomfortable we can add a fine shirred yoke of some transparent material."

"Yes, please do."

"And the sleeves—oh, the sleeves! Have you seen the slashed sleeves that are so fashionable just now?"

"No, I have not."

"You will like it, Prudenza, I promise. You and Matteo will make such a handsome, fine-looking couple on your wedding day."

—⁓—

The date of the wedding became a bone of contention in the Cecchi household. Both Matteo and Zenobi had hoped to celebrate it as soon as possible after arriving in Florence. But it was already early May and the *calendimaggio* was in progress, the great May festival culminating with the feast of the city's patron, John the Baptist, on June twenty-fourth.

Zenobi did not want the marriage to take place during the distractions of the festival, which meant that it could not be solemnized until after the *festa di San Giovanni,* still nearly six weeks away. Maddalena however was glad for the extra time to devote to sartorial matters. Matteo spent a good deal of time sulking. For Prudenza and *Zia* Teresina the delay provided for many precious exchanges in which their mutual love and trust flourished and the kindly older lady did so much to soothe Prudenza's fears at entering into this union.

Prudenza filled many quiet hours with reading, playing her

lute and lovingly going through the contents of her bridal *cassone* where she found many small trinkets and notes from her mother, tucked away amongst the linens. But this life of quiet expectation was not without diversions. More exciting to be sure, were the many festival activities—parties, theatrical entertainments, and contests of all sorts. Zenobi saw to it that Matteo escorted his *fidanzata* to these events, to which *Zia* Teresina was always invited as well. Gradually she absented herself, thereby hoping to allow the couple to get to know each other better.

Zenobi did not disapprove, either. In fact he insisted that Prudenza become familiar with the ways of the Florentines, their rituals, and celebrations if this was to be her home now. There was always, of course, his desire to show her off. In this he was rewarded, for invariably she quickly became the center of attention, and although Matteo was proud of her he was noticeably irritated and became increasingly jealous. He grew to resent all of the attention to her beauty and grace—those same qualities that had so captured his heart. He was simply becoming increasingly frustrated by the delay of the wedding.

Meanwhile Zenobi was busy at his *botegga* experimenting with the new dyes from Ancona, and returned home each evening cheered by the results. But he was not so preoccupied with matters of business that he was distracted from his son's approaching marriage.

As the plans progressed, excitement in the Cecchi household escalated: Even Matteo seemed to resurrect from his moodiness. But Prudenza was actually happy to be separated from the commotion. She spent hours writing the long letters she promised to her parents, sharing with them in great detail the events of this time since leaving Ancona. As always, she found great comfort and joy in playing her beloved lute, singing softly to herself in late afternoon as twilight began to darken the cloister. Before retiring she often read and reread the sad story of those doomed lovers, Francesca and Paolo.

These peaceful times were punctuated by the endless festivities that mark *Calendimaggio* in Florence. On these occasions Matteo was proud to escort her. The jousts, parades, and religious processions through the streets multiplied in number and grandiosity as the feast of the Baptist approached. The largest event was the *calcio*, a football match in which four teams representing the four oldest of the major churches of the city competed. It was preceded by a grand procession with members of the guilds proudly displaying their banners in the colors of the competing teams: red for Santa Maria Novella, green for San Giovanni, white for Santo Spirito, and blue for Santa Croce. The procession preceding the game included large cannons; artillery on wheels were paraded through the street and fired whenever a team scored. With each blast of the cannon a wave of frightened pigeons swept across the field momentarily darkening the sky.

On days between the matches there were other festivities, both secular and religious. Public *piazzas* offered a variety of entertainment: giants walking on stilts, fire-eaters, tumblers, and musicians. Not to be outdone, however, were the more solemn occasions when relics from the *duomo* were carried in procession through the streets with much incense, tinkling of bells, and chanting of popular hymns by foundlings from the Ospedali degli Innocenti.

Excitement and noise reached a feverish pitch by the time of the feast itself. The crowd was dense and noisy but Matteo did his best to open the way for Prudenza as he pressed through, carefully leading her by the hand. This time *Zia* Teresina chose to remain at the convent out of the noisy crowd. Prudenza was excited with an almost childlike reaction to the festivities. Though Matteo had seen the *calcio* many times this was different. He was with the young woman he was about to marry. She was beautiful and good, and she was his trophy. Moreover there was no guardian, no chaperone, and he felt free to hold her close to him as they pressed through the crowd. Surely no one could find fault with that now. He needed to protect her.

The day itself was filled with a dizzying display of games, contests, and frenetic excitement that continued after the game and well into the night. Elaborate feasting, singing and dancing climaxed with a grand display of fireworks, after which the revelry continued into the morning hours on barges in the Arno. Soon enough St. John's Day passed into memory and all attention now turned to the wedding, which was prompting disparate reactions from all concerned.

Maddalena was increasingly preoccupied with perfecting the costumes of both bride and groom as well as planning elaborate banquets and entertainment. For Prudenza it meant enduring endless fittings with the *sarta* who had been engaged to alter her gown—the wife of the same tailor who was dressing Matteo for the occasion. Since their shop was in Borgo San Frediano that meant crossing the Arno at the Ponte alla Carraia each time. She came to dread these excursions, not only for the ordeal of the fitting but for Maddalena's retelling each time the history of the bridge. By now Prudenza could have related the tale in her sleep.

She dared not express her resentment of these excursions that she considered to be merely a futile exercise in satisfying Maddalena's excessive desire to be recognized among the wealthy merchant class. Secretly Prudenza thought, "These proud, vainglorious Florentines! Will I ever fit in here?"

The delays brought about by Maddalena's attention to endless details caused Matteo to become more irritable and impatient, given to sudden fits of temper. For the final fitting of his wedding attire, while Maddalena patiently looked on, he pranced back and forth in the tailor's shop, adroitly turning on the ball of one foot with a grace that his mother could not believe, and resumed his route back to the mirror where he stopped to preen. At one of these passes before the looking glass he interrupted his vain posturing to survey his profile more critically—from his shapely, muscular calves to the cut of his beard. He suddenly flew into a rage when he noted that the beautiful velvet cape did not conceal the slight hump on his left shoulder as he had hoped it would. In a fit of pique he cursed the little tailor, pushed him into the corner, kicked over the work table, scattering all manner of tools of his craft across the floor of the shop, and bolted out the door.

Shocked, and cowering helplessly, the mild-mannered *sarto* said nothing to Maddalena but gathered up the remnants of his trade from the floor. It was left to her to attempt to restore the vanquished little man's dignity while attempting to cover for her son's outrageous behavior. He would hear of this when she returned home!

Ironically, as Matteo's petulance increased daily, Prudenza withdrew more and more, grateful for the tranquility of the convent and the hours spent with her aunt. With the trust and love that bound them came also the realization that soon her mentor must depart. The woman who had been her oracle, her sage, the source of almost sibylline wisdom, would soon have to leave her pupil.

Prudenza was about to enter into the fullness of womanhood and, just as she had done in her childhood when things troubled her, she erected about herself a bulwark of detachment, deliberately seeking solitude in daydreams. Numbed to the troubling circumstances around her, she was almost unconscious of the passage of time. Yet when propriety required, she was able to summon—almost mechanically and without effort—the proper skills and behavior that the nuns at San Salvatore so successfully instilled in her.

Nonetheless, her mind was awash in a flood of emotions—some ambivalent, others precisely identifiable. She felt undeniable gratitude for the comfort and warm welcome of the Cecchi family but, at the same time, lonesomeness for her parents, *Fra* Tommaso, and even her dog Lupo. She experienced fear, excitement, and even guilt. Guilt for vanity over her beauty—something she had not been so aware of until she recognized the envious stares of other young girls not as blessedly favored. The almost seraphic air of remoteness about her behavior now made her all the more desirable to Matteo. It would be a challenge to his manhood to breach the chasm of her remoteness, not unlike the challenge that drove him from one bandit to the next in pursuit of the alum. He became obsessed with the thought of this final chapter in his conquest.

At last the nuptial celebration was at hand and the day was perfect. Maddalena could not have wished for a more beautiful one, bright and sunny yet not too warm. Prudenza looked radiant in the gown upon which Maddalena bestowed such careful attention to detail. But she walked almost trance-like, outside herself, a spectator observing her own performance in the drama about to unfold. It was not unlike that evening when she stood by as her father as Matteo signed the agreement that determined the course of her life.

Outside the door of the great church the notary read the marriage agreement and the two parties affixed their signatures. Nothing escaped Maddalena's scrutiny. As she made her last inspection of the bridal couple, she tucked in place a stray sprig of the ivy that had escaped from the crown of roses on Prudenza's head, and looked on her son with a mother's pride. They were indeed a handsome couple. Prudenza, so very young—just sixteen—looked truly radiant.

For Matteo, her ambitious, worldly-wise son, this was the coveted opportunity to win the approval of his father that so long eluded him. Although his physique might be flawed, he did look dashing in his wedding garment, all scarlet and white, the traditional colors of Florence's Signoria. The chastened tailor had corrected the flow of the cape so that it hung in graceful folds of rich turquoise tastefully ornamented with touches of gold to contrast with the colors of his doublet and trunk-hose.

Just before entering the church, Zenobi presented Matteo with a small roll of parchment. He broke the wax seal and read aloud:

> *To my dearest brother in Christ. On this the day of your marriage, I send you my fervent prayers and wishes for a happy union. May God bless you with health, happiness, and children to grace your table. I am, as always, your devoted brother, Fabrizio.*

Matteo threw the letter down and stomped on it angrily. "Ha! That eunuch in his dank cell. Must he always haunt me— even from far away? What does he know of the longing, the desire, that restless burning in the loins?"

"Your loins! Is that all you think of? You are about to take to yourself a most pure and precious spouse. Mind your blessings and..." Maddalena tactfully interrupted, not wishing Prudenza to hear Zenobi's exchange with his son.

In a more rational moment Matteo had to admit to himself that, had it not been for Fabrizio's decision to live out his life in the monastic enclosure he, as the next born, would one day take over the family business. Even if Matteo inherited it now only by default, at least he should be grateful for that. But must Fabrizio always overshadow him, even on this day when he was about to realize his dream?

For Prudenza the long trek down the aisle was reminiscent of the day of her arrival in Florence. She found strength in imagining that her parents were there beside her, for she had by this time cultivated a level of experience that allowed her to drift safely aloft the deeper dynamic of the day. She could react to the beauty of the surroundings and respond properly, behaving predictably according to the dictates of protocol.

Standing apart like a witness of her own future, she was only vaguely aware of the music and the many candles, for Zenobi had obviously secured an exemption from the sumptuary laws. Against the elaborate floral display that filled the air with a heady fragrance, the Mass proceeded and Prudenza went through the motions.

When the services were over, the celebration moved out into the *piazza* and down the street, not the back alley they followed the day she arrived, but down a main thoroughfare to the Cecchi home. An army of guests followed—including many of Zenobi's faithful employees, no doubt aware that a free meal awaited them. They were not disappointed, for the trestle tables that Zenobi had ordered placed in the courtyard, were heavy with a sumptuous array of roasted fowl, meat pies, cheeses, fruits, and endless quantities of fine wine.

The wedding party and specially invited guests were directed to the great room, which under Maddalena's direction had been transformed into a veritable bower complete with a pergola erected in the center. Here the bride and groom were enthroned and received lines of wellwishers.

Zenobi and Maddalena laughed and chatted away happily, too, as they greeted the guests. After all dispersed, except family and the closest of friends, the traditional procession formed to escort the bride to the home of the groom. In Matteo's case this was an apartment separate from, though connected to, the home of his parents. Prudenza had not before seen it and was impressed with this fine place that was now her home. Here, amid a noticeably less formal, more relaxed ambience, the revelry took on a more exuberant character.

The wine flowed more freely as the moment came for the bride and groom to ascend to the bedchamber—the expectation of the crowd being the consummation of the marriage.

Prudenza paused at the foot of the steps and after a long and tender embrace said her final farewell to *Zia* Teresina who reminded her, "Do not forget Coletta's locket."

Extracting it from its hiding place inside her bodice she assured her aunt, "I would never forget it."

"May God be with you, my child, and bless you with much happiness."

"I shall miss you very much, *Zia* Teresina."

"And I you as well."

"Please recount the events of these days to my dear parents. But I beg you not to reveal to my mother what was done to the wedding gown she made for me. Promise?"

"Of course, I promise. Now go, and do not be afraid. What you are about to do is beautiful and blessed by God."

Prudenza fought back tears as she turned to Matteo and allowed him to lead her to the top of the stairs. As he opened the heavy door to the bedchamber she was struck by the richness of the draperies that covered the walls and the sight of a large bed with snowy-white sheets upon which had been scattered rose petals— the same color as the pale yellow ones in the crown she wore. She was comforted by the sight of her *cassone*. At least there was one familiar thing here. Her nightdress was spread out waiting to receive her, and there in the bed she spied something glittering in the light from the candles. It was the traditional gold florin, a talisman said to insure the fecundity of their union.

She heard Matteo close the door behind them and realized that, for the first time since she met him, they were truly alone. He had waited so long for this moment that he could hardly restrain his passion any longer. In his eagerness he seized her almost roughly, holding her so tightly to himself that she let out a soft cry that caused him to relax his embrace momentarily.

He tried to be gentle as he lifted the wreath of flowers, the symbol of maidenhood, from her head. Her hair at once fell into a rich cascade of coppery bronze like the leaves of the beech tree in autumn. It highlighted the fair skin of her shoulders and sent him into a frenzy eagerly exploring her body with practiced hands and hungry mouth. She shuddered, whether with fear or passion she was not sure.

The lacings of her bodice easily yielded to his deft hands, revealing to him the vision that he had only been able to fantasize about as he sat across from her in the coach that day. In no time at all her lovely gown lay about her feet in a cloud of blue velvet.

The speed with which he disrobed her brought to mind Coletta's remark that Matteo had undoubtedly "had" other women. His skill indeed betrayed considerable experience, for he had by this time handily undone his doublet and hose and with one swift move scooped her naked body into his arms and deposited her on the bed. His swarthy body felt hot and rough against her soft skin and she instinctively clutched Coletta's locket tightly and tried to shut out the sound of his labored breath and the sight of his face—almost plum-colored now. The veins in his temple pulsed visibly with each thrust into her chaste flesh.

As her own body reacted she tried to remember all that *Zia* Teresina told her about this moment—that fright would turn to pleasure. There was nothing gentle about his ardor now and even her ability to escape into the security of her dreamworld failed. She nearly swooned in the intensity of that moment when fierce pain and pleasure combined, leaving her weak and hurting. She recalled Coletta's words: "It may hurt at first." Indeed it did. But it was an exquisite pain unlike anything she had ever felt—something primal, physical yet strangely spiritual. There was a sudden rush of something warm and an awareness of crimson on the otherwise spotless sheets. At once her thoughts returned to the day she had pricked her finger and bloodied the pristine linen of the sachet she was making for her mother. Coletta was right: He had had other women.

"This 'wifely duty,' will it always hurt so much?" she whispered to herself.

She had not meant for him to hear but he obviously did, and with words that seared as much as the pain in her body he responded, "None of the others have ever complained! You will get used to it."

She fought back the tears as she tried to console herself

with the thought that, yes, there have been others, but I alone am his wife. But...am I special to him? Is his satisfaction as great as my pain?

She lay quietly for a long time, exhausted, perfectly still and silent until he was spent and his heavy breathing signaled that he was asleep. He did not stir as she crept from the bed—even when the florin fell noisily to the floor. She hoped it was not a portent.

She wrapped herself in the embroidered shift that Caterina made especially for her wedding night and crossed the room to where a candle flickered in the imperfect glass above her *cassone*. Looking at the distorted image in the mirror, she could not identify with the person she saw there as she slowly said aloud, "You are Prudenza Maria Cecilia Beltramonto no longer. Henceforth and forever in the sight of God and the world, for better or for worse, you are *Signora* Cecchi!"

CHAPTER 12

Signora Cecchi

"Madama, mia! Mamma!"

Prudenza bolted upright in bed, disoriented and frightened by a sudden loud clap of thunder. The storm had sent a loose shutter banging in the wind and drove the heavy rain like needles against the windowpane. *"Mamma, dové sono?"*

"Cara, mia moglia, you are here, safe in your own bed with me, Matteo. It is only a storm." As she felt his arm about her she was jolted into reality with the words he spoke. *"Mia moglia,"* he had called her "my wife." It was the first time she had heard these words spoken of her.

The two sat quietly for a time, Matteo attempting to calm her, still trembling in his arms. She shuddered, self conscious of her nakedness and unnerved by the grotesque figures created by flashes of lightning. Through the window where the wind had now torn the shutter completely from its hinges, fantastic images materialized in surreal blue flashes creating weird shapes on the ceiling that came and vanished with dizzying speed.

Not sure if she was awake or dreaming, she tried to rationalize…"they have no physical reality, and yet…" Matteo reassured her, "Do not be afraid, Prudenza. It is only a summer storm and they usually pass quickly." He gently urged her to lie down again, her head on the cushion next to his, and pulled up the sheet to cover her.

After a bit Matteo's heavy, regular breathing indicated that he was again asleep, his arms still protectively around her shoulders. As she lay still, her eyes fixed on the ceiling, the strange light show gradually began to subside. With one last burst of light Prudenza caught sight of her lovely wedding gown in a heap on the floor where, in their moment of passion, she had abandoned it last night. One last glint of light reflecting the threads of the brocade sent a pang of guilt through her. How careless she had been not to hang it up.

Gradually the storm became less intense, the lightning ceased and the sound of thunder diminished, leaving only the steady, calming sound of gentle rain that finally lulled Prudenza into a deep sleep.

It was midmorning when she awoke to find a smiling Matteo standing over her, already fully dressed. Sunshine was pouring through the same window where the lightning had worked its fiendish display only hours before. He bent over to kiss her before he opened the windows wide. She shielded her eyes against the brightness and, still a bit disoriented, asked, "Was I dreaming? Was it a nightmare, Matteo?"

"No, *cara*. You were simply startled by the storm that passed through during the night. These sudden summer storms are often very noisy. But see," he gestured to the now-opened windows, "It is beautiful. The stones of Florence have been washed clean and they glisten in the light. Your new city awaits you, *cara mia*. There is much that I have planned for you—for us—today. But first you must rise and prepare to meet the servants of your new household. They are very eager to know you."

A soft knock at the door announced a maidservant with a basin of lavender-steeped water. Matteo slipped out of the room as the young girl entered and bowed slightly. "For your toilette, *Madama*."

"*Grazie, Signorina*. I do not know your name."

"Ginevra, My name is Ginevra, *Madama*." She blushed slightly as she announced herself. The pinkness of her cheek betrayed a certain shy modesty that Prudenza could identify with. Yet there was something about her dark-Mediterranean beauty that suggested Ginevra might be more knowledgeable, or at least initiated, in the ways of the Cecchi world. She appeared to be about Prudenza's age, yet despite her apparent reserve there was something in her eyes and demeanor that suggested experience beyond her years—not unlike Coletta. Yes, that was it!

As Prudenza processed this observation she was only vaguely aware of Ginevra's voice until the maid repeated, *"Madama, would you like me to help you dress?"*

"Oh, no, that is not necessary." But sensing that Ginevra was disappointed she asked, "Would you like to help me choose a proper gown from the *armadio*?"

The girl's large dark eyes betrayed wonder and delight as she surveyed the assortment of garments hanging there. Her eyes locked upon a pale-violet velvet. Prudenza shook her head. "Oh, no. It is much too rich, too formal. Today I am to meet my servants and I must wear something simpler, appropriate but not too elegant."

With that Ginevra removed a less ornate gown of pale-yellow color. "It suits you, *Madama*. It is like the color of the morning sunrise."

"But the sun has long since risen, Ginevra; and I am a late bird today—not up with the larks." Nevertheless she accepted the maid's choice.

Just as Ginevra fastened the last lacing of Prudenza's bodice and stepped back to admire her mistress, Matteo appeared at the door accompanied by another serving girl carrying a tray with bread rolls, honey, and watered wine.

"To break your fast, *cara, mia*."

Ginevra had discreetly slipped out of the room and Matteo dismissed the serving girl. He decanted the wine and symbolically broke the bread, offering some to Prudenza, and taking a morsel for himself. As they shared the simple meal he related to her the plans that he had laid for the day.

"It is important that the mistress of her house become familiar with her home and meet the household servants." As he spoke he drew aside a heavy drape, revealing a door that she had not noticed the night before. Although it was obviously an antechamber to the master bedroom, the squeak of tired rusty hinges and the musty smell that emanated from it suggested to Prudenza that it had not been used in some time. He beckoned her to enter, and led her through to a door on the opposite side that opened onto a long hallway leading to a great room where the household servants had been instructed to assemble to meet their new mistress. They stood in an orderly line opposite the door as Matteo presented them, one by one to Prudenza, making some comments about each as he did so.

First came Antonella, the cook and mistress of the kitchen. She was a portly, middle-aged woman with a ruddy face and the kind of rounded full cheeks that defy aging. No sagging jowls to betray her years! It crossed Prudenza's mind that the fullness of the cook's frame testified to her culinary skill, and at the same time gave her plump bosom a kindly, maternal look—more motherly than Maddalena. Her soft gray eyes twinkled as Matteo introduced her and she smiled a warm welcome at her young mistress. Prudenza repeated her name, "Antonella, I am happy to know you."

"If you please, *Madama*, call me Nella as the others do." Age and stature among the servants had given her the right to make such a request.

"Yes, I shall, if you wish it, Nella."

While they still spoke Matteo was already moving on to the next, which was Ginevra. Despite her youth, her prestige in rank resulted from her closeness to the mistress of the house whose most intimate needs would be conveyed to her. Although she and Prudenza had already had a brief encounter earlier, Prudenza was happy for this opportunity to study the young girl more closely as Matteo presented her. Although Ginevra was petite of stature, she was pleasingly buxom, though not out of proportion. Her olive skin and dark eyes suggested perhaps origin in the south. And there was something slightly comical about her heavy black curls as they resisted capture under her small white cap. A rebellious strand over her forehead gave her a mischievous look that belied her obvious attempt to be very proper as the occasion warranted. Prudenza's theory of her maid's southern origin seemed to be contradicted by what she heard Matteo say next.

"*Signora*, I give you your maidservant, Ginevra Dattali. She will attend to your every personal need. I assure you that *Signorina* Dattali is a very proper young lady from a good family in Rignano sul Arno—not far from here. He felt compelled to indicate her good breeding since their close relationship undoubtedly meant that the *Signorina* would be privy to much of the activity of the household. But Prudenza heard only the last bit, "Rignano sul Arno." It came to her like a flash—that is where Coletta now lived with her new husband. She was thrilled and excited to think of the possibility of reaching her dearest friend through this connection.

By this time Matteo was already moving on to the next servant, an older man named Berardo. He was the gardener and brought a small bouquet that he shyly presented to Prudenza. She felt an immediate liking for the man and at once began making conversation with him, asking questions about his garden. Did he have a garden of simples? What herbs did he have? Her questions revealed a considerable knowledge of medicinal plants. Berardo was visibly pleased and invited her to frequent the garden often where he would be delighted to share with her his knowledge of such things.

Next came Maria, the laundress and seamstress whose husband died young, leaving her with six children to support. With little flesh on her large-boned frame, she had the tired, haggard look of one who had worked long and mightily. Her arms were muscular from lifting baskets of wet wash, and her large hands were lined with thick blue veins. Matteo explained that his mother hired Maria in order to help her support her family so that she could keep her children from being taken to a foundling home. In her kindness Maddalena had equipped a small room for her next to the kitchen.

Prudenza was awed and inspired by the woman and at the same time felt guilty for the luxury in which she lived.

Matteo continued, "*Signora* Maria, besides her washing and sewing, has a loom on which she weaves many practical things. She will teach you, Prudenza."

Prudenza pondered what this last remark might mean for she had no desire to learn to weave.

Matteo continued through the line of servants, even the scullery maids who came daily to help Antonella with more menial chores. Finally he came to the youngest, the stable boy, Luca. He was pleasingly shy and a bit tongue-tied—probably just nervous, Prudenza assumed. He looked so innocent.

With the last introduction made there came a sudden shift of mood and Matteo stepped forward, assuming the spotlight, and made a show of formally presenting the keys of his house to the mistress. Addressing the servants he announced, "*Signora* Cecchi, *mia moglia,* is mistress of the household, and you are to be obedient to her." With almost theatrical timing he bowed to Prudenza and drew from a pouch at his waist a set of large keys, and presented them to her with a flourish. "To you, *Signora*, I entrust the keys of our household. You will keep them always hanging from your waist. To you it is charged to let no disorder, turmoil, or distress enter this home."

Prudenza was surprised and moved by this gesture for, although she knew well that it was the custom of the time that the mistress of the house was keeper of the keys, she would not have thought her volatile husband capable of handing over control to his very young and inexperienced wife—and with such a public display of gallantry. The unexpected courtliness on his part required an equally gracious response, so with the *politesse* of one well-bred, she accepted the jangling mass of keys and quickly attached them to her belt. In truth, she disliked their weight and even more so dreaded the accountability that they might represent, knowing that her husband's volatile outbursts of temper were never far from the surface of his disposition. She sensed that, symbolic as the keys were, they were a weighty responsibility.

She thanked Matteo courteously and dismissed the servants one by one, remembering each by name and making a friendly wish or comment to each. When Luca, the last to go, left, bride and groom stood in a long and loving embrace. Then with playful solemnity he announced, "Now, *cara*, *Signora* Cecchi, mistress of the house, you must become familiar with the house over which you rule. I will lead you."

She was curious and eager to do so, for she had never been in his apartments before the marriage. He offered his arm, commented on how lovely she looked and she, like a child embarking on a new adventure said, "Lead on, *mio marito*." It was the first time that she had called him "my husband" and she liked the sound of it.

During the presentation of the servants she had observed some of the furnishings of the great room. The hall itself was not as spacious as that of the elder Cecchi's home, but it was well appointed. She was intrigued by the large andirons in the great fireplace. They were grotesquely carved animal heads with their fangs bared threateningly. The room's furnishings were massive, but tasteful; a large table, benches and chairs, all heavily carved in the style of the period. Her eyes were drawn to a large and beautiful tapestry hanging on the outside wall, a depiction of the hunt. She made mental note that one day she must ask Matteo its origin.

Matteo began the tour by retracing steps back through the corridor leading to their bedchamber. In her fear and anxiety of last night Prudenza had not noticed the door just to the right of the large bed. It opened into a small but pleasant room with a window that overlooked the courtyard below. Before she could inquire of its purpose Matteo began to explain. "This will be your little sitting room, a parlor where you can come to escape, to consort with your maid servant. Or perhaps you will even think of it as your little chapel."

His home was admittedly more modest than those of the great aristocratic families of Florence who built their own chapels in their *palazzi*; but here, at least, was a place of quiet retreat.

"*Grazie a Dio*, Matteo. I will hang on the wall the little crucifix that *Zia* Teresina gave me just before she returned to Ancona." Though Matteo said the bit about a chapel half in jest, he realized his devout wife was serious and he must not offend her.

The room was sparsely furnished, for Matteo had little use for it before he was married. He much preferred the frenetic activity of his father's place of business. As Prudenza surveyed the room she took note of a large comfortable-looking chair with a small footstool nearby, a pair of stools, one tall and the other squatty, and some empty shelves. It was these that caught her eye as she asked, "Where are the books?"

"Books?"

"Yes, these bare shelves cry out for books. They will do nicely for mine. I cannot wait to see them there. But I don't see a desk or a writing table."

"No—not yet."

"May I please have one? I have promised to write many letters to my parents and I…" She broke off without explanation, for she was about to say something about keeping a journal. But considering his suspicious nature she thought better of it.

"Of course, of course you shall have a desk; I will see to it at once."

"*Grazie,* Matteo."

Things were going so well that she considered asking him

for a lectern for her music. She determined that the taller of the two stools would serve her well as she played her lute, and she would make a sort of corner shrine for *Fedele*. But something told her not to pursue the subject of the music stand just yet.

The only touch of elegance in the room, giving it at least a modicum of refinement, was the large and beautiful rug on the floor. It stood out in such contrast to the starkness of the furnishings that Prudenza felt curious as to its origin and decided that one day she would ask Matteo if it is somehow related to the rich tapestry she had just seen in the great room.

As they moved back into the bedroom a wave of embarrassment swept over her as she realized that the wedding gown left so carelessly on the floor had thoughtfully been placed in the *armadio*; the room had been tidied up and the bed linens changed. She blushed at the possibility that Matteo might have announced his conquest by that indelicate and demeaning old custom of displaying the bloodstained sheets to prove the consummation of their union. She could not bring herself to ask. It was all so vulgar, so embarrassing. The condition of the room gave evidence that Ginevra had already assumed her responsibilities. All was neat and orderly.

From the bedchamber they passed to another bedroom that Matteo explained was for guests. It was large but not so well appointed as the master's room. They did not tarry there but quickly descended the narrow stairway leading to the kitchen. Nella was already busy at the hearth where a large caldron of soup made almost musical sounds as it bubbled away, filling the air with a wonderful aroma, at once rich and spicy. A young boy was turning a spit containing several plump chickens, sending short bursts of fat into the flames that exploded like small rockets.

The warmth and the delightful aromas brought on a momentary feeling of homesickness for her mother's kitchen back in Ancona. But this was no time to indulge in such thoughts. As if she sensed Prudenza's feelings, Nella seemed pleased with her young mistress's interest in things culinary. Although her own mother was a fine homemaker, Prudenza had never shown the slightest interest in domestic matters. She preferred books and music to mortar and pestle, but she knew to show an interest and respect for the older woman's efforts.

Nella's motherly demeanor touched Prudenza and she diverted attention from the tears welling up in her eyes by asking, "What is that, Nella?" pointing to a long wooden container with a shapeless gray-white mass that looked much like a balloon. "That is a kneading trough, mistress, where today's bread is rising and will soon go into the oven."

Just across the room Prudenza spied a low door through which she could see into an adjoining room that contained a bed and several large tubs. She assumed it must be the room that Matteo's mother created for Maria. And sure enough, there was a loom in the corner.

Matteo reached for Prudenza's arm and began gently guiding her out to the garden, into Berardo's domain. It was filled with colorful flowerbeds and potted citrus trees, now beginning to show their fruits. There were small lemons, not yet golden, and the orange trees were heavy with little green orbs beginning to show a slight blush on their cheeks. There was a dovecote from which shy white heads peeked at the newcomers and soft cooing sounds suggested the presence of young inside the small nests. Completing the picture was a fat orange cat dozing disinterestedly in the warm sun.

On one side of the garden, near the wall, Prudenza spied several beds of herbs and immediately turned to inspect them, running her hands gently over their foliage to release their pungent fragrances. As she did so she was able to identify each by name; a feat that did not go unnoticed by Berardo. He was pleased that his new mistress showed such interest in his handiwork.

Quite unselfconsciously Prudenza continued, almost as if speaking to herself; "pennyroyal, henbane, oleander, the Pater Noster pea..."

Matteo was a bit bewildered by this rush of information. It revealed a side of his bride he would never have suspected, and though he did not share her enthusiasm for such things he watched with pride and some amazement as she spoke with Berardo of strange-sounding things—nightshades, she called them. Berardo, on the other hand, beamed with delight. No one had ever taken such notice of his efforts before, even though he had often been called upon to produce infusions and poultices to cure the ills of the other servants, to ease their toothaches and bathe their bruises.

More than once he had provided a tonic for Maddalena who sometimes suffered from stomach ailments.

As Matteo attempted to move on to the last stop before *pranzo* Berardo, generally so quiet and retiring, made bold to say to his new mistress, "Please, *Signora,* do visit my garden often. You are always welcome here and I would be honored. And my lazy old cat, Tigre, would allow you to pet him, too." Almost as if he knew he was being spoken of, the cat deigned to open one eye a crack and purr loudly as he resumed his nap.

"I would be pleased to, *Signore* Berardo. You must teach me the secrets of the art of herbals. I do have some knowledge, but I still have much to learn."

"Happily, I will do so, *Madama.*"

With that Matteo announced, "We must stop at the stable briefly before *pranzo*. I have a surprise for you there."

Young Luca met them at the door and ushered them along lines of stalls where most of the horses' heads were deep in their feedbags, oblivious to the intrusion of these strangers. Only one, a beautiful chestnut mare, appeared to notice them and did so with enthusiastic neighing. Matteo pointed her out proudly, saying, "This is Mea, my faithful mare. She took me to you, *cara*, to your father's house in Ancona."

Matteo was pleased when Mea nuzzled Prudenza's face affectionately as if to welcome her into the family. Luca quickly handed her an apple to give to the mare.

Next to Mea's stall was another with a beautiful silvery-gray palfrey. Luca called her Stella, for the nearly perfect white star on her forehead. Matteo explained that she would be Prudenza's horse.

"But, Husband, I have never ridden."

"You will, *cara*. I have arranged for Luca to teach you so you must come to the stable often so that Stella knows you and you establish a relationship with the animal. You will love her. I picked her out for you myself because she is so beautiful and gentle. As he spoke he stroked the horse's sleek, shiny coat while Prudenza said nothing—struck dumb by this last announcement. Fortunately the awkward silence was broken by Zenobi's appearance at the entry of the stall. There was an unmistakable look of delight on his face.

"Oh, my children!" He rushed to embrace Prudenza and

then Matteo in an uncharacteristic show of emotion.

Matteo was curious as to the cause. "Father, what brings you here at this time of day when you are usually in your *bottega*?"

"I could not wait. I had to tell you. The words came from his mouth like a torrent as he explained, "The silks, the first batch of silks! They have been dyed and the colors are brilliant, exquisite. The Beltramonto colors again radiate from the Cecchi silks. It is a marriage of sorts, for all to see as they hang from the *travi* shimmering in the sunlight, almost as if they were on fire."

For one brief moment Matteo was nearly moved to tears, seeing his old father so happy. Zenobi continued on with words Matteo thought he would never hear from his father's lips. "Son, you have not only brought sunshine into my gray old existence in the person of this beautiful child, the daughter of my dearest friend, but with the alum you have also secured the future of the house of Cecchi. You have made me a very happy man, Son, happier than I could ever deserve."

Matteo could hardly believe his ears, so long had he waited for his father's approval and praise. And he was doubly happy that it should come in the presence of his bride.

Zenobi continued, "I thank you, Son, and I thank God for you both." Turning to Prudenza he added, "And now, Daughter, I have not forgotten my promise to you the day of your arrival, that I would take great pleasure in sharing with you the beauties of Santa Croce."

"Nor have I forgotten, Father."

"Then tomorrow we begin; in the morning when the light from the east illuminates the *cappella maggiore* and the frescoes come alive in the bright sun. But for now I must return to work, and you," turning to Matteo, "you must take your wife to *pranzo;* it is nearly time. With that he attempted an almost youthful bow to Prudenza—as sprightly as his gimp legs would allow. *"A domani, cara figlia!"*

"A domani, padre mio!"

There was a lightness of step in the old man's walk that Matteo had not seen in years. For Matteo, all of the scheming, the hardship, and the anxiety endured in order to reach this moment was forgotten. He, too, was happy—happier than he had ever before been.

Prudenza was finding her place in the family, and had no difficulty in calling Zenobi *Padre*. She knew that her own dear father would approve, too. And true to his promise Zenobi called for her early next morning to begin instructing his eager student in the glories of the great church that was so dear to him. His explanation of the frescoes in the splendid apse actually filled the first week's lessons.

Zenobi proved a fine tutor and as Prudenza grew to love this place the bond that she felt so spontaneously at their first meeting was developing into a deep and genuine filial love. The days turned to weeks and then months, marked off by the old man's lessons. She could almost trace it by degrees associated with specific visits.

September ended with Zenobi's heartfelt account of the life of the great Leonardo Bruni—once chancellor of the city—who lay buried in the church. October began, appropriately enough, with the fresco cycle of the life of Francis of Assisi in the Bardi chapel. Zenobi explained that he—even as a layman—could be a member of the Franciscan's so-called Third Order and as such had the privilege of burial inside the great church.

Donatello's magnificent Annunciation quickly became Prudenza's favorite shrine by far. The youthfulness of the virgin appealed to her greatly so that on successive visits to the church she never failed to stop to utter a prayer there.

With Zenobi's lessons she felt an increasing sense of belonging, of finding her place in the Cecchi family. Her experiences were carefully noted in her journal and in the long letters to her parents and *Zia* Teresina. She was happy, no longer traumatized by the sexual advances of the husband she was actually beginning to love.

While Matteo was away at work she spent much time becoming acquainted with the house over which he had so publicly given her charge. The servants seemed happy and were reliable, which meant she had a good deal of free time to explore her home.

The *loggia* at the top of the residence soon became her favorite retreat. From here she could see over the red-tiled roofs of Florence, across the Arno and far into the beautiful hills surrounding the city. She loved the vista for it reminded of the times she spent back in Ancona gazing across the sea into infinity. Into this tranquil setting she began to take her lute and spend hours lost in her music, the sounds wafting out over the rooftops.

One day when she visited Berardo in the garden the old man presented her with a gift, a small goldfinch in a wicker cage. She was delighted with the little songbird and thrilled when he demonstrated his beautiful warble—so clear and joyous sounding.

"Oh, Berardo, how can I thank you? He is beautiful! But he must have a name…I know. I shall call him Angelo, for he does sing like an angel."

Angelo quickly became her companion. In her sitting room she prepared a little perch for him near the window, and on the *loggia* he could enjoy the freedom of the outside. He was never far from her. And one day, as she played her lute and sang, the little bird joined in, at first seeming to imitate her sounds with his chirping and then entering into what almost seemed a friendly competition. On the warm summer afternoons they indulged in veritable singing duels on the *loggia*—with Ginevra as audience, playfully called upon by Prudenza to pass judgment on the winner.

Ginevra was gradually assuming a place of importance in Prudenza's life. She was much more than a servant. Before many months the two had begun to share innocent secrets and ambitions, and revealed something of their personal experiences. Although they were from vastly dissimilar backgrounds, when they were in the privacy of Prudenza's sitting room they could put aside the formalities of the mistress/maidservant relationship and behave like the young girls they were.

Ginevra was delighted when Prudenza began to call her Gina. Gina, however, could not bring herself to call her mistress Pru, as she was invited to do. While Gina dutifully fufilled all of her obligations as servant, the two spent many happy hours laughing and chatting together much as Prudenza and Coletta had done. Soon Prudenza began to give Gina little gifts, tokens of friendship that Gina treasured. She in turn kept her mistress apprised of the climate and the inevitable tensions that arise in any family situation.

As the months passed Zenobi became more and more attached to his daughter-in-law—a fact that Matteo had not failed to notice. The praise that he so desired and fed upon no longer came in such abundance. To his troubled mind this meant only one thing. His wife had supplanted him in his father's affections and, indeed, even in the loyalty of the servants.

Despite his halfhearted efforts to overcome his jealousy and insecurity Matteo feared that he was losing ground in his father's affections and, just as it once was his brother Fabrizio who overshadowed him—or so he thought—now it was his wife. That was doubly humiliating!

He turned to his mother for consolation and advice. Maddalena wisely avoided taking sides and counseled her son to neutralize the tension by paying more attention to his wife. "Be a husband to her! Be glad that she is happy in the family. Take her out. Show her off to your friends just as you did in the weeks before the wedding."

It seemed good advice so he lost no time in following it. He marched up to the *loggia* where he knew he would find her with her lute and the bird. She was surprised and pleased to see him—he had never before come to her there.

"Matteo, what a lovely surprise. Please come, sit with me."

"*Cara*, I have been thinking. It is already September and we have been husband and wife for two months—very happy months. And now it is time I have a surprise for you."

"Yes? A surprise? Oh, tell me, Matteo."

"But If I tell you, *cara*, he teased, it will no longer be a surprise, will it?"

"No. You are right. But could you not give me a little hint?"

"Well, perhaps just a little."

"Do then. Please go on."

"All right. Tomorrow evening you must dress in your finest gown and..."

"And what?"

"You will see soon enough. We will go out into the city."

Without revealing anything more he kissed her and left.

Prudenza looked lovely in the ivory brocade that she chose to wear to this surprise outing, and Matteo felt very proud as he escorted her out of the house and through the *piazza*. As he did so he began to reveal the secret. "We are going to celebrate the *Festa delle rificolone*, the feast of lanterns."

"I have never heard of this feast. Tell me about it."

"It is a tradition in Florence that on the seventh day of September, the eve of the birthday of the Virgin Mary, people gather in the *piazza* near the Ospedale degli Innocenti, the foundling home across from the monastery of the Serviti, to hear the orphans sing pious songs. The celebration takes its name from the lanterns that the children carry."

"It sounds delightful."

She recognized that they were walking in the general direction of the church of Santissima Annunziata, which bordered the foundling home. Prudenza knew the *piazza* and thought it the lovliest in the city. The sun was just beginning to set as the children, all holding small lanterns mounted on sticks, began to file out from under the column-borne arches of the beautiful arcade of the foundling home. As they did so their sweet voices filled the square, reverberating against the buildings that enclosed it. Prudenza was delighted and noted that the children carried different-colored lanterns that matched their robes. There were white and blue and a dark yellow—almost the color of saffron.

She was delighted that she recognized some of the popular hymns that they sang and was able to join in the singing. Matteo had no musical ear but even he could recognize the sweetness of her voice as she joined in *Vergine bella, Madre di Giesù*. As the singing continued into the night the lanterns of the children sometimes swayed with the rhythm of their songs, creating a sort of sacred light show. It was an altogether lovely surprise.

Suddenly Matteo's mood changed as he noted some young men staring at Prudenza with lust in their eyes. He had to admit she was a vision. But she was his woman and they had no right to look upon her with such obvious desire. He struggled with a mixture of pride and jealousy, pondering how to react. Just then one young fellow threw a handful of sweetmeats at Prudenza and Matteo's anger flared. In a moment she was being showered with flowers and Matteo was by now furious. Prudenza did her best to calm him, trying to avoid a street fight over her and was able to convince him that they should simply leave quietly. Reluctantly he agreed.

As the months progressed Prudenza was becoming more and more comfortable in her role as wife and mistress, Matteo was making sincere effort to deal with his jealousy, and she spent many hours writing letters to her parents. The only cloud over her existence was the realization that her father was not well. Caterina did not want to alarm her daughter, but felt she must tell her of Alfonso'a severe headaches that sent him to his bed sometimes for days at a time. Prudenza longed to be able to go to him, but there was no possibility of that. Instead she sent him herbal remedies that Berardo helped her to prepare and she prayed earnestly for his recovery.

The winds from the North were a reminder that fall was turning into winter and soon the great fireplaces would be called into service. In the streets below vendors could be heard peddling their roasted chestnuts as their tantalizing fragrance wafted upward. Prudenza would soon see her adopted city dusted in a covering of glistening snow. The *pifferi* began to come down from the hills and she could hear their *cennemelle*, those out-of-tune little reed instruments accompanied by their wheezy, rustic bagpipes. The streets soon reverberated with strains of that popular Christmas *lauda* that she had learned as a child, *Cristo é nato e umanato*.

As Christmas approached she was occupied with the preparation of proper gifts for her husband and new family. At the same time she was lonely for her parents who for the first time would be alone for the holiday back in Ancona. She hoped that *Fra* Tommaso would call on them.

Matteo had long since determined what his gift to his wife would be. And as they gathered around the fire to celebrate the feast, there appeared before her a very large and shapeless parcel bearing her name. What could it possibly be?

THE LOOM

CHAPTER 13

The Loom

The sharp winds from the north finally ceased and the snow that had earlier blanketed the city and surrounding hills of Florence was now encrusted with a slick layer of ice. It crunched noisily beneath the feet of worshippers who ventured to make their way across the cobbles at this late hour, for it was Christmas Eve. In the reverential stillness the ringing of the great bells of Santa Croce seemed amplified, answered by those of a dozen other churches reverberating through the chill night air.

Despite the cold Prudenza felt warm and secure on the arm of her husband as the two Cecchi couples carefully made their way across the *piazza*. Inside the church was ablaze with candles. Their light filtered through clouds of incense already rising from golden censors in the hands of acolytes who stood ready for that moment when, at the stroke of midnight, the prior began the procession to the elaborate *presepio* where he placed in the manger an image of the Christ child.

The great organ thundered in the vast expanse of the church and in response the choir intoned, *Puer natus est nobis*, the joyful news that "A child is born for us!" The Mass unfolded with all the splendor and solemnity that Santa Croce could offer on such a festive occasion. At its close, while the strains of the last hymn died away, friends chatted gaily and wished each other a *buon natale.* They pulled their mantles tightly about them in anticipation of the blast of frigid night air that awaited them as they left. Most could be seen to walk briskly, undoubtedly spurred by the thought of homes where warm fires, mulled wines, and all manner of Christmas delicacies were sure to await them.

The Cecchi family was no different. In fact Matteo seemed especially animated, energized by something he had hinted at for days—much like a child. It was some sort of surprise for Prudenza, who was pleased to see him so happy, more carefree than he had been of late. Perhaps, she thought, he has taken note of my hints that I would like to have a dog. I miss Lupo so much. On this night especially, I remember what a presence he was at last year's Christmas celebration as he lay at my feet while I played my lute and sang. A dog would be such a good companion for me now since Matteo is obliged to spend longer hours away at work.

As usual Maddalena had outdone herself in her preparation of the great room. The air was fragrant with the pungent scent of fresh-cut greens and spiced wine that mingled ever so subtley with the understated perfume of melting beeswax. Large garlands of juniper festooned the mantle and, in the center of a huge and prominently placed wreath of holly, the mystery of the nativity was represented in beautifully carved figures.

"Come, Prudenza, look!" Maddalena smiled as she pointed out to her daughter-in-law the shepherd with a wooly sheep wrapped tenderly about his shoulders. "This was my favorite figure when I was a child. All of these figures were my grandmother's, Prudenza. One day they will be yours, my dear—yours to pass on to your children."

When all were warmed inside and out, Matteo took advantage of a brief lull in the conversation to move closer to his wife's side. He bowed stiffly, took her hand and led her to a large object placed at the side of the hearth, and formally announced, "To you, my wife, in remembrance of your first Christmas as a member of the Cecchi family, I present this token of our union."

"Matteo, I am truly touched. Thank you." She did note, however, there was no wagging tail to suggest the presence of a puppy inside. Nonetheless she slowly began to peel away the covering, even as Zenobi and Maddalena looked quizically at one another—which suggested that the contents would be a surprise to them as well.

Prudenza could not help thinking of that earlier gift from her father on her thirteenth birthday when the prize was her precious lute. As she proceeded to lift the second silken cloth that had been so carefully arranged to conceal the contents of this gift, a chilling thought crossed her mind like an ominous shadow. "That earlier present that Matteo gave to me the day after our wedding brought with it a requirement, a much unwanted one. It was the palfrey, Stella. She is a beautiful animal, but with her came the mandate to learn to ride."

She offered a silent prayer, "Please, God, let this be different," and gave a resolute tug to the last remaining corner of the cover. As the wrapping fell away she struggled to contain her emotions for, there before her, was an apparatus that stared mockingly at her, seeming to grin with large wooden teeth.

"It…it is a loom!"

"Yes, I know. It is not just any loom, it is your very own loom, Prudenza. I had it made for you."

The words stuck in her throat as she managed to say, "I thank you, Husband. I…I do not know what to say, Matteo."

"Then let me," he continued, obviously pleased with himself. "The loom is a symbol, like the hearth, a symbol of fidelity: It represents the consecration of our marriage vows."

Just as she had never had any desire to learn to ride in the hunt but made a supreme effort to fulfill her earlier charge, so now came another gift with a requirement. Somehow the significance of this one was more alarming. She was conscious of Matteo's voice rambling on in the background but she was lost in her own thoughts. "Why would a prosperous silk merchant ask his wife to sit and weave like a peasant woman?"

Emerging as if from some vast distance she heard his voice continue, "Don't be afraid, Prudenza. You will learn. Start with something simple."

Must he be so patronizing? she thought.

Zenobi shook his head in disbelief and Maddalena attempted to conceal her reaction by hastily refilling everyone's goblet. Obviously pleased with his surprise, Matteo rewarded himself with repeated drafts until he had drained the last crimson drop of wine and then turned to the grappa. At this point Zenobi wisely took matters in hand. Snuffing out the candles one by one he reminded, "It will soon be dawn so let us all retire now. *Buona notte e buon natale.*"

Prudenza was glad to put an end to this ordeal and as she climbed the stairs to their bedroom she prayed with all her might that Matteo would not come to claim his marriage rights this night. He was already intoxicated, and she could not help noticing that, as he staggered out, he snatched the half-filled flask of grappa from the table.

She uttered a heartfelt "Thank you, God," when she heard him stumble up the stairs and fall into bed in the room just next to theirs where, of late, he often slept. As she lay awake a long time reflecting what this strange episode could possibly mean, she fingered Nonna Costanza's ring and invoked the assistance of the brave grandmother she never knew, but with whom she felt such a close bond that she now often talked aloud to her.

Maybe it is just that I have been spoiled by my kind and indulgent parents. Father never suggested that I should ride, other than in a coach. It was a small one, a very modest one, to be sure, but...Oh, Nonna Costanza, you know that I have always preferred music and books to the outdoor life. Is it wrong for me to feel so? What must I do now? Will this thing, this loom, be a noose about my neck, my incubus? As she drifted off to sleep her thoughts were in far away Ancona, of her parents, *Zia* Teresina, *Fra* Tommaso, Coletta—even Lupo. "Do they miss me as I miss them?"

Matteo arranged to have the loom delivered to Prudenza's quarters where it sat for several days, as welcome as an ox in a lady's chamber, before she dared to touch it. She resented its leering presence that so dominated the room that it seemed to her there was no longer space nor even air to sustain her in this quiet retreat. In her troubled mind such pleasantries as reading, music, and even innocent converse with her faithful maidservant had been crowded out of her life, effectively suffocating her, depriving her of the comforts that sustained her in her isolation.

Gina watched her closely as one day she finally approached the rig and walked around it gingerly, scrutinizing it at first only visually. After a time she picked up the shuttle but promptly dropped it when she was startled by a noise on the stairs.

"Go ahead, *Madama*, try. Maybe it is not as complicated as it appears."

"Oh, Gina. I am so afraid. Have you ever...? Can you help?"

"No, *Signora*, I'm sorry. I have never learned to weave but I have watched my mother do so. *Coraggio, Madama*, maybe together we can learn."

Their two heads, one tawny, the other black as jet, bent over the loom as together they struggled with a mass of threads, some yarns of wool, others of silk. At first it seemed that the more they worked the more hopelessly tangled the strands became; but with each passing day they did make some small progress, separating the hanks feeding the weft and the warp. It helped to make a game of it so Gina made up a simple ditty like a nursery rhyme. "This is the way we lace the weft, lace the weft—over, under, over under the warp, warp, warp." It helped to laugh, and sometimes they did giddily, but clearly a more skilled hand was needed.

Prudenza prayed daily that Matteo would not come to inspect her progress—at least not yet, for she had not even begun to investigate the treadles that she supposed might make it possible to create patterns. For now she was satisfied at least to have sorted out the most basic of functions. Doggedly she approached the dreaded loom daily, while in her heart she longed to pick up her lute instead. It now stood silent and neglected in the corner. This mindless to-ing and fro-ing with the shuttle was unbearably boring, so Gina read aloud in an effort to divert her.

Even little Angelo ceased his cheerful singing and only chirped a little as he cocked his golden head to the side quizzically, obviously not knowing what to make of the steady click and clack of this noisy new intruder.

After some time Matteo appeared one day at the door of her little sitting room. He rarely came there, usually not venturing beyond the bedroom, so she was startled at his unexpected presence.

"Matteo! What a surprise!"

Gina slipped from the room unobtrusively as a proper maidservant should when the master calls upon his spouse.

"I have come to see how you like your Christmas gift, *cara*. It would please me to see your progress."

Prudenza held her breath as he approached the loom, knowing he would survey her pathetic attempts with a critical eye accustomed to the work of the skilled weavers of his father business. She watched as his face flushed, and she could see by the ripple of his fleshy cheeks that he was clenching his teeth.

After what seemed an interminable moment of suspense, he pointed to the shawl she was attempting, pulled from it several slack threads and waved them threateningly in her face. "This is not satisfactory, Prudenza. It looks like a child's work." She shuddered as he turned abruptly and, losing control of his voice, thundered at her, "This is how you treat my special gift to you?"

"I am sorry, Matteo. I am trying; truly, I am. It is just that I have never done this before and there is no one to instruct me."

There was a menacing chill in his voice as he slowly and with exaggerated enunciation, accused her. "If you spent more time at this loom and less time making up useless verses and singing with that infernal lute of yours perhaps..."

She dropped to her knees and, as his fury grew in intensity and volume, covered her ears, fearing to hear any more of his ranting. Even little Angelo tucked his tiny head under his wing. Matteo stormed out of the room and only after the sound of his angry footsteps faded into the distance did Prudenza, too shaken even to cry, rise from the floor and begin to breathe freely.

"This is the first time that he has ever spoken to me like that. It was as if I were his horse. No. I have never even heard him speak to Mea in this way."

Gina quietly crept back into the room and attempted to comfort Prudenza. "Come, *Madama*, play your lute and sing. It will make you feel better."

"Oh, Gina, I dare not."

"Nonsense. I will watch when he leaves the house and you can safely sing your heart out. Please try."

"But I must not. My music would become a sinful indulgence, an illicit thing that must be concealed from my husband. I would be a disobedient wife."

"No, no. You would not," Gina dared to contradict. She had lived in the Cecchi establishment long enough to have made some shrewd observations as she skillfully worked her way up through the ranks of servants until she had reached the elevated station she now held. She had heard the rumors, the inevitable gossip and idle chatter of the other servants and she could with confidence say, "Your mother-in-law, *Signora* Maddalena, has never sat around weaving for her husband, jumping at his beck and call. And it is well known that your gentle father-in-law has never raised his voice to her."

"I suppose you are right, Gina. You are such a sensible girl...will you please help me through this?"

"Of course, I will. I have an idea, *Madama*. Listen." She pulled a small stool directly in front of Prudenza and, pointing her finger at her mistress like a tutor, began to quiz her. "Do you remember that first day, when your husband introduced all the servants to you?"

"Of course. How could I ever forget? That was when he gave me the keys to his household."

"Well, then you must remember when he introduced Maria he mentioned specifically that she was a skilled weaver, and that his own mother, Mistress Maddalena, had provided Maria with a loom which she keeps in the laundry next to the kitchen."

"Yes. Yes, I do remember now. Do you think Maria could teach me?"

"I'm sure she could. But there is a problem. The lower ranks of servants are not permitted to come to the upper part of the living quarters. And there is no way that we could transport this monstrous apparatus down to the laundry. We must think of something to divert your master's attention and sneak Maria up here to help."

"Do you think it can work?"

"I know a way!" She leaned forward and in a conspiratorial whisper unfolded her plan. "Nella will help us. You see she and Maria are good friends. Nella is kind, and she likes you very much, *Madama*. Besides, she is safe."

"What do you mean, she is safe?"

"I mean that by virtue of her long service here Nella has

earned some privileges, and she would never be suspected of anything."

"I think I see. Go on. What are you suggesting?"

"Sometimes, when things are very busy at work your husband does not come home for meals, but stays at the *botegga*. He usually tells Nella when he will not be here for *pranzo*. She will tell us and then I can safely bring Maria to you."

"Oh, Gina, are you sure? Are you not afraid? If he should find out I fear what he might do to you, or to Nella and Maria."

"No. I am not afraid."

"Oh, do be careful, Gina. I would never want to hurt you."

It took only a few of these clandestine visits from Maria for her to sort out the problems with the loom and Prudenza was able to make some progress. She was grateful that Matteo had been kept unusually busy at work—though that unfortunately meant that Zenobi's health was failing and he needed his son's assistance more than ever. For Prudenza, however, Matteo's absence not only provided long periods for her to spend playing her lute, it also meant that weeks later when he finally came by to inspect her progress, she had successfully produced a significant length of cloth that even he had to admit was well done.

With smug satisfaction he reminded her, "You see, I told you that if you put aside your useless music and attended to your loom you could do it. I am pleased."

"Pleased to think you were right," she wanted to say, but managed to hold her tongue, and instead swallowed hard as she pronounced words that she knew were mostly false. "I am happy that you approve of my work now."

Matteo's behavior had aroused some unknown reserve of independence within her that throttled her conscience into submission—at least temporarily. Her better judgment told her that what he was demanding of her was unreasonable. Once or twice she had even overheard his mother admonishing him to cease this ridiculous behavior.

Prudenza was growing stronger. She had only to remind herself that she was the daughter of Alfonso and Caterina Beltramonto, upright and God-fearing people. And there flowed in her veins the blood of Nonna Costanza who had risked her life to marry the man she loved. So even as Matteo stood looking down over her, smirking, convinced of his victory, Prudenza's thoughts were fabricating a far different scenario.

I know I am able to match wits with this demanding husband of mine. His uncontrolled temper may erupt in an instant like a volcano, but I believe he can be tamed. I have observed how readily praise can turn his head. Poor thing! How vulnerable he truly is. I will survive, even if I must re-invent myself—try a new scheme. I have never attempted seduction but...smiling demurely she looked directly into his eyes and invited, "Matteo, Husband, will you come to me tonight? Please? I long for you."

In response he could only stare at the floor and blink sheepishly, acutely aware that of late he had neglected his rights and duties as a husband. Instead, like a pouting child, he insisted upon sleeping in another room.

"Please, Matteo? Will you come to me? Tonight?"

After a long anxious silence, "All right, tonight then. Yes, tonight. I promise."

Over the months, since he had first so passionately bedded her, his ardor had waxed and waned. He could be incredibly gentle, ardent, even lustful. Gradually the fear and trauma that Prudenza first experienced gave way to gratification and she even learned those things that aroused him to almost unbearable pleasure. In this last, she sometimes sought the advice of her clever maid. Now as she contemplated this new strategy she literally stiffened her spine as she spoke the words aloud. "I will beguile him! Oh, God knows I do try to love him as it is my duty. Perhaps I can disarm him, neutralize his rage, his jealousy. He will believe that I am simply submitting to him and it will make him happy. I will play upon his insecurity like I play upon my lute. Only it will be a different music."

In a while he did return to their marriage bed nightly, alternately gentle and tender, but sometimes rough. It was on those nights, when he reached the point of being almost crude and hurtful, that she recognized he was having problems at work. He would not speak of it with her for that would suggest weakness. Instead his actions betrayed him. He had to assume more responsibility now that Zenobi had all but retired from his position as head of the business. Matteo knew that the workers hated him and he in turn was abusive in his treatment of them. To make matters worse, when things became difficult, the old scourge of his stuttering returned to humiliate him, sometimes sending him into violent rages. Matteo Cecchi simply did not tolerate embarrassment and humiliation. Invariably he found his ultimate refuge in drink, which only aggravated the situation, and prompted Prudenza to feign sleep, as she silently prayed that he would go to his other bed alone.

All in all, however, she was learning to handle the situation, and her fears began to lessen. Now on those nights when he came to her respectfully she even dared to suggest, "Before we lie together, let us pray, Matteo."

"Pray?"

"Yes, pray."

"Pray for what?"

"Pray that God will be pleased with our union."

"You think He cares?"

"Of course He cares."

"Then why do we need to pray?"

"That He will grant us happiness and prosperity."

"Oh. Yes! Make us rich."

"Perhaps that, too; but more importantly, give us peace, concord, fertility. A child."

"A boy, you mean."

"Yes, a boy! Come then; let us get on with it."

—⟳—

As she had promised, Gina kept watch like a faithful sentry while Prudenza spent blissful hours with her music. Angelo regained his voice and warbled away happily again. She still attended to the loom, investing just enough time to add satisfactory length to the cloth, for Matteo now came periodically to inspect her progress. Her life had become like a seesaw. The lute was her reward after hours of this boring and irksome occupation. In a way it was not unlike the balancing act of her marriage. Learning to love this man required constant diligent effort—just as did the loom. The peaceful and beautiful hours with the lute came to represent the happy times they shared when he was gentle and loving. Now and again she was even able to carve out time to revisit her beloved Dante—though her preoccupation with the ill-fated Paolo and Francesca left her strangely unnerved.

Meanwhile there was that other gift that came with a charge. The horse! Learning to ride was not as onerous an obligation as the loom had been for it meant that she could leave her quarters, to which she had become confined by Matteo's decrees. Besides, she genuinely liked young Luca, the stable boy. He was patient and gentle with her and never ridiculed her awkward attempts to learn the rudiments of horsemanship. Just as Matteo said, Stella was a gentle, docile animal, a beautiful horse. She seemed to sense Prudenza's trepidation as Luca first handed the reins to her. The mare nuzzled her as if to say, "Don't be afraid of me. I am your friend."

An added incentive to her visiting the stable more frequently was the opportunity that it afforded to stop by the garden and chat with Berardo. And since she always paid a call to the kitchen to find an apple or a carrot for Stella she could visit with Nella and Maria, too. It never failed to lift her spirits.

One morning not long after Prudenza had advanced from simply holding the reins and walking the mare about in the paddock Luca announced that it was time to mount the animal and ride slowly.

"Do you think I can, Luca?"

"Of course you can, *Signora*. You are ready and it is clear that Stella likes you. Besides, I will stay at your side and you need only walk her slowly."

As he spoke he placed the saddle on the horse's back and cinched it snuggly. He offered his cupped hand to Prudenza to step into as he helped her mount. She easily adjusted her position behind the pommel as she had observed others do and settled in as if she had been riding all her life. Then, playing the knight of old carrying his lady's silks into the joust, with a sudden flourish of an imaginary cape and an exaggeratedly profound bow, Luca playfully trumpeted, "*Brava, Signora*! My lady."

Continuing the innocent charade Prudenza responded with an equally exaggerated gesture, "I thank you most kindly, my good squire."

After some time walking the horse at a leisurely gait she complained of a slight dizziness and fatigue and asked Luca to help her dismount.

Just as he had periodically checked on her weaving Matteo also came to the stable from time to time to monitor her progress with the horse. At the very moment when Luca was assisting her to dismount, Matteo appeared at the entrance to the paddock, just in time to see his wife faint and fall into the young man's arms. His frown was so deep and dark that his black eyebrows nearly met in the middle of his forehead and, though he said nothing, it was clear what he was thinking. He took a few brisk steps, swooped his wife up into his muscular arms and carried her away, presumably to her bed. He remained at her side until she regained consciousness and then called for Gina to stay with her. There was coldness in his voice as he took his leave. "I must go now, Wife, but we will speak of this later." With that he was gone.

Gina stroked Prudenza's forehead and began to question her mistress. "Forgive me, *Madama*, for being so personal; but I must ask: have your courses been regular lately?"

"I cannot remember. I think, perhaps not. Not really."

"How many days since your last?"

"It was...let me see...the bleeding ceased on the last day that Maria was here to help with the loom. That was..."

"That was nearly seven weeks ago. Let's count." Together they ticked off the days 'til they reached forty-nine. "I think it may be too soon to know for certain, but I do believe, *Madama*, that you are going to have a baby!"

"A baby!" She bolted upright in bed and almost as if struck dumb could say no more, but listened attentively as Gina cautioned, "Let us keep it between us at least for two more weeks to be sure, and then you must share the good news."

"Yes. Until then, Gina, it will be our secret."

CHAPTER 14

A Contest of Wills

Easter was early this year, the end of March, and it seemed that spring came to Florence almost overnight. For Zenobi the warming of the weather and the bright skies brought with them renewed energy, and the old man predicted, "I believe the almond trees will bloom by Easter. No more fasting then, my children. It is time to celebrate." Turning to Prudenza he inquired, "Daughter, do you know our custom of the *scoppio del carro*?"

"*Scoppio*? The explosion? No. What is that? It sounds dangerous."

He laughed at the suggestion. "Oh, no, far from it. It is a very joyous thing. You will see. When we go together on Easter Day for the celebration I will explain it to you."

As promised, on Easter morn, Zenobi proudly led his little family to the *piazza* in front of the *duomo* where already in the early hours a crowd had begun to gather.

Placed squarely in front of the now-opened giant doors of the cathedral, between the church and the baptistry, stood a tall, elaborate, and brilliantly ornamented construction that looked like an altar mounted on wheels. The *brindellone* he called it. It had been towed there by a pair of freshly scrubbed, gilt-hoofed white oxen around whose necks hung garlands of colorful flowers.

There was an air of excitement and anticipation in the crowd and, before Prudenza could even formulate any questions, Zenobi began to explain. "Long, long ago some crusaders brought back from the Holy Land flints that they claimed to have taken from the holy sepulcher itself." At that thought he devoutly crossed himself and continued, "They enshrined them here at the little church of Santi Apostoli where, to this day, they are guarded in safekeeping."

"Oh, Father, have you seen them?"

"Oh, no. But I believe the tale. Each year, in the early hours of Easter morn the flints are carried to the cathedral where they are concealed in a paper dove that is released at the moment of consecration, to fly down a wire from the high altar, through the open doors of the cathedral, to strike the *carro* and explode the fireworks inside."

Prudenza's eyes grew large as she observed, "Nothing like this happened in Ancona. But what does it mean, Father?"

"Oh, it has significance. If the explosion is a big one it means that there will be a good harvest this year."

Then, just as Zenobi had explained, it happened, sending hundreds of pigeons swooping through the sky, and casting a shadow like a momentary cloud passing overhead. Prudenza was not prepared for the explosion and sank backward in a faint, with Matteo catching her just in time. Maddalena had observed that she looked a bit pale but blamed it on the lack of air, for the crowd was dense by now. She ordered, "Quick, Matteo. Let us get her home and to her bed—out of this crowd." In her usual take-charge mode Maddalena suspected the cause of her daughter-in-law's recent fainting spells and sent for the midwives.

After a time, the doctor and midwives confirmed her suspicions. Prudenza was pregnant! There had not been such joy in the Cecchi household in years. Maddalena had nearly given up hope of ever having grandchildren, and Zenobi worried that the business he had worked so hard to establish might not remain in the family.

Matteo was so beside himself that he ran out into the streets, shouting right and left, to anyone who would listen, "Look at me! Look at me! I, Matteo Cecchi, will soon be a father." As he continued his excitement grew so uncontrolled that he nearly choked on the good news, and the tangled words that tumbled out sounded like the crowing of a mad rooster. In his moment of excitement the dreaded old stuttering had returned and some young boys in the street were quick to make fun of him, embellishing their cackling with somersaults, folding their arms and flapping them like roosters' wings—all of which would ordinarily have angered Matteo to the point of violence. Only his pride in what he considered his "accomplishment" spared the urchins his anger.

When at last he had exhausted himself with his senseless escapades in the street he came to his wife and embraced her with a kind of gentleness not usually expected of him. "Thank you, *cara*. Oh, thank you, thank you, thank you! I am so happy—and I hope you are, too."

"Yes, of course I am happy, Matteo." Her joy, however, was tempered by the realization that childbirth was still a mortal hazard; and she longed for her mother to be with her now. "I must write to tell my parents, Matteo. They will be so happy."

"Of course." He clicked his fingers to summon Gina who was dispatched to bring parchment and pen.

"*Si, Signore* Cecchi, at once." She stayed in the background after delivering them in case her mistress needed her, glad that she could share in this joy and very pleased with herself that she had been the first to suspect Prudenza's pregnancy. She watched as her mistress was absorbed in writing the letter.

> *Dearest Mother and Father,*
>
> *I write to you with news that I know will gladden your hearts, for I am beside myself with joy as well. I cannot wait to tell you that in a few months you are going to be grandparents. Yes, I am expecting a baby—probably in the early days of December. God willing he will be a healthy boy, and I shall call him Alfonso Eduardo after you, dear Father. Please pray for me and for the baby that all goes well and that I am delivered of a healthy child. I admit to some fear, Mother dear, and I do hope that you will come to attend me at the birth. You would be such a comfort to me.*
>
> *Matteo is absolutely delirious with joy and Zenobi and Maddalena are likewise thrilled at the prospect. Please be assured that they are exceedingly kind and caring and they share their joy with you. I send my deepest affections and long to hear from you.*
>
> *Your loving daughter, Prudenza*

After some days, as Prudenza was working at the loom, Gina brought to her the missive that she eagerly awaited. She was excited to see the clear, rounded letters of her father's neat hand-writing, but noted at the same time a certain unsteadiness in it, too. As she broke the orange sealing wax, the familiar elaborate letter "B" impressed upon it shattered into small shards and fell to the floor. She opened the letter hurriedly and began to read, half aloud, yet to herself:

> *My dearest child,*
> *Your letter has just arrived and I hasten to respond to say that there are hardly words to express the profound happiness that your good news brings to your mother and me. Together we pray for your health and for the baby's, as well. And we send our thanks and congratulations to your husband and to my dear old friend Zenobi and his wife Maddalena.*
> *Now we share an even stronger common bond in this grandchild in whose blood the houses of Beltramonto and Cecchi are combined. God be praised, and may He be with you always.*
> *Your father, Alfonso Beltramonto*

Beneath his signature she recognized her mother's script, and as she read on Gina noted a change in her mistress's counte-nance, as if a cloud had suddenly obscured the brightness.

> *My dearest daughter,*
> *I must add a hurried note before I seal this. Please know that my heart and mind are with you in this won-derful, and yes, frightening. time. And were I free to follow my own wishes, I would hasten to your side. But I must tell you that I fear I cannot do so, for your father has not been well, and I must not leave him. He would not want me to tell you this for fear that you should worry, but I think you should know. I am torn between my duties to my husband and to my child. Please do not fret over this news. And I beg you not to reveal to him that I have told you.*

*My great consolation is that you are being well
cared for by a loving husband and his good parents. Please
be assured that although I cannot be with you physically,
in spirit I am always at your side, Prudenza.
Your loving mother, Caterina Beltramonto*

Gina could not help seeing the tears in Prudenza's eyes as
she let the letter fall into her lap. "*Madama*. Are you all right?"

There was a long pause during which Prudenza seemed
absent, and then, "Yes. Yes, Gina. Just some disturbing news."

"I am sorry. Is there anything I can do for you?"

"No, not really." But after a moment, "Yes. Yes there is.
Please bring me paper and pen."

Without explanation she wrote what appeared to be a hasty
note, sealed it and gave it to Gina with instruction, "Please see that
this is placed in the first post to leave Florence."

"At once, *Madama*."

"Thank you, Gina and, oh...please do not mention it to
anyone."

"Of course not, *Signora*."

After a few days Prudenza shared with her maid the alarming news of her father's illness as well as her own disappointment
that her mother could not be with her for the birth of her child.
Though she realized that she could never take the place of Prudenza's mother, Gina determined to bring her mistress as much
support and comfort as she could. As the pregnancy progressed
she read to her, massaged her swollen feet and aching back, and
ever so carefully loosed the lacings of her mistress's bodice as the
baby grew in her swollen belly.

There were times when Prudenza seemed far away, lost in
thoughts of who knows what. She had never discussed her early
life with her maid; but now she often prattled on, half-audibly,
about people Gina did not know. A friend named Coletta seemed
to be very much on her mind. "I miss her so, Gina. She was like a
sister to me. You know, Gina, she was with me at so many important times in my life. She calmed me when I was so frightened at
the time of my first blood. She helped me overcome my fear of *Fra*
Tommaso when I went away to school at San Salvatore, and she
cried with me when Father came to take me home from school.

You see we feared we would never see each other again. And when I was so terrified at the prospect of marriage and leaving home she was there for me, always encouraging me."

"She does seem a wonderful lady, *Madama*."

"O, she is, Gina, the best of friends. When I left Ancona she gave me her precious locket that I always wear." As she spoke she drew it from her bodice and caressed it lovingly.

The young girl was obviously touched by these very personal revelations and silently pondered how she might locate this friend of her mistress. It would bring such consolation to her now. She remembered that Prudenza once mentioned that Coletta married a man from Rignano sul Arno.

Gina could be artful if need be, and this was the time to call on those skills. Silently she began rehearsing the plot in her mind. "I remember when the young *Signore* Cecchi introduced the servants to Prudenza that first day, when he came to me he mentioned that my family originated from Rignano. He could not know, of course, that my brother still lives there on the old family farm. I must try to get *Madama* to talk of her friend some more. Perhaps that way I can help."

"Did you say, *Signora*, that your friend Coletta was married?"

"Yes. She was married to a very nice young man named Giampaolo. I don't remember his last name; you see I met him only once, at Christmas when Coletta brought him to our home. I remember that he is tall, fair, and had an extremely pleasant manner."

Gina was processing all this information, formulating plans, thinking, "There isn't much to go on but, after all, Rignano sul Arno is a small place. Everyone knows everyone else. And how hard should it be to find this Giampaolo who is so tall and fair? I must write to my brother at once."

Meanwhile Maddalena was keenly aware of Prudenza's disappointment that her mother could not be with her, and she did her utmost to fill the role of mother to her daughter-in-law, though she sometimes overreached the limits and imposed her own will. Still Prudenza was immensely grateful. As the months passed Caterina sent more and more lovely clothes that she had made for the baby and soon a beautiful finely carved cradle arrived. It was

Alfonso's gift, lovingly made with his own hands.

As the time for the birth approached, Maddalena was busy preparing the birthing room and early one morning announced to Prudenza, "We must secure the wet nurse soon so that she will be available a soon as the baby comes."

Prudenza paled at the mention of a wet nurse. "Oh, no, Mother. I will nurse my baby myself."

Maddalena seemed horrified at the thought. "No never! You must not even consider it, Prudenza. It is unseemly for women of our rank to so do. Women from better families always employ wet nurses. Sometimes the infants are even sent away to the home of the wet nurse for as much as two years—until they are weaned. We will not do that. I want my grandchild here. We must have a live-in wet nurse."

"But look, Mother, You see how my breasts are swollen: I have plenty of milk and I long to feed my baby from my own body."

"No." Maddalena had decreed it, and it was becoming clear to Prudenza that there was little she could do to gainsay her willful mother-in-law's directives.

In the meantime there was good news from Gina's brother. He had located Giampaolo whose surname, he reported, was Alessandrini, and whose wife was indeed named Coletta. Gina wasted no time in sending off a letter to Prudenza's dear friend and as she awaited some response from Coletta she learned that Maddalena had already taken steps to find the wet nurse. She left very early one morning, saying that she would return in two days.

As she passed through the kitchen she issued orders to Nella. "Please see to it that Prudenza eats well. She should have the choicest of foods now as her time approaches. She will need all her strength for the birth. I am going to Prato today to find a wet nurse. I must interview the girl, but I shall return the day after tomorrow."

In Prato, Maddalena had acquaintances who assembled some likely candidates for the job. They were probably poor peasant women who had recently lost their own babies. It was very important to Maddalena that the girl she chose should be healthy and of good character, for it was said that the nurse's milk imparted something of her character to the baby.

She found the young candidates at the local foundling home and after some preliminary questions concentrated on one pretty young woman with coloring not unlike Prudenza's. The girl was obviously frightened by the older woman's commanding presence and the barrage of questions that came. "Come. Let me see you. Now turn; turn around. How old are you? And what is your name?"

"My name is Lucia and I am nineteen years old."

"What was the cause of your baby's death?"

The question touched a still very raw emotion in the poor girl as tears welled up in her eyes. "He was born with the cord wrapped around his neck. The midwives tried to save him but it was too late. His little body was all cold and blue."

Maddalena was touched by the girl's obvious sorrow, but proceeded nonetheless to the ultimately sensitive question. "I must ask you, my dear, was the child illegitimate?"

The girl was offended but not surprised by the question. "No, *Madama*. My baby was not illegitimate. I am a married woman and have a two-year-old daughter."

"Good. I am glad of it. Now I must examine your breasts."

Lucia had not anticipated this degree of scrutiny. She had no choice but to loose her blouse and reveal her distended breasts, so engorged that when Maddalena pressed them even slightly droplets of milk trickled down from the tender nipples, staining her simple shift.

"That will do," she announced, as if the young woman had any control over the function. "I see that you are adequate." As she discreetly wiped the milk from her hand she pushed on with the questioning. "Can you commit to living in our home in Florence until the infant is weaned? Perhaps as long as two years."

Lucia was speechless for a moment. She knew it was uncommon to be a live-in wet nurse, but it had its privileges. Yet, there was the specter of this demanding woman who would undoubtedly be watching her closely. But the money was good and her family was very needy.

"It is a difficult decision, *Signora* Cecchi. Two years! That is a long time to be away from my husband and my little girl."

"Yes, I realize that; but I must know."

Finally after an anxious pause Lucia responded, "Well

then, yes, I will commit to your agreement."

"Good. Then gather your things and prepare yourself. I will send someone for you the day after tomorrow. Do not tarry, for I expect the baby will come within the next few days."

"Goodbye, *Signora*. And thank you."

"Be assured, Lucia, that you will be well provided for under our roof."

"Again, I thank you, *Signora* Cecchi."

Almost as if she controlled the fates as efficiently as she did her household, the first signs that the babe was about to come did, in fact, occur as Maddalena had told young Lucia, "in a few days." The pains began in the early hours of the morning, and to Prudenza it seemed as if at that moment the clock had stopped. She was not comforted by her mother-in-law's announcement as they moved her into the birthing room. "Since it is your first baby it could be a long labor."

The midwives were summoned and went about their business with a quiet efficiency that bespoke many years of experience, and was also a comfort to Prudenza. Anna, the older of the two women, had soft gray eyes so like those of her mother. With a manner especially kind and sympathetic she bent low over Prudenza and whispered, "*Coraggio*, young one. It will be over soon and you will be so happy with your little *bambino* that you will forget the pain."

By turns Maddalena and Gina sat at her bedside holding her hands, wiping her brow and speaking softly. Prudenza's overwhelming sensation was of one long and agonizing pain as this child struggled to come out. Hours passed and she was becoming weaker, more and more exhausted by the extended labor. The passage of time seemed marked only by the gradually changing light in the room. She was vaguely aware of church bells ringing somewhere, but not certain if it were the morning or the evening *angelus*. The candles slowly burned down, leaving only shapeless puddles of softly dripping wax on the floor, their flames now spent—not unlike Prudenza's strength.

Despite her confidence in the midwives' skills Maddalena was growing alarmed as the hours dragged on and she watched the color drain from Prudenza's drawn face as, with fists and teeth clenched, she struggled mightily for the breath to give voice to each successive and more wrenching pain. While Gina kept loving vigil, Maddalena sent a worried message to Berardo to prepare some herbal palliative that might bring relief to Prudenza and hasten the coming of the infant.

Suddenly Prudenza gasped loudly and let out a piercing cry as she twisted in agony.

"It is coming; the babe is coming," Anna announced. "Be brave my girl, be brave." Then after one gigantic and indescribable spasm the baby emerged to cries of joy from all assembled there.

"It is a boy!" Prudenza remembered hearing the midwife say; but she was too exhausted to do more than whisper, "God be praised. Matteo will be so pleased."

Soon the first cries of the baby mingled with the general exaltation in the room and once the midwives had completed their ministration to mother and baby, Maddalena summoned Matteo to meet his little son. He was speechless for a time but then, gently caressing the silky dark fringe that ringed the baby's head like a halo, he collected himself enough to observe, "He has his father's black hair."

As the infant gave a hearty cry, Zenobi, who had been standing behind his son, added "and his father's loud voice."

With that Matteo passed the baby to its grandfather whose joy was too deep for words. As he held the little one in his arms he raised his eyes heavenward and Prudenza observed huge tears trickling down his cheeks. She thought of Simeon who once long ago also held a child. The sight of the old man's peaceful countenance brought to her mind the ancient prophet's words. "Now, Oh Lord, you may dismiss your servant in peace."

After the men reluctantly left, the infant was again placed in his mother's arms—but only briefly, for Maddalena immediately summoned the wet nurse. "Prudenza, this is Lucia who will nurse your little boy. She will be near at all times so that when your baby cries she can immediately comfort him." So saying, she took the baby from Prudenza and placed him in Lucia's arms.

It was a very difficult moment for Prudenza as the young girl shyly came forward. By now she was resigned to the fact that her mother-in-law, for all her kindness and good will, had definitely taken charge and, despite the throbbing in her own tender breasts, she knew she would never nurse her little son.

Reluctantly she surrendered the baby to Lucia and watched as the child instinctively sought the young girl's breast and began to nurse. Prudenza could not help noticing how Lucia's sad eyes quickened when the baby was placed in her arms. And as much as she was saddened by Maddalena's decree, she could not feel jealous of this poor young woman who had so recently experienced the loss of her child. Prudenza had to be grateful that her own little son was alive. Too weak to protest she soon gave way to sleep.

—m—

Christenings, like funerals, were among the few occasions when workers were welcomed into their employer's home. As usual Maddalena arranged everything, insisting that the baby be baptized soon.

"But why so soon, Mother? Can it not wait a bit? My baby is healthy, there is no danger to him, and I want to go to my son's baptism."

"No. You must rest, Prudenza. You have lost much blood, and are far too weak, my dear. The midwives have cautioned that you must not go out now in this winter cold. You might take a chill."

The question of godparents was the occasion for a real contest of wills. It was an important decision, a solemn commitment, for the act introduced a note of spiritual kinship. For these reasons there was no doubt in Prudenza's mind that Coletta and Giampaolo should be the baby's godparents. It had now been more than a year since she last saw them, and she did not know how to reach them. There was still no answer to the message that she had secretly sent to her mother asking her to try to locate Coletta. Time was important now. She must try to convince Maddalena to wait, so she summoned all her strength and courage and spoke directly to her mother-in-law.

"I want my dear friend Coletta and her husband, Giampaolo, to be my son's godparents and my little boy should be named Alfonso Eduardo Zenobi—for his two grandfathers. My mother will try to locate Coletta for me, so we must wait until I can reach her. I know she will be so happy to be my son's godmother."

Maddalena said nothing but a faint wry smile crossed her face as she turned to leave. Her parting words left Prudenza uneasy. "We will speak of this later."

—w—

Although confined to her bed—on pretext of regaining her strength—Prudenza was aware that beneath her quarters, preparations for the christening festivities were being made in the great room. The days were long and time passed slowly, despite Matteo's daily visits to his wife, as well as Gina's efforts to divert her mistress. Fatherhood seemed to bring out a surprising gentleness in Matteo that was noticeable not only as he stood gazing admiringly at his little son asleep in his cradle, but also in his attitude to Prudenza. He was at once proud, tender and serene—though he said nothing about the christening.

Lucia came at regular intervals to fulfill her obligations, so it was a surprise when a mere week after the baby's birth she came to the nursery unusually early one morning to collect the infant. Maddalena awaited her in the next room, and quickly took him to her quarters where she wrapped him in the beautiful christening gown that Caterina had sent. The tiny infant looked even smaller now, lost in a cloud of frothy white lace. He began crying when she wrapped him in yet another layer, this time of fur. She beckoned to Lucia to follow her as she joined the small society that had been waiting below, and they made their way out into the cold and across the *piazza* to Santa Croce.

At the priest's question, "And who stands for this child?" Maddalena stepped forward, accompanied by one of Zenobi's business associates, from a good and wealthy family—not like Prudenza's peasant friends from the country.

Responding to the priest's question regarding the baby's name he poured the water over the squeeling infant's head and pronounced the words. "I baptize you Lorenzo Benedetto Matteo Cecchi, in the name of the Father and of the Son and of the Holy Ghost. Amen."

—m—

Back in the nursery Prudenza stretched out her arms to receive her child, now divested of his baptismal robe. "My sweet little angel, my *bambino*, Alfonso. Alfonso, like your dear grandfather."

Maddalena handed the baby to his mother saying, "No, Prudenza. Here is your son, Lorenzo."

"No, no, Mother. That cannot be."

"But it is. He has just been baptized. His name is Lorenzo."

"Oh, there must be a mistake. I wanted him named for my dear father."

"His name is Lorenzo."

"Why?"

"My father had no sons."

"Nor did mine."

"But my father did have a brother named Lorenzo."

"But there is no one in my relationship by that name."

"There is now, my dear."

CHAPTER 15

The Contract Revisited

Gina was uncharacteristically quiet as she folded the baby's clothing and placed it in the chest at the foot of the bed—almost mechanically. By now Prudenza had come to know her devoted maid so well that the relationship between them was one of friendship, even sisterhood. In her keenly perceptive way Prudenza could not help noticing that Gina had not been her usual high-spirited self for some time now and she determined to find what was troubling her maid. "Gina, you are mumbling to yourself as you work. Is something troubling you?"

"Nothing, *Madama*. Nothing—just a slight headache, and it will soon be gone."

"Are you sure that is all? Is there something you want to tell me?"

The young maid tried to conceal the real reason for her mood but inside Gina was desolate. For all her best intentions and efforts she had not been able to reach Coletta in time, and now it was too late—too late at least for the christening. Several months had passed and still there was no word from Prudenza's old friend.

Gina seemed not to hear her mistress. As she continued laying away the baby's little shirts in neat stacks she muttered half audibly, "I must do something. I cannot bear to see my mistress so sad. I see how she weeps when she thinks I am not watching. I know she must wonder why such a good friend as Coletta has not responded. I know what I will do. It may not be proper but this cannot go on. I will write to Prudenza's mother. The letter that my mistress asked me to post to Ancona for her; I'm sure it must have been to ask her mother to find Coletta and tell her of her desire for Coletta and Giampaolo to be the baby's godparents. But why had *Signora* Beltramonto not answered either? Something is very wrong! I must get to the bottom of it."

Prudenza knew better than to question her maid further if she did not want to confide in her just now. It was Gina's nature to take action. Perhaps it was a trait she had learned growing up in a large family, being the only girl with five older brothers. In any case it was an attribute that served her well as she worked her way up through the ranks of servants in a system subject to a rigid kind of hierarchy in such households. Beginning as a scullery maid when hardly more than a child, in just a few years she had risen to the envied position of maidservant to the mistress of the household. In scullery she had dutifully kept the bowls scrubbed and the pewter polished. But while her hands toiled, her mind was free to roam. During those hours spent peeling potatoes and scrubbing pots she had learned to keep her thoughts to herself while forming astute observations of the behavior of others. It was dear Nella who first recognized Gina's potential and helped to school her in the art of finding her way through the unwritten code of servant behavior.

While Gina watched the post for a response from either Coletta or *Signora* Beltramonto Prudenza slowly regained her strength. The color was coming back to her cheeks and she spent hours cradling her little son in her arms, singing softly as she rocked him; sometimes just humming in a low, gentle tone, soothing little lullabies, *ninna-nannas*. At other times they were jolly little tunes perfect for bouncing the babe on her knee. Gina realized that her talented mistress made up both the tunes and the words. She observed, too, that the happy little songs with the nonsense syllables were the ones she sang as she surreptitiously loosed the windings that bound the infant's legs so tightly. She delighted to see him gurgle a sort of baby laugh as he wiggled his tiny feet freely and almost seemed to dance to the rhythm of his mother's singing. But Prudenza knew that her all-seeing mother-in-law would not have approved so she had to be cautious.

Gradually she began playing the lute more as she sang to baby Lorenzo. She was even finding it easier to call him that, though in her heart he would always be her little Alfonso. At these times when she accompanied herself on the lute it was Gina's privilege to rock the cradle and Angelo added his cheerful warbling to the concert.

To the relief and joy of all it seemed that fatherhood wrought a change in Matteo. It brought out a sensitivity that surprised even Maddalena and somehow alleviated some of the tensions in the household over the christening incident. However when Maddalena's deception became known to Zenobi, but only after the fact, he was quick to voice his disapproval of his wife's interference, even daring to chastise her for it.

Prudenza, in an effort to forgive, tried to believe that her domineering mother-in-law's intentions were good. In any case it helped to lose herself in the hours she spent with her little son. She was usually able to overcome resentment, though she still felt pain at the sight of Lucia nursing her baby, while her own breasts throbbed, involuntarily disgorging the very nourishment intended for her son, leaving his mother with only the embarrassing telltale evidence on her shift.

—m—

Months passed until finally one morning as Maddalena passed Gina on the stairs she casually announced, "O, Gina, the post has arrived and there is a letter for you—from Ancona, I believe."

"*O, grazie, Signora.*" She tried not to appear over eager but as soon as Maddalena passed out of sight she rushed to retrieve the missive and sought out a private place to read it. She knew it had to be from Prudenza's mother for it bore the familiar Beltramonto monogram on the seal. In her haste, as she broke the seal she tore the paper slightly at the edge and shards of wax fell to the floor around her.

As she read tears came to her eyes and she sat silently for minutes, trying to comprehend the reality of the message. Could it be? She read again, hoping her eyes had deceived her at first. But no, there it was in Caterina's clear bold hand. "Coletta is dead!"

Slowly regaining composure she read aloud to herself as if the sound of her own voice would verify that the words that stood out so cruelly on the page were in fact true. She understood now why Prudenza's mother had not been able to tell her daughter. She read again, more slowly this time.

> *Prudenza's dear friend is no longer. Coletta is dead. She died bringing into the world a little daughter who survived her. Coletta's last instructions to her husband were that the baby should be christened Prudenza after her dearest friend.*
>
> *My heart aches for her husband, Giampaolo. He is desolate and in his grief is simply unable to respond to the letter you addressed to Coletta in my daughter's behalf. And I, I confess, have been weak. Knowing my daughter's condition I feared the news would be too shocking for her to bear at this time so close to the birth of her own dear child. I simply could not bring myself to tell her.*
>
> *I thank God that she has such a loyal and loving maid as you obviously are, Gina, and I pray that in your kindness to Prudenza, and your good judgment, you will know the right time to share this sad news with her.*
>
> *With sincerest thanks to you, I am,*
> *Caterina Beltramonto.*

The secret of this sad news weighed like a stone on Gina's heart and for days she went about her duties almost mechanically, all the while trying to maintain a joyful countenance. She had always been open and honest with her mistress and now this was like living a deception, if not an outright lie. She doubted how much longer she could contain this awful secret. At the same time, however, she believed Prudenza suspected something. After all, she must surely question why her dearest friend had not responded to her—even if only to say she could not come to her. I know she wonders why, and it must hurt her terribly.

Now that the weather was warm again, Prudenza spent more and more time on the sunny *loggia* playing her lute and singing to her baby while Gina rocked the cradle and Angelo chirped a little descant. To all appearances it was a charming scene of domestic bliss. Over the many hours spent thus Gina had become acutely familiar with the sound of her mistress's voice and of the lute, which almost seemed to be an extension of Prudenza's very self. Even though she could boast of possessing no particular musical gift, Gina thought she noted a change in the sound of her mistress's voice—subtle but different. In the early days it had seemed to her a very pretty, delicate sound. There was a kind of youthful, maidenly sweetness about it. But now somehow it sounded richer, fuller, with a kind of warm resonance she had not noted before. Was it somehow a reflection of Prudenza's maturing as woman and mother? Whatever it was, it was beautiful and Gina loved to contemplate it as she lost herself in the gentle to-ing and fro- ing of the cradle.

Suddenly, only a few days after the letter arrived, Prudenza surprised Gina by announcing, "Something is wrong, Gina. I know it. Something has happened to Coletta. She is like half my heart and I know she would have written by now."

Gina was questioning in her own mind: is this the right time, or should I continue this charade? As she pondered the question she had put to herself, Prudenza continued to speak. "I had this dream last night, Gina. I saw Coletta all in white in a light so bright I could not..."

Before she could finish Gina interrupted, "*Madama*, Coletta is dead!" She hardly recognized the sound of her own voice and she immediately regretted that she had uttered the news so bluntly. But perhaps it was best that way. She could contain it no longer. Sooner or later her mistress must know. "She died in childbirth at almost the same time that your little son was born. I am truly sorry, *Madama*."

The color drained from Prudenza's face and after an awkward moment she broke the long silence. "Why was I not told?"

In the weeks that followed Gina observed Prudenza's heroic efforts to channel her grief through her attention to her son. At first it seemed strange to her that her mistress had not actually wept at the news of Coletta's death, but over time she began to understand that there are some sorrows that are just too deep to express in words—or even tears. The lute wept for her now.

Despite her efforts to be brave it became known in the household that Prudenza had suffered a great loss, and her devoted servants attempted in their small but sincere ways to bring her comfort. Dear old Berardo not only sent flowers from his garden almost daily, but he also prepared phials of curatives made from the herbs that he so lovingly attended; potions of his own making that were guaranteed to help raise her spirits. Gina was amazed and, in an almost maternal way, was actually surprised at the manner in which her mistress was handling her grief. Prudenza was no longer the timid girl she had been at the time of her entry into the Cecchi family: She was becoming a strong woman.

—⟡—

In a humdrum sort of way a year had passed and once again spring came to Florence. It seemed as if overnight the city had transformed into one large flowering tree whose gentle fragrance lingered in the warm air. The hours spent on the *loggia* were glorious. Life went on in the household, the passage of time marked only by the baby's development, his first teeth, his cooing and babling attempts to speak. Not surprisingly his first word was "*mamma*."

Matteo came at fairly regular intervals to see his son. Maddalena continued her clucking over the baby who had now begun to laugh, and although Zenobi was his usual kind and loving self, the passing year had left him visibly more frail. Life in the Cecchi household had become a peaceful, albeit monotonous, existence.

Gina was shrewd—some would say *furba*—though she never used her gift of discernment for other than good, especially as it related to her mistress. She could not help but suspect that Matteo's attention to his wife and son might be prompted by questionable motives. She saw the way that he studied Prudenza as she cradled little Lorenzo. Indeed Gina thought she looked like the lovely paintings of Madonnas she had seen in the churches of Florence.

As she watched Matteo study this picture of his wife and baby she believed he somehow felt himself outside this tender scene. A chill seized her as she recognized something in his demeanor that suggested he was jealous of his beautiful wife's attention to their son. It appeared that he found some satisfaction in the radiance of Prudenza's beauty, but this was not enough for him; he would not share this with anyone—not even his little son.

Sure enough, within days of Gina's observations Matteo came calling in midafternoon. Prudenza seemed pleased. "Matteo, what a pleasant surprise. Come sit with us."

"I cannot stay. I come on business."

"What business, Husband?"

"You! As you are my wife, you must behave according to my wishes"

Prudenza did not reply, fearing that he was teetering on the brink of another of his sudden outbursts of anger—though she knew not why.

"From this day I forbid you to go outside of this house."

"But why, Matteo?"

"It is not yours to question me. I am the master of this household."

"But think; am I forbidden to fulfill the obligations of my religion? May I not attend Mass and go to confess?"

Although Matteo had never been much afflicted with religion himself he realized that perhaps no harm could come if he allowed this concession. Grudgingly he admitted, "Well, then go to your dismal church and confess your many sins! But you must take a lady companion." Without waiting for his wife to respond he wheeled around and left as swiftly as he had come.

Prudenza suspected, and Maddalena confirmed, that Matteo was again having difficulties at work. The laborers felt no respect for him and resented his often-dictatorial—even physically abusive—ways. He was so unlike his noble father. To make matters worse, as his troubles compounded the old demon stuttering, about which he was becoming more and more sensitive, returned to plague him. Children in the streets hooted, at him, imitating his faltering speech, which only made him bellow at them the more. He was aware, too, that even while the workers toiled at the dyeing vats they mocked him, and cursed him under their breath. Sadly, he carried his problems home and soon tensions again mounted in the household, as well.

One day as he climbed the stairs to call on his wife and son he heard Prudenza singing a little *ninna-nanna* to the baby. He paused outside the door.

> *Tan – tan – ta – ra – ra – r*
> *Ra – ri – ra – ra*
> *Nino mio, Nino, mio.*
> *Fa la mamma bel bambino*
> *Chi –chi – ri chi*
> *Cu – cu – ru – cu…*

Like a bolt of lightning he burst into the room and bellowed, "How dare you mock me so?"

"Husband, what do you mean? I am not mocking you." So frightening was Matteo's fury that she feared for her baby and instinctively clutched him more tightly to her breast. In an instant Gina had seized the lute and was standing close to Prudenza's side ready to protect her mistress and the instrument.

Too angry to say more Matteo stormed out as furiously as he had entered, shouting a threat, "You will pay for this disrespect." He kicked the now empty cradle, sending it careening across the room as he departed. Prudenza burst into tears, frightened, hurt by his treatment of her, and embarrassed that her maid should have observed this cruel display.

She need not have worried about Gina. Such behavior would only galvanize her determination to protect her mistress and the little one she had come to love so much. Regaining composure she suggested, "Come, *Madama,* let us go somewhere safe. I know that Mistress Maddalena is working with the servants as they prepare the spring hangings in the great room. Let us go there. Your husband will not dare to behave so in the presence of his mother."

"Perhaps you are right, Gina."

"I know I am. Now dry your tears and we will find safe refuge until his anger has passed. You carry the baby and I will bring the lute."

Maddalena looked surprised when they entered the room. "What brings you here at this time, Daughter? A little visit from my darling grandson?" Chucking the baby under the chin she tickled his fat little neck. He squirmed and gurgled, causing Prudenza to forget, at least for the moment, the disturbing scene from which she had just fled. Putting on a brave face she fabricated a reason. "We are visiting the house, *Signora* Maddalena. My son should get to know his home, don't you think?"

"Indeed! *Brava,* Prudenza, what a good idea. And it is good for you, too, my dear. I'm sure that Nella and Maria would love to see the baby so why don't you visit them in the kitchen too? And while you are there go out into the garden. It would make Berardo so happy. He asks me daily about your health." Maddalena obviously knew nothing of her son's latest proscriptions.

"Thank you, Mother. I will."

Maddalena could not have known how right she was. The little excursion did indeed please Nella and Maria and dear Berardo. Perhaps more importantly it was a happy distraction for Prudenza, too. Such an innocent diversion helped her regain her equilibrium.

"I feel better now, Gina. Thank you. You always seem to know what is best! Let us go back to the *loggia* to enjoy the sunshine while it lasts, for the afternoon is passing all too quickly."

As they climbed the stairs, Prudenza noted something strange like bits of golden fluff on the steps, a substance so light that it floated as the movement of her skirt stirred the air ever so gently. It was light, almost like powdery dust, but instead of being dull and gray it looked like a tiny golden trail of gossamer. Prudenza hurried ahead and let out a cry as she found the source. "Feathers. I see feathers! *O, Dio mio. Dio mio.* Poor little Angelo!"

In their haste to escape Matteo's wrath they had forgotten to take the little bird with them. By the time Gina had caught up with Prudenza she found her bending over her precious songbird, his tiny head twisted off, his body lying on its back, all cold and stiff, with spindly legs up in the air like the broken spokes of a diminutive wagon.

"How could he? How could he do this, Gina?" By now both mother and son were crying. "Oh, Gina, stay close! I am so afraid. I fear that my husband is jealous of the things that mean most to me. I fear for my baby and I fear for my own life."

Before she could respond Matteo appeared as suddenly as

he had left. His movements by now had become alarmingly swift and stealthy. He was scowling so menacingly that his heavy dark brows almost met in the middle of his forhead as they often did when he was enraged, and his face was flushed with purple blotches. Standing there triumphantly with arms akimbo he laughed unrestrainedly, a hoarse, almost barbaric sound full of anger.

"You have done this!"

"Yes, I have done this," he responded proudly, still laughing.

"Why? Why have you done this? Poor little Angelo."

Then making fun of her he repeated in a falsetto, mincing around on tiptoe like a ballerina. "Poor little Angelo, poor little Angelo..."

"Stop it! Do not taunt me with your cheap burlesque."

For one brief moment Matteo knew not what to say, so stunned was he by his wife's fearless confrontation. But Prudenza had not finished. "Yes, poor little Angelo. What did he ever do to offend you? He brought cheer and beauty to this place that is becoming like a prison to me."

"I'll tell you what he did. This damnable bird distracted you. You spent all your time singing with him, singing to my son— silly songs that will turn him into a weakling if you continue."

"Matteo, please, please..."

"He took you away from your loom. Look! The coverlet you began to weave for the baby...nearly a year ago, just look."

She had to admit she had begun it during her pregnancy and it still remained unfinished. There was time though. She would complete it when the weather turned cold again and she could no longer enjoy the out of doors. Now perhaps it would be better to try to reason with him. Realizing that nothing good can result when both parties are spewing angry words, she pondered a new approach. Her voice was controlled now as she asked, "Husband, why are you so cross with me? I have given you a fair son, have I not? Is this my reward?"

"Do not speak to me of rewards. I OWN you."

"How can you say that?"

"How? Let me show you. I BOUGHT you—and at great price." With that he pulled from his shirt a roll of parchment and brandished it in her face. "Do you not remember this?" Then rolling his sleeve up he bellowed, "See this?" He pointed to the scar still visible on his arm where he and Pichino had mingled their blood in a compact that had sealed the agreement for the alum. As he unfurled the document before her she could see that there was even a bloodstain on the corner, though it had by now turned an ugly brown.

"This is how I bought you. I toiled and toiled and took insults from those damnable smugglers—all to win you so that I could earn the praise of my father. And this is how you thank me?"

Yes, she remembered all too well that evening when her life had been signed away in her very presence. Her loving father could never have suspected the cruelty of this man to whom he committed his daughter through what he believed to be an honest agreement. Good and kind Alfonso Beltramonto had been deceived by this crafty man who was her husband.

It was clear in her mind now. He has always been jealous of his older brother, so I was the trophy bride that he believed would win his father's affection. And now that I am his wife, and he recognizes that Zenobi loves me like a daughter, he is jealous of me, too. Where will this ever end? Now it is our son of whom he is jealous. I am to him no more than chattel acquired to win the praise of his father. Not once, even in the beginning, has he ever spoken to me of love. With this she buried her head in her hands and wept bitterly as Matteo fled still raging as he departed.

Meanwhile in her practical and quiet way Gina disposed of the dead bird and cleaned the feathers from the stairs. Prudenza collapsed into a chair and began to croon softly to the baby:

> Mio giocondo bambino
> Suo riso é paradiso
> Per la povera mamma
> La povera mamma.

"Yes," thought Gina. "*Povera mamma* indeed."

Matteo took the document with him as he descended the stairs, shouting like a mad man. "Come and see! *Mio tesoro!* Come and see my treasure." His voice somehow sounded even more ominous in the darkness as it echoed off the walls of the great room when he entered. He threw the document to the floor before the hearth and prepared to burn it. As he set about lighting the fire he heard a shuffling sound behind him and was appalled to see his father entering the room. For a brief moment Matteo was alarmed at the prospect of being caught in the act, but reminded himself that the old man's eyesight was so dim that he probably could not see his son. His hearing, however, was sufficiently acute so that Matteo's raging had roused him from sleep. Now he was cautiously feeling his way through the dark room, bumping into furniture and along the wall for security as he sought the source of this disturbance.

Matteo watched him for a moment, contemplating some means of escape. He had so systematically and successfully hidden his deception from the old man up to now and was not about to be found out at this point when in a matter of moments the fire would have consumed the evidence in the document. He dared not try to flee through the door where Zenobi had just entered; the best he could do for now was to hide.

"What is it? Who is there?" the old man called out.

Matteo concealed himself behind a drape and held his breath as he listened to the sound of Zenobi's felt slippers softly shuffling across the stone floor. Against the background of their rasping sound he muttered under his breath, "Curses! Why did the old man have to come just now? One more minute and I could have thrown that damnable evidence into the fire and no one would ever have been the wiser."

At that moment Zenobi's foot caught on the corner of the document and the stiff parchment made a rustling sound that startled him. With difficulty he stooped to retrieve the object and as he did so Matteo's heart pounded so hard in his chest that he thought surely his father must actually hear it. He attempted to calm himself with the thought, "He cannot read it; I am sure. He is as shortsighted as a mole."

The fire by this time was blazing brightly, lighting up that part of the room and Zenobi moved slowly and cautiously toward it drawn like a tired old gray moth attracted to the light.

Just as Matteo was comforting himself with the assurance that his father's rheumy old eyes could not possibly make out the writing, he heard the old man's feeble voice speaking the words Matteo had so hoped to expunge forever.

Item: *Signore* Beltramonto will pay the sum of one thousand gold florins to *Signore* Cecchi for the purchase of alum from the mines of the Fratelli Bosi.

"Who are the Fratelli Bosi? I have never heard of them." He read on.

Item: The said *Signore* Cecchi agrees to waive the usual dowry due him at this time, the one thousand florins being payment in lieu of the dowry for *Signore* Beltramonto's daughter, Prudenza Maria Cecilia..."

"Why, this is a legal document! My son has bargained, traded ill-gotten goods for this sweet and innocent girl."

Item: *Signore* Beltramonto will process the alum and produce the dyes by April 1537 when *Signore* Cecchi will come to collect them. At that time *Signore* Cecchi will return to Florence with his bride..."*O, gran Dio*, Can this be?"

The old man's frail body seemed to crumble like dry husk as he collapsed into a chair and began weeping—at first softly, but as he read the words over again, his weeping turned to convulsive sobs. "What have you done, Matteo? This is a sin, my son. You have not only betrayed the good name of Cecchi, you have made your father a party to illegal doings. You have dishonored a good, humble, and beautiful young woman, the daughter of my dearest friend. You are a smuggler, a liar. Oh, God forgive! I must seek absolution."

As he watched the old man shuffle away, Matteo was frightened and angry with himself; angry not because he had hurt his father, but because he had so carelessly left the document about. Just one more minute and...Oh, why did the old man have to come in just when he did? Well, what was done was done and he would just have to ride out the situation.

—ᴍ—

The sun was full up and the day was bright. Maddalena wondered where her husband was. "Zenobi! It is late. Time to rise, Husband. The day is warm and the sun will do you good."

As she opened the door to his room she was alarmed to see him lying on his side, his knees drawn up to his chest; he was shaking and breathing with difficulty.

"Zenobi, what is it? What is wrong? You are ill?"

"Yes, I am ill."

"I will send for a doctor at once."

"No."

"Then at least let me call Berardo. He will prepare medicine to relieve you."

"No! No nostrum or doctor can heal my illness. It is a wound too deep for any medicine."

"Zenobi, what kind of talk is this?"As she stroked his forehead it was clear that he had a fever; his head was burning. "Surely Berardo can provide something to…"

"No!" He again said emphatically. "It is spiritual healing that I need, Wife. Please send for my old friend *Fra* Filippo. I must seek absolution from my sin."

Though she did not understand this talk of sinning, she did her husband's bidding. The good friar came quickly when he heard that his old friend was sick and it seemed to Maddalena that he spent an inordinately long time with Zenobi while she fretted and lamented outside the room. She had to admit, however, that Zenobi seemed quieter and more peaceful after the friar's visit.

Maddalena could not imagine what had upset her husband so. Although he seemed at peace since the friar had come, with each passing day it appeared to her that he was gradually withdrawing from this world. Since that day when he first took to his bed he never again left it. It was like standing by helplessly watching a lovely plant die, leaf by leaf. Although it was difficult to realize that he did not wish to share with his wife the cause of this strange and sudden affliction, Maddalena attended him lovingly for more than six weeks.

Sunday morning was bright and beautiful when she came at the usual time to bring his simple collation. "Zenobi, Zenobi!" She called pulling the heavy drape aside. "Have you slept well? It is already late."

As the sunlight shone on him, Maddalena noted a slight smile upon his lips such as she had not seen in weeks, and his eyes were wide open as if looking at some celestial vision above the bed. She felt his hands; they were cold but his countenance was beatific. Falling on her knees at his bedside she wailed loudly, *"O Dio! Dio mio.* He is gone! Zenobi Cecchi is no more."

CHAPTER 16

Requiescat in Pace

"What was that?"

"What, *Madama*?"

"Listen, Gina, don't you hear it? It seems like muffled cries, soft weeping."

"Perhaps it is your little Lorenzo waking up."

"No, Gina, I know my baby's cries."

By now the weeping became loud sobbing punctuated by cries of *"ahimè, Dio mio, ahimè."*

"Something is wrong, Gina, I must go! Please come with me."

"At once, *Madama.*"

The sound was coming from the private quarters of her in-laws, but Prudenza paused outside the door, questioning momentarily if she should enter uninvited, and called out, "What is it? Are you all right?"

There was no answer—only a continued low moaning from inside. Cautiously she opened the door a bit, careful not to intrude lest her presence was unwanted. What she saw dispelled all such concern for propriety. Prudenza was momentarily shocked at what met her eyes. It took only a glance to realize the truth that Zenobi was dead. Her immediate and overriding reaction was concern that Maddalena needed her daughter-in-law now, as she never had before.

Her mind raced. Matteo had to be found and little Lorenzo tended to. Lucia must be told at once to keep the baby in her care until Prudenza called for him. Without waiting for instructions, Gina set about the duties at hand.

What Prudenza observed was indeed a pitiful sight. Her beloved father-in-law lay cold and dead on his pallet while Maddalena was crouched on the floor like a piece of crumbled foolscap. This woman—her dominant mother-in-law who was always so forceful, authoritative, and in control—was now like a helpless child. Her loud sobs diminished to a softer but constant wailing—a sad, hollow sound. It reminded Prudenza of those dismal foggy mornings in Ancona when mournful horns on the shore warned approaching ships in the bay. Soon, however, the voice began to rise and fall in a weird pattern, almost like the howling of a solitary wolf baying at the winter moon. Maddalena was keening over the corpse of her beloved husband. The sight aroused deep-and-instant compassion for this woman who had often made Prudenza's life difficult. She was so pitiful in her grief.

"Mother!" Prudenza was aware that she had never actually addressed Maddalena that way, nor had she ever embraced her so tenderly. Without thinking she suddenly found herself crouched on the floor, cradling her mother-in-law in her arms and rocking her gently to and fro, almost the way she did her little Lorenzo when he cried. As she did so the poor woman's tears came in such abundance that they formed small rivulets down her cheeks and fell onto her already tear-stained bodice.

The two women remained there crouched on the floor, weeping together, until Prudenza was jolted by the sound of her husband's voice. Gina had run through the house in search of Matteo to announce that his mother needed him now. Prudenza was grateful to see him standing over the two of them, still locked in each other's arms so that when he extended his hands to raise his mother, he also raised his wife.

The situation momentarily elicited the best from Matteo. Remembering that his father was a deeply religious person, he at once sent for his father's old friend and confessor, *Fra* Filippo, who came immediately. Although *Fra* Filippo was a Dominican he was well aware that Zenobi was a devout member of the Compagnia of Santa Maria at the Franciscan church of Santa Croce where the company maintained a burial vault.

While the good friar tried to calm Maddalena, Matteo sent

word of Zenobi's death to the prior of the confraternity. As was their custom they came immediately to fulfill the ritual obligations to a member.

At the sight of the *fratelli* in their humble garb Maddalena felt a deep regret that she had not called them earlier while her husband was still alive. They could have come and kept vigil at his bedside to pray with him, to prepare him for the inevitable. That might at least have brought Zenobi some solace in his last days. Now, seized by a sense of guilt, she trembled and began repeating over and over, "I have been selfish. I have been selfish. Oh, Zenobi, forgive me!"

By midday Prudenza had still not left Maddalena's side, as she tried to assuage the poor woman's remorse. "No, Mother, you must not speak of guilt. You know your good husband would not wish it. You must not reproach yourself; you have done no wrong."

In the end it was perhaps only exhaustion that finally stilled Maddalena's lament—that and the tincture that Berardo sent to calm her nerves. At first she did not want to drink it and repeatedly pushed away the cup as Prudenza lifted it to her lips. Finally Matteo commanded her to drink it and, just as the wise old gardener promised, the mixture worked its magic and she fell into blessed semi-consciousness.

Late in the day, shadows crept like long gray fingers across the floor of the great room and candles flickered around the bier where Zenobi's corpse had been laid. A respectful somber quiet settled over the house as one by one the servants heard the news of Zenobi's death and came to pay their respects. By evening Maddalena began to emerge from her stupor. She had ceased her keening and now instead withdrew into a profound silence, exhausted mentally and physically from her hysterical weeping.

Seated at her side Prudenza recalled happier times when as a family they celebrated in this same great room. She would never forget the day of her arrival in Florence, or the pomp and jubilation of her wedding day. The sorrow she felt now was every bit as intense as the joy of those happy occasions. Yet despite the profound sense of loss she felt, she found comfort in the quiet dignity with which the members of the confraternity tended to their funerary rituals. Their respectful behavior reflected the long tradition of caring for the deceased members of their company. Ministration to the dead was a most sacred obligation of confraternal life. They had prayed aloud in unison that morning as they completed the ritual washing of the corpse, which they then dressed in the simple gray tunic with a cord about the waist.

The sight of this garb elicited the first sign that Maddalena was returning to her usual dogmatic self as she accosted the friar in charge. "Why must you clothe him so? This is the dress of a pauper."

"It is our tradition, *Signora* Cecchi. It is written in our sacred rule that a deceased brother must be dressed in the habit of our company."

"Words, words, words. That is your rule, just meaningless words!" She paid no heed to such an excuse and, despite her exhaustion, reached deep into some unknown reserve of strength and continued her protest. "Do you not know that my husband, Zenobi Cecchi, was a wealthy silk merchant well known not only in Florence but even abroad. Merchants came from far away places in search of his silks."

"Yes, *Signora* Cecchi. Your husband's work is well known and respected…"

Moving closer to the brother she continued her interrogation which, had it not been for the intervention of *Fra* Filippo, would have likely only mounted in volume and intensity. The good friar's love for Zenobi gave him the authority to silence this unfortunate outburst and Maddalena responded with the docility of a child as he led her to her seat next to her daughter-in-law.

How like this woman, Prudenza thought, always so concerned with externals. Poor Maddalena!

Matteo became conspicuous by his absence from the scene. He had slipped away, unable to watch the preparation of his father's body. Anyone with eyes to see could understand when Maddalena began prattling away, insistently repeating, "Where is my son? And where is the *drappelone*? Matteo should insist that the proper symbol of mourning be hung at the door. Oh, where have you gone, Matteo?"

She began pacing distractedly and once again approached the brother in charge. "Should I not be given an allotment of fine black silk for my mourning veil, and for my daughter-in-law too?

My husband was a silk merchant!" She commenced repeating like a mantra, "My husband was a silk merchant! My husband was a silk merchant..."

Prudenza understood all too well. In her efforts to avoid the appearance of a pauper's funeral Maddalena insisted on a certain amount of pomp, but her lack of success left her frustrated and disconsolate. She needed Matteo to speak for her. Perhaps a man—especially the heir to the business—would have more authority. But where was he now? The dulling effect of Berardo's brew had worn off completely and Maddalena was becoming angry with her son for his neglect.

Perhaps more than anyone in that assembly Prudenza understood. Almost as if by his forceful handling of the immediate situation earlier that morning, Matteo had exhausted the limited resources of his compassion. She was quite sure that he was closeted away somewhere, in his narcissistic way battling his own demons. No one was above him now! He had risen to the position of master of the family business, and that realization energized him, at least momentarily. Yet the prospect of dealing with the day-to-day administration terrified him, as did the thought of facing the same workers he had so alienated by his harsh treatment of them. The thought tormented him.

Prudenza resolved to take the place of her negligent husband and stay at Maddalena's side throughout the day, trying to coax her to rest and drink the broth that Nella sent up to her—but to no avail. Failing in her attempts to manage her own husband's funeral as she had always so efficiently managed important events in the household, Maddalena resorted to indulging in her own grief!

At the onset of darkness the brothers knelt around the bier and began the prayers of the vigil that continued throughout the night as they chanted in a solemn, low voice their simple version of the Office of the Dead—endless Paters and Aves punctuated by their traditional music, the *laude.*

Day was just dawning when a solitary brother stood at the head of the bier and in a loud, clear voice intoned the traditional *lauda,* signifying that the funeral cortège was about to begin.

Chi vuol lo mondo desprezzare,
Sempre la morte dea pensare…

He who wishes to despise the world
Must think always of death.

Four young brothers, now hooded, grasped the corners of the unadorned bier and, led by three others—one with the cross and two with candles—went out of the room, down the broad stone steps, through the garden and into the street. As Zenobi Cecchi made his last trip from his home, his servants lined the way, their heads bowed in respect for this fine man. Even the oldest of them could be seen to wipe a tear on the sleeve of his homespun smock and whisper a prayer as the bier passed by.

Following her instinct Prudenza located her husband cowering in his room, his knuckles white as he clutched a half-empty flask of grappa. In only a few stern but well-chosen words she shamed him into going to the side of his grieving mother, where he belonged. On wobbly and reluctant legs he did so, taking a position on Maddalena's right with Prudenza on her left.

The entire brotherhood joined the procession and continued singing their simple hymns as they proceeded into the *piazza*. Their voices, augmented now by those of friends and employees, reverberated throughout the cobblestone streets just as the morning sun worked its magic, glancing off the façade of Santa Croce in great rich rose and ochre swaths of brilliant light.

At first it appeared to Prudenza that Maddalena did not really want to be comforted just now; she preferred to wallow in her pitiable state. Instead she siezed the opportunity of Matteo's closeness as well as the cover of the singing to chide her son as they made their way through the *piazza*. "Why did you not do your duty and insist that there should be a *drappelone*? Surely you could have obtained exemption from the sumptuary laws to have more candles."

Matteo maintained a sullen silence while Prudenza made a valiant effort to restore some dignity. "Hush, Mother!"

She could not help recalling the many dreaded visits to the *sarta* who altered her wedding garment under Maddalena's critical eye. Silently, but sincerely, Prudenza pitied her mother-in-law, that she should be so disturbed by these truly inconsequential matters. She vowed to try to be a true daughter to this domineering woman whose real weakness became so evident in this time of sorrow. "God help us. How I pity her."

The funeral cortège retraced steps that Prudenza recalled so vividly from a far happier time, the day of her arrival in Florence. And, just as Zenobi's employees had then lined the *piazza* awaiting a glimpse of the bride of Matteo Cecchi, the *piazza* was again filled by workers from the Cecchi establishment. The prevailing emotion, however, was now one of genuine sadness at the passing of this much-loved man. Through the crowd there now ran another current, unspoken yet palpable—fear at the prospect of life under the erratic and ill-behaved son of Zenobi Cecchi.

As they passed through the tall doors and into the coolness of the church the procession turned abruptly to the right, toward the now-opened crypt of the brotherhood where longtime members and former officers like Zenobi were privileged to be buried. It was near the wall, not a prominent place, and certainly not adorned with statuary like the burial vaults of nobles. It was, appropriately enough, an unostentatious resting place for one who was a follower of the beloved Poverello of Assisi.

The opening of the vault was like a gaping hole in the pavement of the church. The sight of it brought tears to Prudenza's eyes and she had to admit, I am grateful now for the voluminous veil that Maddalena insisted upon, for I can conceal from her my tears. She needs me and I must be strong for her. At the same time from behind the veil I can watch my husband. Why does he not at least show some sign of compassion for his mother—some emotion at the loss of his father? I see none. His face is cold and unfeeling, like chiseled stone. In contrast, Zenobi's countenance was peaceful, almost beatific, still marked by the same faint smile that Maddalena observed when she found him dead in his bed, the gnarled and bony fingers of his hands peacefully crossed on his breast.

The loss was great for Prudenza. The strong bond between her and her father-in-law that was clear from their very first meeting remained a blessing and a comfort to her; yet it was also the agent that fed the tortured maunderings of her jealous husband's twisted perception of reality. His behavior made her fearful, and now as she must say farewell to this beautiful man who had been her protector, to whom could she turn?

It could never be really farewell, however; for the very sights and sounds in this church that were so dear to him would to her always be alive with the precious memories of the many lessons he taught her as he shared the beauties of this place. Her mind momentarily returned to those happy times, but she was brought back to the present as the singing of the brothers ceased, and she heard, as if coming from some distant place, the voice of the priest intoning in the austere Latin of the church, *"Requiescat in pace."*

She felt a gentle spray of holy water as the priest blessed the corpse and the body of this dear man was lowered into the crypt. Again the words, "Rest in peace. Sorely tried in soul and body, Zenobi Cecchi, may the angels lead you to Paradise." *In Paradisum deducant te angeli..."*

Despite the sadness she felt at the loss of this dear man, Prudenza knew a joy that she had shared with no one as yet. Under the voluminous folds of her mourning gown she placed her hand on her swollen belly and felt the unmistakable stirring of a new life within her. One precious life had ended, but another had begun.

CHAPTER 17

The *Gobbo*

Gina crept into the room cautiously, noting that the blinds were still drawn and the bed was undisturbed, just as she had prepared it for her mistress the night before, the sheets still smooth and un-wrinkled. As her eyes gradually adjusted to the darkness she noticed a sliver of faint yellowish light escaping from the little sitting room where the door stood slightly ajar. She was touched by the sight that met her eyes as she moved closer. Her mistress was seated at her writing desk, still fully clothed in her mourning attire, lacking only the veil that lay in a crumpled heap on the floor next to her. She no longer had need of it to conceal her grief. It was clear from her swollen eyes that here in the privacy of her own space she had at last given vent to her own deep emotions at the loss of this man who had become a surrogate father to her. Up to now she had disciplined her emotions, keeping them pent up for the sake of her needy mother-in-law.

The two large candles on her writing table sputtered in the draft from a crack in the leaded window nearby. Their nearly spent wicks gave evidence of what had been a long solitary vigil, while the parchment before her was stained by an errant drop of ink that she had carelessly allowed to fall from her quill. It was evident that Prudenza's mind was far from the scene for she made no response to her name when Gina gently called, "*Madama*!" So she called a second time—softly in order not to unsettle this poor discomfited soul any further. Finally, her mistress turned toward the voice, making no effort to conceal her reddened eyes. Moving closer Gina gently admonished, "*Madama,* it is already morning and you have not slept at all. You must rest."

Staring into space as if in a trance she muttered, "I cannot find the words to tell him. Gina. I cannot find the words to tell him!"

As she drew close enough to embrace her mistress's slumping shoulders Gina observed the unfinished letter that had engaged her mistress through the night. The "him" to whom Prudenza referred was of course her father, Zenobi Cecchi's closest friend. The fruits of this long nocturnal vigil were distilled into nothing more than a salutation of three words on an expanse of blank page. *"My dearest father…"*

Only days after Zenobi's funeral Gina reminded her mistress that although Matteo had forbidden her to leave the house and had even taken back the keys he so ostentatiously bestowed on her in the presence of the servants the day he introduced her to the household, he did make one concession—albeit reluctantly. He grudgingly allowed permission for Prudenza to attend to her devotions in church. Motivated by her deep concern for her mistress Gina suggested that such an outing would be good for Prudenza. She could escape the gloom that had descended upon the Cecchi household. And so began the devout daily pilgrimages to Zenobi's burial place, visitations that brought some solace to Prudenza.

Inside the church that Zenobi loved so much, his friend, the old sacristan, still toiled away. Painful knees and aching joints may have slowed his movements, but age and infirmity had not dulled his curiosity. His eyes were ever observant as he dusted the statuary, polished the candlesticks and fussed unnecessarily over the linens. He hardly took his eyes off the two figures in black as he muttered into his long beard, "Ah! There they are again. It must be the hour of *tierce.*"

Over the weeks since Zenobi Cecchi's death these two figures had become regular visitors to his grave; so regular, in fact, that the sacristan had little need of a clock now to remind him of the time of day. Their appearance meant that it must be nearly nine o'clock, time to make the painful climb up the steps to the bell tower to announce the midmorning hour of prayer. The simple exertion caused beads of perspiration to glisten on his baldpate, an attribute he jocularly referred to as his natural tonsure. The effort rewarded him doubly though, for from his vantage point he could not only observe the silent pair as they paid their respects, but he could maunder half-audibly as in his monologue he retraced their movements. "Ah, there they are! They always enter the church by a side door and creep silently to the tomb where they kneel with heads bowed for a long time, obviously lost in prayer. Surely one of them must be Zenobi's widow; but who is the other?" Invariably they completed their devotions by lighting a solitary candle before they departed—quietly as they came.

The days wore on, marked by these regular visitations, the phases of the moon that Gina faithfully noted, and the passing of notable feast days. Since her responsibility to her mistress included attending to her linens and her most intimate personal needs, Gina suspected that once again Prudenza was pregnant, and ventured to suggest to her, "*Madama.* I believe the news of the baby you are carrying would bring much comfort to *Signora* Cecchi, your mother-in-law."

Prudenza was caught off guard by this unsolicited suggestion from her maid and waited an awkward interval before responding. For one anxious moment Gina feared that she might have overstepped the boundaries of propriety. But Prudenza did not seem to be offended.

"I know you are right, Gina. It is selfish of me to keep it from her any longer; but it has been a great comfort to me to preserve my secret for a time."

At that Gina affectionately patted her mistress gently on her ballooning stomach and pointed out the obvious, "You really can no longer conceal it, *Madama.*" They laughed together, realizing that it was the first time in weeks that they had done so.

"Gina, I confess that, although I do care for my mother-in-law, I admit that I have become resentful of her selfishness, her display of self-pity as she indulges in her grief. I know it is wrong of me! God forgive me."

"He does, *Signora.* He does forgive you. It saddens me to see you torture yourself with such thoughts. You could relieve yourself if you would share this news with her. I am sure it would bring some joy to her troubled soul—or at least some distraction."

"I do pray over it, really. I ask God each night to help me to forgive her, and still I cannot seem to release these feelings. They only seem to grow and I fear the effect my troubled mind may have on the baby I carry."

"If you cannot do it for her sake, *Madama*, then do it for your own. It will bring you peace. Promise me?"

After a long and thoughtful pause she agreed. "All right. I promise."

—〰—

Ever since the day they first met, Prudenza was impressed by the uncomplicated, simple wisdom of her maid. She was not trained in the refinements of scholarly debate or the sophistry of theologians. Indeed, she barely possessed the rudiments of reading and writing when she came to Prudenza. But she had been an apt pupil, hungry to learn from her mistress who secretly tutored her in those skills. Although Gina never seemed to err in practical matters, this was the first time she had ventured into the realm of spiritual advice and, somehow, the self-assured way in which she did so gave Prudenza the courage to share her secret with Maddalena.

The news that she was about to become a grandmother again did indeed help to heal the rift between the two women. Moreover, Prudenza came to realize that the breach existed mainly in her own mind, for Maddalena expressed deep gratitude for her daughter-in-law's solicitude. It stood out in such contrast to her own son's blatant dereliction just now when she needed him most. And just as Gina in her homespun wisdom predicted, the bond between Prudenza and Maddalena grew, though it would never be the same as that which Prudenza felt so spontaneously with Zenobi. That had been like a full-blown blossom from the beginning; whereas, she realized, this was a relationship still in the bud. It needed careful nurturing, but she was determined to cultivate it as assiduously as she nourished the babe within her.

While the news of the pregnancy was a source of joy to the women, it elicited only lukewarm response from Matteo who was daily more isolated and self-absorbed, stewing over the responsibilities he so recently inherited. The dynamic within the Cecchi household was slowly changing. The growing, yet unspoken, covenant of the women was becoming the counterpoise of his deepening isolation.

Matteo seldom came to call on his wife now and, in truth, Prudenza found it a welcome relief from his unpredictable outbursts of temper. Days passed in relative calm and before long the cold winds and rain marked the beginning of November when pious Christians paid special homage to their dead. They could be seen walking respectfully in little pilgrimages to cemeteries, while silently fingering their beads, laying flowers on tombs and, in some cases, leaving offerings of food. At Prudenza's urging, Maddalena began to join her and Gina in their visits to Santa Croce, which were becoming more difficult for Prudenza as the time of her delivery approached. By month's end Maddalena recognized that it was time to call the midwives.

Prudenza was happy to see the familiar, loving face of Anna who had been so kind to her the last time. Anna, however, had some misgivings and quietly remarked to her companion, "It is too soon, only about a year since the first baby and she is still weak. Had she been permitted to nurse her son this would not have happened so soon. But it has, and we must do all for her that we can."

Soon it became apparent that the midwives' concerns were for naught. By the time the sun broke over the hills on the thirtieth day of the month, labor had begun and Maddalena and Gina assumed their vigil with the young mother. Unlike Lorenzo's coming, this was a swift and easy birth. Just as the bells of Santa Croce sounded the hour of *tierce* on this St. Andrew's Day, the baby emerged—all pink, healthy, and bawling—not a weak, whimpering sound but a lusty howl from deep within his little lungs. Another boy! Prudenza could only say, "That will please my husband, I hope."

"Husband, indeed!" Maddalena huffed with indignation. "Where is he? Where is Matteo? Why is he not here to greet his little son and thank his wife for this gift?"

Although Gina entertained the same questions, her position did not permit her to verbalize them as Maddalena did so freely, making no effort to conceal her indignation at her son's neglect. While Gina still pondered the thought, Maddalena drew her away from the bedside to where Prudenza could not hear and whispered, "Please go and find him. Tell him of his son. If you cannot locate him, question the servants. Have they seen him? Do they perhaps know where he has gone? It would be best to begin in the stable. Go! Hurry!"

"At once, *Signora*."

It took only a short time for Gina to report back. "Luca tells me that he heard *Signore* Cecchi speak of going to watch the lions."

"Watch the lions?"

"Yes. The lions."

"Where? What lions?"

"It had been announced that on this day there would be a spectacle in Piazza della Signoria. It is said that a bull and two greyhounds would be brought there and two lions would be released to set upon them."

"Merciful Savior!" Maddalena crossed herself as she muttered in disgust at the thought.

Gina continued, "Luca told me that the master seemed very excited and as he left said something about it promising to be a bloody contest, for the beasts had not been fed in several days."

"That is barbaric! We must not tell Prudenza."

"Of course not, *Signora*."

Up to now Gina had little occasion to deal with, or even speak to, this formidable woman, but the fact that she so freely shared her feelings with the young girl marked a certain new level of trust. There was other evidence too, that Maddalena was softening. This time she made no mention of employing a wet nurse. Perhaps she was just too weary to argue. She did, however, venture to suggest that the baby be christened Andrea, since he was born on the apostle's feast day. But she did not object when Prudenza countered. "No, Mother. He will be called Piero."

"Why, Prudenza?"

"Piero was the name of my mother's father and I know it would please her greatly if her new grandchild were named for him."

"Then it shall be so."

While this discussion ensued, the peace of the household was noisily disrupted by the clamor of Matteo's return. Servants scurried out of his way as he bolted up the stairs toward Prudenza's quarters, two steps at a time, while shouting angry imprecations, *"Maledzione! Dannazione."*

The instinct for self-preservation had taught the servants to take cover when Matteo unleashed his anger. Yet the urge to seek safety was equaled by curiosity concerning what caused this latest outbreak. So from their various places of security behind closet doors and draperies, they strained their ears to listen to his crazed monologue as he continued to ascend the stairs.

"Blood! There was supposed to be blood. They promised a spectacle." There was a breathless pause as he negotiated two more steps. "I saw no blood. Only huge beasts cowering like mewling kittens." He continued his ranting narrative as if the mere sound of his own voice confirmed for him that what he had seen—or more correctly—had not seen—was not merely a hallucination. By now he was panting, periodically gasping to gain his breath.

Inside the kitchen where Luca had come, attracted by the fragrance of Nella's honey cakes, he hid with her behind the door, hoping to learn more from this latest outburst. When it appeared that Matteo had caught his breath sufficiently he continued his narrative. "They were roaring in their cages that looked like huge hen coops."

"Oh, yes," Luca remembered. In a whisper he recounted the promise of the spectacle as it had been announced, sparing no details about the animals being starved for two days before the event.

Meanwhile Matteo carried on, his voice becoming more difficult to hear as he moved farther up the stairway. "They should have torn those dogs apart in a minute. But no, what did they do? Nothing!"

The steps gave out a creaking sound under the punishment of his boots as he repeated, "Nothing! Dumb stupid beasts. One jumped on the bull's back and then retreated into his cage. Neither of them paid any attention to the vulnerable greyhounds! They simply returned to their coops like frightened chickens. Unbelievable. *Dannazione!* A waste of time. I cannot..."

He was brought up short by the sight of his mother planted deliberately in the center of the stairs, her arms outstretched on both sides to prevent his passing. In her most imperious voice she demanded, "Where have you been?"

"Must I report my every move to you?"

"How dare you speak to your mother in that insolent tone?"

"Is it so important for you to know where I was?"

"Yes! It is indeed important, as it should be to you as well."

"Why?"

"Why, indeed!"

As she spoke she moved down a step, still standing over him but coming closer to his face as she waved a condemning finger before his nose. "While you were pursuing your loathsome diversion, your wife has given you another child, a healthy, beautiful boy."

With an impulsive jerk of the head meant to signify a studied lack of concern he simply grunted, "Huh! Another sniveling crying machine, mewling for its pap. It might as well be a toad!"

"How could you speak so of your own flesh and blood?"

"To me, *Madama*, it is just another mouth to feed, while my wife babbles and coos over..."

"Enough! Your sainted father would be saddened by your behavior."

Only at the mention of his father did Matteo seem to react. After all it had been the desire to earn his father's praise that brought him to this impasse.

"You may be the head of your father's business, but you are still my son!" Maddalena had little time for his purported concern for "another mouth to feed" and as if he were still a child she seized his arm in a surprisingly firm grip and propelled him, protesting angrily, in the direction of the birthing room to see his son.

—◊—

She was relieved to find that Prudenza had fallen into a deep sleep after the exhaustion of the birth. Matteo showed little reaction to either his wife or his new son and continued muttering, "Another mouth to feed."

"Is that all you can say? Another mouth to feed? Then go to your work and earn your family's bread. Go!"

It was an inauspicious beginning of life for the beautiful baby that lay in the cradle. Piero was a sweet, chubby little baby, truly a joy to rouse his grandmother from her grief over Zenobi's death. There was relative peace in the household, too, as Matteo spent more and more time at work and, as Maddalena suspected, seeking his pleasure elsewhere. Indeed, it was reported that he was seen frequenting the *bordello* near the Mercato Vecchio, not far from the Baptistry of San Giovanni.

For Prudenza his absence brought a sense of relief from his angry outbursts and his harping about the loom. She was able to fill her days now with efforts to build a happy life around her little boys. Their development became the measure of time for her as they progressed through their first halting steps and spoke their first words. The days were filled again with music and laughter, and Maddalena came daily to visit. It pleased Prudenza that her mother-in-law obviously liked her young maid, for Gina was indispensable to Prudenza. As the boys grew from babyhood, Prudenza taught them little ditties, read stories to them, taught them their numbers and colors and told them Bible stories.

But having grown up without brothers—in fact with no siblings at all—she was sadly lacking in knowledge of such things as the games little boys play. There was no male influence in their lives. Zenobi was gone, and Matteo could not be counted on. In any case she feared what his influence might be. Gina fulfilled this part of the boys' lives.

Born into a household of older brothers she had been something of a tomboy and delighted in teaching Lorenzo and Piero the games she had played with her brothers as a child. Under her tutelage they progressed from playing with large soft balls to the game of *bocce.* She enjoyed it as much as they did as she tucked up her skirts and demonstrated the basic elements of little boys' sports.

Prudenza was amused no end to watch as her babies gradually lost their baby fat and developed long straight legs that propelled them around the courtyard like young goats. Soon they progressed to rougher play and wrestled on the floor amid squeals of delight when one succeeded in disrupting the match by the strategy of tickling the other. It never failed to end in gales of laughter. The finer motor skills were not neglected either, for Gina had begun to teach them the rudiments of juggling small balls. It was a peaceful time. The boys were developing nicely, though their father took little notice of them.

Lorenzo was a precocious four-year-old whose body was slim and muscular, straight as a reed. He promised to be a tall man and Maddalena noted one day that he was beginning to look strikingly like his uncle Fabrizio. That fact was not lost on Matteo who, for that very reason, began to dislike his son, and treated him badly whenever he did chance to see him. It frightened Prudenza to see the way Lorenzo cowered at the sight of his father, so she appealed to Maddalena to admonish her son for his behavior. Matteo's only response was, "Must he haunt me forever, that pious eunuch? I hate him."

Several carnivals had come and gone since Matteo last visited Prudenza's bed, and though relieved, she began to ask herself if it was her fault. Had she failed in her responsibilities as a wife? Often during tranquil hours she reflected on the passage of time. Her life was in flux not unlike the fickle Arno, that malodorous stream that so sickened her at the time of her entrance into Florence. That was a time when Matteo was glad for the opportunity to steady her in his arms as the coach lurched through the cobbled streets. She pondered how the river was almost emblematic of her marriage. There had been good times and bad, seasons of joy and seasons of aridity! She longed for the kind of life she was privileged to observe in the happy marriage of her own parents, but realized that for her it probably would never be. So with the support of her mother-in-law, her maid, and her little boys she was determined to create a happy world.

More than three years after Piero's birth, Prudenza was not only resigned to her state, she was grateful for the respite of the abstinence imposed by circumstances. But that respite was broken by a most unexpected manifestation of nature. On the night of 27 February 1542, while Matteo was lost in the arms of his favorite Spanish prostitute, Florence was shaken by an earthquake lasting, it was said, the length of a *Pater noster*. Seized by a combination of guilt and superstition he bolted from his pleasure bed and sped into the street half naked, running frantically toward his home. In a fit of fear he vowed rashly that, if God spared him, he would never again visit a *puttana*. He would honor the sacredness of his marriage bed and be faithful to his wife.

Just as dawn follows the dark, by spring Prudenza was again heavy with child. So long as Matteo could claim his marriage rights, a more or less tranquil period followed—though all concerned were conscious that at any moment it might be disrupted. Rumor had it, in fact, that there was serious trouble at work among the Cecchi employees. It was reported that much unrest and murmuring was heard at the dyeing vats. The dyers' work was exacting and Matteo was demanding in a demeaning way that Zenobi had never been. Among the dyers a current of unrest was caused by poor pay for hard work and, perhaps even more so, by the consciousness that they, skilled artisans, were denied the right to form their own guild, and were instead controlled by the wealthy Arte delle Seta, the Silk Guild. The dyers were well aware that even the butchers had their own guild. There was no way that they could take their complaints to Matteo who, they knew, would only become harsher.

They did, however, have a religious brotherhood, named for their patron, Sant'Onofrio, who, according to tradition, had lived in the desert clothed only in vines. In a spot behind Santa Croce the brotherhood maintained an oratory dedicated to the saint where they met for prayer and undoubtedly for discussion of their lot.

A near revolt was set off by a recent incident when one of the workers confused the proportions of madder to indigo and added the silk to a vat too soon. Even worse, he had crowded the fabric in the solution. It was well known that blue dyes required meticulous handling and could easily be destroyed by crowding. The disastrous result of his mistake was equaled only by Matteo's fury at the waste of precious indigo and the loss of the fine silk that was hopelessly mottled. It was a total loss.

Despite the fact that the unfortunate worker was an older man who, in a moment of utter exhaustion at the end of a hard day, made the disastrous mistake, he was made to suffer the indignity of Matteo's fashionable boot in his backside. Matteo knew that the workers were united in their defense of the man he disgraced and, fearing revolt, he ran to his mother like a frightened child, seeking sympathy more than advice. Yet it was advice alone that he received. "Matteo, you are becoming a tyrant with your workers. Your sainted father always enjoyed the loyalty and support of his men."

"But..."

"Listen to me! You have alienated your men by your treatment, your temper, your uncontrolled outbursts." At that he began to pout like a peevish spoiled child. This was not at all what he hoped for and expected. But Maddalena had seen enough of his behavior in the home and his treatment of his wife, and could only surmise the lengths to which he might go with his workers. As she spoke, Matteo hung his head, his chin nearly touching his chest, and his lower lip protruded noticeably.

"Do not sulk. It ill becomes a man."

"What shall I do, *Mamma*? I must do something before the dyers take it upon themselves to damage the equipment, or even do harm to me."

"Try some kindness for a change! Be forgiving. All is not lost. Do not sacrifice your person and the good name of Cecchi for a couple ounces of indigo—no matter how precious."

"Then, tell me what I must do."

"The *calendimaggio* has begun and people are in a celebratory mood. In a few days it will be June, and on the ninth day of the month the dyers will celebrate the feast of Sant'Onofrio. Do you not remember how your father allowed them to celebrate it?"

"Yes. I remember. They called it the Palio of Sant'Onofrio. The poor fools raced their heavy old draft horses down the *corso* while the finer people made fun—taunting them with insults and cat calls."

"Well, do not belittle the idea. A little revelry might go a long way to release some of the tension. Let the workers hold their *palio* and race their horses down the *corso*. I believe such innocent entertainment can do no harm."

Although his mother's suggestion was not what he had expected and hoped for, he would at least honor her advice, but not without reminding her that he had seen the colorful festivities in Siena when fine horses were raced around the *campo*, and he knew what an exciting spectacle it was. Even the bareback riders in the donkey races at Montepulciano were superior to anything that the dyers and their draft horses could offer.

"Well, as you say, Mother. I will let the poor fools have their fun."As he departed, Maddalena could only shake her head and utter a fervent prayer. "Oh, Zenobi, guide him. May God move his heart to be more like you."

Although he was not amenable to the idea of the race, Matteo announced a day of celebration honoring the feast of their patron. There would be no work that day! And as Maddalena predicted, tensions eased a bit as the men made preparations for their festival.

In order to keep an eye on his workers during the race, Matteo positioned himself where he could best observe the antics of these rough men as they attempted to become nimble jockeys on their massive draft animals. To distinguish himself from the noisy peasants he dressed most ostentatiously in his best doublet and cape. His behavior, however, did not match the elegance of his attire. Despite his mother's good counsel he grew progressively more ill mannered as the day wore on, hurling tactless and insulting shouts and hisses—especially when a rider was thrown by an animal more accustomed to pulling drays.

He soon became the object of interest to a group of ragged urchins who were quick to comment on his appearance. Vain as he always was, he had been careful that morning to arrange his cape to conceal the curvature at the top of his spine. Although his preoccupation with the deformity was entirely out of proportion to its actual size, over the last few years he had become increasingly sensitive about the hump sprouting there. He had simply allowed his tortured mind to bestow upon it a magnitude far greater than warranted. Yet one sharp-eyed little ruffian in tattered shirt and bare feet had spied it and began yelling, "*Gobbo! Gobbo*! Come and touch the humpback for good luck."

Soon a pack of young boys, and even some older men, rushed to touch Matteo's hump, hoping for good luck. His face was so inflamed with anger that the veins in his temples threatened to burst as he attempted to escape the aggressors, while breathlessly cursing at them. Finally he was able to fight his way through the dense crowd and literally ran to the safety of his home.

"I will kill them. They must pay for this!"

Once home his anger was still so great that he could respond only with uncontrolled physical violence. Without pausing to think he bolted up to Prudenza's sitting room where her little boys sat on the floor at either side of her stool as she began to tune her lute. She was just turning the pegs with her right hand, as she plucked the strings with her left to test the pitch, when Matteo burst in, nearly knocking Gina to the floor.

He sprang at Prudenza like a crazed animal and as the children burst into tears of fright he tore the lute from her hands and with a movement so swift that neither she nor Gina could react in time, he smashed the lute sharply against the corner of the marble mantle and cursed vehemently as the instrument shattered, making a hideous sound. It was a jangled reverberation of dissonance—so strident and grating that Prudenza could only cover her ears to shut out the cacophony, and close her eyes in horror and disbelief.

As Matteo raised the pitifully fractured skeleton to strike it again he cursed, "Damnable instrument! You have been my adversary since the day you first robbed me of a moment of intimacy with my bride. Now is my vindication." Turning to his wife he boasted, "There. You see!"

"Matteo, why?"

"This thing has always been my rival, but it is not quite dead yet." In an instant he gathered up the splintered remnants and set about the final destruction. With fiendish glee he laughed as one by one he fed the beautiful ribs of the lute into the fire, relishing the crackling sound of the flames as the glossy wood of the maple seemed still to be alive with sap that hissed and spat as it was consumed. And just as the design of the lute had alternated the reddish maple and the white ash, with sadistic relish he consciously alternated feeding the slender spokes into the flames where both quickly turned to ashes. The strings curled in the heat of the fire, twisting and writhing like hideous black serpents, while the delicate pegs fell through the grate and became cinders.

Prudenza looked on helplessly and in disbelief as the flames flickered almost daintily through the lacy design of the carved rose that had adorned the belly of the lute, until gradually it too was consumed, the last trace of her *Fedele*!

CHAPTER 18

The Cradle

Only the laughter of the children penetrated the gloom that invaded Prudenza's world after the destruction of the lute. She made a supreme effort to respond as normally as possible to the antics of her lively little boys, but when they were out of sight she was again crestfallen.

Gina knew her mistress was grieving, mourning *Fedele* as truly as friend mourns the death of friend. But she did so mutely now, her voice taken from her. Gina understood well that her mistress needed somehow to find expression for the multitude of emotions she must be feeling. She was determined to help—but how? To find the answer she called on all the resources in her considerable arsenal of wit and good sense.

While Gina pondered a course of action, she was keen to observe a change in Matteo. He projected a curious newfound air of confidence, due undoubtedly to his "victory" over the lute, his perceived rival. He strutted and swaggered about the home arrogantly now, and although the change in his behavior was a welcome relief, the clever maid was mindful that it was undoubtedly only transitory, a shortlived respite likely to be disrupted at the slightest whim.

Eventually Prudenza's melancholy abated somewhat and Gina determined it was time to intervene more actively, perhaps even a bit boldly. Early one morning she entered the room where Prudenza sat mutely in the semi-darkness and, without awaiting the customary daily instructions from her mistress, she threw open the windows and breezily announced, "I have been thinking, *Madama*; you have not read anything lately. And indeed, how could you, it is too dark and stuffy in here to do so."

Before Prudenza could protest, she went about arranging shutters and draperies to admit the maximum sunlight, and continued chattering away. "Perhaps the sunshine will raise your spirits and you can enjoy your books again. I remember how you used to sit by that window and read—even aloud sometimes. You shared some of those stories with me, *Madama*, and I miss that."

Her well-intentioned remarks brought only a feeble nod that she chose to ignore, as in mock horror she pointed to the cloud of dust motes that floated in the beam of sunshine. "It is time to clear the cobwebs, let the light shine in, *Madama*."

This elicited only a listless, "Thank you, Gina. I know I must try." Although her heart was not in it, to please her maid she rose and walked slowly toward the bookshelf next to where the lute once stood in the corner. There was something warm and comforting about the books, the smell of aging paper and the scent of the fine leather binding. As she ran her fingers along the tops of the books her hand was drawn, almost as if by a magnet, to the volumes of Dante—volumes that *Fra* Tommaso gave her years ago, in a happier time when she was a schoolgirl at San Salvatore back in Ancona.

As she removed the *Divina Commedia* from its place, the thick layer of dust that she brushed aside to reveal the title embossed on its cover sent a pang of guilt through her. It reminded her of how long it had been since she spent time with her favorite author, an old friend who had been with her through earlier hard times. As her fingers passed over the glossy binding, the book easily fell open to the well-fingered pages of the *Inferno, Canto* V and her eyes rested upon the words, "*O anime affannate, venite a noi parlare…*" "O wearied souls! Come to speak with us…"

It was like an invitation, but one Prudenza could not accept. Turning slowly while still pointing to the open pages, she explained, "Do you know, Gina, why I stopped reading here?"

Gina, of course, had never actually read Dante herself, but she suspected the reason, since Prudenza had often related to her the tragic story of Paolo and Francesca. Cleverly hoping to break through Prudenza's silence she pretended not to understand. "No,

Madama. Why did you cease reading there?"

"I put aside that tragic story because I had begun to identify with Francesca, so hopelessly trapped in a loveless marriage. I had to put her aside because I knew the outcome for her and I dared not contemplate a similar fate for myself. I cannot die yet; I must think of my children, Gina, so it is better to abandon the poet."

"But *Madama*, can you not go on to a happier part of the story?"

"There is no happier part for Francesca. She is in hell where there is only violence—violence against nature, violence against art. I have had enough of violence!"

Gina understood that Prudenza was not just speaking of the poem now, and was wise enough not to pursue the matter further at this time. She was grateful however, that her efforts had at least penetrated the bulwark of silence that so isolated her mistress.

During the long periods of reflection on her situation, Prudenza had come to perceive Matteo as a victim; a victim of his own deep-seated insecurity, a flaw so profoundly rooted in his being that he could not help himself. It fueled a jealousy that only seemed to increase until it threatened to consume him. Reminding herself that Gina had actually witnessed Matteo's outbursts there was no need now to hide the fact of his bad treatment of her. She began to speak openly of it with her maid—though at first still attempting to make some excuses for his behavior for, despite his ill treatment of her, she felt pity for him. "If only I could unlock the power that holds his spirit captive. It is truly a malady of the mind that seizes him, and I want to help him. I must try but I do not know how."

Gina listened attentively and after a quiet interval suggested, "Perhaps, *Madama,* Berardo can prepare some remedy to calm Signor Cecchi."

"I have thought of that Gina, but I must not reveal that it is my husband for whom I seek his help."

"You need not tell him. Berardo is kind and understanding and he will not ask."

"You are probably right. He is a master of his art, I know. So...I should at least try. It can certainly do no harm."Gina felt pleased that she had at least sown a seed of an idea that she knew her mistress would ponder.

—m—

The old gardener was weeding a plot of phlox in the shaded side of the garden and did not notice Prudenza until she greeted him. "Oh, *Signora*, forgive me. I did not see you."

As he emerged from the flower bed to the gravel walkway that wound between neatly manicured hedges of fragrant herbs and flowering begonias, he rubbed his soiled hands on the canvas apron that he always wore as he worked.

"Welcome, *Signora*. Welcome to my garden." He gestured to a nearby stone bench and when she had settled there he began: "What is your pleasure today? Some lovely lilies for you? They suit you well, if I may say so; they are modest, beautiful and so fragrant. Or perhaps these asters. They are the first of the season, which tells us that autumn will soon be here."

"Oh, They are lovely, Berardo, thank you, but..."

Just then she saw that Lorenzo was in the garden, on the sunny side where he was playing with Tigre, the lazy orange cat that made his home there. When he noticed his mother he called out, "*Mamma*," and started toward her.

"No, no, Lorenzo. Stay and play with the cat. I do think he likes you." She was relieved to see him return to teasing the animal, waving about a string with a tiny ball that bounced this way and that. She smiled at the dizzying display of orange paws thrashing and flailing about in the air as the cat pursued the evasive orb. For a long moment she was silent, admiring her firstborn who was growing into such a tall handsome lad. When she was sure he was again fully engaged in his game with the cat, she pursued her mission with Berardo, speaking in a low voice now. "Berardo, I have come seeking your help, your knowledge."

"Of course, *Signora*. How may I serve you?"

In her effort to conceal the identity of the person who was the object of her concern she continued cautiously. "One of my household, Berardo, is seriously tormented in spirit, caught in a dark state of mind. Surely in your store of knowledge you have some restorative, some elixir to relieve mental distress, to cure a dark humor."

"Indeed, *Madama*, I do. It would please me to place my humble knowledge at your disposal."

"Oh, thank you. I knew you would help."

"There are actually many possible treatments that may relieve a troubled spirit and restore balance to a distressed mind. But one must be careful to use them properly. It requires knowledge or the malady might only become worse." Pointing his forefinger directly to his heart he promised, "Do not worry, *Signora*. Berardo is here for you."

With that he began reciting a catalog of possibilities while running his hand over a stand of catnip that, judging from a flattened spot in the middle, suggested it must be a favorite spot of Tigre's. It gave off a strong, pungent fragrance as the old man stroked it and explained, "We must begin simply; possibly with a modest tea made from catnip leaves. It works as a mild sedative and may induce a relaxed state." Moving on he continued, "Or, I could blend a potion containing some oil of bitter almond that has the power to soothe and even sedate slightly." Pointing to a patch of greenery with pretty pink and white flowers he warned, "This is dogbane. Do not be deceived by its innocent beauty. The juice from its milky stem is very poisonous; but I know its secrets. Handled properly it has been known to induce a state of tranquility and, who knows, it may well be the answer to your friend's malady."

Prudenza was duly impressed with his knowledge, but he had only just begun. "Many plants that are beautiful to the eye, like foxglove—or that give off a marvelous fragrance like jasmine—can actually be poisonous."

"Really?"

"Yes. But..." like a good teacher pausing for emphasis to insure his student's complete attention before he revealed the pearl of wisdom, he continued, "The secret is in the root. Although the nectar of the jasmine flower is poisonous, I can make for you a medicine from its dried roots that may actually bring about the result you desire."

Prudenza was captivated and pleased.

"Come with me, please, *Signora*. Let me show you my store of dried preparations from which to choose." He led her to a corner of the garden and into the small shed where he dried his herbs. The air inside was heavy with a mixture of odors coming from a variety of scruffy-looking spikes and bushes hanging from the ceiling beams in various stages of dehydration. He spoke of them like old friends, gently stroking them as he moved along, all the while regaling Prudenza with his knowledge of their medicinal properties.

He guided her to a shelf filled with an array of odd-shaped jugs, bottles, and amphorae containing already processed herbs, ready for use. For a moment she was overcome by a strong nostalgia. She was transported back to her father's *botegga* where he had so lovingly shared with her his vast knowledge of the properties of the dyes he imported, dyestuffs contained in a variety of receptacles so like these. She was brought back—somewhat reluctantly—to the present by the awareness that Berardo was putting a question to her. "Do you think, *Signora*, perhaps it would be best to begin with the bitter almond?"

"If you think so, Berardo. Yes, yes, that would be good."

"I can blend it for you today and perhaps make a tincture from the jasmine as well. I will send some catnip, too. Your maid can easily brew its tea for you."

Just as they emerged from the drying shed they were startled by the horrible shrieking sound of an animal in distress. Above its cries Prudenza recognized the voice of Lorenzo crying, "Please don't! Please stop, Father."

She was horrified to see Matteo holding the cat by its tail, swinging it wildly in a great arc over his head all the while laughing fiendishly.

At the sight of Prudenza with Berardo he dropped the protesting animal and it took swift refuge in a small safe chink in the wall, still hissing loudly at his tormentor. Then, in a decidedly combative manner, Matteo bellowed, "And what brings you here, Wife? Seeking some foolish magic potion? Or is it the old man's attentions that draw you?"

"Matteo, stop! How could you say such a thing? Berardo is my friend—your own father's faithful servant, respected in the household."

Enraged that she should dare speak to him thus he quickly bent down, appeared to extract something from under a stepping-stone, and in a flash with his right hand he seized Prudenza by the hair and jerked her head back sharply. As she opened her mouth to protest he commanded, "Here. Try this! Here is a REAL remedy from the garden for you."

She recoiled as she saw in his left hand, a slimy garden slug, covered with mud and mucous, dangling over her open mouth. "Go ahead," he commanded, "Eat it. Swallow it. Feel it slide down your delicate gullet!"

Her revulsion was so great that she retched involuntarily, soiling both her bodice and Matteo's shirt, which only angered him all the more. Meanwhile Berardo attempted to comfort Lorenzo who had unfortunately witnessed the whole disgusting incident and was crying hysterically. Trembling with fear he clutched at his mother's skirt as he pleaded helplessly, "Stop! Please do not hurt my *mamma*."

Prudenza was humiliated, sickened physically and emotionally that her son and her gardener had to witness her husband's brutish behavior. In one last burst of anger Matteo threw her to the ground and sped out of the gate, cursing as he went, leaving her to apologize for his bad behavior. With Berardo's help she struggled to her feet and, mindful of her appearance, walked unsteadily to the fountain, dipped her handkerchief in the water and attempted to clean her soiled dress.

There was little reason now to hide the identity of the person for whom she had come to seek Berardo's assistance. The kind old gardener understood and could only shake his head and murmur in disbelief as he watched her leave with as much dignity as she could muster. "*Povera Madonna!*"

Berardo, so devoted and trusted, would never report the incident in the garden to others, knowing that it would only further afflict Prudenza's already burdened heart. Nevertheless, knowledge of Matteo's bad behavior soon spread among the servants and, more importantly, reached the ears of his mother who sought out Prudenza to hear the full account.

Gina recognized that the humiliation to which her mistress had been subjected more or less cancelled out any progress she had been able to affect through her ministrations. She could only watch sadly now as Prudenza retreated in embarrassment and shame.

With frightening clarity Prudenza perceived a pattern in the progression of her husband's jealousy. At first it was jealously of his brother Fabrizio, whom Prudenza had never met, yet she knew of his fabled good looks. But she had begun to question, "Was Fabrizio really so comely? Or was this also just another invention of Matteo's sick mind, like his obsession that Zenobi preferred his eldest son?" Even now, with his brother miles away in a monastery, Matteo persisted in this almost sadistic self-torture that had sent him on the crazed odyssey trying to win Zenobi's approval by bringing back his trophy bride.

"I was that trophy, that prize! But, oh, how quickly the laurel wreath of his victory faded, and instead he saw me as a rival for his father's affections. There have been signs along the way. I should have recognized it I suppose; but what could I have done?"

"You cannot blame yourself, *Madama*."

Prudenza started at the sound of her maid's voice. She did not realize that she had been musing aloud and was not aware that Gina had entered the room. Her embarrassment was only momentary as she quickly reminded herself that there was no need to keep up a pretense with Gina.

Both young women were aware that the conventions that governed their roles as mistress and maidservant had been blurred for some time—though they never actually discussed the fact. There was an unspoken realization that their relationship had evolved into something deeper, more personal. They were friends unfettered by codes of behavior or tradition. Freed from inhibitions, Prudenza related a sequence of abuses that she had held in denial for so long. The effect was like a cleansing bath. Gina was patient. Perhaps, God willing, in the unburdening, Prudenza could regain her voice. She listened with sympathy, wisely saying little lest she impede the inventory that Prudenza began to reveal—first in halting, incomplete, and almost incoherent fragments.

"The sailors. I remember the sailors."

"Sailors?"

"Yes, sailors—on the ship that brought us from Ancona to

Rimini. His harsh treatment of the sailors. And his sullenness…"

"Sullenness?"

"Yes. The way he always withdraws from social intercourse when he is no longer the center of attention. And his stammering…"

"Stammering?"

"Yes, Gina, surely you have heard him trip over his own tongue when he is distressed. It sends him into a fury, causing him to rage. Oh, he can be so charming when it serves him; but he can use that charm to deceive, too. Indeed, he deceived even my dear, wise father."

"Deceived?" Gina was becoming a skilled interrogator by simply repeating her mistress's cryptic declarations. And soon the mere verbalizing of these secrets that she had kept for so long hidden in the darkness, released a torrent of long-suppressed tears. Like the devoted confidant that she was Gina gave her complete attention to her mistress at these times. Sitting at Prudenza's feet she listened attentively but said little, as her mistress's words now began to flow with abandon.

"There was Angelo, the pathetic, headless little songbird. What had he ever done to offend?"

"Nothing, *Madama*."

"And the lute! Oh, Gina, how can I ever forget the anger in his eyes, his voice? His cursing? You heard him call it 'that damnable instrument.' He admitted his jealousy of it—calling an inanimate object his rival! Is that not a symptom of a sick mind?"

"Yes, I fear it truly is, *Madama*."

"It is clear to me now that no one, no person, no thing has offended him, yet his malady grows stronger, more frightening by the day. Gina, I have come to believe and fear that he hates and must destroy whatever it is that I love. Oh, what will be next? I fear that in his demented condition he is transferring his jealousy of his brother onto his own firstborn. Indeed, even his mother has noted it. Where might this lead? Especially now since Lorenzo witnessed the incident in the garden. The poor child is terrified of his own father; and how can I blame him? He is just an innocent little boy whose unfortunate likeness to his uncle Fabrizio has made him the object of his father's wrath. Think of it, Gina, he is jealous of his own son—his firstborn! Is this to be the child's birthright?"

Gina could only shake her head in response, unable to offer any answer.

"And now since he destroyed the lute he has begun to shun Lorenzo, and in an obviously calculated manner he fawns upon Piero…Piero, the son whose birth he missed in order to watch the bloody contest with the lions."

Gina had, in fact, witnessed this behavior only a few days earlier when she had seen Matteo whisk little Piero off his feet and hold the frightened child high above his head, as he bellowed, "*Ecco*! Behold the scion of the house of Cecchi!" It was all such a transparent and pathetic demonstration of his effort to strike out at his absent brother by promoting Piero whose position in the family, like his own, was that of second child.

"What will happen next? I live in fear for my babies. I love my little boys and I must protect them from their father. But how? What can I do? It seems no remedy can release him from the grip of this horrible sickness that has ravaged his mind. I am afraid and I…I find myself wishing he were gone from our lives. Perhaps it is the only way!"

"Gone, *Madama*?"

"Yes, gone."

Prudenza's large eyes were opened wide now, her pupils strangely dilated, fixed in a glassy, smoky-green stare that Gina had never before observed. It was as if she beheld some otherworldly object in the distance that momentarily paralyzed her. With her eyes thus fixed on some phantom she spoke slowly, deliberately and in a strangely hollow, emotionless voice, "Gone? Dead. I mean dead! God forgive me."

For a long interval neither woman spoke. The silence was like a thick darkness, almost suffocating. Prudenza appeared momentarily shocked at the severity of her own admission, and questioned if she should go on. Finally she broke the long silence with another pronouncement equally startling to Gina. "Do you think it would cheer him to learn that he is to become a father again?"

For once Gina was so taken by surprise that she could make no response.

"Yes, Gina, ever since the earthquake and the destruction of the lute, Matteo has visited my bed—almost nightly. Unwelcome visits they are to be sure. His behavior almost conducted like business, coming as it were to collect a debt I owe him, and with little gentleness. He is often rough and hurtful and I am relieved when he leaves."

"Then why do you submit, *Madama*?"

"Because I pray that it may somehow help him."

Gina did not dare reveal her doubts that the arrival of a third child would be cause for joy to Matteo. Nor would her position allow her to prevent her mistress from revealing the news to her husband.

Knowledge of Prudenza's condition left Matteo menacingly withdrawn and ominously silent, as if calculating his next move. As he pondered his strategy, Prudenza's life settled into a dull routine broken only by the welcome visits of Lorenzo and Piero. In the days and weeks that followed, Gina brought the boys more frequently to their mother's quarters to distract and to cheer her. Matteo, however, remained closeted away, silently brooding over this latest development.

The deadly dullness was broken one day when Gina brought to her mistress a letter from Ancona, bearing the familiar monogram of Beltramonto. It seemed well timed to bring some cheer into this otherwise dismal period. She watched as Prudenza opened it eagerly and began reading. But it quickly became apparent that the news was not good. She read aloud.

> *Your father is ill, very ill, Prudenza. And he calls for you. The old pain behind his eye has become persistent and he suffers from intense headaches and periods of unconsciousness. None of the doctors' remedies have brought him any relief and they tell me that he has not long to live.*
>
> *Please come, my dear. He loves you so, Prudenza, and I know it would give him great comfort to see you before he dies. And I too should love to hold you in my arms again, my dearest daughter. In the name of God, do answer at once.*
>
> *Your loving mother, Caterina*

Too stunned even to cry, Prudenza's hand went limp allowing the letter to fall into her lap and slide softly down the folds of her skirt 'til it reached the floor at her feet.

"I must go, Gina. I must go at once. They need me."

"Of course, *Madama*."

"But I will need my husband's permission."

Without hesitation she rose, determined to seek him out, wherever he was. She found him at last, blurry-eyed and brooding in the semidarkness of his room. He seemed surprised at her coming and had little time to react as she relayed the contents of her mother's message and boldly asked permission to go to her. Clearly this would not be easy, but she was resolved to find a way.

He delighted in stating the most obvious obstacle. "How will you go? You have no money of your own."

"I know, Matteo. I will need money and I am asking you, as your devoted wife, to provide what I need to make the trip."

"And you cannot go alone!" With a contemptuous curl of his lip he sarcastically added, "Such a refined and proper lady as you are must always have a woman companion."

"Yes, I will need such a companion. I am sure that Gina would be glad to accompany me."

Making his first acknowledgement of Prudenza's pregnancy he struck the final blow. Seizing a half-empty wine bottle he pounded the flask so vehemently on the table that it shattered, cutting his fingers badly. With bloodied hand raised as if to strike her he bellowed, "No! The answer is emphatically, no!" With contempt and sarcasm in his voice he added, "Not in your condition, *Madama*." He had never shown the slightest regard for her "condition" until now when it provided a useful excuse to deny her request. "What might happen to our baby?"

"Our baby?"

"Yes, our baby!"

There was no reasoning with him now; so without excusing herself she turned abruptly and did the only thing she could think of at the moment. She sought out Maddalena who attempted to comfort her and promised to intercede with her son.

Despite his mother's plea he steadfastly refused until at last it was too late. The dreaded message came. *"Gone, Prudenza! Your father is dead."* There was no point now in asking to attend the funeral, since by this time her father would already have been buried. She wept for her mother now so alone, and retreated into her own grief.

In anticipation of the birth of her baby, the cradle was brought to her room and stood there now an icon, a reminder of her dear father whose gift it had been before Lorenzo was born. She caressed the smooth wood, tracing the delicate carvings with her fingertips as she thought of her father whose hands produced it so lovingly for the grandchild he never saw.

These were the kind of late-autumn days when each seemed a miniature eternity, and the leaden shade of the skies matched Prudenza's spirit. Once again it was November, the month of the dead, the season when nature even seemed to retreat to a lifeless state. The trees released their colorful foliage, leaving the only persistent green to be seen in the cypress. Yet even the cypresses were an emblem of mourning for the dead.

At that moment however, the sudden stirring of life within reminded her that nature was only dormant—not dead—resting, preparing for new life.

CHAPTER 19

The Mole

Her heart was beating a veritable tattoo in time with the noisy swish of her abundant petticoats as she bounded up the stairs toward *Signora* Maddalena's room. Gina was responding, not without some trepidation, to a summons. She could hardly imagine what the mistress might want of her, but one did not keep this willful woman waiting—ever. With some anxiety, she knocked at Maddalena's door.

A determined voice invited, *"Avanti. Avanti subito, Signorina."*

Maddalena sat in a large chair, not unlike a throne, with a countenance that matched the urgency in the voice that bade Gina enter.

A bit ruffled at the sight, the young maid attempted a hurried curtsy that was little more than an awkward and comical bob, but it brought a welcome smile to Maddalena's face and relief to Gina who had anticipated—God knows what. Anything could happen in the Cecchi household these days. The obligatory courtesies having been completed, Gina stood silently awaiting her orders.

Sensing the young woman's uneasiness Maddalena made benign attempts to relax her with polite pleasantries about the weather and the children's play, but then suddenly turned the conversation abruptly to the point at hand. "Gina, Mistress Prudenza is very fond of you I believe."

Unaccustomed to hearing such pronouncements from this dominant woman, Gina was flustered and responded feebly, "It would seem so, *Madama."* She shuffled her feet nervously and with her eyes modestly downcast added, "She is a very kind and generous lady."

"Oh, silly child, there is no need for you to be embarrassed. I have observed how loyally you serve her, and for that I am deeply grateful. You have no need to fear what I have to say to you, my dear."

Gina relaxed visibly and managed a heartfelt, "*Grazie, Signora*. Mistress Prudenza has been very kind to me and I would do anything for her."

"Anything, Gina?"

"Yes, *Signora*, anything."

"Then listen carefully, for I have a plan that will require your help."

Gina's anxiety was melting away like the last frost under the Tuscan sun in springtime, as she responded to Maddalena's indication that she should be seated. In a gesture that meant, "I give you my complete attention," she pulled a stool directly in front of Maddalena and waited expectantly.

"I was deeply touched by your loyalty to Mistress Prudenza and the care and attention that you have shown in her bereavement. I trust you, Gina. If I did not I would not share my plan with you."

"*Grazie, Madama*. I am truly honored. But you must tell me what it is that you wish me to do."

"I have been contemplating the situation and am well aware that my daughter-in-law has suffered a great deal in the last few years. She loved her father-in-law, my good husband, Zenobi, in a special bond. He has left us and now her own dear father has died. Not only does she mourn him, but I know she is deeply troubled by the realization that her mother is alone back in Ancona."

"Yes, *Signora*. I too worry—though I have never met *Signora* Beltramonto."

"Prudenza was so kind and loving to me at the time of my dear Zenobi's death. No blood daughter could have been more solicitous and caring, and now I want to comfort her in her grief. I worry that the burden of her sorrow may affect the baby that she is carrying."

"As do I, *Signora*."

"And I am aware, too, that my son will not permit her to

go to Ancona now. I can only imagine the pain this causes her. So I have been thinking what it would mean if we could bring her mother to her."

"Oh, *Signora*, do you think that is possible? How?"

"We must present the idea to Prudenza very cautiously. For that I rely on you, Gina, to lay the groundwork. You must plant the idea ever so subtly in her mind."

"I will do my best."

"We must act quickly, though. How wonderful it would be if *Signora* Beltramonto could be here for the birth of the baby."

The very thought of it excited Gina. "Oh, yes, yes! I know that would bring such joy to my mistress."

"I leave it to you then, Gina, but remember; be subtle! Prudenza is very intelligent and she must not know we have plotted this."

"I will do my best, *Signora*, I promise."

"And be assured that I will do my part to make it happen."

Gina left this surprising audience with a light heart, her pulse quickening at the thought of Maddalena's suggestion. She at once began thinking how she might bring this delicate suggestion about. She had the good sense to recognize, however, that she must not rush headlong into the plan. Restraint did not come easily to her but she reckoned that this matter must be approached most delicately, yet soon. At the same time she acknowledged a certain satisfaction—even pride—that *Signora* Cecchi should have taken her into her confidence and placed so much responsibility in her hands. It was exhilarating, but a bit frightening too. She dare not waste precious time indulging her own satisfaction in this new-found recognition. Instead she crossed herself and uttered a heartfelt, "*Gran Dio.* May heaven help me."

Soon enough her prayer was answered—quite unexpectedly. One glorious spring morning Gina came upon Prudenza standing by an open window watching her two little boys boisterously cavorting at play. There was a smile on her face as from the courtyard below came shrill yelps, howls, and squeals of delight.

"Oh, Gina, are they not beautiful little boys? I am so blessed and so grateful. With each passing day I find more pleasure in their development, and I thank God for that. May He always keep them safe."

"Amen I say to that, *Madama*. They are indeed precious—boisterous as little boys should be—but indeed very precious. And may I say they have something of their mother's grace and charm too."

Prudenza breathed a small but audible little sigh and whispered wistfully, "My father would have been so proud of them, so happy to see his grandsons. But alas…"

Barely able to contain her enthusiasm at this incredibly well-timed opportunity, Gina fairly blurted out, "But, *Signora*, your mother could see them. Think what it would mean to her to see her grandsons."

"Oh, I know, Gina. But I fear that could never be."

"Why not, *Madama*? A visit with your mother! Just think of it!"

"But how? My husband…" She thought better than to finish that thought aloud.

"How, *Madama*? Remember how you have often said to me when I was in doubt about something, 'Nothing is impossible with God.' So you must believe it yourself. Do you not?"

"Yes, I do, but…" Gina dared to interrupt, lest she lose the momentum of the argument she was carefully building. "And it would be good for you, too, *Madama*. Think of it. How long has it been since you saw your mother?"

"More than eight years."

She began to detect a sudden flush on her mistress's cheeks that had so recently known only the color of grief and sadness. Was this perhaps a chink in Prudenza's conviction that it would never work?

"I should love to see my mother once more, to comfort her and to be held in her dear arms again like a little child."

"God grant you will, *Madama*. You will!"

Gina was bursting with satisfaction and more than a little pride that she had introduced the thought of a possible visit from Prudenza's mother. She could not wait to report to Maddalena who was obviously well pleased as she listened to the excited young girl's account.

"I do believe, *Signora* Cecchi that a word from you now would be timely, for I know she would respect and honor your wishes in this."

"Of course. I will do my part. But remember, we must not let her suspect our plot."

"She trusts and respects you, *Signora* Cecchi, and I believe your assurance that her mother would be a welcome guest here would convince her of the possibility."

Despite the difference in their age and station, the two women were united in a kind of "holy" collusion, an unlikely pairing to be sure, but it was clear that both were pleased. Gina even thought she noted a slightly mischievous twinkle in *Signora* Cecchi's eyes as she announced, "I will go to her now." Looking back over her shoulder she added, "You have done well, Gina. Thank you."

There was genuine concern in Maddalena's voice as she entered Prudenza's room. "You look weary, Daughter."

"I am well enough, Mother. Just tired."

"You must consider yourself, Prudenza. You have suffered much in these last months and you owe it to yourself and to the baby you carry to take care."

"Thank you, *Signora*. I do. I rest and, thanks to Nella's ministrations, I eat well, too."

"That is good, but it isn't enough, Prudenza. You must feed your soul as well. What would bring you joy, lift your spirits, Daughter? Tell me."

"Well, you know I grieve the loss of my father but nothing could ever bring him back. My greatest joy would have been for him to see his grandchildren."

"That, of course, I cannot change, Prudenza. But what of your mother?"

"I worry for her. She is so alone now, and…my husband will not hear of my going to her now."

"I know, my dear, and I understand your disappointment. Although I do not approve of my son's behavior, I do believe it is right for you to remain here. It would be dangerous for you to travel now in your condition."

"That is what Matteo says. But I know that his refusal is not really based upon concern for me, or the baby. He is not happy, *Signora*, at the prospect of another child."

"I fear you are right, but we must not let his temper spoil our joy over the gift of this new life. I have been thinking, perhaps we could invite your mother to come here—to be a guest in our home. Have you ever thought of this?"

"Oh, *Signora*, I would love that but…"

"No buts, Prudenza. If we act promptly perhaps she could even be here in time for the birth of your baby."

"That would be a dream too precious to be true."

"Nonsense! Let us invite her. I am sure that her longing to see you must be great. And I understand fully her loss and her loneliness."

Prudenza noted the tears that welled up in Maddalena's eyes at the allusion to Zenobi's death. "You must write to her at once, Prudenza; there is no time to lose if she is to be here for the birth."

"I will, *Signora*; I will at once. I do know that in her last letter to me she spoke of her loneliness, the empty house, just one servant and the gardener now. Even my faithful old dog Lupo has died."

"Just think how the antics of Lorenzo and Piero would delight your mother."

"Yes, and how my little boys would love her. I want them to know her."

"Do you think, Prudenza, that your father's business would keep her in Ancona?"

"I hope not." After some reflection she added, "I know that in these last years, as father's health was declining, my cousin Filippo—we called him Pippo—apprenticed to father and gradually assumed more responsibility for the business. Pippo has always been my favorite cousin. He is dear and considerate of my mother. She speaks often of his kindness and support, and of her affection for his lovely wife, Bianca."

"I am glad to hear that. It should make things easier."

"Mother was never really involved in my father's business anyway. And I know she trusts Pippo."

"Then let us do it, Daughter. Write! And I will extend my invitation to her at the same time."

Many anxious days passed as the three women awaited Caterina's response; but when finally her letter arrived, the news was not encouraging. Although she was grateful for the invitation she was hesitant and worried about leaving Ancona. Moreover there was the problem of a companion for the trip; now since *Zia* Teresina had died, who would accompany her?

Maddalena intervened with another letter stressing Prudenza's need for her mother now, her sadness, and the imminent birth of her baby. And as for the matter of the companion, Prudenza had anticipated the problem and wrote to Pippo who happily assured her that he would hire one of the most trusted employees of the Beltramonto business—in fact his own younger brother, Fabio—to see Caterina safely to Florence.

There was immense jubilation in the household when finally word of Caterina's acceptance came. Prudenza was overjoyed and like a little child could only repeat over and over again, "My mother is coming; my mother is coming." In her excitement one day she actually twirled about in a spontaneous attempt at a little pirouette that nearly toppled her as she lost her balance—so heavy was she with child. It was a performance greeted on all sides with gales of laughter.

Meanwhile Maddalena was especially busy preparing suitably comfortable quarters for Caterina while Prudenza prepared her boys to meet their grandmother.

Such a flurry of activity did not escape Matteo's notice and his suspicious nature would not rest until he had determined the cause. He would not ask directly, however, for he did not want the women to know he cared or, for that matter, that he even noticed. It was a new strategy for him and it required a new solution. Soon enough what it was would be quite evident to all.

—⁓—

One day as Maddalena was hurrying up the stairs to Prudenza's chamber she was suddenly startled by a figure that literally seemed to spring out of the shadows, coming before her with such suddenness that she let out a startled cry. What she saw before her gave her even greater pause as she collected her wits and overcame her fright. Who was this creature whose legs seemed to fold beneath him and then suddenly propel him into the air, springing like a toad?

"Who are you?"

The poor pockmarked creature, his mouth hanging open stupidly replied, "Tuccio."

"Tuccio? What are you doing here?"

His shifty, piggish little eyes squinted as he attempted to answer, but speech did not come easily. Through a gap in his blackened teeth there escaped a persistent trickle of drool down his chin that caused a sort of lisp when he spoke.

"The mashter. I sherve my mashter."

"Master who?"

"Your shon, I do believe."

"And what could you possibly do for him?" No sooner had she asked than she realized. Of course, he is a spy. He was eavesdropping outside Prudenza's room. "Be off with you."

Without a word he scurried away as suddenly as he had appeared.

"What next? To what depth of indignity will this troublesome son of mine stoop? I must warn Prudenza, and tell Gina, too."

Gina had, in fact, already run into Tuccio earlier that day in the lower regions of the house. He was walking furtively, partly springing toad-like and partly slithering in a way that sent a shudder through her. Clearly he was up to no good and she must watch out for him. Her mistress was too kind and trusting and might easily be moved by his pitiful appearance. The servants of the household all loved Prudenza but this new one could be a canker in their midst.

—ɷ—

Maddalena and her young accomplice looked on with great satisfaction as their plan was about to be realized. Prudenza's spirit brightened at the prospect of her mother's arrival and the servants had been instructed to do their part to make this visit perfect. Nella promised to prepare a special feast of welcome and Berardo offered to fill *Signora* Beltramonto's room with sweet herbs and flowers from his garden. Nothing should be allowed to cloud this day.

Prudenza was not told the time of her mother's expected arrival, but all the rushing about the house and the animated conversation that was immediately hushed when she appeared, told her that the time was being kept a surprise. She knew it must be imminent

Maddalena thoughtfully arranged that the meeting of mother and daughter should be unattended by anyone else. She and Gina met Caterina first for the proper exchange of courtesies and led their guest to Prudenza's apartment, leaving her there alone before the door.

Caterina's heart pounded as they climbed the broad stairs and she had to pause momentarily on a landing to catch her breath.

Fearing that the climb was too much for her Maddalena, inquired, "*Signora* Beltramonto, are you feeling ill? It has been a long trip, I know, and you must be very tired. Perhaps we ought to wait until tomorrow. You should rest first."

"Oh no, *Signora*, no! I am well, really."

Gina understood. "It is the excitement, is it not, *Signora?*"

"Yes. It is the excitement of seeing my daughter after all these years—so much emotion."

When finally they reached Prudenza's door Maddalena stepped aside and motioned to Gina to do so, too. "We leave you now, *Signora*. This is truly a sacred moment for you and your daughter alone."

After rapping gently the two quickly retreated as the voice from within responded, *"Avanti."*

At the familiar sound of her daughter's voice, that same sweet melodious voice, Caterina's eyes filled with tears, tears of joy, tears of anticipation. Her hand trembled visibly and she was forced to pause a moment to gain control before turning the handle and pushing the door open gently. She gasped at the figure she beheld there. Two women, mother and daughter, stood frozen in a moment of profound silence, their voices stilled by emotions simply too precious for words. It was Caterina who finally broke the spell with a single word, "Prudenza."

At the sight of her mother still framed in the doorway came the simple childlike response, *"Mamma."*

The two rushed into each other's arms and after a long tender, silent embrace they grasped hands, holding each other at arm's length. Each scrutinized the other, hungrily observing every feature, every detail of countenance, of change, of transformation. Prudenza noted with satisfaction her mother's still straight back, the elegant posture that contributed so to her always regal bearing. Only a few silvery wisps at the temples, gave evidence of aging. With satisfaction she reflected, Caterina Beltramonto, my mother, is still a beautiful woman at fifty-three.

To Caterina her daughter seemed at once the same, yet different. Her lovely hair, still the color of burnished copper, was now worn in a more matronly style. And the clear green of her eyes was still flecked with golden lights, probably made brighter than ever by the sheer excitement of the moment. Her body was youthful, that of an active twenty-four-year-old, and the rounded curves of her plump belly only made her all the more beautiful. However, with the keen scrutiny of a mother, Caterina could not fail to note something about her look that suggested another kind of change deeper within—one that would reveal itself only in due time. For now mother and daughter were ecstatic. "My little girl. My baby is a woman!"

—ᵚᵚ—

Despite the joy that she felt at the news of her mother's coming Prudenza was anxious about the meeting. So much had happened in these years that they had been apart. "Will my mother approve of me? And how will I explain Matteo's absence—or worse still—his behavior if he does deign to appear?" But for now all inhibitions and worries dissolved, overcome by the absolute bliss of this reunion.

—ᵚᵚ—

Meanwhile Tuccio continued spying, rewarded by pitifully small payments from Matteo, whom he considered his master. Though measly sums, they were undoubtedly more than he could ever have known before, and sufficient to encourage him to go to great lengths in his surveillance of Prudenza. Although he had never even met his master's wife, he had come to think of her and her friends as his adversaries, and he searched out every possible opportunity to carry out his assignment. In only a short time he became familiar with every imaginable hiding place: cupboards ample enough to contain his twisted little body, draperies sufficient to wrap himself in, closets and landings on the stairs where the late afternoon hours provided dark shadows. Little by little from these vantage points he could report laughter coming from Prudenza's quarters, the number of visitors and the length of time that each stayed, and even the food they were served.

Of this last he was doubly pleased since he learned a way of turning this to his advantage as he observed the remains of the repasts that were returned to the kitchen. While Nella and her assistants were occupied with serving the other members of the household, he foraged through the remnants. Indeed, he concluded from these that the ladies must have very delicate appetites. As he gorged on these delicacies he muttered, "Well, all the better for me."

—⁓—

Prudenza had never revealed to her parents the problems with her marriage, nor the treatment by her husband. She suspected, however, that her mother must wonder why several days after her arrival in Florence, she had still not seen her son-in-law. It was a gross infraction of courtesy that Matteo seemed nowhere to be found. For a few days, at least, Prudenza could make excuses that his work kept him away. Although her maternal intuition could not so easily be deceived, Caterina determined that she would not question her daughter on this sensitive point, for it would only embarrass her. In any case she believed Prudenza would confide in her in her own good time.

She did not have to wait long. While visiting her daughter only a few days after her arrival Caterina asked, "Prudenza, there is something I am longing for."

"What is it, Mother? Anything you wish."

"I long to hear you play the lute again, and to sing. I miss your sweet voice and the sound of the lute, your dear father's birthday gift to you before you went away to San Salvatore. Please, Prudenza, will you play for me?"

It was a simple request but came with the suddenness and force of a thunderbolt that caught Prudenza off guard, struggling awkwardly to find credible excuse. Instead she remained speechless, groping for words to extricate herself from this impasse. She was not accustomed to dissembling and lying had never been a part of her experience. The best she could manage was a feeble protest. "Oh, *Mamma*, I have not played in some time and I am horribly out of practice, I fear. With the babies coming so close together I have had little time to keep up my music. Please forgive me."

All true enough, but not really convincing! Something was lacking in her daughter's protest that warned Caterina not to pursue the point just yet. She would be patient. Gina, on the contrary, determined that *Signora* Beltamonto should know the truth and at the first opportunity to seek her out alone, she would relate the story of the lute. And so she did.

The incident of the destruction of the lute only convinced Caterina that her misgivings about Matteo were justified. She had met him only a few times when he came to Ancona for the betrothal and again when he returned to take his young bride back to Florence. Despite her husband's assurance that Matteo came from a good family, she always had strange feelings about this man. For now she would wait and observe, but she was anxious for her daughter's well-being.

Maddalena was quick to sense the fragility of the situation and, hoping to spare Prudenza the embarrassment of having to discuss her husband's absence she took the initiative, chastened her son and literally brought him bodily to greet his mother-in-law. Like a pouting, sulking child he grudgingly made the briefest of feeble salutations, realizing that his own mother was standing by, critically observing his behavior in this exercise that she imposed upon him. No one in the present company—especially Caterina— could fail to observe that he fulfilled only the barest rudiments of civility, and that in a most perfunctory manner. Caterina was left to contemplate the question, "Oh, Alfonso, is this the man to whom we gave our precious daughter?"

A few days later Prudenza encountered Tuccio for the first time. It was a lovely day and on a sudden impulse she decided to take a walk in the garden. There she would have an opportunity to introduce her mother to Berardo and to pass by the kitchen where she would introduce Nella. She opened the door so quickly that she nearly toppled the creature cowering on the other side.

"Oh, forgive me."

He said nothing. No one had ever asked his forgiveness before—for anything. His only response was a thin-lipped grimace that she took to be an attempted smile.

"What is your name?"

"Tuccio."

"And what, may I ask, are you doing at my door?" though she knew very well she caught him in the act of spying. The thought almost amused her as she considered, "Spying! What could you possibly expect to hear? I have done nothing wrong."

As she studied the poor sniveling creature now crouched at her feet he stared up at her with squinting little close-set eyes. Indeed, she thought, there is a porcine look about him—even to the coarse hairs protruding from his ears. Yes, poor thing, he looks a bit like a bristling pig.

He was frightened and momentarily struck dumb at the sight of his master's wife. Even he could recognize that she was a pretty one. At this he sniffled and wiped the drool from his chin on to the sleeve of his filthy smock, already mucky from repeated use.

Without thinking Prudenza instinctively reached into her pocket and gave him her own clean white handkerchief. As she did so a single tear trickled down his upturned face, adding to the watery mix on his already-grimy cheek. He was touched, not accustomed to kindness, especially from a gentle, lovely lady.

As Prudenza studied him she observed from the color of his skin and some peculiarities in his speech the he must be the offspring of Turkish slaves that had in an earlier time been bought as cheap labor in wealthy homes of Florence. They were regarded as chattel, often listed in a family's inventory along with domestic animals. Given Tuccio's unfortunate deformities Matteo was probably able to obtain his services for very little cash. She could only imagine how he was being treated by her husband.

Without a word Tuccio tucked the handkerchief in his pocket, quick as a ferret, and slithered away. Looking after him Prudenza made mental note to instruct Maria to give him a clean shirt. "So what if the poor creature was spying on me. I have nothing to hide, and he has feelings, too."

Gina, however, cautioned her mistress to take care. "Do not be too kind, *Madama*. He is pathetic, yes; there is no denying that. But he is not to be trusted."

—ℳ—

Soon enough her premonitions proved to be true as Prudenza's mother became the victim of a series of harassments. They were minor disturbances at first: childish adolescent pranks like spiders placed in her bed, a dead mouse on her pillow, and strange rattling noises near her door at night. Not wishing to alarm her daughter, Caterina approached Gina who had already proven herself wise for her age. On the basis of the trust that Maddalena had placed in her, Gina made bold to suggest that Caterina confide in the elder *Signora* Cecchi.

It was a delicate situation to be sure, but one that Caterina could no longer avoid. If, as Gina suggested, she confided in Maddalena she might insult her hostess, show herself ungrateful for the warm hospitality she received. On the other hand she was driven by concern for her daughter and the soon-to-be-born child. She really had no choice; she would speak to Maddalena, even though it meant she believed her host's son to be the perpetrator of these acts.

Maddalena realized how difficult it must be for Caterina to approach her on this sensitive matter. Caterina could not have known of Maddalena's already-strained relationship with her son. She had all too recently suffered the insult of Matteo's behavior and neglect at the time of Zenobi's death. Moreover, she had even been witness to some of his brutality in the treatment of others. Even his own children! Prudenza had not realized, nor for that matter had Maddalena herself, how deep was the hurt from her own son's treatment of her and indeed of the ruination he had brought upon the entire Cecchi household.

It was clear that these disgusting pranks were the work of Tuccio. Matteo would never touch such things as spiders or dead mice, but he was most certainly the instigator. He was using this poor simpleton to affect these tricks that were becoming more serious now, even dangerous.

As Tuccio reported all the comings and goings of the women, Maddalena realized that the increasing seriousness of his pranks was fueled by Matteo's awareness of his mother's growing friendship with—of all people—his own mother-in-law. It was more than he could tolerate. He had always turned to his mother for support: She had been his advocate with his father, his ultimate salvation when all seemed lost. But now Caterina's presence was about to rob him of even this consolation. To a more rational creature it would seem inevitable that the two lonely widows might be drawn together by the common experience of their recent losses as well as by their love for Prudenza and the children. Instead of being happy for his mother's consolation in her newfound friendship, the knowledge of it drove Matteo to use Tuccio to make Caterina's life so miserable that she would of her own accord leave Florence.

Mindful that she was the cause of this growing tension, Caterina one day announced to Prudenza, "My dear, I believe the time has come that I must return to Ancona."

"But, Mother, why? Why now, especially, when my baby is so soon to be born? And my little boys—they have become so attached to you and will be heartbroken if you leave us."

It was clear to Maddalena that her intervention was needed now. Never one to be thwarted by obstacles, she determined she must prevent Caterina's departure. But how? Surely there must be a way!

Fortunately, as the heavens ordained, all thought of Caterina's departure was abruptly dispelled when wrenching pain awakened Prudenza early on the morning of 26 May, an unmistakable sign that the baby was about to arrive. Not surprisingly Matteo was once again nowhere to be found as Prudenza's labor began. This birth, at least, would occur in happier circumstances. The young mother was surrounded by the three women she loved most and comforted by the gentle ministrations of the now-familiar midwives. Despite the pain, Prudenza felt happy, deeply loved and cared for, which helped make this a relatively easy and swift birth. It was made all the more joyous by the news that this little one was a girl, a beautiful, healthy little girl whose delicate soft fringe of hair was the same unusual color as her mother's. As the baby lay sleeping in her arms, Prudenza recalled Matteo's sudden return to her when he was frightened by the earthquake. Silently she prayed, "Blessed be the earthquake that gave me this precious daughter."

There was general rejoicing of all concerned, save one, as

expected; yet Matteo's absence could not dim the happiness. Indeed, there seemed to be an unspoken understanding that it was better this way. In order to forestall any unpleasantness, Maddalena sent a strongly worded admonition to her son. "I command you; do not dare to speak of another mouth to feed. You must thank God for the gift of this beautiful little daughter."

His only reaction to the admonition, however, was to create a new mantra. "This one will cost me a dowry as well!"

The weeks preceding the baby's christening were filled with preparations, for this must be a suitable celebration effected in the style for which Maddalena Cecchi was well known. This time Prudenza was deemed strong enough to attend, and her little boys would be present to welcome their sister into the family and into the fold of Mother Church.

An all-pervading sense of warmth, of safety, flooded Prudenza's soul as she stood proudly amid the extravagant bank of flowers that Berardo contributed and watched the priest anoint the infant and pour the holy water over her head as he intoned, "I baptize you Coletta Caterina Maddalena Cecchi, in the name of the Father and of the Son and of the Holy Spirit."

Prudenza stepped forward and pinned onto the frothy baptismal robe that literally engulfed the tiny body, a small token painted with violets and ivy. She offered a fervent silent prayer that her precious daughter would possess the qualities of the dear person for whom she was named. "May she be a model of those virtues."

The festive christening provided a welcome distraction from the threat of Caterina's possible departure, one that Maddalena was quick to utilize while searching a solution that would keep Prudenza's mother in Florence. She worked quietly, questioning friends as well as servants—in particular Maria. As a widow with six children to support Maria could never forget the elder *Signora* Cecchi's generosity that allowed her to work so that she might keep her children from the foundling home. As a longtime widow she was aware that Florence was full of widows. It had much to do with the marriage patterns. Husbands were usually much older than wives, hence care of the elderly in the city became primarily a matter of looking out for women.

Maria was aware that in the quarter of Santa Croce, near the little church of San Piero Maggiore and not far from the Cecchi home, there was an institution known as the Orbatello. Her longevity in the household allowed Maria to approach Maddalena to make a suggestion. "It is a home for respectable widows, *Signora,* not a religious institution, but one administered by the state. Certainly *Signora* Beltramonto would qualify. She is more than respectable; she is indeed a virtuous woman."

"I am grateful to you for this knowledge, Maria; but I must know more about the place—what amenities does it offer? I could never recommend such a place to my friend Caterina if it did not meet my own expectations."

"I am told, *Signora,* that it is a safe and pleasant place, well run."

"I will need to know the procedure for application to the Orbatello. I have no experience in this sort of undertaking so I will need help."

"Why do you not ask *Fra* Filippo?"

"A fine idea, Maria. I will send for him immediately. There is no time to lose."

As expected the good friar readily agreed to look into the matter and after only a short time returned to report. It seemed to Maddalena a good sign that he was able to do so so quickly. Surely that must mean good news. As she entered the *sala* however, her spirits flagged a bit at the sight of the old priest's face.

"Please tell me you bring good news, *Fra* Filippo."

"Alas, *Signora* Cecchi, I fear not."

"Why? What has happened? Surely *Signora* Beltramonto is a virtuous woman and she is a widow of advanced age."

"All that is true, but my sources tell me that only a Florentine, or one whose family has paid taxes to the city for twenty-five years is permitted to enter the asylum. Obviously since *Signora* Beltramonto is not from Florence, nor is her family before her, she would be denied entrance."

"But there must be a way. Surely from time to time exceptions are made to rules."

"It may be so, *Signora,* but I do not know that."

"We would not really 'break' any rules, just perhaps interpret them differently. Remind the officials that by her marriage to my son, *Signora* Beltramonto's daughter is now a citizen of Florence. Is there no hope that this might be resolved? It would be such a perfect solution if Prudenza's mother could remain here."

"I have already given the situation much thought, *Signora*, and I believe we may have a very legitimate reason to solicit such an exception—*Signora* Prudenza's condition, the babies, and the fact that her mother would be of such help and consolation in her present state."

The old friar obviously knew something of Matteo's bad behavior, as did much of Florence by this time, but he would not be so indelicate as to speak of it with Maddalena.

"Perhaps if we had someone to represent our case to the authorities…"

"Yes, go on. What are you saying? Can you think of such a person?"

"What would you say of asking *Ser* Ugo da Cristofano? He is a respected notary and a man of some influence."

"Indeed. And a devoted friend of my husband—a wonderful idea *Fra* Filippo! I am quite confident that he would agree and could, if required, draw up a suitable petition to present to the Signoria."

"And he knows my daughter-in-law. In fact he presided over the legalities of the betrothal and the wedding. Oh, *Padre*, please present my plea to *Ser* Ugo immediately and pray that he agrees."

"I will do my best. Legal documents are beyond my poor comprehension, but prayer—now that is another matter!"

"Hurry, *Padre*. The christening is over and Caterina may make plans to depart soon. There is no time to waste."

"I go at once, *Signora*."

"God be with you, *Fra* Filippo. And do bring me good news."

Devoted friend that he was, the old friar went directly to *Ser* Ugo to present Maddalena's request. He was accustomed to a devout life lived strictly by the rules and customs of his order, and so was somewhat surprised at the ready compliance of the notary who assured him that he knew that such exceptions were not unusual.

"Rules can be bent, *Fra* Fiippo. Surely for the family of such an honest, respected man as Zenobi Cecchi there should be no problem."

Ser Ugo was right. Just as predicted, permission was granted and it was agreed that Caterina could be admitted to the Orbatello. Maddalena was thrilled at the news but at the same time was sobered and somewhat embarrassed by the realization that she must now present the idea to Caterina behind whose back she had made these plans. She had to admit that perhaps her motives were not the purest, for she would miss her new friend terribly if she returned to Ancona. This time it was Maddalena who needed help and she knew instinctively where to turn.

"I will enlist Prudenza's help. I know she would want her mother to remain and surely if she pleads with her to stay, Caterina will say yes. She is happy here so close to her daughter and her grandchildren."

Even before *Ser* Ugo returned with the good news Maddalena presented the plan to Prudenza who was delighted and suggested that if her mother could be taken to visit the Orbatello, to see for herself if the place is as desirable as *Fra* Filippo believed it to be, perhaps her mother would agree.

So it was arranged. On the appointed day *Fra* Filippo and *Ser* Ugo accompanied Maddalena and Caterina to the Orbatello to see for themselves. Maddalena watched her friend anxiously to determine her reactions, but Caterina showed no strong inclination one way or the other as they inspected the apartments which Maddalena found to be quite complete and comfortable. It was only when the director of the place introduced the question of children that Caterina's face brightened noticeably. Yes, children and grandchildren of the widows could stay here with their *nonna*—boys up to the age of twelve after which they were apprenticed to a respectable trade. Girls might stay indefinitely—if need be even until they married. Lorenzo and Piero could, of course, come to visit. With that realization Maddalena knew that the plan was a success. Soon *Signora* Beltramonto would become a resident at the Orbatello, which meant that she could come and go freely to the nearby Cecchi home and be with her precious daughter and grandchildren as often as she wished.

They could not wait to share the good news with Prudenza. As the two grandmothers approached her room their hearts were gladdened by a sweet sound that had not been heard in some time.

Ninna nanna, bella bambina
Gioia della sua mamma!

Prudenza was singing again!

CHAPTER 20

Madonna Chimerica

"Are you sure? Are you very sure?" Matteo seized Tuccio by the throat and was mercilessly shaking him much as a terrier would a rat. "If you have deceived me you will most certainly feel the fury of my boot on your lazy arse."

Tuccio seemed not even to hear Matteo's threat, so excited was he to report the fruit of his nefarious work. Springing up and down while literally foaming at the mouth he soldiered on through his report with difficulty, fairly choking on his own spittle as he did so.

"I am sure what I shaw, mashter."

"Master!" Matteo savored the word, rolling it smoothly over his tongue as one might relish a fine wine. "Oh, how I love being called master—even if it is by an idiot. Go on. Tell me again."

"Yesh, I shaw it; I shaw it mashter! She hash left; her mother hash left, dressed for travel. Luca carried her bag to the coach."

Matteo struck the table so hard with his tankard that its contents sent a rosy spray into the atmosphere while, with his free hand, he pumped the air and triumphantly bellowed, "*Benissimo! Finalmente vittoria*. My plan has worked. This is good news." Pushing a rusty cup to the disfigured little wretch he commanded, "Drink. Drink to our success, Tuccio."

There was no way, of course, that in his fastidiousness Matteo would have allowed Tuccio's mouth to befoul his own fine tankard. As the poor creature drained his cup like one dying of thirst, Matteo threw him a small coin and dismissed him with another command. "Now watch my wife and her maid. Go! And leave me to savor my victory. My plan has succeeded: She has left here— that miserable meddling old woman has left." Leaning back in his chair he laughed almost hysterically, loudly proclaiming, "Matteo Cecchi will not be deceived."

It had not escaped the notice of others in the household that Matteo had of late developed a certain fastidiousness in both behavior and dress. It was a daintiness inconsistent with his often loutish behavior, just another of the conflicting aspects of his character. Believing that Caterina had in fact returned to Ancona, he became more relaxed, less cantankerous with his workers and less petulant and quick-tempered with Prudenza than he had been for some time. It was not unlike the period of uneasy calm after he destroyed the lute.

Spying, however, was not exclusively the weapon of Matteo and his pathetic little slave. Without being charged to do so, Gina had taken it upon herself to increase her watchfulness, vigilant lest her kind mistress would be too forgiving of Tuccio's behavior. So from her post at a second floor window overlooking the garden gate she watched daily, noting Matteo's pattern of departure for work and the hour of his return for *pranzo*. His absence from the home allowed for a few carefree golden hours during which Prudenza, her maid, and the two grandmothers could enjoy each other's company. Whether reading, attending to their needlework, relaxing with a game of tric trac or just casually chatting, these times were precious.

When the weather was inclement or the sun simply too hot to remain in the garden these clandestine visits removed to the protection of the *loggia* where one could always count on a good breeze. But more often pleasant sunny days found the women in the garden while Lorenzo and Piero played leapfrog, teased the cat or romped under Gina's watchful eye.

Only a few weeks after Caterina's apparent departure, the women were gathered near the fountain in the garden where Prudenza was singing softly to her baby, swaying to and fro as she cradled little Coletta in her arms. Caterina was bent over her embroidery hoop dealing with a stubborn knot and Maddalena was dozing over the book that had fallen into her lap. From the flowerbed where he was gathering some blossoms Berardo looked on with deep satisfaction at this picture of contentment. As he did so, however, his kindly smile suddenly turned to a look of alarm as the gate flew open and Matteo staggered into the garden, clutching his side and swearing loudly. He was obviously in great pain, his face drawn and pinched and, his mouth strangely contorted.

Prudenza had not seen him enter and was terrified at the sound of his voice spewing forth a volley of profanity, damning the scene he had come upon. Whatever the cause of his obvious physical pain, it was quickly surpassed now by force of his rage, for in one shocking instant he faced the realization that he had indeed been deceived. His mother-in-law had not returned to Ancona as he believed, and to make matters worse his own mother was now a part of this scheme to deceive him. He momentarily forgot the pain in his side as he approached Prudenza with upraised fist and screamed, "What loathsome collection of damnable hens is this that dares to deceive me?"

Despite Berardo's attempt to diffuse the explosive situation before anyone should suffer bodily harm, the shock was so sudden and great that the women were frozen in fear, unable even to attempt to escape. Only the brave little boys rushed to their mother's side in a childish but sincere attempt to protect her, for Lorenzo had not forgotten that earlier assault upon his mother in this place.

Whether it was the stabbing pain in his side, some small long-suppressed remnant of shame, or simply the excessive anger that weakened him—the cause mattered little now—Matteo fell exhausted. For the moment at least he was incapable of doing anyone physical harm. Now prostrate and writhing in agony, with his teeth clenched he could summon only enough strength to snarl at his wife, "You will pay for this, you disobedient woman, you slattern!"

Almost as an after thought he added, "and you, Tuccio, you worm—worse than worm—you took my payments, my protection, and turned on me deliberately. I will kill you! But only after you grovel in the dust at my feet."

Caterina now knew she must, at least for a time, forego these precious visits to her daughter, lest Matteo fulfill his threat. Gina, meanwhile, assumed an almost maternal stance, ready to do battle if need be to defend and protect her mistress and the children.

Maddalena's bewilderment was great. She was torn between maternal instincts and disgust for her son's churlish behavior, which she had now observed with her own eyes. She had to admit, "These are no longer idle words. He means it. I know his wife and even his own children are in grave danger now." Instinctively she invoked the intercession of her beloved saintly husband. "Oh, Zenobi, from your place in paradise I beg you, watch over us, protect us. And in your father's love, heal our son. I fear this is a malady beyond the reach of medicine to cure. God help us!"

Nonetheless, Maddalena consulted the most notable doctors in Florence concerning her son's affliction. As she did so it was increasingly evident to Prudenza that the situation was taking a great toll on her mother-in-law who had once seemed almost invincible.

For Prudenza sleep now came uneasily and only intermittently, as she was besieged by nightmares that caused her to scream in the night, thus awakening herself. In her caring way Gina had begun to sleep in the small bedroom adjacent to Prudenza's where in earlier times Matteo had often collapsed after excessive carousing. More and more frequently now she was awakened to find Prudenza sitting on the edge of her bed trembling, her nightclothes sodden from cold sweat. "It was that dream again, Gina—that same awful dream!"

"Perhaps, *Madama*, it might help to talk about it. What is this dream that so upsets you?"

"I cannot..."

"But, *Madama*, you yourself have often reminded me that when our fears are seen in the light of reason they often disappear much as night phantoms vanish in the sunlight."

"I know, Gina. You may be right. It isn't that I do not trust you but...Oh, you must promise not to tell anyone. Promise?"

"Of course I promise."

"Well, in my dream...no, in my *dreams*—for there are two that keep returning. In the first I see Matteo lying on a pallet, writhing in intense pain, moaning pitifully, calling out for help. I am seated at his side but cannot reach him."

"Go on, *Madama*. Why can you not reach him?"

"I try. Oh, Gina, I do try but he is surrounded by bars that enclose him inside his bed like a cage, and no matter how hard I try to reach through to comfort him, I cannot touch him. I cry out for help. That is when I awaken myself. And now I have awakened you as well. Oh, I am so sorry, Gina!"

By now she was holding her mistress in her arms like a frightened child, rocking gently to and fro. "But *Madama* you say that there is another, a second nightmare."

"Yes. It is terrifying and comes upon me like a flash. It is blood; there is blood all about, nothing but blood. I try to escape it but cannot. I am choking, drowning in a pool of blood."

"Oh, *Madama*, my dear *Madama*. Perhaps it is just the shock of this last outbreak. It may signify nothing more than exhaustion..."

"I fear it is more, Gina. It is a portent."

"If that is the case then we must seek help. There are people who are endowed with the gift of reading dreams."

"Do you mean interpreting the dream or fortelling the future?"

"Perhaps both."

"Oh, Gina, that is fortunetelling and it is forbidden by our religion."

"I know that, but forgive me, *Madama*. I still see no harm in it if it can bring peace of mind to you. You need not act on it. I'm sure that in a city like Florence we can find such a person to explain the meaning of these troubling nightmares."

"Oh, Gina, it frightens me so. You must be careful."

"Trust me, *Madama*. We will find a way."

With the efficiency that Prudenza had come to expect of her maid, Gina returned in just a few days with news. "I have learned that there is in the city a seer who reads dreams so accurately that people come even from far away places to consult her in secret."

"Her? The seer is a woman?"

"Yes. She meets her clients in a modest little retreat just inside the walls of the city, near the blacksmith's shop at the gate of San Frediano."

"I do not like this idea, Gina."

"Don't worry, *Madama*. I am told that she is modest, discreet, and has a good reputation. She is even consulted by priests and doctors seeking direction."

"But how can I do this when I am not permitted to go outside my house. You were there—you heard when my husband forbade me to do so. He even took back the keys he had once given me. Besides, you know that Tuccio watches my every move."

"I have thought of that, too. The answer is simple. You must go in disguise."

"If Matteo should ever discover this I fear he might kill me, and you as well. It would not be so bad for me to die, but it would leave my babies orphans. What would become of them?"

"He will never know." Suddenly standing shoulder to shoulder with Prudenza she announced, "Look *Madama*. We are nearly the same size. I can bring you some of my clothes and no one will suspect it is you dressed like a servant."

"Ah, you make it sound easy, but have you thought of this? Your hair is black as jet and mine is like copper. It will never work."

"You could wear a veil like a widow."

"No. No widow would be out roaming the streets in her mourning attire."

Gina did not give up easily. She appeared to be energized by the challenge of this stratagem as she moved on to a more audacious solution. "Then we will make a hood for you—like the kind that are attached to ladies' mantles. We can fashion one that is so close fitting that it will hide even your abundant curls."

"I do not think so…"

"And if that does not work, I know a way of coloring your hair so that it will be as dark as mine."

"And how do you propose to accomplish that?"

"I do know how, *Signora*, believe me. When I was a little girl my brothers and I often did it to my youngest brother who had unruly blond curls that we dyed in this way when we played at being gypsies. All that is needed is some charcoal and some ashes made from butternut bark. I will pulverize them together and when the mixture is smoothed into the hair around your face—the part that might show under your hood, you will be transformed. You will see."

"It sounds bizarre. Even if that works, Gina, there is the principle of the act itself. Fortunetelling is wrong. It would be a sin."

"Not necessarily!" Gina was becoming a master at the art of casuistry. "Just remember you need not act on what the seer says. There is always the possibility that these dreams are nothing, that they signify only a reaction to the difficulties of these last months. I believe that merely hearing this will relieve you."

She recognized that Prudenza's resistance was wearing down and it was time to play her ace card. "You heard your husband's threat. You owe it to yourself and your babies to seek this help. Besides, have you forgotten that I said even priests, and doctors seek out her understanding of their dreams? Will you agree to do it, *Signora*?"

Too beaten and tired to resist, Prudenza reluctantly nodded in agreement.

"Trust me, *Madama*. Her place, I am told, is secluded, sheltered. If it will make you feel better, I will search out some of the smaller, less traversed streets on the other side of the Arno where we will be inconspicuous in our disguises."

"As you say, Gina."

"We must avoid the commerce near the Ponte Vecchio and cross the river at the Ponte alle Grazie. From there we will take some of the narrow alleys that lead to Piazza Santo Spirito."

Prudenza was dazed, listening only half attentively now as Gina unfolded her plan. "If you wish we can stop in the church there where you can pray for God's blessing. No one will suspect us. From there it is only a short distance to Borgo San Frediano where we will be well concealed in the shadow of the overhanging eves in the narrow street. Just past the church is the seer's place. You see, it is not so difficult."

Over the next few days Gina gradually smuggled into the house the clothing needed to disguise her mistress and went about collecting the ingredients for the crude mixture of dyes for her hair. They agreed to leave on a midweek morning, early enough to avoid Maddalena who would certainly not approve. Nor had Prudenza breathed a word of the plan to her mother.

The transformation of her mistress as a maidservant in a simple cotton dress and mantle, her hair pinned tightly to keep it tamed within the hood, was nearly complete. Finally came the moment to apply the disagreeable mess of powdered dye to the only part of her hair that was visible around her face. As she brushed the ashes into her mistress's hair, inevitably some particles fell on her cheeks and nose, giving her a dirty face. Siezing the opportunity to lighten the situation, Gina held a looking glass up to her mistress and despite the gravity of the situation they burst into laughter at the sight.

Satisfied that the transformation was complete, the two set out, for there was no time to waste. They went quietly and quickly down the stairs and past the kitchen where Nella was kneading the breakfast bread. She gave them a knowing look and traced a discreet sign of the cross on her lips, signifying her pledge of silence, for she had assisted Gina to prepare the ashes and charcoal the night before.

Berardo was busy in his drying shed and did not see the two as they silently passed through the garden gate and out into the street where, if anyone should question them, Gina would say this was her older sister, come to visit.

This was a strangely haunting recapitulation of that earlier escapade when Prudenza had stolen away from home before dawn to seek *Fra* Tommaso's advice. Only now the disguise was more efficient than the old canvas she had childishly improvised. But the stakes were higher, more dangerous to be sure—especially if Matteo should ever learn that she had violated his mandate to keep her locked up in the home.

Much about the route Gina devised brought back myriad memories. They crossed the Ponte alle grazie, the same bridge by which Prudenza first entered Florence as a young bride on her way to meet her in-laws; only this time they were going in the opposite direction. Carrying the market baskets that Nella thoughtfully provided, they passed unnoticed through small alleyways, quickly crossed busy Via Maggiore, and slipped into Piazza Santo Spirito, melding easily into the crowd for it was market day. Vendors were busy setting up their wares while women noisily jostled one another in their quest for the choicest produce. Eager to be done with this disagreeable venture, Prudenza elected to continue on without visiting the church.

Shortly they came to a crude tent-like construction—nothing more than a canvas roof stretched upon wooden poles jutting out from a stone wall behind. Gina announced under her breath, "We are here, *Madama*. This is the seer's place."

"Are you sure, Gina? It is so small, scarcely larger than the *armadio* in my bedroom."

The interior of the place belied the seemingly improvised appearance of the exterior however. It was apparent that the grimy film that covered the walls was the accumulation of years of the same noxious fumes that still filled the tent as they poured from the dimly lit oil lamp. Prudenza shuddered to think of the number of clients who had come here before her seeking the prognostications of this person. But her fears and expectation of something sinister were somewhat abated by the seer's kindly face. She was an ordinary-looking woman seated behind a small table from which she motioned for the two to enter and take a seat.

"Welcome, *Signore*! I am Madonna *chimerica*."

It was obvious to Prudenza at once that this was no name, simply a title describing her profession, a lady visionary! She was relieved to think, "Perhaps it is best to avoid identity—hers as well as mine!"

Before leaving home Prudenza requested that Gina do whatever speaking was necessary. In a cautiously well-rehearsed dialogue Gina, not surprisingly, performed flawlessly in her assumed identity. Prudenza, meanwhile, sat mutely, her eyes downcast, but her ears alert to catch every nuance in the voice of the seer.

Of the vision of Matteo contorted in pain, thrashing about in his cage while his wife sat helplessly on the outside, the *chimerica's* pronouncement was not comforting. Softly and mysteriously she merely said what Prudenza already knew. "You want to free him from his illness, but you will never succeed. You are powerless to do so for he is caught in the grips of a sinister force."

The suggestion of diabolic power sent a horrible chill through Prudenza's body. As if the seer recognized this she was quick to add, "You must realize, however, that you have in no way caused his malady. His affliction comes from a dark humor deep within him."

Passing on to the other terrifying dream the seer reacted even more strangely, becoming still as stone, her eyes wide open but fixed on some far-off object. She spoke slowly as if in a trance, her voice hollow and expressionless, coming from a distant place. The message was enigmatic and not at all comforting. In measured cadence she began a kind of rhythmic incantation. "You cannot staunch the flow of this blood. You cannot staunch this flow of blood. It is not in your power to do so. More serious action is required."

Gina attempted to probe, "What kind of action, *Signora*?"

Only with noticeable reluctance did the seer continue, now speaking in hesitant and fragmented bits that came with extraordinary effort. The words issued from her mouth like a halting and terrifying litany punctuated by long silences between pronouncements: "purging...ministers of dark science...poison...blood letting, Yes, he must be bled to draw out the corrupt matter that poisons his mind and racks his body."

With that she appeared to awaken from her trance and dismissed the women abruptly, refusing even to take payment. They left heavy-hearted, haunted by the seer's words and wondering what she had seen that caused her extreme reaction. Added to this was Prudenza's feeling of guilt as her conscience accused her of the sin she believed she had just committed. The only thing successful about this venture was the fact that they managed to return safely and without their ruse being detected.

Meanwhile in the care of the doctors that his mother summoned, Matteo gradually regained his strength; but Maddalena was troubled that he now spent so much time away from the *botegga*. Fortunately the trusted older workers, who were so well-schooled in their art, carried on production without him, actually grateful that he was out of the way. During these absences, Matteo spent much time watching the progress of the Mercato Nuovo, the New Market near Por Santa Maria. Unlike the nearby Ponte Vecchio where butchers, blacksmiths, and green grocers noisily plied their trade, this new market was intended by Cosimo I for the purchase and sale of luxury goods and for moneychanging.

Matteo managed to beguile himself with the thought that this was finally his opportunity to be accepted into the *Seta,* the silk merchant's guild of the Calimala—that distinguished society of artisans who dealt in foreign goods; mainly textiles sent to Florence for finishing. He was certain that by now, for it was 1547, with the acquisition of the Beltramonto colors and the restoration of the superior quality of the Cecchi silks, his acceptance into this august company was all but certain.

More self-absorbed than ever, he was obsessed with matters of personal appearance and convinced himself that he must be a living advertisement for the Cecchi silks. Even Maddalena, who was not entirely without aspirations to social rank, was embarrassed by his latest obsession, seeing him turned out so foppishly.

"Is this the legacy of the family business that Zenobi so carefully and honestly built? What would he say now at the sight of his son decked out like a strutting peacock? He looks ridiculous, like a *pappagallo* in these brilliant colors."

He even added a cape with a border of miniver suitable for a king or even a pope. To complete this extravagance he now bedewed himself so generously with fragrance of musk that his mere presence infected the atmosphere around him.

His obvious ambitions and aspirations were dashed when admittance to the Calimala was denied him. All of his posturing could not dispel the reputation he had earned, for Florence was not so large that his treatment of his workers and even of his family could be concealed. Matteo Cecchi had by his own bad behavior excluded himself from the Calimala.

CHAPTER 21

The Cautery

The punishing August sun so completely dried the Arno that the rocks lining its bed lay exposed like parched fossils from another era, creating steppingstones. One could conceivably cross the river without fear of getting wet. The city was eerily quiet while inside their shuttered houses Florentines remained captive, awaiting the relief brought by sundown. For the Cecchi family the confinement became almost intolerable as the entire household braced for yet another outbreak of violence. Strangely none came, at least for a time. Matteo locked himself away in another part of the house where soon enough his ranting began. He could be heard at any time of the day or night as he hurled invectives at real or imagined adversaries within hearing. Soon passersby who ventured out in the evening paused to listen, and it was whispered about that a madman was imprisoned in the Cecchi house.

The women sought each other's support and seemed to draw strength from the hours spent together. The only blight on this otherwise steadfast sisterhood was Maddalena's occasional absence from their company. Although none would speak of it, it was apparent that the situation took an enormous toll on her. As the gossip spread so did Maddalena's spirit ebb away.

According to Nella, Matteo refused to eat. He touched none of the food she sent by way of Tuccio who, it was quite obvious, had filched the food for himself, for the remnants were clearly visible on his grimy shirt.

Prudenza could no longer stand by and do nothing while

her husband seemed to be willing his own death by starvation. So against the advice of her mother and Gina, she approached his retreat and, while standing outside his door, attempted to reason with him. Reasoning soon grew to pleading as she tried to make him consider the consequences of his behavior for the well-being of his family. After days of her pleading, his ranting began to subside and at last she heard a raspy sound from within as he attempted to raise the bar that reinforced his door. A scraping, grinding sound mingled with his groans as he struggled to heave the heavy beam from its slot. From the other side Prudenza considered, Should I try to help? Perhaps push the door from this side? She trembled at the possibility of the physical violence that might result.

Her fear dissolved into shock as the door finally opened and she was nearly overcome by the stench that issued from inside the room, the rank and fetid odor of accumulated vomit and urine. Before her stood a shadow of a man, still wearing the same fine garments in which he had postured and paraded himself, but now soiled, torn and hanging slack on his emaciated frame. It was clear to Prudenza that his self-inflicted starvation and the ceaseless screaming brought on by the disappointment of failure to be admitted to the Calimala had taken an alarming toll on both his mind and body. She could only wonder if this was the same proud and fastidious man who has always placed such importance on his appearance.

Any feeling of fear, hurt, or anger on her part was in an instant swept away by another overwhelming emotion. Not love surely, only pity! She wept as in the dim light from within the filthy room she took stock of the pathetic scene. His once-muscular frame now looked withered. He was slumped and stoop-shouldered, making the hated curvature of his spine more noticeable than ever. What flesh he still had hung flaccid, slack on his bent frame. From his jaundiced, hollow-cheeked face now framed with unkempt, matted hair, the eyes that looked out at her were vacant, giving him a spectral look that was terrifying. Within a few moments he collapsed and lay before her in his own feces.

She was sickened at the sight and hurriedly left to call for Berardo who, with the help of another manservant, washed Matteo, clothed him with clean linens and moved him to a room near Prudenza's where he lay pale and whimpering, white as the sheets of his bed. Against the advice of all in the household Prudenza took up her post at Matteo's side and announced her determination to nurse her husband back to health as a dutiful wife should. For this she would employ all the skills of her faithful gardener's catalogue of curatives.

Most of all she prayed—a feverish, distracted sort of prayer. While she struggled to forgive Matteo his past offences, at the same time she begged God to restore her husband's health. She invoked the two fathers who had been such devoted friends and support to her and she thought more and more of Nonna Costanza. Surely from paradise they must look with pity upon this tragedy.

—✺—

Over the ensuing weeks, Maddalena continued to fade from the scene, which meant that Prudenza's support system was now reduced to just her mother and her maidservant. While they attempted to comfort and support her, they also advised her—for her own sake and that of her children—to give up her efforts to heal Matteo, for indeed it seemed hopeless. Caterina argued, "He had such unrealistic aspirations, my dear. Remember it is said, 'The higher one seeks to climb, the farther he may fall.'"

Gina, on the other hand, expressed similar thoughts but in homely words of the proverb, "*Chi piscia contro il vento, si lava la camicia.*" (Who pisses against the wind washes his own shirt.)

"Gina!" Prudenza was momentarily shocked at such a crude pronouncement from her maid.

"Forgive me, *Madama*; but it is true. I cannot feel sorry for him, for he has brought it on himself."

"Mother, you must know that Gina was brought up with a gaggle of rowdy brothers. Please excuse her."

Although Caterina crossed herself unobtrusively and uttered a quiet, "*Santa Madre di Dio*," Gina, that acute observer of human nature, could not fail to notice the upturned corners of *Signora* Beltramonto's mouth. It suggested that she undoubtedly subscribed to the same sentiment—albeit in more dignified language.

—〰—

Despite all their admonitions Prudenza persisted in her bedside vigil, growing visibly more thin and pale by the day. Out of concern for her mistress, Gina brought to her some of her books, hoping to ease the tedium of her self-imposed routine. Day after day Matteo continued to turn and toss restlessly on his pallet as if in extreme pain. Whether real or imaginary, Prudenza could not be sure, but it mattered little. She attempted to quiet him with doses of laudanum and other sedatives, which he sometimes refused to take.

"Get away from me! Go away."

"Please, Matteo, take it. You will feel better."

"No. Go away." With that he struck her arm, spilling the medicine on himself, and began cursing again—signifying that he was gradually regaining strength. With it, however, came ever stronger, dreaded reactions. "I know you hate me! Admit it!"

"No, Matteo, I do not hate you." Though to herself she thought, I hate what you have done to our family, but I do not hate you.

There was no point now in argument, for it would only precipitate more abuse. Reluctantly Prudenza recognized that although there were no physical bars around his body as she had seen in her dream, there was an invisible obstruction, an impediment just as real. The nightmare had come true. She tried to distract herself with the books Gina brought her but found herself obsessively returning again and again to the story of Paolo and Francesca. She could relate to their sad tale now more than ever.

There was little time now to spend with the children. More than anything she was grateful for the calm presence of her mother and the loving ministrations of her maid with whom she knew that Lorenzo, Piero, and little Coletta were safe and secure. She took comfort in the realization that the only good thing about Matteo's state is that, with him out of the way, her mother could come and go freely.

For Caterina the situation was doubly painful as she observed her daughter's plight and at the same time witnessed Maddalena's deterioration, which grew more complete by the day.

She sometimes sat for hours, withdrawn and silent, now and then breaking her silence with incoherent babbling. It was almost as if the illness that afflicted her son had now invaded her mind as well.

With so much time on her hands now, Prudenza's thoughts returned again and again to the *chimerica's* predictions. No matter how much she tried to silence those pronouncements, the seer's words kept coming back like a persistent drumming in her brain. "Purging…corrupt matter…dark humor…You cannot help him. There is a dark spirit within…" Finally she could no longer resist the realization that he must be bled. In her anxiety she called out, "Gina, Gina. Please come. I need you." Her cry was even more distressed than when she awakened from the night terrors.

Without hesitation Gina opened the door to Matteo's room, which up to this time she had not been permitted to enter, and rushed to the side of her mistress. "I am here for you, *Madama*. What is it? What can I do for you? Tell me."

"You must call a doctor, Gina. Please hurry."

"At once, *Signora*." And the maid was off.

Gina realized it was a difficult decision for Prudenza, knowing how much she feared that the physician would advise bleeding, and how violently Matteo would undoubtedly react. For her the very concept of bloodletting was irretrievably associated with the *chimerica* and was nothing short of voodoo medicine. She was vaguely aware of the relationship of astrology and medicine, but avoided learning more since, like necromancy—in which she had already dabbled—it, too, was forbidden by the church. She made feeble attempts to silence her delicate conscience with the thought that she might be refusing him the treatment that could cure him or at least bring some relief to his spirit. How can I refuse him?

Gina returned with the doctor who came with several assistants in tow and presented them to Prudenza who had been awaiting them in the great room. She recognized the chief physician by his ostentatious garb of red silk. He was Benedetto Maiano who had also attended Zenobi in his last illness. Educated at the great university of Padua he was well-known and respected in Florence. Perhaps he could help.

"*Dottore*, I thank you for coming so promptly; I pray you can bring physical relief and some spiritual solace to my good husband."

"We will do our utmost, honorable lady."

"Then let us proceed." With that she led them up the stairs to Matteo's room where Tuccio had sneaked in during Prudenza's brief absence. At the sight of the doctor he scampered away as swiftly as his twisted legs allowed.

Matteo lay bleary-eyed and quiet, his body splayed on the bed, still under the blessed influence of the laudanum that Prudenza had administered. As they entered the room the doctor and his three assistants took positions around the bed, looking very grave as they did so. The doctor asked Prudenza to leave the room—for which she was, despite her anxiety, most grateful.

For the most part the diagnosis was made on the basis of observation, for which the doctors took what seemed to her an extraordinary amount of time. After an interminable wait Matteo began to curse and scream, indicating that he was awakening from his drugged stupor. Although she was embarrassed by it, Prudenza was at the same time grateful, for now the doctors would see him as he really is.

Finally the physicians emerged from the room and the grim-faced Maiano announced what Prudenza most feared. "He must be bled, *Signora*. It is the only way that the dark humor will leave his body."

"*O, Dio mio*! I feared this."

"There is nothing to fear, *Signora*, and everything to hope for."

"If you say so, *Dottore*. (Oh, God, where is Gina? Where is my mother? I need you.)"

The doctor continued. "There is one thing I must ask you, *Signora*."

"What is that?"

"Although it is a science, this is a treatment that should only be undertaken at an auspicious time."

"What do you mean? How can you know when the time is right? He is sick. He needs help right now!" She did not like Maiano's posturing as he launched into a discourse intended to educate her in the basics of cautery. She was already aware, without the help of science, that Matteo's illness was of the mind. As she turned all this over in her head she bit her tongue and politely listened to the doctor pontificate, seemingly impressed with his own erudition.

"We must determine the seat of the illness and its duration. But I sense, my good lady, that you are uneasy with this procedure. I assure you that your husband's condition will improve with this treatment, but we cannot proceed until we know the critical days of the month when the planets affect the crises in human illness. For this we must draw up his astrological chart. There are things that I must ask you."

Oh, dear God! What am I to do? It seemed clear enough to her what the problem was, so why dabble in the occult? The doctor's patience was being tried as she stood silently for what seemed to him an intolerably long time while she turned the situation over again and again in her mind. I am but a simple girl from Ancona who, to be sure, possesses some modest knowledge of herbal medicine, but I dare not argue with this learned man. God forgive me, I have no choice. Finally she addressed the doctor, "This auspicious time, as you say. How will you determine that?"

"For that we will need your help for we must know the year of *Signore* Cecchi's birth, the date of his conception, the time of day of his birth. We will study the confluence of the planets, the phase of the moon, and consult the chronicles to learn of any significant events on that day. Only then can we decide how to proceed."

"*Dio mio*! I know only that he was born in the year 1503. I know neither the day of the week nor the time of his conception. Only his mother could tell you that."

"Ah, of course, *Signora*, the Lady Maddalena will know. We must speak to her."

"But..."

"Yes?"

"She...she is not quite herself. You know—worry over her son. It has distracted her, left her..."

"Please, *Signora*, you must realize how important it is that we speak to her or we cannot proceed with the treatment."

"As you say, sir, but I beg you, be gentle with her. She has suffered so."

"Of course."

"Please follow me then."

The door of Maddalena's room stood partially ajar and before entering Prudenza paused and called softly, "My good mother, I bring you guests. May we come in?"

"Guests at this hour! Who can it be?"

"You will see. Your old friend, Father Zenobi's physician, *Dottore* Maiano."

"*O, Dottore, s'accomodi.*" Her face brightened, indicating some recognition. Then turning to her daughter-in-law she ordered, "Please, Prudenza, send for some wine for our guests." It seemed a remnant of the ever proper and hospitable hostess Maddalena had always been. Prudenza breathed a sigh of relief. So far, at least, Maddalena was behaving more or less naturally.

With the niceties attended to in a babble of benign pleasantries, Prudenza decanted the *vin santo* and held her breath as the doctor began his interrogation. As he did so his first assistant stood poised with pen and paper, the second held a large and impressive tome whose beautiful binding showed signs of much wear, and the third merely stood gaping and wide-eyed like a curious child.

"*Signora* Cecchi, we have just come from visiting your son."

"Oh, yes, Matteo. How very kind of you."

"Not at all, *Signora*."

"And how do you find my good boy?"

"He is, I fear, a very sick young man, *Signora*."

"Oh, he will be fine, I know."

"He will of course, if we can attend to him properly."

"Then you must do that."

It was clear to Prudenza that she was beginning to fade as she began absentmindedly to toy with the lavaliere that hung from her neck. Lifting it for the doctor to view she exclaimed in a thin, reedy little voice, "You know Zenobi gave me this when we were married."

"How lovely."

"Zenobi will be sorry he missed you. He has gone to Prato on business, you know."

Fearing that things were about to fall apart, Prudenza interjected, "Mother, the doctor would like to ask you some questions. Do you feel well enough to speak with him?"

"Well? Of course I am well. What is it you want to know, *dottore*?"

"*Signora* Cecchi, do you remember when your son Matteo

was born?"

"What a foolish question! Of course, I remember."

"Then can you tell us when it was?"

"When?"

It was as if that word sent her careening far into the past, to a happier time. Her eyes glazed over and she began rocking, singing, as one would to a baby—at first softly, but then in full voice. At the same time she began raising and lowering her knee rhythmically as if bouncing a baby upon it. Prudenza had often heard her sing this little ditty to Lorenzo and Piero when they were babies.

> *La mia nonna é vecchiarella*
> *Mi fa ciao, mi dice ciao,*
> *Mi fa ciao, ciao, ciao.*

Obviously with the question about his birth she had regressed with ease into a time of innocence long past. *Dottore* Maiano attempted to cover his alarm while his first assistant scrambled to write something in his book. In an effort to spare her mother-in-law and hasten the end of this agonizing ordeal, Prudenza intervened. "Mother, the doctor would like to know exactly when Matteo was born."

"Yes, *Signora* Cecchi. Can you remember?"

"Of course I can remember." With that she broke into song again, even more lustily than before. "*Mia nonna é vecchiarella, ciao ciao. . .*"

"Your daughter-in-law tells me that he was born near the beginning of this century, perhaps in the third year. Is that correct?"

"Yes, that is correct. Prudenza would never lie to you."

"I'm sure she would not. Then you concur that Matteo was born in 1503. Can you tell me in what month?"

"*Ciao, ciao, mi fa ciao...*"

"Mother, do you remember in what month?"

"That is easy. All eights! All eights! It was the eighteenth day of the eighth month of the year and at eight o'clock."

"Ah! That means he was born under the sign of Leo." With a signal from the doctor the assistant clutching the book began frantically leafing to find that date in the chronicle. Was it an auspicious or a portentous day? Running his finger down the page he stopped abruptly and blanched noticeably.

"Tell me, what does the chronicle record on the eighteenth day of August in 1503?"

"It is…"

"Yes? Go on." the doctor was growing weary of this business.

"It is, I fear, a portent. Perhaps best to speak of it in private, *dottore*."

Realizing that Maddalena was in no condition to understand it anyway the doctor insisted. Prudenza steeled herself, her spine straight and her jaw set, dreading to hear what the chronicle contained for that day. The doctor was losing patience and commanded sternly, "Read!"

"On this day, in Rome, Pope Alexander VI Borgia died."

"*O Dio!*" This time even the doctor's voice quivered.

Prudenza had not heard of the Borgia Pope who, according to *Dottore* Maiano, was said to be "the very devil in the papal tiara! Two mistresses, and nine children!"

Prudenza was shocked and, but for the sake of her mother-in-law, would gladly have bolted from the room. She tried to close her ears as the young man read on. "The Pope died of the tertian fever, the scourge of Rome in the heat of August. His body quickly decayed, his face turned the color of mulberry, his lips swollen to grotesque proportions, his tongue…"

"That is enough. God help us. Our work is cut out for us. It was an evil day on which to be born."

None of this had registered with Maddalena who continued to smile benignly as she again began bouncing the imaginary baby on her knee. Prudenza was almost grateful for her mother-in-law's deranged state. She was pitiful but in her own little world she seemed content—even happy. "I almost envy her!"

Dottore Maiano was ominously sober-faced as he took his leave and announced, "It is serious, *Signora* Prudenza, very serious. Your husband must be bled, but first we must determine from which vein to draw the blood, and whether it should be by incision or by leeches. When we have studied his chart and his condition more thoroughly we will return in a few days.

"In the meantime you must take care of yourself, too. Your

mother-in-law needs you now more than ever, and you are looking very pale. You must be extremely tired from your vigil. It is useless for you to remain by his side at all hours. Your being there has not caused your husband to improve one bit. You would do better to take care of yourself now. Think of your children, your mother, and the elder *Signora* Cecchi."

"Thank you."

As the doors closed after him Prudenza stood alone, facing the realization that Matteo must be told of the doctor's return to treat him. She thought it best to wait until the last moment and perhaps to administer some drug in hope of making him more compliant.

The days of waiting while the doctors consulted tomes of astrological readings and poured over pharmaceutical theories seemed endless until finally *Dottore* Maiano and his apprentices returned, bearing with them the dreaded instruments of their profession. This time Caterina was at her daughter's side while Gina tended the children, careful to keep them out of earshot of the anticipated outcries that were bound to come from Matteo's room.

Despite his rather ostentatious dress the good doctor assumed a gentler demeanor as he explained the procedure to Prudenza. "First we must apply a cautery to the skin in order to direct the bad humors in his body to a specific place, the better to treat them, to draw them out."

"And what is this thing…this cautery, as you call it?"

"It is called *cantarella*—known also as the Spanish fly. In exceedingly minute doses it can be used as an aphrodisiac. We will create a slightly stronger, yet still very weak, dosage that we will then apply to the skin over the diseased part of his body as a blistering agent."

"But it will hurt then, will it not?"

"Yes, *Signora*. But it is necessary. The pain will be minor compared to the sickness that now holds him in its grip. Some discomforts of medical treatment are inevitable, but we must recognize that they are, in the end, beneficial."

Hoping for support from her mother, she objected, "It will only bring on another severe outbreak that may be worse than the others."

"We do not know that, my dear. I fear we must trust the

physicians." Then turning to Maiano, "*Dottore,* I do not think my daughter should watch this procedure."

"You are very wise, *Madama.* It would be best for you both to wait outside."

As the doors closed, shutting the women out in the anteroom, the first sound to be heard was that of objects being dashed against the walls, accompanied by a fusillade of curses mingled with the sound of shattered glass. In reality it required only a moment before the commotion subsided, for the three well-trained assistants quickly restrained Matteo while *Dottore* Maiano prepared the cautery.

After much study he had determined that if Maddalena's recollection was correct, and Matteo had been born in mid-August, his astrological sign was Leo, and Leo governed the heart. Since medical practice decreed that the cautery should be applied over the afflicted organ the doctor exposed Matteo's chest and applied the *cantarella*.

The brief quiet was shattered by bloodcurdling screams and wails from inside the room—exactly the reaction Prudenza had feared. The pain must have been horrific, for it sent the medical team from the room like a volley. Although they struggled to maintain some remnant of dignity, no mask of propriety could possibly cover the shame of their failure.

"*Signora* Prudenza, we will return in two days when we have had time to evaluate the success of our treatment."

"Success? You call that success?"

"It will subside, *Madama.*"

Prudenza's thoughts were less forgiving. "You cover yourself, but in the meantime you leave us to suffer the effects of this so-called cure. I beg you, sirs, please do not continue this treatment. Just allow us to carry on our humble ministrations."

"But there is another possibility, another approach. Please, *Signora* Beltramonto, try to convince your daughter to allow us to try again."

"Perhaps it is wise to follow the doctor's suggestion, Prudenza, to let the remedy take its course."

"I cannot bear it, Mother."

"Gina and I will be at your side, and you know Berardo will stand ready to assist with every nostrum known to him."

"I am too weary to argue. Very well, Mother, but just one more time."

Precisely at the pealing of the morning angelus two days later the doctor and his apprentices arrived, this time carefully guarding a vessel tucked inside a wicker basket. Prudenza wondered what strange object this could be, but Caterina suspected: Leeches! In her daughter's fragile condition she realized it was best not to tell her. "Come, Prudenza, I think we should wait here in the antechamber."

The room was sparsely furnished, just a few chairs and one large credenza. Its polished marble top was crowded with an array of bottles, decanters, jars, and vases containing the tinctures, and powders intended to bring some relief to Matteo. Prudenza restlessly paced the length of the room, pausing only now and then at the window to see if the children were in the garden. The sight of them there with Gina and Berardo brought some comfort.

Inside the sickroom the apprentices quickly went to work applying the stronger restraints that they had provided this time, while *Dottore* Maiano went about the dreaded business of the leeches. Surprisingly there was no verbal outcry this time. Matteo lay still—not serene but petrified—almost catatonic. With dilated pupils he anxiously followed the doctor's movements as one by one he removed the slimy wriggling worms from the receptacle where they had been guarded as carefully as if they were precious jewels. He arranged them meticulously on Matteo's chest which was still nearly raw from the cautery. This time his entire body convulsed and shivered uncontrollably as the disgusting muck from leeches left a cold slimy tracery outlining ribs now so prominent after his self-inflicted starvation.

Gradually the leeches began their work, and as he felt the tightening, the drawing sensation his revulsion grew so great that his back arched and in a sudden surge of almost superhuman force he broke the restraints. He tore the leeches from his chest, and threw the doctor and his assistants to the floor amid a welter of medical instruments, broken restraints, strange surgical utensils, and the hated leeches—now plying their way through the mangled remnants.

Before the stunned physician could react, Matteo threw open the door and burst into the room where Prudenza and her mother were anxiously pacing the floor. He seized Prudenza by the arm and, pitching his entire weight against her, threw her against the credenza, sending pills, liquids, crystals, and shards of shattered glass on the floor. The blow had been so unexpected and came with such force that the pointed corner of the marble credenza struck Prudenza sharply in the abdomen, sending her crying in pain as she lay in a heap on the floor clutching her belly. "My baby! Oh, God, my baby."

Up to now she had told no one but her mother and Gina of her pregnancy.

With the sudden rush of something warm and wet she knew that the baby had been expelled from her body as she lay helplessly in a pool of blood. Just as suddenly she realized, "Oh, God, it is the other nightmare! It is MY blood, not my husband's."

Caterina rushed to her side, lifted her sodden skirt and gasped at the sight of the tiny, but fully formed fetus—just barely alive. As she gathered up the pitiful trembling creature the pulsating blue veins visible under the baby's transparent skin were the only hopeful sign of life.

"Dear God grant that we may save the baby."

"Mother, please baptize the baby."

As Caterina examined the fragile little body more closely she exclaimed, "Prudenza. It is a girl!"

"A girl! Mother, I would that you baptize her Francesca, dear unfortunate Francesca. My poor, untimely born babe, Francesca."

Dipping her hand into a pitcher of water that stood on a nearby table, Caterina sprinkled the infant's head, and as she uttered the familiar words of Baptism, the baby made a feeble cry. At the same moment Prudenza lost consciousness.

Caterina at once instructed Gina to fetch the midwives who came quickly to minister to Prudenza and the baby and to find a wet nurse. There was no time now to recall Lucia from Prato, and Maddalena was in no condition manage things.

As she gradually awoke from unconsciousness Prudenza whispered, "If my baby dies, my husband is a murderer!"

CHAPTER 22

I Corinthians 7:39

It was an altogether pitiful sight—the tiny babe swathed in robes fashioned by the grandmother who now watched anxiously beside the cradle made by the grandfather the baby would never know. Little Francesca labored visibly for each breath, her life suspended in a fragile balance while in the adjoining room the young mother struggled with a tangle of emotions: guilt, anger, fear, and love.

As the midwives shuttled back and forth between mother and child their exchanges were guarded. Their reports to Caterina given in hushed voices lest Prudenza should hear, and their responses to Prudenza's inquiries were suspiciously evasive.

Once again an uneasy quiet descended over the household. Closeted away in his quarters Matteo, utterly spent from this last outburst, was unaware of this latest addition to his family. In yet another part of the house Maddalena sat blissfully detached from the human drama that was so painfully being played out all around. Prudenza could only be grateful that in her blessed state Maddalena was spared the sight of her son's collapse and the possible undoing of the Cecchi dynasty. Meanwhile the servants went about their tasks in a respectful silence, and those closest to Prudenza sought every means to ease the situation.

Though her body gradually gained strength, Prudenza's mind was growing increasingly troubled. She was convinced that Matteo's condition and the untimely birth of her baby were her fault. "God is punishing me for having consulted the occult, and now, because I have concealed my sinful activities from my dear mother, I am therefore deprived of her comfort and good counsel as well."

She could confide these thoughts only to Gina whose estimation of Matteo Cecchi had long since plummeted to a depth that propriety forbade her to express to her mistress. As her opinion of him declined so did her determination to support Prudenza increase.

After anxious weeks of watching, praying and nursing, one bright October morning the midwives entered her room with cheerful faces and no longer spoke in whispers. "*Signora* Cecchi, we are happy to report that baby Francesca is now breathing easily and is nursing hungrily. We believe she is out of danger. The crisis has passed and she will live."

"Oh, thank God! Thank you for caring for her so faithfully. Please, please bring her to me now. Let me hold her. I long to see my baby."

She noted a troubled look on the faces of all. Finally Anna, the older midwife who had attended Prudenza in her three previous births, broke the awkward silence. "*Signora*, there is one problem."

"Problem? What is that? Tell me…" she was becoming agitated and insisted. "Please do not keep anything from me."

"Your baby will live, but…"

"But what?"

"But, the injury. When your abdomen was struck so sharply the blow fell on the baby's back and resulted in a deep bruise—an injury to her spine. As a result her little legs are paralyzed, and she will probably never walk."

"*O Dio*! It is my fault."

"No, *Signora*, you must not think that. There was nothing you could do." As the midwives left to fetch the baby Gina intervened. "You simply must not blame yourself for your husband's behavior."

"But I…"

"Alas, *Madama*. Please listen to me. Although I do not have your delicate conscience I think I understand that only the consolation of the faith in which you have been so strictly brought up can relieve your mind now."

"I know you are right, Gina."

"I promise you that when you feel well enough I will see you to church where I believe you will find peace."

"Oh yes, please. I must seek absolution."

"We can go to Santa Croce."

"No! I...I might be recognized. Remember, my father-in-law had such close ties there. We often went together to study the paintings. I was married there and he is buried there now. It would bring back a multitude of memories—both happy and sad."

"Very well, then, what about San Marco? It is farther away but I think no one would know you there."

"Must we go in disguise as we did when we consulted the seer?"

"Certainly not. There is no shame in visiting a church, and your husband is so ill that he will not even be aware that we have left the house."

"True, but there is Tuccio. Remember?"

"Well, you could wear a veil if it makes you feel more secure."

"Yes, a veil. When may we go?"

"Perhaps as soon as tomorrow if you feel well enough."

"Yes, yes. I am eager."

Just as Gina was departing, Anna entered the room with the baby in her arms and noted, "I do believe that I detect a bit of color in your cheeks, *Signora*."

When Gina came early the next morning to do her usual ministrations she found Prudenza already awake, completely dressed and ready to go. "Do you think we should take some small, less-traveled streets?"

"No, *Madama*. Forgive me, but I must disagree. You need not go like a criminal, like a thief in the night." It was a measure of Prudenza's growing confidence in her maid that she did not argue the point. "Very well, then let us go now, quickly."

For Prudenza the trip was like an abridged account of her life since coming to Florence—but in reverse, reliving so many varied experiences. They were all fraught with memories, some joyful, others painful reminders of the steps along the course of Matteo's collapse. "I should have recognized the signs along the way."

Although Gina managed to distract her mistress with innocuous but cheery conversation, after a time it was clear that Prudenza had lapsed into serious preoccupation with the business at hand and preferred to remain quiet. When finally the unadorned façade of the church came into view Gina announced, "We are here, *Madama*."

For a moment Prudenza hesitated, as if unable to cross the threshold.

"*Coraggio, Madama*. Come, soon all will be well."

A few tentative steps and they were inside the church where the musty coolness and the residue of incense and candle smoke conjured a comforting sense of permanence, of constancy. It was comforting even to Gina who slipped unobtrusively into a pew near the rear door. She watched anxiously as Prudenza walked slowly but resolutely to the second altar on the right as if drawn by some invisible magnet. There she sank to her knees before the image of the Madonna, and buried her head in her hands for a long time.

Gina surprised herself at the ease with which she, too, found herself uttering a prayer. "Holy Mother, please, I beg you, comfort my mistress. Though I am far from pious, I beg you to hear her prayer, to look upon her purity and let her find peace."

After a long time, Prudenza rose, rang the little bell that indicated someone desiring to confess and approached the confessional box where she knelt on the penitent's side awaiting the arrival of the confessor. A thick curtain separated her from the white-garbed friar who answered the summons. Grateful for the anonymity she began: "Father, I come bowed with guilt. I fear I am unworthy of forgiveness..."

The voice from the other side interrupted, "Stop. Stop, *Signora*! You offend almighty God if you do not trust in His infinite mercy."

With that she began to sob. Again came the reassuring voice. "Calm yourself now, *Signora*. Tell me simply what it is for which you seek absolution. Bring your burden to your savior."

As he spoke a strange and indefinable calm seemed to permeate her whole being, causing her to pause and consider how this disembodied voice from the other side could bring such comfort, like a balm on her spirit. Gradually the sobbing ceased. Again came the voice. "Be calm. Be at peace my child."

"My child..." Even though the priest continued to speak Prudenza heard nothing more, but continued to replay in her mind the words, "My child, my child."

She was mystified, momentarily struck dumb and embarrassed, too, that she could find no words to respond. From her post in the rear of the church, Gina shifted uneasily, wondering what was happening.

From behind the curtain the voice continued, "God is forgiving, my child." Again there it was, that refrain, "My child."

It was like a voice from the past, the ghost of a voice she had never expected to hear again. "Only two people addressed me this way, my father and…No, it cannot be. Have my emotions so clouded my memory that I should imagine this?"

Again she heard a voice, but this time it was her own, though she hardly recognized it for it was the tiny voice of a frightened child. "Father, could it be that you are from Ancona?"

"No. I am not from Ancona but I did live there for many years."

"Are you…Could it be that your name is Tommaso?"

He was patient with her. "Yes, it could be. Indeed my name is Tommaso and I have come from Ancona to Florence where I was born. It is not so unusual, for I am a Dominican priest and I have come to work here at San Marco where I live with my Dominican brothers. My ministry is here in Florence now. But how is it that you ask me these things?"

"Father, in Ancona did you know the Beltramonto family?"

"Yes. Yes, I knew the family well."

"There was a daughter."

"Yes, her name was…"

"Prudenza!…*Fra* Tommaso, I am that Prudenza—no longer Beltramonto—but Cecchi, the wife of Matteo Cecchi."

It was now his turn to be silent. As she waited, terrified that she might have overstepped the bounds of propriety with her questions, she could almost hear her heart pounding within her.

Finally he spoke again, "Prudenza, my child, what has brought you to this troubled state?"

His question effectively broke the dam that had so long held back all the pain of her husband's abuse and her exaggerated perception of her own guilt. At last she was able to unburden her anguished soul. Slowly she recounted the events since she had last seen him standing on the quay in Ancona, his hand raised in benediction as the boat carrying her away to Rimini made out to sea and his figure grew smaller and smaller, eventually fading from sight entirely.

Recounting the jumbled narrative of her life history brought blessed relief to her soul, but her peace was short lived as she asked herself, "What will he think of me now? I am no longer the innocent who once matched rhymes with him."

Almost as if he read her mind he called out in that familiar old manner that recalled their wordplay of years ago in the days of San Salvatore. "Prudenza, Remember our contests? *Nocciolo.*" Like a reflex she responded *roccolo*, but was immediately embarrassed, for it was not a perfect rhyme. Typically his word, meaning "two intimate friends—like twin souls," was a gentle affirmation, validation of his continued concern and affection for her. But hers was faulty, *Roccolo* a trap, a snare. Both seemed to recognize it for what it was, an appropriate commentary on her life since leaving Ancona. There was about it an aspect of dark humor and, despite the gravity of the situation, both laughed aloud at the ironic appropriateness of it.

From where she stood, Gina could not have heard the exchange at the confessional but she heard the laughing and gasped as she saw the priest pull aside the drape.

"*Gran Dio*, what is happening?" She could not possibly have comprehended what passed in the silence as the steady, comforting eyes of the priest met those of the penitent, still reddened from weeping. Unabashedly they stared at each other, apparently making no excuses for the obvious fact that each was assessing the changes wrought in the other by the passing years. Not even the touches of gray at his temples could dull the joyful truth that this was indeed her old friend *Fra* Tommaso.

"Prudenza, for what you have told me of your sufferings, I am truly sorry. But I urge you to take comfort in the thought that sometimes we can only suffer the growth of those we love. You have tried to do that, tried heroically."

"Tried, yes. I believe I have tried, Father, but I cannot say that I have ever really loved him. Nor do I think he ever loved me."

"Nonetheless, continue your efforts. Go in peace in the knowledge that you have tried and, if you have failed at times, you are forgiven. Pray for guidance and return to me when you need counsel. I will always be here for you."

As the two women retraced their steps to *casa* Cecchi, Prudenza was silent. It was not a troubled silence as before, but a peaceful, tranquil one that even Gina dared not break. What she had just witnessed was sacred, and some things are simply too precious to talk about.

Revitalized by the experience, Prudenza resumed her self-imposed vigil at her husband's bedside, no matter how difficult. This was not the result that Gina had hoped for. Nevertheless she held her tongue as she watched her mistress administer the poultices and various remedies that Berardo tirelessly created—all to no avail. Matteo's condition only grew more serious.

Finally the kind old gardener suggested, "*Signora*, I fear that your husband's illness is beyond my power to cure."

She recognized that this admission must be truly difficult for the old man. "Berardo, you have always been here for me with your knowledge, and above all your friendship and…"

"*Signora*, forgive me for interrupting, but there is one remedy left that may hold the key to his cure."

"Pray, tell me, Berardo, what might that be?"

"Theriac, *Signora*."

"Theriac. I do not know that drug."

"No. It is not one drug, it is a compound of many drugs; far more than I have here in my modest garden."

"That many!"

"Yes, as many as sixty or more."

"*O, Dio*! Where could we possibly find such a thing? We must try."

"There is, I believe, a *speziale* across the Arno, in Via della Chiesa, who might be able to provide the necessary ingredients. They must be ground, pulverized into a fine powder that can be made palatable by mixing it with something sweet, like syrup. They say the theriac originated in Venice—some influence from the East, I suspect. It would please me greatly, *Madama,* if I could mix the drugs with honey from my own bees. Think of it, *Signora*, they collect their nectar from the very blossoms in this garden that you love so much and, God willing, they may hold the secret to the cure we seek."

"Oh, Berardo, how can I thank you?"

A tear slid down his weathered cheek as he responded, "To accept my help is more thanks than I could ask."

"Then let us not waste time. Shall I send my maid to the druggist or do you prefer to go yourself?"

"Please allow me to go, *Signora*. But…" He seemed uneasy and fidgeted uncharacteristically as he added apologetically "I…I will need money, *Signora*. It is costly, I fear."

In her excitement she had not considered this reality, but tried to cover her concern. "You shall have it, Berardo. Gina will deliver it to you." Her heart grew heavier with each step as she slowly climbed to her room. "Where will I find the money? I have none of my own, yet I must somehow." Instinctively she turned to Gina who promptly suggested, "Perhaps your mother…"

"No, never, Gina."

"Then is there anything in the household that you might sell? Think!"

"Has it come to this? My pride would not permit me to do this. And anyway, what valuables there are in the home—the silver, the carpets, the paintings—they are not mine. They belong to my mother-in-law."

"But she…forgive me, *Madama*, but she is in no condition to know."

"Gina, I could never do this to her. We have had our differences in the past but she has been good and kind, and I have grown to love her."

"What about jewelry! Have you any jewelry?"

"My jewels are my four babies."

"Yes, but there must be something of monetary value."

Instinctively Prudenza closed her hand into a fist as if to prevent any possibility of removing her wedding ring, Nonna Costanza's ring that had become such a symbol of strength. "No, I could never part with it."

"Nor would I suggest it. But what about the locket with the violets?"

"Coletta's locket? It is precious to me, Gina, precious as was her dear friendship. It would be a betrayal to part with it."

"From what you have told me I believe your friend Coletta would want to help you."

"Probably so."

"Be reasonable, *Madama*, Coletta is not here to help, but the locket is!"

With that Prudenza retrieved it from the little rosewood box, the very box that *Ser* Ugo presented to her on the quay in Rimini the day she arrived—a gift from Zenobi. Reluctantly she had ceased wearing the locket for fear that Matteo might destroy it as he had other objects that she treasured. She fingered it lovingly for a moment and as it caught the light the deep green of the ivy shimmered in the sun. Handing it quickly to Gina lest she hesitate and change her mind, she said, "Go, then, go quickly and sell it if you can."

"No, *Signora*, I will not sell it. I know a pawn shop, the Monte di pietà, where it can be kept in deposit, secure until we are able to retrieve it."

"What ever would I do without you, Gina?"

With the locket tucked safely in her pocket Gina was on her way and Prudenza was left to contemplate what she had just done. "O Coletta, forgive me! I know you understand. It is like those days back at San Salvatore: You were always there for me in my time of need."

The whole intricate scheme was completed with amazing speed. By the time Gina returned with the money, Berardo had already retrieved the choicest honey from the comb and quickly went to work with mortar and pestle, pulverizing the drugs into a fine dust which he then carefully stirred into a thick, sticky but aromatic mess.

Prudenza took it immediately to Matteo who, as she feared, rejected it at first. "Just taste it, Matteo."

"No!"

"It is pleasant and sweet. You have always loved sweet things."

Only very gingerly did he accept a spoonful of the concoction. Clearly the honey had not sufficiently masked the bitterness of the herbs and he threw the expensive mixture in her face with yet another accusation. "You are trying to poison me."

The theriac had not worked. The locket was gone and, despite Gina's assurance, she knew there was probably no hope of ever retrieving it. The rebuff was doubly hurtful, considering the emotional cost to Prudenza.

"What to do now?" Like an answer *Fra* Tommaso's departing words rang in her consciousness. "Return when you need counsel. Remember I am here for you."

She retraced her steps to San Marco—this time alone— and found him at prayer. He greeted her warmly and led her to a bench in the cloister garden where they could speak quietly. Prudenza relayed her story, ending with a plea. "What shall I do now, Father?"

"I believe you know the answer, Prudenza. You are a good soul and you have been well-schooled in the beliefs of our religion. Remember the sacredness of your marriage vows."

In stunned silence she asked herself, "Is this the same *Fra* Tommaso that I used to know? So detached, so unfeeling?" In her disbelief she somehow found voice to question him, "Do you remember your advice to me about marrying Matteo?"

"I do. And it may well require you to be truly heroic."

"You asked me if I remembered the fourth commandment, 'Honor thy father and thy mother.' I did, and I still do. But look where it has brought me. And what do you say now but that I should continue in this miserable state?"

"Yes, I say, go to him. Pray, ponder the word of God in scripture. You will find there all the strength that you need. Did not the voice of God instruct Eve at the time of the fall, 'Your desire shall be with your husband, and he shall rule over you.'"

"What kind of heartless theology is that—that you say he must rule over me? It is easy for you to say this as you sit in the tranquility of this holy place." Shocked and embarrassed that she had spoken so disrespectfully to her old friend, she ran from the cloister in tears. "Dear God, what is happening to me?"

Despite the disappointment and humiliation she returned again and again to seek his counsel and each time it was the same. She left downhearted and confused by his apparent lack of sympathy. In an earlier time their innocent bouts had merely been a test of skills in rhyming, done for sport. But now their meetings were becoming exercises, like debates on more serious matters of theology. But there was something else. Just as back then she had honed her skill with words, now her sparring with him over the admonitions of St. Paul seemed to arouse in her a newfound resolve to improve her lot.

He threw down the gauntlet. "Consider, Prudenza, 'Wives, be subject to your husbands, as you should in the Lord.'"

And she rose to the bait, "Oh, yes. But do you read on? 'Husbands love your wives. Treat them with gentleness.'"

So it went each time, yet she continued to return. Despite her initial disappointment she had the feeling that her old friend was leading her somewhere. Strangely enough he did not appear to be offended by her apparent impudence and she felt herself becoming stronger. After each visit she returned home determined to do as she had been admonished, and filled the long hours of bedside vigil pondering St. Paul as *Fra* Tommaso had suggested. Her life had degenerated into a thankless dull routine of watching, praying and administering food and medicine to her husband—all the while aware that the eyes of Tuccio were following her every move.

Then one day her contemplation of St. Paul bore fruit in a strange and most unexpected way that *Fra* Tommaso could never have predicted. She was in the kitchen preparing Matteo's gruel of minced chicken and broth when Paul's word to the Corinthians came to her. "A wife is tied as long as her husband is alive. But if he dies...?"

CHAPTER 23

The Spanish Fly

"If he dies...what then?" She shuddered at the thought, her body actually turning icy cold at the significance of her own words. Clutching the bowl of food tightly she literally fled from the kitchen as if flight would miraculously banish the temptation from her mind. Yet much as she attempted to free herself from this gripping thought the words only pulsated more loudly with each step as she climbed. "And if he dies..."

"May God forgive me. It is wrong even to think so—it would be murder—a sin, a grave sin. How would I confess to *Fra* Tommaso? What would he tell me of such a temptation?" It required only moments for her to answer her own query. "I know. He would just continue to tell me to ponder Saint Paul. I have grown so weary of that tiresome apostle! I fear my old friend has abandoned me, left me to find my own way out of this hell."

By the time she reached Matteo's room her body was physically bent, reflecting the burden of conscience that she bore. She paused at the threshold to collect heself and entered the room mentally prepared to meet Matteo's usual refusal to eat what she had brought. "Why does he so predictably accuse me of poisoning his food? Is it possible that he knows my thoughts, my temptation? It would be so easy now. Perhaps even kind to...No, I must not even think it. And yet...?"

Surprisingly Matteo said nothing. As he reluctantly took some of the gruel, Prudenza looked down on his pitifully wasted body and contemplated, "He is but a hull, an empty pod enclosing a tortured soul. I could free him. It would be so easy."

As he took another spoonful it was clear that his trembling hand could not even convey the food to his mouth now, so she knelt beside his bed, lifted his head with her left hand and fed him with her right—just as she had so often done for her babies when they were small. "He is utterly dependent now. It would be so easy. Just one more spoonful." There was not even the faintest glimmer of life in the eyes that looked up at her so vacantly. "Yes, it would be a kindness to let him go. One more spoonful, Matteo."

"Oh, God, I am just deceiving myself. I would be ending his life. No matter how I may try to justify it, I would be killing him. It would be murder. All these words, these thoughts, these excuses—all justifications! Just so many specious arguments to deceive myself. What am I to do? I cannot bear it any longer."

To divert her mind, she went about tidying up the room, opening the blinds, smoothing the bed linens. "At least I can try to make him comfortable for now." As she proceeded to make some order out of the boxes and vessels on the table next to the bed her eyes came to rest on a glass vial containing a white powder.

"*Dottore* Maiano must have left it." She picked it up gingerly, turning it in her hand and tried to read the label. There, written in fine notarial script were the words *cantharis vericatoria*. Beneath it a coarser hand had inscribed the word *cantarella*. "I remember now. He called it 'the Spanish fly.' This...this was the cautery that the doctor had first applied to Matteo's chest that caused such a violent reaction that the doctor and his assistants bolted from the room. In their haste they must have left it behind. Then the thought occurred, *It is good. No one could trace the purchase of the cantarella to a speziale. There would be no evidence!*

Matteo was sleeping now. His breathing was labored, coming in uneven gasps that caused his still-scarred chest to heave up and down, producing a loud guttural sound. "He is so pathetic. It would be a kindness perhaps..." But all the specious arguments in the world would not release the guilt she felt now as she looked down on his spent body. "He is no longer a threat. It would be cowardly to take his life now. Am I thinking of him or am I just acting out my own revenge for what he has done to our family? Yet there was that haunting reality that I have so often seen him rise from ravaging illness and with inexplicable, almost diabolic, strength go on to terrorize those for whom he should have had the greatest affection. It could happen again. I must not let it!"

The sunlight streaming into the room now shown brightly on the glass vial, exaggerating the pure whiteness of its contents. Holding it up to the light Prudenza reflected, "It looks so harmless, so pure. Just a white powder." She uncorked the container and brought it slowly and carefully to her nose. "It is odorless. I remember *Dottore* Maiano said that it was once used as an aphrodisiac. Perhaps if I used just a little…"

Then the words came again, like a drumming in her brain, one that she could not silence. "And if he dies…this could be the key to freedom, freedom for my children. Freedom for me. What should I do? I need counsel. O *Mamma*, *Mamma*, I need you." She started toward the door, hesitated for a moment, then turned, grasped the vial and quickly deposited it in the pocket of her abundant shirt.

In the quiet of her sitting room at the Orbatello, Caterina Beltramonto was startled by the sound of her daughter's voice from outside the door. "*Mamma*, may I come in?" Her delight at the prospect of a visit from Prudenza quickly turned to alarm as she considered what could possibly cause her daughter to leave Matteo's bedside at this hour?

"*Avanti*. Come, Prudenza."

Standing there on the threshold, her body was framed in the doorway and the light from inside the room illuminated the look of terror in her eyes. Caterina recognized at once the tiny beads of perspiration that always caused Prudenza's hair to form tight little tendrils about her face when she was nervous. In an earlier time they gave her a kind of cherubic look; but this was different. The expression on her face now belied the angelic. Caterina was suddenly struck by the hollowness of her daughter's cheeks. The slant of the fading light made her delicately sculpted cheekbones stand out now in a way that gave her face an almost unattractive angular look, one beyond her twenty-eight years! There was tension about her mouth and from beneath a furrowed brow two glassy green orbs stared out blankly.

"Prudenza, what is it?"

In an instant she collapsed in a heap at her mother's knees, buried her head in the folds of Caterina's skirt and gave way to wrenching sobs that came like spasms as between gasps she laid bare the painful thoughts that tortured her. "Is it just a temptation, *Mamma*? Please say that it is just a temptation. I am so weary. I do not know...I can no longer endure..."

Caterina instinctively stroked her daughter's head as she had often done when as a child Prudenza had been frightened by a bad dream. But this was no childish fantasy. Caterina was too perceptive not to realize the frightening truth of the situation. "She is asking my advice—no, my permission—to take her husband's life. God help me!"

"*Mamma*, I do not wish to burden you with responsibility for such an act, but..."

"It is not that simple, my dear." Caterina was mentally tabulating the many abuses she had observed since coming to Florence, and God only knew how many there had been before her arrival. She did not need to be told the indignities, the shame, the pain to which Matteo had subjected her daughter and the children. "Prudenza, I need to think, to pray."

In the protracted silence that followed, time seemed to stand still. Prudenza's sobbing gradually subsided, her breathing became less spasmodic and Caterina was seized by her own troubled thoughts now. As she always did in moments of decision she addressed Alfonso's spirit. "Are we the perpetrators of these abuses our daughter has suffered? Are we actually the guilty ones? Had we not agreed to that irregular dowry settlement this would never have happened and our daughter could be happily married, living near us back in Ancona. *O Dio*, how can I help her now?" Her mind raced in search of answers. "Our daughter is a good woman, a devout person of faith. Indeed it is her faith that has sustained her thus far—but how much more? If, as she says, it is clear that Matteo is dying, then it might be mercy not to prolong his ordeal. Yet even in the throes of severe illness that brought collapse, there have been those inexplicable surges of energy that only brought further abuse. It could happen again."

The silence was shattered by Prudenza's question. *"Mamma,* what are you thinking?"

"I...I'm here, Prudenza."

"What do you say?"

Her voice sounded hollow and devoid of compassion as she reluctantly answered. "I say no, Daughter. Do not do it."

It was not what Prudenza had hoped to hear as her mother continued. "Please believe me that you are beloved above all else in my life. You know that I would gladly give my life to help you, to free you from the terror with which you now live."

"Then why..."

"I confess that my motives are not the purest. I wish I could say it is because what you suggest is wrong. But in truth it is because I am afraid for you..."

"But, *Mamma,* I do not fear God's judgment."

"It is the judgment of the law that I fear."

With an almost eerie calmness in her voice now, Prudenza spoke. It was the kind of unsettling calm that comes of having resolved a seemingly hopeless situation. It was clear to Caterina that her daughter had made her decision. Though she attempted to sound resolute, a mother's ears could not fail to recognize the fragility of her daughter's argument as she continued to explain. "God knows that I do this for my children, though I realize that it may mean that I must sacrifice my life so that they may live free of this horrible fear that controls our lives now."

"And Matteo? What of him? What of his soul? Will he die unshriven?"

"He is miserable in mind and body, already dead within, like the husks of the lupines along the roadside in autumn. Only dead stalks remain where once there were colorful blooms."

"Please believe in the depths of my love for you, Prudenza, when I say, 'No. I do not condone what you propose.' I beg you not to do it, but although I believe it is wrong I honor your sincerity and the devotion that moves you to take this great risk for the sake of those you love. I will stand by you, Daughter, though, God forbid, it means you must forfeit your life. I pray God to protect you and give you strength. Go now, and do what you must, but do it believing that you do it for the right reasons."

Prudenza found herself back in the Cecchi residence with no recollection of her walk back from the Orbatello. She was obsessed by one thought alone: "I will do it. I must do it, regardless of the cost to me, but I must do it quickly before I lose courage." For once she did not share her thoughts with Gina. It would place her in great danger. "She is like a sister to me and I must protect her. None of my faithful servants should know."

Resolute in her decision as she thought herself to be, her momentary resolve was still fragile enough to be shaken by the thought of the children: "Should I speak to my sons of this? Lorenzo is eleven, and in some ways an old soul. He remembers the sight of his father's abuse of me in the garden, and his torturing the cat. I have seen bruises and welts on his body and, although he would not speak to me of their origin, I know they are the visible reminders of his father's longstanding jealousy of Fabrizio, to whom Lorenzo unfortunately bears such a resemblance."

"And Piero—at one time the favored second child—even he bears the marks of his father's physical abuse. It is only by the watchfulness of Gina that little Coletta has been spared. Her injuries are not as apparent, but a mother knows the signs. She is a very serious child and speaks little, which is unnatural for one so young. I know she has been scarred emotionally by the situation. And poor little Francesca's broken body is a constant reminder to me that I must do this. But how? Which is worse, to leave the children motherless or to allow this abuse to continue? I could not bear the thought that my babies should be *gitatelli*—throwaways sent to a foundling home."

Prudenza sat cold and motionless, unconscious of the passage of time, her mind racing through the possible consequences of what she was about to do. Like a sudden glint of light in the darkness the words of *Dottore* Maiano came to her. He had said that the *cantarella*, if administered in the smallest of doses, can be an aphrodisiac. If I can administer the *cantarella* in the tiniest of doses over a period of time, his death may seem to have come naturally and I will not be suspected. The children will be out of danger and no one will know. All will be well.

Today Matteo surprised me by taking a bit of the gruel—*pollo battuto* Nella had called it—chicken beaten, ground almost to a paste. Of course! Why had I not thought of it before? An obvious casualty of Matteo's deteriorating health had been the loss of so many rotted teeth. The *pollo batutto* he can swallow without difficulty. I will mix the tiniest bit of *cantarella* with the chicken. It is odorless and he will not detect it. But I must do it when Nella, dear sweet Nella, is not in the kitchen. Since she spends most of her life there I must work at night, after the household is safely out of the way, asleep.

For once there was no warmth and no fragrance in Nella's kitchen, not even a trace of residual aroma from countless meals prepared there. The hearth was cold and the well-scrubbed kettles were hung in orderly rows above, ready for the next day's labor. Whether it was from the terror of what she was about to do or simply because the fire had gone out, she shivered almost uncontrollably as she looked about. "I have never seen Nella's kitchen so dark and cold."

Her rational voice reminded her, "It is January and to be expected, I suppose."

She was startled when from the candle she held unsteadily a warm drop of melting wax fell on her hand. It was like a reminder that there was no turning back now. "To plan such a thing, even to think such a thing for a moment, is in itself a sin, so whether I do it or not, I am guilty, I have sinned…"

As she rummaged through the cupboard in search of some cooked chicken that Nella usually kept on hand, she thought she heard a sound from the adjacent laundry room. "It is nothing—just nerves. Yes, my nerves. No time to look now. I must hurry. Ah, there it is. Bless you, Nella, for providing so well."

She went to work quickly with mortar and pestle mashing the chicken vigorously until it reached the consistency of a smooth pulp. Satisfied that it was sufficiently soft she was suddenly gripped with the realization that this was the moment of the ultimate decision. Closing her eyes for an instant she breathed deeply, crossed herself, then reached into the recesses of her pocket and withdrew the vial. Her hand shook so uncontrollably that the powder spilled sending a fine spray around the bowl and onto the table. Terrified that she might have contaminated the surroundings she quickly wiped it away. This time she steadied herself by holding the spoon with both hands, measured a small amount of the white powder, dropped it into the mixture and watched it disappear into the chicken as she gave it a vigorous stir.

Then covering the bowl with her hand she started for the door, only to remember the soiled spoon. "There must not be a trace." She scrubbed it thoroughly and returned it to its hook, surveyed the kitchen critically for any evidence and, satisfied that all was as she had found it, she literally ran up the stairs to the security of her quarters where she placed the bowl on the window sill to keep it safe and cool until morning. Still fully dressed, she collapsed onto her bed; but sleep eluded her for what seemed like hours.

The moonlight seeping through the cracks in the blinds streaked the walls with eerie blue light. It was a cruel reminder of another time when, lying on this same bed on her wedding night, she had been so frightened by the light show from a violent summer storm. "Then Matteo comforted me. He held me passionately and for the first time called me his wife." Now however there was no one to comfort her; her only companion the condemning moon as it shone on the vessel on the windowsill. "Is it the key to my freedom, or my own death warrant?" Finally overtaken by sheer exhaustion she fell into a profound but troubled sleep.

With the first signs of sunrise she rose, grasped the vessel and left the room before Gina could find her. She did not pause before Matteo's door but entered quickly, as if hesitation might cause her to recoil at what she had determined to do. Surprisingly he was awake, staring vacantly at the ceiling.

"I have brought you food, Matteo, the chicken like that you ate yesterday." He offered no resistance, even reached out for it. His uncharacteristic docility brought a nearly paralyzing wave of guilt over her. "He is so helpless—perhaps I should not…"

In a moment she heard a voice, as if coming from afar—disembodied—yet she recognized it as her own. It was saying gently, almost sweetly, "Take some, Matteo. It will help you. That's right, just a spoonful, Husband." Now it was her hand that trembled as she struggled to maintain control by reminding herself, it has no taste, no odor. Only the aroma of chicken.

With his head now tilted back and his nearly toothless mouth opened wide he looked like a baby bird helplessly waiting for its mother to feed it. Again from outside herself she heard, "Just a spoonful, Matteo. Just a spoonful."

Suddenly the air was rent with the most terrifying scream

she had ever heard, even from Matteo. He was clutching frantically at his throat, howling like a wild animal writhing in pain. In a moment his body contorted in a succession of convulsive fits until it was constricted into a ball, and he sought relief by attempting to roll from side to side. Still screaming he now clawed at his stomach but, just as suddenly, he lurched backward violently, his spine arching in the opposite direction like a taut bow.

"*O, Dio mio*. It was not supposed to be so. It was just a little bit." She sickened as from every orifice of his body there came horrifying proof of the deadliness of this innocent looking white powder. From his mouth spewed bloody vomit while his bowels involuntarily disgorged their contents, befouling his sheets with stinking, blackened feces. His fierce cries gradually ceased but only because he could no longer breathe sufficiently to give vent.

"It was not supposed to be so. God help him. God help me. What have I done?"

The screaming roused Gina who literally bolted into the room in time to see him lapse into a coma, and witness the last extreme hemorrhage, a discharge of bloody urine that soaked the bed and filled the air with a stinging acrid odor.

"Gina, run for the doctor."

"Perhaps, *Madama*, it would not be a wise thing to do."

"How can you say that? Look at him." She realized at once that her clever maid suspected the truth. He was expiring before their very eyes.

"*Madama*, the doctor may suspect…"

"But I must, Gina. Perhaps there is yet something they can do for him."

Alone and horrified Prudenza watched Matteo expire as the deadly Spanish fly did its work. By the time Gina returned with the doctor and his assistants, there was nothing they could do but testify for the records, "Matteo Cecchi is dead! Dead at the age of forty-six—neither young nor old—but dead, wasted."

His ravaged body was a pitiful sight, made all the more so by the irony of the bright January sun now illuminating his corpse so that the ghastly effect of the poison stood out in even more horrifying bold relief. The doctor and his assistants silently took up their familiar places around Matteo's bed, all the while exchanging knowing looks. Maiano held a silken handkerchief to his nostrils as the assistant with the book began scribbling vigorously while the younger one stood, ghastly white and gape-mouthed, on the verge of fainting.

The sickening sight and the overpowering stench in the room heightened the realization of what she had just done and sent Prudenza into shock. The large muscles of her body suddenly cramped in seizures like convulsions that made it nearly impossible to walk or to talk. Yet even in that state it was clear to her that *Dottore* Maiano suspected her, for she heard him say, "There must be an autopsy."

The assistants were eager to remove the body and tend to it at once. The doctor said nothing, neither to Prudenza nor her maid, as he soberly followed the makeshift litter with Matteo's body in the silent procession as it moved quickly down the back stairs, hoping thereby to avoid alarming the other occupants of the house.

However by midmorning word of Matteo's demise soon circulated among the servants, bringing little sympathy for him, but great concern for Prudenza and her children. No tear was shed for him except by one who, from his hiding place on the landing, witnessed the silent column descending the stairs. The pathetic, mishapened little mole would now have to find a new master.

In the dank and gloomy laboratory at the rear of the doctor's quarters they laid Matteo's still-warm body on the cold marble slab provided for that purpose. Maiano was now surrounded by several others who had been called in very quickly to witness the autopsy. He did not see his youngest assistant seek out a dark corner where he was retching violently. The room was cold and as Maiano slit the body with a deft swath of his scalpel from shoulders to sternum, down the front of the abdomen, and exposed the visceral cavity, a small but perceptible wisp of steam actually rose from the opening...the last breath of Matteo Cecchi.

Meanwhile Gina managed to help Prudenza to her room where she bathed her mistress's feverish brow and massaged her stiffened body in an attempt to rouse her from a near catatonic state brought on by shock and the paralyzing effect of conflicting emotions. By evening the combination of Gina's tender ministrations and Berardo's sedatives brought some relief and finally Prudenza sank into blessed unconsciousness that lasted throughout the following day. By the end of the second day she began muttering in jumbled, broken phrases. Clearly she feared the worst. "The doctor...he..."

"Hush, *Madama*. Do not try to speak. You must rest."

"But, Gina, the doctor knows."

"Knows what, *Madama*?"

"He was silent but I saw his look. He knows I was alone with Matteo. He suspects me, Gina,..."

"But, *Madama*, there is no evidence left behind. No poison in the room."

"What do you mean? What about the bowl of chicken?"

"Gone! Dashed on the rocks in the Arno."

"How?"

"I took it inside my apron as I ran for the doctor and threw it as hard as I could into the river. Then as I crossed over the bridge I paused a moment and watched as it shattered against the stone of the fish weir."

"Oh, Gina, God love you."

The knowledge brought only a temporary but anxious quiet to the house. There was the matter of how to tell Maddalena that her son was dead, and there was a funeral to plan. Prudenza was in no condition to take on these responsibilities, but suggested that Gina go to the Orbatello to inform her mother, and to ask that *Fra* Filippo be called into service once again.

Across town in the solemn chambers of the law, *Dottore* Maiano made his compulsory report to the authorities and presented his findings from the autopsy. The report was concise and left no doubt as to the cause of death. Extreme diarrhea, excessive vomiting of blood and necrosis of the gastric membranes had caused such severe loss of blood supply that the soft tissue of the body was literally burned. Moreover, there was a telltale congestion of blood in the genital and urinary organs. The concluding sentence simply read: "Cause of death: poison."

Although it was not the doctor's role to imply guilt, especially when it concerned a member of such a prominent family with whom he had been closely associated for years, the evidence was so overwhelming that he ventured his professional opinion quite unsolicited. "I believe that such instant, complete and catastrophic damage to the body could be the result of only one thing: *cantarella*—the Spanish Fly. Matteo Cecchi was murdered."

Meanwhile, back in the Cecchi residence, the second anxious day had passed uneventfully and now in the semi-darkness of Prudenza's room Gina prepared her mistress for bed. She brushed Prudenza's hair until it cascaded down her back and over the shoulders of her night shift. In the flickering light from a candle at the bedside she noted that the bronze of her mistress's hair was now shot through here and there with strands of gray.

"Matteo's fault! The jealous brute." Her vigorous poking and prodding of the fire was as much a statement of her disgust with him as it was an attempt to coax some warmth from the logs. They were just beginning to glow brightly when, from the corner of her eye, she saw Prudenza sink to her knees at her bedside and bury her head in her hands, lost in silent prayer. Climbing into bed she pulled the coverlet up high under her chin and began issuing a series of orders that sounded all too much like the last wishes of a dying person.

"It is just a matter of time now, Gina. I know it."

"No, *Madama*, it cannot be. Remember they have no evidence." But even in her distracted state Prudenza could not fail to note the lack of conviction in her maid's voice.

"Please take care of my babies. And poor Maddalena! Perhaps it is a blessing that she will not understand what has happened. She lives in a cacoon of memories of a happier time that shield her from harsh realities. For my own dear mother the pain and sorrow will be great, Gina. Comfort her, be gentle with her, Gina, and remind her that I alone am guilty."

"Do not speak of guilt, *Madama*."

Suddenly the silence of the night was broken by the sound of commotion in the garden below and loud but indistinct talking—voices of men.

"*O, Dio*, Gina, they have come for me. You must go! Flee from here; go immediately. I fear for you."

"Do not worry for me. If they question me, I will lie. I will simply say that I know you were asleep in your bed at the time your husband died."

"I will not ask you to lie. You must not perjure yourself."

"No, *Madama*, I will not leave you. I must stay. What will happen to the children if I go now?"

"My mother will…"

By now the sound of boots on the stairs grew closer.

"Gina, as your mistress I *command* you to go."

"And *Madama*, as your friend I *refuse* to go."

"Don't be foolish, Gina. Can you not hear, they have reached the landing and it is only a matter of moments…"

Before she could finish the thought the pounding at the door began. Prudenza quickly removed Nonna Costanza's ring from her finger, kissed it and thrust it into Gina's hand. "Take it, please. You must. They will only take it away from me in prison. I beg you go now and pray to my grandmother for me. She will protect you, too."

As the pounding grew more insistent, she embraced Gina, pushed her through the door into the passageway leading down the back stairs, and managed to draw the drape over the door only a moment before the guards entered her room. Realizing the need to stall for time she mustered a kind of stoic resignation and very slowly asked her accusers, "What is it you want with me? By what authority do you enter my home and awaken the entire household at this untimely hour?"

"By order of the *Otto di Guardia*," barked the oldest of the three policemen, a swarthy man obviously impressed with his own importance and annoyed at being called upon in the middle of the night. He stepped forward and loudly announced, "Prudenza Beltramonto Cecchi, you are under arrest for the murder of your husband."

As he did so he seized her roughly, pulled her hands behind her back and began to bind her wrists together. Although the indignity of it was humiliating, she was almost glad, for it would buy time, precious time allowing Gina to escape.

Swift as a swallow Gina had flown down the stairs and into the garden, but before passing through the gate she turned for one last glimpse of the window where, through her tears she could see a bright reflection from the fire she had so carefully laid—her last service to her mistress. Her tears were flowing as she quickly closed the gate and disappeared, swallowed up in the blessed anonymity of the night.

THE BLADE

CHAPTER 24

Inferno

Although the descent down the stairs was slow and painful, it seemed to the prisoner more like a sudden and terrifying plunge into the abyss from which there was no return. "My *inferno*!" More painful by far than the smarting in her wrists, where the angry policeman had bound her so tightly that the shackles were beginning to draw blood, was the agonizing humiliation.

For by now the whole household had been awakened and out from partially opened doors heads of servants peered cautiously. Disbelief turned to horror as they recognized who it was that was being led away by the police.

So overwhelming was the shame and sense of guilt that gripped her now that she could take no consolation in the fact that their sympathies were with her. As they neared the kitchen she sensed that the figures in the shadows must be Nella and Maria, wrapped in shawls, and weeping openly at the sight of Prudenza, still in her night shift. Her long hair hung loose over her shoulders and her eyes were downcast—not so much in modesty as in shame. Over her nightdress a coarse blanket thrown about her shoulders served as a hastily contrived cloak. Whether it was a reluctant concession to modesty or just a makeshift protection from the cold January night air, Prudenza was grateful, for at least it concealed the crude manacles that by now were digging more deeply into her wrists. In her weakness, progress was slow and the guards were becoming increasingly impatient. The youngest of them began complaining aloud. "Could this not have waited until morning?"

"Watch your words or you..."

"He is right," the oldest of the three interjected, as if the seniority of his gray hair provided immunity. "Who made this accusation that sends us out into the night like this?"

Clearly annoyed at the interruption of their sleep the three began arguing loudly. "Yes. Who made the accusation? May he rot in hell."

"It must be someone important."

"I'd wager someone with firsthand knowledge. Damn him!" Eager to get on with their miserable task the chief guard commenced barking at his prisoner, "Can you not walk any faster?"

Prudenza's felt slippers were slight protection from the numbing cold of the stone stairs and, as she groped to find her footing, several times her legs folded helplessly beneath her. Unable to reach for the balustrade for support she struggled to maintain her balance until finally the chief guard commanded the youngest to lift her up. When they reached the garden and the guards opened the door the blast of cold night air felt like needles against her skin and she struggled for breath.

The torch that the second guard carried fouled the otherwise clear night air with the stink of tar, and the drops of hot pitch that fell on his hands from time to time brought forth a volley of obscene language the likes of which Prudenza had never before heard—not even from Matteo.

From the corner of her eye she recognized the bent figure of Berardo emerging from his little room at the edge of the garden. He commenced coughing and choking from the acrid smoke of the torch and shielded his eyes for a moment. As he adjusted to the light and comprehended the scene being enacted before him, he made no effort to hide the tears that began to stream down his face, following the deep furrows in his leathery cheeks. He crossed himself devoutly as Prudenza had so often seen him do, and murmured, "*Madonna*, I fear it is your *via crucis*."

Despite the fact that Berardo's neatly manicured paths through the garden were so familiar to her, progress was slow and difficult for all feeling had left her feet by now and the darkness was profound, as black as ink. Although the moon was full, it was so completely obscured by thick clouds that the gloom could almost be felt like a pall. For this she uttered a silent grateful prayer:

"Thank God for the darkness. May it protect you, Gina."

Just then the mournful hooting of an owl broke the silence and from a distance another answered, prompting the youngest of the guards to observe ruefully, "At least he has a mate waiting for him to return, warming his nest. But for us, not even a *puttana* out in this foggy soup."

As her captors pushed her out into the street, behind them the gate slammed shut noisily, undoubtedly rousing neighbors and certainly disrupting the seedy nightlife of the street. At that moment Prudenza spoke for the first time. "Where are you taking me?"

"You will see soon enough."

Within minutes one of the guards seized her arm and guided her sharply to the left, making her acutely aware of where she was. "This has to be Via della Giustizia."

She was conscious that above and to the left of them rose that huge looming bulk of Santa Croce, the resting place of her dear father-in-law and the repository of so many memories.

"They must be taking me to the Stinche." But only minutes later they turned again, this time onto Borgo dei Greci and she recognized Piazza Sant'Apollinare. "*O Madonna,* this leads to the Bargello. *Dio mio,* they are taking me to the Bargello, to the dungeon!"

By now the first light was beginning to streak the sky and the guards were becoming more and more irritated by the slow progress of their prisoner. Though still pale the early light was sufficient to outline the tower of the Bargello, so harsh and overpowering. Somehow the very solid squareness of it seemed unforgiving—an appropriate symbol of the seat of the Council of Justice, the condemning arm of criminal justice in Florence. How ironic, she thought, as her eyes wandered across the way where the skyline was pierced by the graceful and delicate spire of the Badia, that ancient monastery where for centuries monks sent their prayers heavenward even at this hour. At the thought of it, she murmured under her breath that monastic entreaty, *"Deus in adiutorium meum intende..."* (O, God, come to my assistance.)

Finally the chief of the guards deigned to speak to her. "We are here."

He began pounding the base of his torch against the huge door of the prison, depositing as he did so, large globules of tar from his nearly spent torch. From inside some muttering could be heard and in a moment the tired hinges rasped and groaned as, under the weight of its mass, the great door slowly opened. There was a short but inaudible exchange between her captors and the night watchman and Prudenza was ordered to enter. As she stepped over the tar-spotted doorsill she caught a glimpse of the courtyard where a fire burned in the center.

"Oh God, how I long to warm myself, but I know it is not for me. Shall I never be warm again?"

Shortly the mammoth door clanged shut noisily, announcing that her captivity had begun. Their business apparently done, her captors made for the fire where several other guards seemed in a jovial mood, undoubtedly helped by the flagon they passed as they warmed their hands. She was now the jailor's charge. There were no explanations. After all why would there be? She was just another disgruntled woman. Holding a lantern on high, the jailor stepped forward and commanded sternly, "Follow me."

By now fear and apprehension had so sharpened her powers of observation that she began to note every detail of the narrow passageway as the flickering light revealed what seemed at first like gaping holes in the walls. She soon realized that these cave-like recesses actually housed prisoners, criminals who would be her neighbors. A sickening feeling seized her as she recognized, "These are to be my companions in this dreadful place."

Some stared glassy-eyed and mute, uncomprehending at the sight of this young woman—yes, a beautiful woman. Others, toothless and foul-mouthed, hurled insults as the guard hurried her past. He stopped abruptly as they came to a dead end before a low door through which the jailor had to stoop in order to enter. Above it was inscribed, "*Lasciate ogni speranza, voi ch'entrata...*"(Abandon all hope, you who enter here...)

"Oh, God, is this to be my home?" It smelled of mold and urine and had no apparent source of light. A crude and makeshift sconce on the far wall was empty, the drippings of tallow that stained the floor beneath testified to some prior occupant's existence. As her eyes gradually adjusted to the darkness she noted with some relief a small, narrow window hardly more than a crack high up in the wall.

Realizing that they were alone now in the cell, she recoiled as the jailor came nearer—so close that she could feel his hot breath on the back of her neck. It reeked of sour wine and garlic and, although her stomach began to churn, she recognized that he had approached her in order to free her hands. As he loosed the rope that bound her, it slid to the floor and she felt blood begin to pulse again through her bruised wrists and hands. She began to massage them and as she did so, stared at the mark on her finger where Nonna Costanza's ring had been ever since Matteo placed it there on the day of her betrothal long ago in Ancona. As the jailor closed the door behind her, Prudenza fell to her knees next to the straw pallet and prayed aloud, "O, Nonna Costanza, help me, help my mother, my babies. And keep Gina safe."

CHAPTER 25

Flight

"Run, run! I must run. But where?" In her distraught state Gina's usually dependable instinct had deserted her so that it was without a sense of direction that her young legs propelled her over the stones now slippery with dew. In the darkness she crashed blindly into an obstacle that felled her to the pavement.

"*O, Gran Dio*! I have dropped it, I have lost the ring." She began groveling frantically on the cold stone, chiding herself for being so clumsy. "It is my one remaining connection with my mistress. I must not lose it. *O, Madonna Santa Maria*, in the name of your Son, please help me to find it. There is no time to lose."

Remembering her mistress's last words to her she raised her eyes to the heavens and added, "Nonna Costanza, come. Help my mistress." Just then her right hand came upon some obstacle and, there it was, standing upright, caught in a deep crevice between the paving stones. "God be praised." She crossed herself and then slipped the ring on to her own finger. "No. No, I must not wear it... I know that bandits and outlaws carouse in the streets at all hours and God help me if they should see it. Better to hide it in my deep pocket"

At the thought of the danger she was in, she began running again, darting blindly through deserted alleyways, until finally, in a deep, sheltered doorway she paused, breathing hard. Over the loud beating of her heart she heard an unmistakable sound. "I know that sound well. It is the clang of the garden gate, the Cecchi garden. That means that I...I am not that far away. *O Dio*, I have been running in a circle."

As she so often did when she attempted to stiffen her resolve she spoke aloud to herself. "Stop! Think, Gina. Where are you? If the garden gate has closed that means the police have taken her, they have left the Cecchi house and are now in the street. Surely they will take her to prison. But where? To the Stinche? No, I think not. The Bargello, it must be the Bargello."

The thought sent a shudder through her. "That means that they will proceed to the west, probably along the Via della Giustizia, so I must avoid it. I must go north, yes, north immediately. But which way is north? Without the moon I cannot tell. North. North would be away from the river, so the Arno must be at my back. But I cannot see the river from here."

In her confused and disoriented state she turned around slowly several times, her eyes searching for some landmark. Finally she caught sight of the faint outline of hills in the distance. "Those hills—I know those hills. They are across the Arno, to the south of the city so I must flee in the opposite direction."

Although there was some comfort in knowing that the Arno was now at her back, she grew more and more cautious as at each cross street she peered warily to the left and to the right, before darting quickly in a vaguely northern direction. Finally she came upon something familiar. "It is Sant'Ambrogio." The sense of recognition was, however, small comfort for in the openness of the little *piazza* before the church she felt nakedly visible and unsafe. "I must not linger here. I must keep going. But where? I cannot just keep running forever."

Her aching feet and legs forced her to slow her pace a bit now as, still aiming north she found herself in more familiar territory. Suddenly there opened in front of her a vast *piazza*. Its graceful colonnades on three sides told her that it was Santissima Annunziata. "Perhaps I can hide in the church for a bit—at least long enough to plan an escape route." She tried the huge doors of the church but they were unyielding. "Of course, it is too early. But I have to rest somewhere. Where can I hide?"

Pale streaks of amber light were beginning to break through in the east. "Soon it will be dawn, and I must find a place to hide." A rustling sound nearby startled her, sending her like a shot into a still shaded corner under the colonnade of the Ospedali degli Innocenti. Relieved to see that it was only a rat foraging for garbage she gave in to fatigue and fear and collapsed into a heap, pulling her skirts close about her. In her distress she had not realized until now how very cold she was, and she began to cry. "Here I am—thinking about myself when it should be *Madonna* Prudenza. Oh, God, forgive me and guard her."

By now the early morning sunlight was flooding the square and Gina was awakened by the sound of church bells nearby. "I...I must have fallen asleep, and now it is daylight! I dare not stay here." She crept cautiously to the great doors of the church again. "Locked, still locked! It must be the bells of San Marco that I hear." Her mind was flooded with memories of the day she escorted Prudenza to San Marco to confess—that strange day when the mistress had met her old tutor. The thought of him roused feelings of anger and resentment in Gina. "He was the one who counseled my mistress to stay, to endure the treatment of her husband. He is the guilty one!" Gina's desire to accuse him, to show him what his counsel had done, was tamed only by the knowledge that Prudenza would want him to know, though certainly for reasons different from hers. "Perhaps he can help."

San Marco was only a short distance away and since no one was yet about she walked slowly down via della Sapienza toward the church as she rehearsed mentally what she might say to the priest to reveal what his insensitive counsel had done.

The ochre stones of the façade looked warm in the early light and were the first encouraging sight after what had been a truly horrible night. "Well, if nothing else there will be some shelter from the cold here."

She slipped quietly inside the door.

"Sicut erat in principio et nunc et semper..." The friars were just finishing their morning office in choir and the sacristan began to extinguish the candles.

"I must hurry. I must find him—but how? She moved quickly to the front and stationed herself just inside the door through which the friars would have to pass. "I must make sure to recognize him, for I saw him only once." Finally satisfied that she had identified him she fell to her knees directly in his path, effectively startling him.

"What are you doing? Who are you?"

"My name is not important! I bring you news of someone you know."

"How can that be? I have never seen you before." Still startled he stepped aside to allow the procession of friars to pass.

"I must speak to you, Father, but in private. Please! It is urgent. In the garden of the cloister, perhaps?"

The look of terror in her eyes told *Fra* Tommaso that this, whatever it was, must truly be serious. He must be discreet.

"No, not the cloister then. It is safer to go into the confessional."

The thought made her uncomfortable, but she was grateful for the privacy it would afford. As *Fra* Tommaso entered the priest's side of the box she knelt uneasily on the penitent's *prie dieu* on the other side of the curtain and began at once to relate in detail the events of the past few days, pausing only to catch her breath and to answer his questions.

"Where is she now?"

"They have come for her—the police. They have taken her away this very night."

"Do you know where they have taken her?"

"No, but I suspect to the Bargello."

"God help her! Do you believe she killed her husband?"

"She did not mean to, Father! I know. I was there. She even sent me for the doctor thinking he could help. You must help her, Father. *Signore* Cecchi, her husband, was cruel to her and even to the children sometimes. I myself have witnessed his brutish behavior." It was obvious to her that the man on the other side of the curtain was stunned by this revelation.

"What can I do, *Signorina*?"

"Do?" At this she lost control of her voice and nearly shouted, "I should think that a man of God would know his obligation. It was you who continued to counsel her to remain with her husband, to continue to be the obedient wife."

There was an awkward pause as she became aware that the voice from the other side did not require an answer. He was speaking to himself now, reflecting somberly. "I have counseled unwisely. Twice I have failed her. First was that night long ago in Ancona when she fled to our monastery in the night, fearing to go through with the betrothal. I was wrong then and now I have failed her again. This good and beautiful young soul...What must I do now?"

Lost in his guilt he had not expected an answer but Gina seized the opportunity and carried on. "Go to her in prison. Surely she must be permitted visitation by her confessor."

"Yes. Yes, of course, I will."

"And her mother, *Signora* Beltramonto. She is in the Orbatello and I know my lady is so worried for her. Please comfort her as well."

"But what of you, *Signorina*? Surely the police must be looking for you. You are not safe. What will you do, and where will you go?"

"I have a brother who lives in the country near here, on a farm east of Florence."

"Where?"

"Rignano sul Arno."

"But that is a long way and you cannot go on foot, and without some protection."

"I can perhaps find help in the countryside, or I can hide for a bit. No one here knows that I have family there except Nella, the cook, and she would never tell. She loves Lady Prudenza so much. They will not look for me there."

"It is not safe, *Signorina*."

"Perhaps some farmer returning from the city with his cart will allow me to ride."

"But you have no money, do you?"

"No, but..."

"Here. Come with me." He stepped out of the confessional box and, looking about cautiously, motioned for her to follow him to the entrance of the church. "You know, *Signorina*, we monks take a vow of poverty so I have no money of my own to give you." Satisfied that they were alone in the church he pried open the alms box near the door, gathered the coins from it and placed them in Gina's hands. "It is for the Lord's poor. God knows your need and He will not object. Take it, *Signorina*."

At once surprised and touched she stuffed the money carefully in her deep pocket, with Nonna Costanza's ring for company. "I thank you, Father, and I know my mistress would be so grateful."

"You have done the right thing, *Signorina*. You have shown great courage by coming here as you have. Your mistress is blessed to have such a good and faithful friend."

"Oh no, it is I who am blessed, Father."

"Now you must tell me your name."

"I am Ginevra Dattali—but my mistress calls me Gina. Please call me Gina, Father."

"I will. You know, of course, that I am *Fra* Tommaso. Now, follow me, Gina. At the far side of the vegetable garden behind the monastery there is a gate that opens onto a road leading directly up into the hills. I will take you there now but we must go quickly, for it is already light."

"You are kind, Father. I thank you with all my heart."

At the gate he raised his hand and said, "I give you my blessing, *Signorina* Dattali. Godspeed, Gina. May the angels guard you on your way."

CHAPTER 26

The Prisoner

Where darkness never yields to light there is no sense of time. Its passing is punctuated only by a cycle of bodily responses—hunger, fatigue, sleep, confusion, exhaustion—in no rational sequence. In such unrelenting darkness circadian rhythm is scrambled, gone amok, and can lead to madness.

To the other inhabitants of this dusky world of the dungeon this newest prisoner was a curiosity. She looked so frail, so quiet and passive when she was brought in. No screaming malediction, no cursing or loud protestations, only silence as she collapsed to her knees aside the filthy pallet that was to be her bed. In some ways this cursed darkness could be a blessing. At least she could not see the vermin that inhabited the straw tick. The other prisoners' reactions to this newest inmate resulted in a most unexpected and strange quiet as they watched, waited and even wagered how long she could remain thus. With their heads pressed against the bars their eyes sought the slightest hint of illumination that might assist their vigil. Their unexpected and eerie quiet was interrupted only by their periodic assessment of her condition.

"*È morto*. She is worm food by now. That's what she is."

"No! She would stink by this time."

They ticked off the days by counting the number of times the guard brought their pitiful rations of watery soup and dried crusts—hers always left untouched. For nearly three days now she had neither moved nor eaten, and even the guards began to worry that she might not live long enough to be taken to justice. For the other prisoners the only diversion from the deadly monotony of their vigil was a disgusting contest to determine which of them could smash the largest number of fleas he had harvested from his bed.

"Eh!"

"*Cosa*? What is it?"

"*Guarda*. Look! She is moving!"

At the far end of the corridor the careless night watchman had left his torch to burn itself out. Even as it sputtered its last it gave off enough dusky light that the curious observers could see a faint outline of Prudenza's body as she attempted to rise to her feet. She was moaning, weak from lack of food and struggled to gain her balance.

"*Ascolta*! Listen. She is talking to someone."

"There is no one there. You must be going mad."

Out of the silence came a little voice like that of a child. "Where am I? I am so cold, and yet…yet my head is on fire. I cannot see…*O, Dio*!" The voice was suddenly energized, like the pitiful scream of one in great pain. "No! No. Go away, Matteo. Why are you here? You are dead." It was as if his image materialized out of the very stone wall before her, as he leered condemningly and called her by name.

"It cannot be. Go away, Matteo. Must you torture me even in death?"

She had not expected that the phantom could speak, so the sepulchral sound of his voice in response made her blood run cold as he accused her, "*Mi hai traduto, Signora* Cecchi! You have betrayed me and I have come to avenge my murder."

"No. I have not betrayed you. I tried to heal you, Matteo. Do you not remember all the long hours at your bedside? I did not mean for you to die."

"Do not lie, *Signora, mia moglia*."

"Your wife? No, I'm no longer your wife; I'm your widow."

She attempted to turn away from the cold gray phantom, but his eyes, piercing like arrows of fire, followed her as she moved unsteadily about in the tiny space that was her cell.

"*Ingrata donna*. Ungrateful woman, did you not enjoy the wealth and comfort of the Cecchi home?"

"Yes, yes. Your family has been most generous and kind

to me. But I have not been an ungrateful woman, Matteo. Think! I have given you sons and daughters, and I have tried to love you."

"Not a true love. *Un perfido amore.*"

"A deceitful love? How can you say that? What was treacherous was the twisted path I trod in order to avoid your rage."

"Repent, damned woman. *Va a mia tomba.*"

"What are you saying? I cannot go to your tomb; I am not free and you are not yet buried. There is no tomb."

"Until my body rests in the grave I will find you and I will haunt you."

"Must you torment me even after you are dead?"

"Sì! Io dico, Va a mia tomba."

"How can I go to your tomb? There is no tomb. You have not yet been buried."

"Ma Io dico, va, e spargi d'amaro pianto."

"I cannot weep bitter tears at your tomb as you command me to. If I weep my tears are not for you, Matteo, but for my mother, your mother, my babies who now have neither father nor mother! You are not yet buried, Matteo. Neither your soul nor your body has found a resting place."

As she addressed the image squarely now it began to fade. "Yes, go! In the name of God, go! If you go and leave me to work out my salvation, I promise that I will attempt to put your body and your soul to rest. There must be a funeral—I will see to it, Matteo."

She rose unsteadily and with hands outstretched before her—like one sleepwalking—she moved forward. In deliberate, slow and measured step, the cadence of a funeral procession, she skirted the periphery of her small cell reverently and repeatedly. Like a spiritual cleansing, an unloading of the unconscious, she would free her soul of all feelings of guilt or anger and at the same time redeem him with honors, with a funeral, even if it existed only in her troubled mind.

"I hear it now. Your soul cries out for redemption. Rest in peace, Matteo Cecchi. You must rest in peace. I will put you to rest. This is Prudenza's last gift to you, my Husband, a noble funeral. There it is. I hear the bell toll. Do you not hear it? It tolls for the passing of Matteo Cecchi. It tolls for you, Matteo?"

In silence she continued to trace and re-trace the perimeter of her cell, and then began to speak again. "Now I see the funeral cortege forming in a grand procession of friends, family, workers from the Cecchi business. They carry you on a beautiful bier covered with a blanket of flowers. And dear, dear *Fra* Filippo and *Ser* Cristofano—they are there, too. They weep, oh they weep for you, Matteo."

"Oh! Now I see my mother, your father Zenobi and your mother. My boys are there too—no, OUR boys, Matteo. OUR boys. Lorenzo so tall and beautiful, and handsome little Piero looking so brave. But...but where are the girls? Where are my little Coletta and Francesca?"

Suddenly she cried out, "Where am I? It is my husband's funeral. I should be there." Then after a moment of calm, "Yes, there I am. But where is my *abito di lutto*? I have no veil, no mourning veil."

With that she began thrashing about among objects on the floor. She picked up the blanket that the guards had given her the night she was arrested and draped it over her head. "Here it is—here is my veil." In sudden panic she began to scream, "But I am not there, I am here, looking down on it. How can it be? Oh, Matteo, Husband, rest in peace. I wanted to give you peace, blessed peace. But you did not find it here in this life. I tried to reach you but I failed time after time even as I contemplated the words of St. Paul. 'Wives, be subject to your husbands.' But do you know what comes after that? Do you know, Matteo? After that comes your part. 'Husbands love your wives, treat them with gentleness.' Did you ever heed that, my Husband?" She paused as if waiting for a response. "No. There was no love in this marriage, no gentleness." After a long pause she continued. "Then I remembered, 'A wife is tied as long as her husband lives. But if he dies she is free. No, that severe apostle has deceived me again. I am not free...not free ever again. So my mind worked! I am not...free."

Spent and delirious she collapsed on her pallet.

—ɯ—

Not far from the Bargello the body of a murdered man was being carried through the street on a simple bier, to receive the last ministrations of the church. But this was a *marcia funèbre* without pomp, for *Fra* Filippo, who had been there in every crisis of the Cecchi family, had thoughtfully arranged for a simple funeral at a very early hour, before the streets would be alive with commerce. By now the demise of Matteo Cecchi was well known to the rumor mongering Florentines, so the kindly old priest wished to spare the family as much anguish as he could. There was but one candle, one priest and the cross bearer preceding the simple bier bearing Matteo Cecchi's body.

It was the custom that workers from a merchant's business should be pallbearers for a member of their employer's family. But for Matteo Cecchi the pallbearers had to be drafted from among the Cecchi workers, for no one would willingly serve. It required all of *Fra* Filippo's diplomatic powers of persuasion to fill the ranks, for there was a distinct hierarchy among silk workers of Florence and the House of Cecchi was no exception. Unless he volunteered, no weaver, spinner, dyer, or other skilled worker could ever be drafted. Only from the lesser ranks of the draymen and young apprentices new to the firm was he at last able to enlist the necessary number—and then only as he appealed to their concern and respect for the family.

As the funeral cortege wound its way through the street to the church the old priest intoned the familiar ancient Latin prayers for the dead. *"Miserere mei Deus; secundum magnam misericordiam tuam."* Like a muted counterpoint to the plea for God's great mercy the grumbling of the reluctant pallbearers punctuated the austere petition with their own thoughts concerning the deceased's need for mercy.

The priest continued, *"Et secundum multitudinem miserationum tuarum, dele iniquitatem meam."* (And according to the multitude of Thy tender mercies, blot out mine iniquity.) His iniquities were well known to them and their *sotto voce* recitation of them was gradually becoming an audible commentary on their feelings for the deceased.

Caterina followed close behind the bier, taking the place that under ordinary circumstances would have been her daughter's. The two young boys stayed close to her side; Maddalena was not there. It was thought better to leave her to the blessed state of tranquility into which she had regressed. She was totally unaware of the events of these last days, so why disturb the fragile world in which she now lived?

It was their love and respect for Prudenza that brought Nella, Maria, Berardo, and Luca to the funeral. They noted Gina's absence and suspected the truth but in a kind of dedicated conspiracy of silence asked no questions.

Just as they reached the church, out from the shadows of a small niche in the wall sprang a frightening looking creature. It appeared to be a woman, yet it was difficult to tell, for the body was covered all over with hair—like Donatello's Magdalene. Yet the crown of the head was bald and smooth as a ripe pumpkin, ringed about with shaggy hair like a monk's tonsure. The creature's eyes were ferret-like, peering out from under bushy eyebrows that showed traces of once ginger-colored bristles, and a scrubby forelock dangled nearly down to its beak-like nose.

At the sight of the priest and the cross the creature erupted into an ear-splitting diatribe of frightening intensity, its range and pitch at once confirming her sex. Obstructing the way of the priest she screeched in a voice as raspy and crackly as dried acorns underfoot in the fall, *"Voglio cantarvi una canzon, prete. Attende bene."* (I want to sing you a song, priest! Listen well)

Not even *Fra* Filippo's stern command of silence could stop her as she carried on in a rhythmic singsong pattern, like children at play. *"Un gatto ha fatto tre uove, Un gatto ha fatto tre uove."* (A cat has laid three eggs.)

"In the name of God, I command you to go away."

"E dentro a queste uove c'erano tre o quattro preti." (And inside these eggs there were three or four priests.)

The horrified mourners waited in silence, frightened at what might follow as she carried on. *"I preti nel porcile e i maiali cantavano messa."* (The priests were in the pigsty and the swine sang the Mass.)

Horrified at the disruption and offended by the shrew's abuse *Fra* Filippo again commanded, "Go at once. Have you no respect for the dead?"

At that moment the tolling of the bell announcing the arrival of the cortege at the church, spurred her to continue this bizarre charade with renewed vigor. *"Le campane erano di burro e le corde di salsicetta."* (The bells were of butter and the bell rope a string of little sausages.)

This last she completed by vigorously miming the ringing of the bell.

The children were terrified and Caterina began to weep. The creature had to be stopped. Some sympathetic bystanders chased the old virago and she retreated briefly into the shadows. But as soon as the cortege resumed its way she began again, chanting—this time adding a frenzied sort of dance, *"L'ucello perde le penne, e il gatto ha fatto uove."* (The bird has lost its feathers and the cat has laid eggs.) Shaking a long bony finger in *Fra* Filippo's face she approached the catafalque waving a branch of mandrake over the corpse. *"La mandragola. La mandragola—mele del diavolo."* (The mandrake, the mandrake—the devil's apple.) Having completely captured the attention of all she bellowed a pronouncement. *"Io ricordo bene. La levatrice mi detto, 'Questo bambino é nato con denti!'"* (I remember well. The midwife told me, "This baby was born with teeth.") At that she curled her lips back, exposing her yellowed fangs in a hideous smile and slowly turned her face for all to see. *"Ecco! E un presagio sinistro! Orrore."* (It is an evil omen. Horrors!)

Even the unwilling pallbearers were terrified, fearing what strange powers the virago might possess. Would she invoke the evil eye on them? For one anxious moment *Fra* Filippo feared that they might even abandon the bier and flee. Just then a quick-thinking observer from the crowd that had gathered, attracted by the commotion, ran into the church and returned with holy water, splashing it liberally in the direction of the hag. Like snow melting under a Tuscan sun she shrank before their eyes, sniveling and writhing on the ground—twisting, contorting and flailing about until she finally fell silent and exhausted as in a trance.

There was a sense of relief as the bier carrying the remains of Matteo Cecchi crossed the threshold of the church, for the hag would not enter the holy. For that matter it was the first time that Matteo had been in a church in years.

As the procession disappeared into the tranquility of the church, there was yet one who followed at a distance, unnoticed. He, too, hesitated at the threshold, then shed a tear—though not out of compassion for his master, nor even in sadness. He was without income now. Where would he go? After a moment he slithered away, dragging his deformed body and disappeared into the shadows.

CHAPTER 27

The Informant

"*Messer, Messer* Latini, you have a caller." The judge did not move. It was clear that he had dozed off. His head was inclined so low that his neatly trimmed beard nearly brushed the official-looking papers scattered atop his desk, so the officer cleared his throat loudly three times. It would not do to let the judge know that he had been caught in this indecorous posture.

"*Messer!* Sir, you have a caller." This time the older man moved and pretended to have heard the first time.

"Yes. Yes, I hear you. A strange time for a caller!"

"He says he has information for you."

"Information?" There was something in the young officer's demeanor that suggested this was no ordinary caller.

Bartolomeo Latini was an honorable man and a wise judge who conducted his affairs in the strictest accordance with the law. Somehow sitting here alone in his chambers and without the trappings of his office, he appeared tired and vulnerable. The weight of his office had taken its toll and the judge did not wear his years well. He did not usually receive callers unscheduled or at this late hour. But there was something about the young officer's voice; perhaps not so much what he said, as what he did not say, that piqued the judge's curiosity as he muttered to himself, "A caller at this late hour? And one who says he has information?"

It was not unusual that in so litigious a city as Florence informants should seem to materialize out of nowhere in hope of extorting money in exchange for information—often bogus at that.

Perhaps this was just another. "Well, send him in."

The venerable judge could never have anticipated what he saw as the informant entered—not actually walking, more lurching, from place to place, almost springing with unbelievable dexterity and speed, despite his obvious deformity. There was an awkward silence as *Messer* Latini observed the creature before him. He could not help noting that the pristine whiteness of the creature's shirt (which he assumed was probably filched from somewhere) suggested that he had taken some measure of care for his appearance. But its unstained condition belied the overall untidiness of the informant's costume and mien.

It was clear that the pathetic figure cowering before the judge was terrified by these unfamiliar surroundings. Although he made some effort to appear nonchalant it was immediately obvious that any attempt to articulate his thoughts could only be impeded by the persistent dribble that cascaded from his slack-jawed mouth. It streaked his dirty face and soiled the collar of his once immaculate shirt. Latini studied the pitiable creature with more than polite routine interest and asked, "What is it that brings you here?"

Struggling to overcome his fear and at the same time to control the impediment of his speech he managed to respond simply, "I...I know shomething."

"You have come here at this hour to tell me that you know something?"

"Yesh." In a kind of rhythmic singsong he began almost to bounce up and down like a child, repeating, "I know shomething, I know shomething."

Bartolomeo Latini was generally a patient man, but this nonsensical display was straining his tolerance and he raised his voice uncharacteristically. "Everyone knows *something*."

"Yesh. But I know shomething important...shomething that you would like to know."

"Am I to guess what this coveted knowledge is? Do not play games with me. I am a busy man with important matters to con..."

"No. You need not guessh."

"Then pray tell me what it is that you know."

"I have knowledge of a sherious act, a murder."

"A murder, you say."

"Yesh! The murder of Matteo Cecchi"

Latini was startled but not surprised, for the Cecchi murder was a topic of much talk in Florence. Not knowing whether or not to take the fool seriously the judge proceeded with caution, attempting not to betray too much interest. The creature simply carried on: "He wash murdered. I tell you, he wash murdered."

"That would appear to be the case."

"And I know who did it."

The judge thought it best not to mention that the wife of the murdered man had already been apprehended. He would play this game with the idiot.

"How is it that you should know who the murderer is?"

"Becaush I wash there."

"And why should I believe you?"

Despite the strange circumstances of this interview the judge was beginning to think that perhaps this fool might really know something, and asked, "So now you have come to tell me who murdered Matteo Cecchi?"

"No. Not yet." At this the creature appeared to contract his twisted body even more and commenced moving his head in the strangest manner. He swiveled from side to side so that his soiled cheeks took turns rubbing against first one shoulder and then the other, further befouling his shirt.

"Am I to believe that you are asking to be paid for this information? That is extortion!"

"Ex...?"

"It means that you are asking the state to pay you for this 'knowledge' that you say you have. It is wrong. Moreover, how do I know that this information is true? Will you at least tell me how you arrived at this intelligence?"

"Shignore Cecchi was my mashter. I worked for him."

"*Signore* Cecchi was your employer?"

"Yesh."

"And just how did you serve your master?"

"I watched. I lishtened."

"Watched what?"

"The mishtressh, Shignora Cecchi...and her mother, too."

At this Bartolomeo Latini lost his patience and raised his voice to a pitch that the guard at the door had never before heard from the judge. "What you mean is that you are a spy. And you want money for…"

At that the idiot began to wimper, "Now I have no mashter, and I have needs."

"And what are these needs of which you speak?"

"Shimple needsh. A bit of bread, a bed to shleep in…"

"What is your name?"

"Tuccio."

"Do you not know, Tuccio, that you can and *will* be called to testify in court, and this you will do *without* pay?

"What if I don't want to?"

"You could be flogged—even worse. You could be tortured."

The creature was so terrified that he made a rapid exit, though with somewhat less spring than before, saying only, "I go now."

At the same time, across town in the Bargello Prudenza was roused from a fitful sleep by the raspy sound of the jailor's key as he opened the door of her cell. Her head burned feverishly and she was not at all sure that she was not again fantacizing.

"Who are you? You have come to take me away to my death, haven't you?"

"No. Your trial has not yet even begun."

"What day is it?"

"It is Monday."

"And how long have I been here?"

"Since full moon, the night of Friday last. Now, no more questions. I have orders from the *Capo della Guardia*. You are to be moved."

"Moved where?"

"You will see."

"Yes, that is what they said to me the night the police took me from my home."

"Hurry on. Gather up your belongings."

She stooped to retrieve the tattered blanket that the guards had thrown over her shoulders on that horrible night. Other than the now-soiled clothes that she wore, it was her only possession.

The climb up the stairs was difficult but even in her weakened state she realized that it could only be better, for with every step the way was becoming more light. It was like resurrection from the grave, after three days in the dungeon, and now at least there was light and the air was not quite so rank as in the dungeon.

As the guard led her through the corridor there was light enough to see prisoners in their cells as they passed and she noted with relief that some were women. At once she felt a strange sorority with them. As she surveyed her new surroundings she was relieved to see that her cell had a window, and although it was small and barred, at least it admitted some daylight. It took only a moment to inventory the pitifully few objects that were the furnishings of her new dwelling place. There was a simple bed, a stool, and a crude table that could serve as a makeshift desk.

Hardly had she completed this survey of her surroundings when the jeering and taunting began. These were the voices of the women prisoners with whom she had naively hoped to find, if not actual sorority, at least tolerance. Their language was shocking to her, even more offensive than that of the men. Despite the din and confusion she tried to imagine how it was that she came to be moved into these new quarters. Had someone made intercession for her that she should be rescued from the dungeon?

What she could not have known was that dear, dependable *Ser* Cristofano had used his influence to request this move. However, in truth it was not a humanitarian act. Rather it was motivated by fear of retribution from their superiors if the prisoner died in captivity. *Signora* Prudenza Cecchi, if left in the dungeon, would surely not live to be taken to justice.

Meanwhile Bartolomeo Latini sat in the dim light of a single dying candle, pondering the significance of the strange encounter with the idiot who called himself Tuccio. "Perhaps he is not so much an idiot as he is artful, scheming and deceitful. He cannot be really stupid, for he has somehow managed to eke out an existence up to now. I fear he is cunning and not to be trusted."

Nonetheless the encounter raised questions in the judge's mind. After some moments of anxious deliberation he called to the officer on duty, "Please bring me *Dottore* Orazio Maiano's autopsy report on Matteo Cecchi." And after a short pause added, "then summon *dottore* to appear here in two days. Perhaps this fool, Tuccio, does know something."

It was the sense of urgency in the summons, as well as a generous degree of vanity that motivated *Dottore* Maiano to appear before the judge in the typical robes of his profession. "After all, my reputation in Florence is well known. I am no mere barber-surgeon, nor modestly skilled practitioner among the many herbalists and apothecaries of this city."

Although there was no one present as he stood proudly before the mirror he announced as if to an audience, "I am *Dottore* Orazio Maiano, trained at the famed school of medicine of the great University of Padua, and physician to some of the most noble houses of Florence."

He was glad that he had donned his doctoral robes for this occasion for Judge Latini also wore his robes of state. Seated at a small desk somewhat lower than the judge was a notary whose task it would be to record the doctor's testimony. It seemed to Maiano that he made more show than necessary as he addressed himself to the task at hand—sharpening quills and endlessly shuffling papers. He ceased only after the judge nodded to signal the beginning of the interrogation. In his finest script the notary guided his noisy pen across the parchment and inscribed the customary beginning:

The statement of *Dottore* Orazio Maiano of the city of Florence, the quarter of Santa Croce, in via dei Fiordalisi, this 12th day of February 1549.
The judge began:

"*Dottore* Maiano, you are a well known and respected physician in our city. Tell us how it is that you came to be engaged to treat the deceased *Signore* Cecchi."

"Yes sir. I will tell you how it came about. I have for some years been the physician and, I think I may say, the friend, of the elder *Signore* Cecchi, *Signore* Zenobi of blessed memory. I have had a long relationship with the family."

"I have reviewed your autopsy report in which you state that *Signore* Cecchi's death was brought about by poisoning. Will you now please elaborate on the case?"

"Yes. On the day of January 15th I was summoned to the Cecchi household to examine the son, Matteo, who suffered from a strange malady of unknown origin. His wife, Mistress Prudenza, had been attending him with the help of their gardener, a knowledgeable *erborista*. After repeated treatments—doses of herbal remedies, various tinctures, and poultices—*Signore* Matteo failed to improve. That is when I was called in, along with my assistants who can testify to the truth of what I tell you. After careful observation I determined that the patient suffered from a dark humor; the only remedy was the drawing out of the corrupt matter by bleeding."

Maiano noted the judge's acute attention to all that he had said and was encouraged to carry on with vigor.

"Although I am a practitioner of the science of medicine, I am well schooled in the astrological influences of celestial bodies upon the human body. Such serious treatment as bloodletting for the purpose of drawing out the dark humor should be undertaken only at the most critical times when the planets affect the crises in human illness. For this we needed to determine the auspicious time. And in order to do that it was necessary to learn certain things such as the date and time of *Signore* Matteo's conception and birth.

"From his mother we obtained that information. We then consulted the chronicles to learn of any important signs or events on the day of his birth and we learned, alas, that it was a day of enormous portent—the death of Pope Alexander VI, Borgia, who, as you may recall, some believed to be 'the very devil in the papal tiara.' This required extreme caution."

"Indeed. And how did you then go about your treatment?"

"On the basis of the knowledge obtained from *Signore* Cecchi's mother we were able to determine that he was born under the astrological sign of Leo, and since Leo governs the heart, the treatment to draw out the dark humor must be applied over that part of the body. We prepared a cautery from the *cantarella*—which is a substance made from grinding a beetle known as the Spanish fly. It cauterizes and burns, but applied in small doses is beneficial and in time can bring relief when judiciously applied topically to the affected area. We placed the cautery on the patient's chest, directly over the heart."

"And where was the mistress Prudenza when the treatment was made?"

"I had explained the treatment to Mistress Prudenza but I suggested that she should not be in the room when we applied the *cantarella*. I must say that she did not favor this treatment. She seemed very fearful so I thought it best that she not witness it. It was a good thing, too, because *Signore* Cecchi's reaction was violent and we were required to leave his room in haste. At that time I recommended that we try another treatment after his chest had had sufficient time to heal. For this second treatment we decided to apply leeches."

Maiano's nerves and the length of his testimony had made him thirsty so he reached for a goblet of water that stood on the table before the judge proceeded with his next question. "How would you describe the behavior of the Lady Prudenza at this time?

"The lady was most attentive to her husband and had over a long period of time attempted to nurse him back to health."

"You have said that she did not approve of the treatment you prescribed."

"No. She did not. She was very anxious and was not at all in favor of the application of the leeches either. But her mother encouraged her, observing that nothing else had helped and there was perhaps a chance that this would be the cure that they prayed for. So she reluctantly gave permission. And again I prescribed that she not be present."

"A wise and prudent decision, I am sure. Please continue *Dottore*."

"This time my assistants brought along stronger restraints to prevent any such outburst from the patient as before. But when the leeches were applied to his chest his reaction was even more violent than before—so much so that I and my assistants were forced to make such hasty exit that we left without even taking our equipment with us. The Lady Prudenza, we presumed, would continue to minister to her husband as she had before we were summoned."

"And did she do so?"

"Yes. It is my understanding that she did, although I myself counseled her to give up these long vigils at his bedside for, clearly, his condition was not improving. She looked pale and weak and her mother, too, attempted to convince her to give up. Yet she persisted."

"There has been a report to the *Otto di Guardi* by one close to the family, who swears that it was she who administered the poison."

"I did not say that, sir."

"No. But you did declare in your autopsy report that it was your considered opinion that Matteo Cecchi was indeed murdered."

"Yes. His condition was such that he could not have taken the *cantarella* himself. It had to have been administered by another."

"When you left the room of *Signore* Cecchi in such haste after the failure of your treatment..."

Maiano winced at the judge's choice of words, obviously resenting the suggestion of failure. *Messer* Latini repeated, this time leaving off the offending word. "When you departed in such haste you say that you left all of your equipment behind in the room."

"That is correct."

"Did that equipment include the poison—the *cantarella*?"

"Yes."

"*Dottore* Maiano, you are aware, of course that *Signora* Prudenza Cecchi has been apprehended on suspicion of murder and is now held in the Bargello. Your testimony in this affair is of extreme importance to the service of justice. You will certainly be called upon to testify further. Meanwhile, you have been very helpful. Thank you. For now you may go."

The jailor did not holler or bark out his words on this morning. Perhaps it was the presence of this particular visitor that caused him to be more restrained. "You have a caller," he announced in a more civil tone than usual. There was also something less jarring about the sound of his approach, announced not by the usual ostentatious jangling of keys, but by a gentler sound—more like the rattling of rosary beads. Before Prudenza could ask who was calling on her he came into sight.

"*Fra* Tommaso! Is it really you?" She was suddenly embarrassed and self-conscious of her appearance. Her gown was torn, she was unwashed, and there was the ultimate indignity of the chamber pot that seemed to stand out so prominently in the room. Her eyes longed to take in the sight of this friend, but sheer embarrassment over her disheveled appearance kept them fast to the floor.

Sensing her disquiet *Fra* Tommaso easily called upon the custody of the eyes that was so much a part of the friar's discipline and training. He simply called her gently by name. "Prudenza. Prudenza, I am here for you. Do not give up hope."

Her only response was silence but the tears that filled her eyes spoke more than her tongue could communicate. The friar came closer to avoid being overheard and whispered, "Prudenza, I bring you news of your dear friend, Gina…"

"*O, Dio*! She has been taken!"

"No. She is safe. She has escaped to the countryside, to the home of her brother."

"God be praised! But how do you know this?"

Still speaking only *sotto voce* he relayed the whole incident of her coming to him at San Marco.

"Thank God! And thank you, Father for what you have done. I love Gina like a sister, and to know that she is safe makes my confinement in this place at least a little less unbearable. Surely the police must suspect her, and I know that Tuccio watched her every move as he did mine. And my mother? How is it with her, and with my babies? What will become of them, Father? Will they be *gettatelli*, throw aways in society because of their mother's sin?"

"No, Prudenza. Gina told me of your mother's residence at the Orbatello and I have gone there to bring her what comfort I can. As for the children, the two little girls may remain with your mother there as long as they wish; even to adulthood, until they are married. The boys, however, may remain only up to the age of twelve. But be assured that we will find suitable place for them in a good family, perhaps to be apprenticed in some respectable trade."

"You know, Father, that what I did—I did to save them. They are my life—even if I must give my life to spare them."

"Prudenza. You have friends who love you, who know the suffering that you have endured, and who will always support you."

"But what can they do for me here?"

"You must speak for yourself, Prudenza. You must have a *procuratore* to present your defense. Your old friend *Ser* Cristofano has sought out one for you, one of the best in Florence he tells me."

"But how can anyone defend me, Father, when I was the one who gave my husband the poison?"

"You must act on your own behalf, Prudenza. You were motivated only by concern for the good of your family."

"Yes."

"You have the right to call up witnesses in your behalf. Your *procuratore* will do this for you. He will undoubtedly call upon those who know the circumstances that brought you to this. They can testify to your integrity, and the manner in which you attended your husband even in his last illness."

"No! No, Father. I must not involve them in this."

"You owe it not only to yourself, Prudenza, but to your children. The knowledge of your heroism throughout the abuse of your husband will testify to the nobility of your motives. And, Prudenza, I will testify, too. You must think about this. But for now I must go. The guards have said only one half hour. But I will return."

"God bless you, *Fra* Tommaso. I thank you with all my heart."

"One last thing, which I know will cheer you."

"What is that?"

"I have obtained permission for your mother to visit you and when I return I will bring her to you."

"Oh, how I long to see her and to feel her embrace, but... it may be too difficult for her to see me like this. My soiled clothes, my tangled hair..."

"You who have sacrificed so much out of love for your children must surely believe that your own mother's love transcends the appearances that concern you."

"You are right, I know. Yes, please bring her...and there is one small thing that I would ask of you as well."

"You need only speak; what is it, Prudenza?"

"Books! May I have some books? My Bible, and my divine poet friend."

"You shall have them."

He raised his hand in blessing just as the guard appeared at the door and announced, "You must go now."

—◊—

Some said he was the finest legal mind in Florence. Certainly so erudite a man as Bartolomeo Latini thoroughly understood the process of the criminal justice system of Florence. Under the law judges could and did conduct investigations. "Surely this case required that the magistrates could systematically go about collecting evidence. But the accused has the right to a *procuratore* who in her defense will call witnesses. Surely there must be those who know the lady well, and have observed her behavior at close range."

"Then there is that simpleton who, without being summoned has insinuated the woman's guilt. This is not a simple case!" The judge's finest sensibilities would prevail. He called out to the guard, "It is time. Toll the *Montanina.*"

CHAPTER 28

The Trial

The deep voice of the great bell of the Bargello brought a sudden halt to passersby in the street who knew the significance of the *Montanina*. It sometimes summoned citizens to public gatherings such as executions, or it might signal a curfew banning from the streets anyone bearing arms. But it was midday now. Ringing at this time of day it could mean only one thing; the judges were being called to assemble for hearings in the great hall. It had to be the case of the woman accused of murdering her husband.

News of the arrest of the young *Signora* Cecchi spread quickly and there was hardly a Florentine within hearing of the bell who did not have an opinion on the question of her guilt. In the weeks since Matteo Cecchi's death, speculation over the case had sustained the insatiable Florentine appetite for gossip. And now, with the trial about to begin, each successive testimony simply provided more grist for the lively mill of rumors and hearsay.

Prudenza, too, was familiar with the significance of the bell, but was blessedly distracted from its full import now, for just as it ceased tolling, *Fra* Tommaso appeared at the door of her cell and, as he had promised, was accompanied by her mother. It was for both women a heart wrenching moment as shame, humiliation, fear, and anxiety simply dissolved into tears when mother and daughter embraced.

Tommaso thoughtfully withdrew into the background to allow this agonizing meeting to play out. After a respectful period he brought the stool near to the bed, invited Caterina to sit, and motioned for Prudenza to take the only other place available, on the edge of the bed. On the floor between them he placed a large hamper from which Caterina began to remove items that she had brought for Prudenza. First a tray of food; cold roasted fowl, fruit, cheese, and some fine bread rolls—so welcome after days of prison fare. On top were some small pastries—not unlike the sweetmeats she had served to her father and his clients when they called on him back in Ancona when she was a girl. Yes, even to her husband she had served these when he came there. As she laid aside the tray so generously provisioned for her she began to find her voice. "*Mamma*, it is so much. You are too generous."

"Nothing is too much for my dearest child, Prudenza, my treasure. It is all I can do now except pray—which I do with all my heart."

"Then, *Mamma*, will you allow me to share with the others who may have no one to bring them food? Please." Caterina could only nod her acquiescence, silently proud of her daughter's generosity. She indicated to Prudenza to remove the remaining parcels from the hamper. "Take them out, Prudenza."

"Clean linens! Oh, *Mamma*, thank you. More clean clothes, soap, and even a small bottle of rosewater."

As she buried her face in the clean sweet fragrance for a long moment, *Fra* Tommaso drew from under his scapular a smaller parcel than that provided by Caterina. "Here, as you requested, Prudenza, I have brought your Bible and your poet-friend to keep you company."

"The *Divina Commedia!* Dear Father, how can I thank you? The time passes so slowly in this place where one's mind has only memories to sustain it. Now I can read again."

At this the friar raised his hand before her face in a warning gesture that said, "Wait! First you must promise me one thing."

"Of course, Father. What is it?"

"That you will move beyond the sad tale of Paolo and Francesca. I beg you, leave the circles of the damned in the *Inferno* and move above, Prudenza. It is time to begin the ascent. This place, this is your purgatory, your cleansing, and if you use it well resurrection awaits you as it did Dante. Read on. Allow him to inspire you, to guide you just as Virgil guided him. Your fate rests in the hands of…"

He was interrupted by the appearance of the turnkey at the door of her cell, signaling time for departure. There was no more time for thanks, tears, or embraces. The iron door slammed shut noisily but the friar, speaking through the bars, finished the thought he had begun. "Your fate rests in the hands of the judges, Prudenza. They will send someone to question you now. You must speak in your own behalf, and you must have the best defense available to represent you, an experienced notary who can argue your case in court as your *procuratore*."

"But, Father…"

"Please cooperate, Prudenza. I will return again as soon as I am permitted to and we will speak more of this. Meanwhile, I pray for you."

———

Just as *Fra* Tommaso predicted, before the sun set on that day a notary appeared at her door, identifying himself as *Ser* Ignazio Pandolfini.

"*Signora* Prudenza Cecchi, I have come to take your statement. I am authorized to record all that you say and you must realize that you are obliged under oath to speak only the truth." So saying he drew from the ample folds of his robe the sacred scriptures and Prudenza did as instructed. He surveyed the cell, looking about for a seat worthy of his dignity. Finding no proper chair, he disdainfully drew the humble stool up to the improvised desk, leaving Prudenza to stand before him in an attitude of submission. Having spent a needlessly long interval inscribing the usual notarial protocol at the head of the page he began.

"I must ask you what it is that has brought you here."

"Sir, you know that as well as I do."

"*Signora*, may I remind you that you are obliged to answer me, just as I am obliged to record your statements."

"Very well."

"Tell me then, how is it that you come to be here?"

"I was brought here by three men. It was night, and I cannot remember much, except that I was extremely cold and very frightened."

"You know that you are charged with the murder of your husband. What do you say in your defense?"

"I have always been a faithful wife."

"You don't deny that you murdered him?"

"As I told you sir, I have always been a faithful wife."

"Answer the question."

"With due respect, Sir, a faithful wife does not murder her husband."

"Did you ever wish your husband to die?"

"Sir, I tried everything in my power to nurse my husband back to health."

"Am I to take this as denial? I must ask you to respond to the question clearly and directly."

Slowly and with exaggerated clarity he began again. "Did –you–poison–your–husband?"

Prudenza realized that it was more than her words that he was noting. He was scrutinizing her physical reaction to the questions and making his own interpretation of them.

"Do you not realize that your silence can be taken as admission of guilt?"

Again he was met with only silence. "And if you persist in remaining silent the judges may resort to torture to arrive at the truth."

"Suffering is no stranger to me, sir."

By this time *Ser* Pandolfini was becoming irritated and impatient with what he interpreted as the prisoner's failure to cooperate—not to mention her lack of respect for his office. Thinking that perhaps a different approach might loose her tongue he assumed an unctuous tone as he resumed questioning. "Surely you must know that you are permitted to call witnesses in your behalf. Do you wish to do so?"

This time her answer came full-voiced and without hesitation. "No! I do not wish to involve my friends."

"But your *procuratore* may do so." His tone became insinuating now as he continued. "Surely he will wish to call witnesses who can testify to your innocence—if indeed you are innocent!"

Prudenza's silence tried his patience. He seemed frustrated by her remote and almost apathetic demeanor, which he interpreted as impertinence. So, unwilling to endure any more of it, without further questioning he abruptly gathered his things and made his exit.

At his next visit *Fra* Tommaso came alone, intent on encouraging Prudenza to speak in her own behalf. "You must defend yourself, present your case and make known the circumstances. You have struggled, endured your husband's jealousy, his anger, and his abuse of you, and your children. There are those who have observed these things and who would willingly testify in your behalf. I beg you, Prudenza, the judges must hear your story."

"But how can I defend myself? It was I who gave my husband the *cantarella*. I did it. I poisoned him."

"The circumstances may allow some clemency in your case. You must make them known. Promise me that if you do not speak in your own behalf you will at least do so for your children's sake. They deserve to know their mother's heroism."

"Their mother's sin, you mean!"

"No. Her love for her children that has brought her to this. Tell your life; write your story, Prudenza."

"How? How can I? I have nothing with which to write."

"If you promise to write I will bring you what you need. Surely the officials cannot object. It is well known that inmates in the Stinche are sometimes actually employed as scribes during their incarceration. You are not asking to be paid for this; you are just telling your story."

"Do you really think that I can? Am I capable of doing it now?"

"Of course you are. You used to write—write very well—and even in verse, when you were back at San Salvatore."

"But that was a long time ago."

"You will, Prudenza. Believe in yourself. It will be your *Commedia*. I will bring you what you need but in the meantime press on with your beloved poet friend."

After a long deep and reflective pause she answered reluctantly. "All right. I will try. I promise."

Despite her promise several long and tedious days passed before she could bring herself to move beyond the *Inferno*. What little light there was from her barred window created a strangely striated pattern on the floor of her cell, but she sought it out hungrily like a moth attracted to a flame. Finally, with some trepidation she gingerly opened the pages to the *Purgatorio* and began to read aloud softly from the first *Canto*:

> *Per correr miglior acqua alza le vele*
> > *omai la navicella del mio ingegno,*
> > *che lascia retro a sè mar sì crudele*
> *E canterò di quel secondo regno,*
> > *dove l 'umano spirito si purga*
> > *e di salire al ciel diventa degno.*
> > > Purgatorio, Canto I, 1

> For better waters now the little bark
> > of my indwelling powers raises her sails,
> > and leaves behind that sea so cruel and dark.
> Now shall I sing that second kingdom given
> > the soul of man wherein to purge its guilt
> > and so grow worthy to ascend to Heaven.

The poet's words seared her consciousness and she began to repeat them aloud like a mantra, "wherein to purge its guilt... wherein to purge its guilt."

Her chanting aroused the interest of the other prisoners who now kept a respectful silence as they strained to hear the young woman who had been so generous to them, and who they had begun to respect. After a time the voice became stronger. "No, no. Wherein to purge MY guilt. I will bide my time in this place of purgation. I will try. And then, maybe...as *Fra* Tommaso says, maybe I may grow worthy to ascen..."

She could not finish the last line.

—〰—

It seemed like eternity before *Fra* Tommaso returned with the promised writing materials. Actually it was only a few days before Prudenza found herself wrestling with words again. The rhymes did not come so easily as they had in the old carefree times when she and the friar made a game of it. The vast blankness of the empty page before her was intimidating. Then almost as if to break the ice and at least indicate her willingness to try, she wrote with large bold strokes across the top of the page:

L'ISTORIA DELLA DONNA PRUDENZA CECCHI,
SCRITTO NEL SUO PROPRIO MANO

THE STORY OF THE LADY PRUDENZA CECCHI,
WRITTEN IN HER OWN HAND

Despite the effort, it seemed to her that her life was but a void, a great wastelend like the pristine page before her—beckoning her to tell her tale.

"You must know that I do this hopeless task only in obedience. I hesitantly put pen to paper, impelled by his repeated admonition, 'Just tell your story.' And so I do, beginning at the very beginning."

> *D'Ancona io venni in la Toscana parte,*
> *privandomi di spassi, e di piaceri,*
> *di quelli che può far natura ed arte.*
> *Non mancavano a me case e poderi,*
> *veste, tappezzerie, robbe e denari,*
> *servitor, fanti e scudieri.*
> *O mancati mi son gli amici cari.*
>
> Lament, Line 7

> I came to Tuscany from Ancona,
> depriving myself of freedom and pleasure,
> those things that are bestowed by nature.
> I did not lack for property or clothes
> tapestries, possessions and money
> or horses, domestics, maidservants and grooms.
> What are missing to me now are my dear friends.

These last words brought home a reality that she had not been able to voice to anyone up to now. "It has not all been bad—my life in the Cecchi family. Up to a point it was good—at least in material ways. To be separated from my father, from Coletta and for a long time also from Mother and *Fra* Tommaso—that has been my deepest pain. And now my dearest Gina has been taken from me; Gina with whom I could share my inmost feelings and fears. We had no need of words. Dear God, how I miss her."

It was difficult to measure the passage of time in this place of confinement. Time was but an indefinable span whose margins were marked off simply by visits from *Fra* Tommaso and the arrival of fresh provisions from her mother. If nothing else the gifts from Caterina's kitchen, which Prudenza continued to share with the other prisoners, had begun to soften their reactions to her whom they had at first perceived as the pampered child of some wealthy person who had probably never known a day's work.

She soldiered on—reading, praying and doing battle with rhyming words while beneath her, in the Hall of the Judges, the trial of *Signora* Cecchi continued. Witnesses for both prosecution and defense were heard as argument and testimony proceeded at an agonizing pace. Soon it would be spring and to pass the time she conjured up in her memory the many blossoming things that would soon scent the air in this season that she loved so much. "Jasmine! When I close my eyes I think I can actually smell its sweet fragrance in Berardo's garden. And the almond trees; they must surely be about to bloom. How I long to see them again."

Soon enough summer would come and in her mind's eye she could see the stones of the riverbed all dried and parched white from the unrelenting sun—white like dead men's bones. She took some comfort, however, in the knowledge that the thick stone walls of the Bargello would tenaciously retain some of the residual cold of the Florentine winter and provide blessed relief from the heat.

—ɯ—

Benedicat vos omnipotens Deus, Pater et Filius, et Spiritus Sanctus. The words were familiar to the young man who had just slipped quietly into an empty pew at the rear of the church, near the main door of San Marco. The familiar Latin signaled that the Mass was over, and as the priest was making the sign of the cross over the congregation the figure in the dusty travel costume crossed himself devoutly, too. He knelt with head discreetly bowed until the early morning worshippers had filed past him, taking holy water from the stoup as they left. He did not rise until he was assured by their chattering that they were now safely out in the street going about their day's business.

When it appeared that the church was empty he walked hesitantly to the entrance of the sacristy where the priest was just divesting, and knocked timidly at the door. Without waiting for a response he announced himself a bit nervously, "Father, I am looking for a friar named Tommaso."

"Well, you have found him, young man. *Eccomi,* I am *Fra* Tommaso, and you are?"

"My name is Giampaolo Alessandrini."

"How is it that you know my name, Giampaolo?"

"I am come here at the request of someone who knows you, Father, a young woman recently come from Florence to my home town, Rignano sul Arno. Her name is..."

"Gina," the friar interrupted. "Is it Gina?"

"Yes, Father."

"Please tell me that she is safe."

"She is, Father, safe in the home of her brother. But she is extremely troubled and anxious for news of her former mistress, *Signora* Cecchi."

"Prudenza."

"Yes. And when she learned that I was going to Florence on business she begged me to find you here and bring back news of her mistress." At this *Fra* Tomasso hurriedly removed his alb, returned it to the *armadio* and took Giampaolo firmly by the arm.

"Come, let us go into the cloister garden where we can talk privately." As they emerged into the cool greenness the only sound to be heard was the gentle cooing of doves from a cote nestled high up under the arches of the cloister. *Fra* Tomasso pointed up to them and remarked reassuringly, "They are the only living creatures here in this quiet place that have ears. You need not fear to speak freely, however, for although they have ears they do not talk."

They sought out a bench in the shade and *Fra* Tomasso began. "I must tell you, Giampaolo, that it does not look good for *Signora* Prudenza. There are witnesses—many of them false— who, hoping to gain some monetary reward, have fabricated strong testimony against her, and at this time I fear that..." He could only shake his head, unable to finish the sentence.

"Father, you must know that Gina wants to come. She believes that she could help if only she could reveal what she has observed."

"No! She must not. It is noble of her but I fear hopeless, and far too dangerous. The authorities have been searching for her and I am convinced that they would not hesitate to subject her to torture to obtain what they want to hear. Please impress upon Gina how dangerous this would be for her, and tell her that it would do little good for Prudenza's cause."

"I will try, Father, but I know that the love she bears for *Signora* Prudenza is strong."

"As is ours for her as well."

After a slightly awkward pause the young man went on timidly. "I, too, have a Prudenza in my life, Father, a little daughter. She is named for *Signora* Cecchi, the best friend of my wife Coletta, who died soon after my little girl was born. You see, I have known such devoted love too—and the loss of it as well. My Coletta has left me but with the gift of a lovely little daughter."

As the friar listened to the young man's story Giampaolo noted a look of sadness on the priest's face. "I thought there was something familiar about you, Giampaolo, and now I remember, as soon as you mentioned the name Coletta. You know your wife was one of my students back at San Salvatore in Ancona, and I met you that last Christmas before Prudenza left for Florence to be married. You must remember how we sat around the fire in the great room of the Beltramonto home, and drank to the health of all, while Prudenza played her lute and sang for us. It seems such a long time ago—a far happier time, to be sure. And now...Giampaolo, you are very kind to do this, to come here. Please tell Gina that I am relieved to know that she is safe, but do try to make her understand that Prudenza would not want her to come as things are now."

"I will do my best, Father."

"Perhaps it will help if you tell her that as Prudenza's confessor I am permitted to visit her from time to time and I will certainly tell her of your visit—quietly, of course, for none must know. It will mean a great deal to Prudenza, for I know how much she loves and misses her friend. May God bless you and keep you safe, Giampaolo."

Fra Tommaso was anxious for his next visit to prison. He would share the news of Gina and Giampaolo and he would check on Prudenza's progress with her writing. He was pleased but noted in subsequent lines of her story a pervasive sense of guilt; evidence that Prudenza believed that she would indeed be found guilty and be executed. She admitted that:

> *Dal primo giorno ch'io entrai in prigione,*
> *sempre fui certa di dovir morire*
> se il luogo suo si dava alla ragione.
> Lament, Line 88

> From the first day I entered into prison
> I was always certain that I must die
> if this cause was just.

As her spiritual advisor Tommaso knew it was imperative for her to face that reality, to acknowledge that she will most likely pay with her life. And he, too, felt the need to unburden himself of the guilt he bore for the counsel that had brought her to this place. In the solitude of San Marco the friar spent many nights in prayer, interceding not only for her but also for forgiveness of his own mistakes.

"Merciful God grant that she may come to realize that her suffering is not without purpose—it is redemptive. Give me the strength to support her to the end in this ordeal. Assist her to continue her life's story so that her children may know her great sacrifice and the true story of Prudenza."

He could not help noticing however that her story began to take on the character of a last will and testament, the instructions of a dying person, the last words to loved ones. Most anguished were her thoughts of her children who would be left motherless.

E tu, Lorenzo mio, sor non ti duoli
  del caso acerbo della madre tua,
   hor di che altro mal doler ti vuoi?
Piglia la cura hormai delle tue due
  sorelle afflitte, che per amor mio,
  ogn'una mostrerà le doglie sue.
E tu sola mia speme, mio desio,
  Piero figluol mio, tu sai ben certo
  che quanto amar si può ti ho amat'io.
Mostrate a ciascheduno chiaro, e aperto
  il vostro gran dolor con negri panni,
  poichè per vostro amor quest'ho soferto
Ti prego, Signor mio, che tu raccogli
  in nelle bracia tue le miei figliuoli
  che della tua salute non gli spogli.
      Lament, Line 31

And you, my Lorenzo do not mourn
  the bitter plight of your mother
  or of that other pain that you bear.
Henceforth take care of your two
  grieving sisters who
  for love of me endure this pain.
My only hope and my joy,
  O Piero, my son, my only hope
  you know I have loved you
  as much as anyone can love.
And now, by the black clothing that you wear,
  show to everyone clearly and openly
  that it is for love of you that I have suffered this.
I beg you my Lord, to gather my children
  in your arms so they be not
  deprived of your blessing.

Surprisingly the turnkey spoke almost kindly on this morning as he ushered in a visitor. Perhaps it was the dignity of the person he escorted. "You have a caller, *Signora*."

She was bent over her improvised writing table and seemed at first not to have noticed his presence. Hearing the scratching sound of her pen on the parchment, the jailor tried again, this time more loudly. "Your priest is here!"

"My priest?"

"Yes." With that he took the huge key that hung from his belt and unlocked the grill. The unpleasant grating sound was like music to Prudenza's ears as she saw her old friend and confidant.

"It is I, Prudenza." Then producing a basket laden with more provisions from her mother, he delivered Caterina's assurances of her love for her daughter, and her prayers, of course.

"I am so grateful, Father. Please look out for my dear mother and my babies."

"Be assured, Prudenza, that they are safe and well. I call on your mother at the Orbatello regularly." Turning his head slightly to see if the turnkey had left, he motioned for her to come closer, and whispered, "Prudenza I have some news for you."

"Pray God it is good news."

"Giampaolo, the husband of your dear friend Coletta…"

"Yes?"

"He has come to see me just a few days ago. He lives in Rignano sul Arno where Gina has gone and he came seeking news of you."

"Rignano sul Arno! Yes, I remember now that Gina has family there. Tell me that she is safe, Father."

"She is, but she is worried and distraught and wants to…"

"No! She must not come"

"I assure you, I insisted that she must not risk it. She is suspected and I hear is being sought. I asked Giampaolo to make it very clear that if she truly loves you, as we both know she does, she will honor your wishes and remain in hiding with her brother's family. He assured me that he would deliver my message."

"Oh, how I long to see her, Father. But now I can at least take comfort in the knowledge that she is safe. Dear Giampaolo, and dear, dear Coletta. She has always been like a lifeline in my time of need. And now she comes to me by way of Giampaolo and

Gina. It makes me both happy and sad."

"I understand, Prudenza."

"And now I bring you other news as well. You must remember *Ser* Cristofano who has long been a friend of the Cecchi
family."

"Yes, of course. It was he who, along with *Fra* Filippo,
greeted me at the pier in Rimini when I came to Florence."

"Well, he is frail now and too old to assume the responsibility of representing you in court, but he has been instrumental
in obtaining the service of *Ser* Vincenzo Taddeo, an officer of the
magistracy in good standing in the powerful Guild of the Lawyers
and Notaries. He is learned in Latin, skilled enough to perform
the work of representation in court and in his position as your
procuratore is determined to call as witnesses some of the trusted
family servants upon whom he knows he can rely to present you in
a favorable light."

"God bless him, and God bless *Ser* Cristofano, too. You
must thank them for me, Father, but assure them that I do not want
to endanger my friends through their kindness."

"I will. But you must understand that it is their sincerest
wish to help you now. I know that the next witness to be called will
be your faithful old gardener, who loves you so much."

"Oh, I hope they will be gentle with Berardo. He is old and
frail and so dear."

"He will not be required to come to court; *Ser* Taddeo himself will call on the old man to take his *depositione*."

CHAPTER 29

The Wheels of Justice

Only a few days later *Ser* Vincenzo Taddeo himself called on the old man in his garden, which was at its lovliest in the warmth of summer. As they sat in the shade of the orange trees, now heavy with fragrant fruit, *Ser* Taddeo inscribed in his finest notarial script: "The statement of Berardo Castelfranco, taken in my presence on this first day of July, in the year of Our Lord, one thousand five hundred forty-nine."

He led with the question, "How, and for what length of time have you known the accused, Prudenza Cecchi?"

"I have known the young mistress Cecchi ever since the day that she arrived here for her marriage to *Signore* Matteo. She was very interested in herbs and already knew a good deal about the art of herbal medicines so she frequently visited me here in the garden. We spent many pleasant hours here discussing the healing properties of plants and herbs."

"Would you please comment on her deportment; how she presented herself on these occasions?"

"Mistress Prudenza was modest, polite and kind at all times. Whenever she came to the garden I always gave her flowers, which she accepted sweetly but she never would ask for them. Only twice do I remember that she asked for anything from the garden. The first time was when she came seeking a remedy for someone in her household who was gravely ill. She was very distressed but did not identify the person. I realize now that it was her husband who had been…"

The old man broke off, too polite to describe Matteo's bad behavior that he had seen on more than one occasion. *Ser* Taddeo urged, "Did you actually ever observe *Signore* Matteo's treatment of her? It is important for you to describe it."

"It is painful, Sir, but I will try. Yes, on more than one occasion I did see the young *Signore* Cecchi physically abuse his wife. Once he attempted to force her to eat a garden slug that he took from beneath one of the steppingstones. When she resisted he threw her to the ground in anger."

By now the old man was weeping as he related the episode that had unfortunately taken place in the presence of young Lorenzo.

Ser Taddeo noted, "You mentioned that there was another occasion when the young mistress sought your help. What was it?"

"This time, Sir, she did not come to the garden to seek it herself, for she was not able."

"How is it that she was not able?"

"It was at the time of the...the incident."

"The incident? What incident?"

"The baby. The last little girl so...so untimely born."

"Please explain."

"I was not there sir, but the midwives immediately sent for medicine to revive the young mistress. *Signore* Matteo, in his last illness had become very abusive, and in anger threw his wife against a table with such force that the babe was expelled from her and she lost an excessive amount of blood. The baby, too, was in danger, her back so injured by the blow to the mother's stomach that she will probably never walk."

The testimony had been very hard for the kind old man but there was yet one important question that *Ser* Taddeo must put to him. To emphasize the gravity of it he addressed the gardener very formally. "*Signore* Berardo Castelfranco, do you believe that *Signora* Prudenza Cecchi used her knowledge of medicine to take her husband's life? Could she have mixed the poison that took his life? Do you think that she murdered her husband?"

"*O gran Dio*, no! No, Sir. Quite the opposite. She did, in fact, pawn a treasured piece of her jewelry in order to purchase some rare and expensive herbs and drugs that I myself could not supply to her from my garden but that I did mix for her once she had procured them. It was a kind of last resort treatment and he rejected it completely, threw it into her face, and flew into a rage. Despite that she sat faithfully at his side, caring for him to the end."

"Thank you, *Signore* Castelfranco. You have been very helpful."

Ser Taddeo requested to hear the testimony of the midwives who attended Prudenza. Anna Balducci, the older of the two, was summoned. Her associate, Emma di Baldo, had since died. *Signora* Balducci took up the story where Berardo's narrative had ended. She confirmed that Prudenza's miscarriage had been the result of the sharp blow to her abdomen where the corner of the marble credenza had struck her so forcibly when Matteo threw her against it that she gave birth spontaneously, there on the floor in a pool of blood.

"*Signora* Caterina sent for my assistant and me at once and we worked day and night to save the baby and the mother. It was only after several weeks that we could confirm that the infant would likely survive. But, alas, the blow had paralyzed the baby's legs."

"Your statement has been most useful, *Signora* Balducci. Thank you."

Not surprisingly the prosecutor for the state pushed on with the case of the Cecchi woman. The Magistrates of the *Ruota* were now assembled in the Great Hall, prepared to hear the next witness whose testimony, it was speculated, promised to be particularly damning to the defendant's case, and might just bring the whole trial to a welcome conclusion. He had been heard from before, but only informally. This time the words of the witness must be officially recorded by the notary of the court and in the presence of the judges. From their reactions it was clear that they were not prepared for what they saw.

With the preliminary details attended to, and the clerk already in his place prepared to record the testimony, the presiding judge indicated to the *procuratore* to proceed with the questioning. "What is your name?"

"*Tuccio.*"

"Just Tuccio? Your full name, please."

"My name ish Tuccio."

"Your family name. Your father's name!"

"I do not know. I never knew my father."

With that the judge indicated to the clerk, "Write Tuccio, *sine nomine.*"

"Where is your domicile?"

"Do mi..."

Clearly the witness did not understand. "Where do you live?"

"I live in the housh of my mashter, *Signore* Cecchi."

"You are aware that your master is dead, are you not?"

"Oh, yesh."

With a sympathetic cock of his head to the left, his face registered a studied look of sadness and he even managed to manufacture a tear as he added, "He wash murdered, you know. I shaw them take him away."

"You saw *them*. Who are *they*?"

"The doctorsh. And after that the polisch took her away, too."

"You say that you know who killed your master. Tell us who."

Recalling *Messer* Latini's reference to torture, the night that he had so unceremoniously called upon the judge in his chambers, Tuccio made no attempt to extort money in return for this information, and answered without hesitation, "It was the misshtressh, hish wife."

"How do you know this?"

"I shaw it. I shaw her prepare the shtuff, the poishon."

"When? And how is it that you saw her do it?"

"It wash the night before he died. I wash in the kitchen."

He then deftly talked his way around what would obviously have been the clerk's next question: "Why were you in the kitchen at this hour?"

"I wash hungry and I went to look for food. That ish when I shaw the lady enter sho I shlipped into the laundry room where she could not shee me."

"How is it that she did not see you?"

"I hid! O, I can hide very fasht. Shee!" Before he even said the last word, he disappeared under the witness box. *Messer* Latini had no desire to see this official testimony go the same route as had his private encounter with Tuccio.

He commanded sternly, "Come out from there at once," and then nodded to the notary to continue questioning. "What did you see in the kitchen?"

"I shaw the misshtressh look around in the cupboardhs and I heard her talk to hershelf. She shaid shomething about chicken. She wash looking for chicken."

"Go on."

"She took shomething from her pocket—it was the poishon, I believe, and she plashed shome in the dish with the chicken. Even from my hiding plache I could shee that she wash trembling, and she shpilled some of the poishon on the cupboard. She cleaned it up carefully."

"And then?"

"She looked about the kitchen one lasht time, took the bowl with the poishoned chicken and dishappeared up the shtairs in the direction of the mashter's room."

"Did you actually see her administer the poison?"

Reluctantly he admitted, "No!" and seemed disappointed, for even he could not fail to recognize that his testimony was far from conclusive.

There was nothing more to be gained by questioning the creature, who actually appeared to be visibly relieved to be dismissed. More reliable and conclusive testimony was needed; the defense must be heard from. Since Tuccio observed all this in the kitchen and at night, the mistress of the kitchen must therefore be called upon to witness. The judges would hear the testimony of the cook, Nella.

"Thus, on the 26th day of July in the year of Our Lord, one

thousand five hundred forty-nine, this statement of the mistress of the kitchen, *Signora* Antonella d'Ubertini of the town of Filigne, was taken in the presence of Giovanni Gherardino, *notaio*. This is what *Signora* d'Ubertini said."

"I came to work in the Cecchi household many years ago as a kitchen maid, scouring pots and peeling vegetables. *Signore* Matteo was very young then. *Signora* Maddalena, his mother, was my mistress; and a very kind one she was. After some years I became mistress of the kitchen."

Eager to reach more relevant issues, the *procuratore* directed his query to recent events in the Cecchi household and probed: "Will you tell us what is your relationship with the accused *Signora* Prudenza Cecchi?"

"The young *Signora* Cecchi, *Signora* Prudenza, is kind and very generous, and of good nature. She has always treated me and the other servants with great respect, generosity and friendship."

"Did you see her often?"

"Yes. Whenever she went to the stable to visit the palfry that her husband gave to her, she always stopped in the kitchen for an apple or a carrot for the horse. And when her husband became so ill, she frequently prepared his porridge."

"Did you ever see her add anything to it—like poison perhaps?"

"No, never. She was so gentle and kind; she would never do such a thing. And when he became so weak that he could no longer feed himself, she fed him as you would a baby."

"On the morning that *Signore* Matteo Cecchi died, did you observe anything amiss in your kitchen? Anything disturbed?"

"No, sir. Nothing. All was as I left it the night before."

"Very well. That will be all."

—◦◦◦—

Messer Latini was troubled over the complexity of this case. Recalling that *Dottore* Maiano's earlier testimony concluded with the failed treatment of Matteo Cecchi with leeches, he believed it imperative to learn exactly what had happened between that episode and the time of the victim's death, a period that was unaccounted for in the doctor's previous testimony. *Dottore* Maiano must return for more statement. So, on the morning of July 28th the doctor appeared before the court in the proper attire of his profession.

As judge, *Messer* Latini began the proceedings: "*Dottore* Maiano, the magistrates have seen your statement given on the 12th day of February in my presence." At a signal from the judge the notary began the interrogation: "Will you now continue to tell us what happened after you and your assistants left the room of *Signore* Matteo Cecchi so abruptly."

"Yes, sir. Some days later, *Signora* Prudenza Cecchi's maid came to me in great haste, ordered by her mistress to fetch us to assist once again her husband *Signore* Matteo who was now *in extremis*. When we arrived at the home it was, alas, too late. *Signore* Cecchi had already expired. We removed his body at once to my laboratory where I performed the autopsy in the presence of witnesses."

"For the court will you please repeat briefly what you recorded in the autopsy report?"

"Certainly. My findings revealed extreme diarrhea, excessive vomiting of blood, and necrosis of the gastric membranes that caused such severe loss of blood supply that the soft tissues of the body were literally burned. Moreover, there was a telltale congestion of blood in the genital and urinary organs. It is my opinion that the cause of death was poison."

"And are you able to determine what was the poison used?"

"I believe that such instant, complete, and catastrophic damage to the body could be the result of only one thing, *cantarella*—the Spanish fly. It is my considered opinion that *Signore* Cecchi was murdered."

"You say that *Signore* Cecchi had been suffering for a long time before this. Is it possible that he may have taken the poison himself in order to end his sufferings?"

"No. His condition was such that he could not have taken the *cantarella* himself. It had to have been administered by another." Despite the doctor's suspicions, he stopped short of making an accusation. It would not be proper. Besides, he had observed the Lady Prudenza's genuine concern for her husband and her objection to the painful treatments that he himself prescribed. It was difficult for him to believe that she might actually have killed her husband—especially by such torturous method.

He was grateful when the judge announced, "*Dottore* Maiano you have been very helpful. You are dismissed for now."

—m—

For Prudenza it seemed that the wheels of justice were turning at an agonizingly slow pace and, as her fate was being determined, she knew very little of the argumentation going on in the Hall of Justice below. In his periodic visits *Fra* Tommaso attempted to keep her abreast of the proceedings—careful, however, to filter the news in order not to alarm unduly, for he was aware that the defamatory *libellus* had been read and the list of indictments was bad news.

Even without the luxury of a mirror in her cell, Prudenza was painfully aware that the passage of time could be measured by the changes in her appearance. She was startled one day and began to weep as she stared into the basin of water brought to her to wash. She could hardly recognize the face reflected there. As she touched her fingertips to her sunken cheeks she murmured, "They are hollow as empty shells. Fear, fatigue, and worry for the fate of my children rob me of appetite, and sleep eludes me for hours at a time. But I must continue to write, for soon *Fra* Tomasso will come again and I know he will expect me at have made some progress."

Despite her best intentions several days passed before she mustered courage to take up her pen again. When finally she dipped it into the inkpot she hesitated in mid-air over the naked expanse of parchment spread out before her. The friar's words came to her: "Just tell us who you are; where you came from. Simply tell your story."

Her hand trembled as she put pen to paper but then almost as if another power guided her hand, she saw the words continue to materialize before her eyes. The suggestion that she should tell her life's story was proving to be wise counsel for, through the exercise, she was gradually coming to terms with her inevitable demise.

Adding to the narrative each day, she began to refer to it now as her lament. Indeed she inscribed a new title page to the manuscript, calling it:

IL PIETOSO LAMENTO CHE FECE LA SIGNORA PRUDENZA PRIMA CHE FOSSE CONDOTTA ALLA GIUSTIZIA

THE PITEOUS LAMENT MADE BY THE LADY PRUDENZA BEFORE SHE WAS TAKEN TO JUSTICE

She appended a note to the reader—should there ever be one. "I must explain why I, a simple wife and mother, should share my innermost feelings, fears and prayers; how it came to be that I write my story. My dear friend, confidant, and confessor has brought me pen and paper and counseled me to tell my sad tale.

> *E subito mi fece lì portare*
> *da scrivere, notando molte cose,*
> *che cominciò ciascun a lacrimare*
> Lament, Line 121

> He brought me at once things to write with
> noting down many things
> that moved everyone to weep.

In the privacy of her cell Prudenza continued to contemplate the words of the poet she so loved. Making her way through the *Purgatorio* she was comforted by his word of admonition.

> *"Non aver tema" disse il mio Signore;*
> *"fatti sicur, chè noi siamo a buon punto;*
> *non stringer, ma rallarga ogni vigore."*
> Purgatorio, Canto IX, 46

> "Don't be afraid," he said. "From here our course
> leads us to joy, you may be sure. Now, therefore
> hold nothing back, but strive with all your
> force."

Time seems to have stood still for her as she inscribed the next words in her own *commedia*.

Settantacinque giorni tra' dottori,
e medici fù visto il caso mio,
e disputato fra procuratori.

Lament, Line 82

For seventy-five days my case was examined
by physicians and lawyers and
disputed among the attorneys.

While Prudenza labored on with her story, the prosecutor for the state continued to build his case against the Cecchi woman, attempting to find witnesses whose testimony might cast more negative light upon the behavior of the accused. For this he called first the laundress, Maria Marcucci, who when asked, "Did you often see the accused?" answered, "Only infrequently. Once the mistress's maidservant took me up to the young *Signora's* private apartments."

"Is that not rather unusual? Why would a laundress be taken to the upper regions of the residence?"

"It was to teach the young *Signora* how to use the loom that her husband gave her for Christmas. She was having difficulty learning to weave and Gina, her servant, took me to her room while *Signore* Matteo was out of the house."

"Then it was in secret, was it not?"

"Yes, I suppose you could say that."

"Hm! Suspicious at best. Is it not possible that there were other secret meetings? Other assignations?"

"I know of nothing but this lesson with the loom. She learned very quickly and I never had to return after only two or three lessons."

"That is very helpful, *Signora*. Thank you."

—ɯ—

The prosecutor then called *Fra* Tommaso as witness. "We know that you and the accused have long been friends, and that you have called upon her in prison a number of times. Tell us what she has told you. Did she confess to you?"

"Sirs, I know well that you are learned in the law, both civil law and the canon law of the church. I need not remind you that, in my capacity as *Signora* Cecchi's chaplain and confessor, any such conversations or confidences are protected by the Seal of the Confessional. For me to violate that privilege would result in my excommunication."

"I need no monk to lecture me on the intricacies of the law."

"Nevertheless, you thought you might try that ploy."

Having no success on that front, the prosecutor called his last witness, Niccolo Mascalzone, *Dottore* Maiano's assistant, who carried the book and whose duty it had been to notate all things surrounding the case. His account was a tiresome rendering of facts that were already familiar to the judges—except for one last remark. "When we arrived at *Signore* Cecchi's bedside, he was already deceased. As it was my duty to take note of all things related to the case I inscribed in my notebook this observation. 'The *cantarella* that we had left behind at the time of our hurried departure, was no longer there.'"

With the satisfied look of a vulture that had just picked the carcass clean, the prosecutor dismissed the officious young man saying, "That is more than sufficient!"

Having been heard from it remained now for the judges to determine the fate of the accused as she attempted to comfort herself with the divine poet's words.

Non attender la forma del martire;
   pensa la succession; pensa che, al peggio,
   oltre la gran sentenza non può ire.
                              Purgatorio, Canto X, 109

Do not think of the torments: think, I say,
      of what comes after them: think that at worst
      they cannot last beyond the Judgment Day.

"And so I await my fate while beneath me the debate
goes on."

—《双》—

"Father Tommaso, forgive me for interrupting your medi-
tation." The apologetic young porter stood sheepishly in the doorway as he attempted to rouse the friar who appeared to be deep in
thought, kneeling at his *prie dieu*, his head buried in his hands.
      "What is it, Brother?"
      "There is someone asking for you, Father, someone who
wants to confess. I take it from the rough cloak and hood that she
is a pilgrim."
      "She, you say?"
      "So I believe, from the voice. I could not see the face so far
buried under the hood. She asked for you specifically, saying 'I can
confess only to *Fra* Tommaso.'"
      "Very well, then. God forbid that I should keep the peni-
tent sinner from being absolved. I go now."
      Of late it was apparent to his fellow friars that *Fra* Tom-
maso moved somewhat slower than usual; his shoulders were decidedly slumped, and deep circles showed under his eyes. Though
no one would venture to say it to him, they understood that the
fate of the Cecchi woman weighed heavily on him. He had known
her since she was little more than a child, had been her tutor back
in Ancona and now, as her chaplain, was preparing her for death.
      With noticeable difficulty he rose from his place to go to
meet the penitent inside the church where the late afternoon sun
dappled the floor of the sanctuary. The church was empty except

for the small figure kneeling before the Madonna at the second altar on the right.

Gone was the friar's youthful vigor and the spring in his step. He genuflected unsteadily as he passed the altar of the sacrament and quietly asked the waiting pilgrim, "You wish to confess?"

From under the ample hood the muffled voice called out, "No. but I do wish to speak to you alone." As she did so she threw her hood back and *Fra* Tommaso gasped as he recognized her. "Gina! You should not have come. Do you not realize the danger to you?"

"I had to come, Father. You know well that I, more than anyone, have witnessed the atrocities and abuse that my mistress suffered from her husband. I was there. I was with her."

"All the more reason that you are being sought by the authorities."

She seemed not to hear—or perhaps more correctly she chose to pay no attention to his words. Her only response was a dismissive gesture, as if brushing away a pesky mosquito.

"Think, Father. I was there when he killed her innocent little bird, when he destroyed her precious lute, and I saw the jealousy in his eyes when she caressed her babies—his babies, too. I have seen the bruises on their little bodies as well."

The friar grasped her hand firmly and said, "Even if, as you say, you have not come to confess, Gina, let us go into the confessional to talk. It is safe and no one will disturb us there."

This time she did not resist the idea. As the heavy drape fell into place and her identity was concealed, she breathed more freely and began, "Mistress needs an eye witness of these events. For that reason I must make myself known. That slimy little Tuccio has probably filled the judges' ears with lies. He is nothing more than a mean, sniveling little spy, a spy paid by her husband."

"Gina, you are…" He broke off abruptly as from a distance he heard a familiar deep rumbling sound that aroused his worst fears. "Do you know that sound, Gina?"

"I…I fear I do, Father. Tell me it is not the *Montanina!*"

"Would to God, it were not." As the somber tolling of the bell continued, its meaning became obvious. "The sun has not yet set, Gina; it is too early to announce curfew. It can mean only one thing."

CHAPTER 30

Deliverance

"It means the judges have reached a verdict, Gina, and if she is guilty they will read the sentence at once. God help her, she needs us now. I must go to her."

Like a flash Gina followed the friar out of the confessional, pulling her hood over her head as she did so. "I will go with you."

"No, you must not. It is still dangerous for you to be found. I beg you, Gina, remain here in the church where you will be relatively safe until I return. Pray, Gina! It is the best service you can do for her now."

"I am not much practiced in that, Father."

Realizing the intensity of the young woman's love for her mistress he anticipated what might happen when he was out of sight, and called out a last minute admonition. "Do not try to follow me, Gina. Do not even think of it!"

It was a motley and raucous crowd that spilled out from the courtyard of the Bargello and into Piazza Sant'Apollinare. Some, sadistically thirsting for the harshest sentence, were shouting obscenities. It was as if the weeks and months since the prisoner's arrest, and the avid speculation that followed, had not satisfied their blood lust. Others were silent, their anxious looks revealing sincere sympathy for the young *Signora*. Still others—many of them women—stood in an attitude of prayer, hoping against hope that the knowledge of the young *Signora* Cecchi's sufferings might win some clemency from the judges. In their hearts, however, there remained the haunting realization that after all, she is just a woman;

what was she to expect? Then there were the spineless ones fearful of expressing allegiance to anyone, neither the accused nor the state. Voyeurs! Their vacant faces reminded the friar of the irresolute that Dante rightly consigns to the antechamber of the *Inferno*, for they do neither good nor bad. They are pitiful!

Still breathless after his trek from San Marco to the Bargello, the friar stepped into the courtyard and with difficulty made his way through the teeming crowd just in time to see Prudenza being led to the great hall to hear her verdict read. Her hands were bound and she walked slowly with eyes downcast, her face sunken and pallid, skin transparent as alabaster. She passed inside the great doors of the Hall of Justice and the catcalls of the crowd suddenly subsided as if an impermeable pall had been dropped over the raucous mob. An unsettling silence prevailed, not from respect so much as from fear that their clamor might drown out the verdict when it was read.

Tension in the crowd was palpable and it seemed to *Fra* Tommaso an eternity until from inside the courtroom an expressionless voice broke the thick silence: "Be it proclaimed this day that the honorable judges of the *Ruota* find the accused, *Signora* Prudenza Cecchi, guilty of having poisoned her husband, Matteo Cecchi."

There were cheers from some, tears from others and yet a dull silence of disbelief for the few loyal friends in the crowd who knew and loved the young woman. Despite the fact that he thought himself mentally prepared to hear the worst, the sheer finality of the words, "guilty of murder," left Tommaso gasping for breath as he awaited the sentence that would follow. The disembodied, expressionless voice continued: "By law the condemned must forfeit her life. Execution by the *ghigliottina di mannaia!*"

"Decapitation! My God, she is to be beheaded!" The noise of the crowd thundered in his ears now, drowning out his voice as in disbelief he repeated aloud to himself, she is to be beheaded. He strained against the crowd that filled the courtyard and milled about noisily trying to catch a glimpse of the condemned as she was led back to her cell. To *Fra* Tommaso she appeared strangely emotionless, drained. "I must find the turnkey."

Attempting to make his way to the jailor's office was like marching against a charge of the Roman Legion. He was jostled and repeatedly pushed against the wall, his white habit now stained by the accumulated grime and mold of centuries, for in his haste he had not taken time to don the black cloak that Dominicans wear in public. One thought only drove him forward. "I must go to her."

In the press of the crowd progress was slow, so by the time he was admitted to her cell, she had already been secured there and stood facing him—almost serenely, he thought. There were no words to express the pain both felt; their silence was eloquent. To the friar her tranquil countenance seemed to suggest relief. Whether it was resignation or shock, he could not say. As if to read his thoughts she spoke first, words of comfort for him. "Father, at least this interminable waiting will be over. Soon an end will come to my tribulation."

His mouth was dry as cotton as he spoke the only words that came to him now—feeble words they were. "Prudenza, you must ennoble the time that remains to you as you prepare for…"

"For my death, Father. Do not hesitate to say it."

He hung his head in a moment of shame, thinking, I have come to comfort her and instead I am the one being comforted. She has become strong in her suffering. He was acutely conscious that as a man of God he should do better than that.

"Do not think, dear Father, that I am not afraid. It is just that I am utterly drained of feeling now. I am numbed; all emotion is gone from me in this moment. But you must not mistake this for courage, for when I least expect it terror comes over me in great waves and I am helpless, like a drowning person struggling to breathe."

An awkward interval passed as the friar pondered what to do or say next. Finally he broke the silence. "Prudenza, there are things you need to know—what to expect, how to prepare yourself. Please allow me to help you."

"Although I know, Father, that the journey of my life is nearing an end now, I do not know exactly what to expect. I need you now more than ever. Please help me to prepare."

"I am here for you, Prudenza; never doubt that."

"I find solace in the thought of my dear ones who have gone before me; my father, my father-in-law, Coletta, and my brave grandmother, *nonna* Costanza. Will they be there to welcome me?"

"They will indeed, Prudenza. In the meantime we will together prepare for the journey that you are about to complete. Think that like your beloved poet your *commedia* will also have a *Paradiso.*"

"But Father, my way is different."

"Yes, the soul's progress to God is different for each of us, but the reward is the same."

"It seems to me, Father, that my journey is not just different, it is the exact opposite of the poet's. He began in the depths of the *Inferno* and rose through *Purgatorio* to enjoy the ultimate bliss before the face of God. It seems to me that I began in paradise. To be sure it was a kind of earthly paradise of love and security and happiness with my dear parents back in Ancona—a place that I loved so much. I have descended here into this pit that you would have me regard as my purgatory. I have tried to use this time as my purification, my preparation for...for, do I dare say heaven? But I am seized with fear that for the evil deed that has brought me here, I will instead be cast into everlasting hellfire."

"You must not think that for one moment, Prudenza. It would be a far greater offense to fail to trust."

"I want to trust, and I try; but I need help."

"Believe, Prudenza, as I do, that we have been brought into each other's lives for a purpose. We have had wonderful, happy times together, but we have suffered together, too."

"You have suffered, too?"

"Of course. Do you not understand that your pain is mine as well?"

"I am sorry, I did not mean to..."

"Over these last difficult months I have come to realize that I need forgiveness, Prudenza, forgiveness for encouraging you to remain faithful to your husband. Now look where my words have brought you! It is the burden that I carry."

"It is not your fault, Father."

"Fault or no fault, please allow me to make the ascent with you. We will prepare together, every step of the way."

In that moment of utter nakedness of soul, she realized for the first time the depth of his vulnerability. The scholar, the tutor she so respected and admired, always knew the right thing to say to comfort her. But in this awkward silence she realized for the first tme, his frailty. This man of God was a child of Adam, too— flawed like the rest of us. It was a look that spoke volumes of an otherworldly love, pure gift.

Finally in a timid voice like that of a small child she broke the silence. "I have never attended an execution, Father." Touching her neck gently as one might stroke a puppy she spoke softly, "It is small, my neck, is it not? Will it be hard to...to...?"

It was a painful and chilling question that deserved an honest response. He steeled himself as he struggled to find the right words, knowing there were no right words.

"Prudenza, it is said that beheading is faster, less long and agonizing than hanging. It is actually a concession to your family's status...a patrician privilege." That his choice of words was unfortunate he realized immediately as she abruptly turned away from him and responded in short, ragged, and passionate questions, allowing no time for his response.

"I should be honored to have my head cut off? And in the presence of that cruel mob? Is that what you are saying? Are you telling me that I am privileged?"

"No, no child,...that is not what..."

"Whether hanged or decapitated, what matter? I should be just as dead one way or the other. Will they display my head for the crowd to revile? Will I be denied Christian burial? Am I to be held up as an example?"

"No, no, Prudenza. You must not dwell on such thoughts." The vehemence of her reaction left him speechless for a moment, fumbling for some word of comfort. When he regained his equilibrium he asked, "Have you never heard of the Confraternity of Santa Maria della Croce del Tempio? They are called the company of the Neri, from the black robe that they wear. They are dedicated to attend the afflicted in their last hours. It is a most solemn obligation. You will be treated with the utmost respect and, Prudenza, I will be there with them, every step of the way, I promise. Let me share in your ascent; make it mine as well as I also ask for forgiveness."

"When will it be, Father?"

"We will know that when the judges have sent their notification to the captain of the Neri. He will then summon members of the company to the Bargello where they will accompany you to the prison's Magdalene Chapel to spend the night in prayer, supporting you, reassuring you. That is why they are called the comforters."

"I should be grateful for that I suppose, but I am terrified."

"Please know that although I am not a member of the

Company of the Neri, I will seek permission to join them in this vigil, and to accompany you to the last. You see, there must always be a priest there to administer the sacrament. And then the procession to…" He stopped abruptly: "It is enough for now. Let us spend these last days well. They are precious. Above all, Prudenza, try to forgive those who have treated you badly—your husband, Tuccio, all those who testified against you. Meditate on the words of your beloved poet:"

> *E come noi lo mal che avem sofferto*
> *perdoniamo a ciascuno, e tu perdona*
> *benigno, e non guardare al nostro merto.*
> Purgatorio, Canto XI, 16

> As we forgive our trespassers the ill
> we have endured
> not weighing our merits, but the mercy of
> Thy will.

"I leave you for now. It is time for you to finish your own *commedia*. It will be your legacy for your children, for all of us who love you. You must tell your story, Prudenza. Let history to be the judge."

"There is yet so much to tell, Father, but so little time."

—·—

She now spent nearly every moment working on her lament and even at night labored over the manuscript by the light of a single tallow candle until her head throbbed and her eyes burned.

To bring the poem to conclusion had now become a race with death and she realized how wise he had been to counsel her to do this, to focus her mind. "O God, I know the moments left to me are few; help me, help me truly to live until I die."

Her great preoccupation at this moment was concern for the loved ones left behind—especially her mother. "When words of comfort do not come I turn to the divine poet and he never seems to fail me. Oh, noble Dante, you inspire me to take up my pen and add thoughts of my mother to this poor *commedia*. I know not how to comfort her; what can I say to her? When the words do not come to me I ask you to speak for me and I find my answer in your words."

> *Quest' ultima preghiera, Signor caro,*
> *già non si fa per noi, chè non bisogna*
> *ma per color, che retro a noi restaro.*
> Purgatorio, Canto XI, 22

> This last prayer, Lord, with grateful mind,
> we pray not for ourselves who have no need,
> but for the souls of those we left behind.

"So then I take up my poor pen again and try to think what it will mean for her who has already lost her husband, her good friend Maddalena and must now see her daughter die in such ignominious fashion? What will she feel?"

> *Quando vedrà la mia testa tagliata*
> *dal delicato mio candido busto.*
> *con la faccia cruente insanguinata.*
> *All'hora sentirà l'amaro gusto,*
> *la mia dolente Madre, e miei Figliuoli,*
> *sentendosi ferir dal duolo ingiusto*
> Lament, Line 25

> When she sees my head
> cut from my pure and delicate body,
> the face all covered with blood?

> In that hour my sorrowful mother and my children
> will themselves be wounded
> by that unjust pain.

Tears blinded her now as she abandoned the pen, giving way freely to weeping—but only briefly. "I must carry on, I must finish this. Soon *Fra* Tommaso will come again to see my progress and at any moment they may take me away to pay my debt."

Tommaso was caught up short as he crossed Piazza Sant'Apollinare, for there in the center of the vast square was a neatly stacked pile of sturdy pine boards, and already workmen were arriving with the tools of their trade to construct the *palco*. "*O, Dio mio.* It can mean only one thing: It is going to be a public execution! She is to be made a spectacle, an object lesson."

—ɷ—

She did not even hear the jailor admit her friend, so intent was she feverishly working at her table, and was startled at the friar's voice. "I am pleased with your attention to your *commedia*, Prudenza."

Then in a futile attempt to lighten the exchange which had gone so badly at his last visit he looked over her shoulder and said, "Who would ever have predicted back when we played those rhyming word games that you would one day write your own *commedia*, and write it in *terza rima* too, like Dante. *Brava, Signora!*"

"No. I say rather, who would have ever predicted that one day I would find myself in these circumstances? What I have written is hardly a true *commedia*, Father. I should instead call it my *tragedia*, for I do write my fear into my poor poem."

Over her shoulder he read her latest addition. The ink was not yet fully dry, and here and there in the margins he detected a stain that must surely be a tear. They were words that revealed the depths of her anxiety.

> *Ogni romor nel cor tremor mi dava.*
> *e per gran pezzo mi batteva il petto*
> *che d'hora in hora tal morte aspettava.*
>   Lament, Line 94

At every noise my heart is seized by fear and
a heaviness pounds in my breast
as hour by hour I await my death.

Try as he might to comfort her now, there was no way to
distract her from the sound of hammering in the *piazza*.

"That pounding, Father, is it for me?"

"Yes, I fear it is."

Mindful of her impertinent and angry response to her
friend at his last visit, she was embarrassed and made a heroic effort to reach deep into the recesses of faith and friendship to find
words to set things right between them. With great effort she managed to produce a wan smile and, speaking with mock seriousness
announced, "I do believe, Father, that they are erecting the stage
for the last act of my *commedia*. It will be the farewell performance
of Prudenza Maria Cecilia Beltramonto Cecchi."

Giovane di età di ventotto anni,
offersi il capo mio alla giustizia."
Sonnet, Line 9

A young woman of twenty-eight years
I offer my head to justice.

It was but a brief respite from the reality of the situation
however. "I know they will come soon to take me to the chapel
for that last vigil and, although you assure me that the comforters
are kind, the thought of their coming for me fills me with terror."
It was a terror poignantly captured in this latest tercet of her lament.

Ed ogni volta ch'io sentivo aprire
la porta della prigion m'imaginava
che in cappella dovessi all hor gire.
Lament, Line 91

Every time I hear the door of the prison
open I imagine that it is the hour
when I must go to the chapel.

By the time of his return the next day, the din of the construction in the *piazza* had ceased and she appeared surprisingly calm. "Father, does that mean...?"

"Yes, It is nearly time, Prudenza. *Coraggio*."

"The day I am to die?"

"No, rather the day that you begin a new life freed from all this pain and sorrow."

"I reckon then it must be nearly August tenth."

"Yes, tomorrow."

"How appropriate that I should die on the feast of a martyr, the great San Lorenzo. My stage must be ready then. Tell me, is it a beautiful *palco*?"

The familiar sound of the jailor's rusty key in the old lock meant that someone was being admitted. It was too early in the day for the comforters. Instead there stood before the prisoner a wizened little woman of undetermined age, with dull, black eyes that looked out emotionless from under shaggy brows as she announced the purpose of her presence. "I have come to prepare you."

It was her thankless assignment to attend to the last *toilette* of women about to go to their death. Prudenza felt almost sorry for her, and wondered what violence she must have had to do to her sensibilities in order to carry out this grisly assignment. Had she simply willed to dull her feelings in order to shield herself from thoughts of sympathy, or had time and repetition successfully subdued such sisterly sentiments?

"Sit here," she commanded, showing no emotion or compassion for what she was about to do. Opening a dingy brown reed basket she produced a huge pair of scissors, so large and rusty that they could have been used to shear sheep.

"Sit still, and don't whimper like a sick puppy. It won't help." So saying, she seized a lock of Prudenza's hair and announced, "This must go, it will make the job of the blade more efficient." In fact, the blades of the shears were so dull that it seemed to Prudenza her hair was being pulled out bit by bit. It was a slow and agonizing process, made even more painful as the crone snickered at the huge handsful of hair that began to accumulate at her feet.

"Dear God, for all those years that I have been so vain about the color of my hair, I offer this sacrifice. How many times my mother brushed my locks so tenderly, and Gina, too, stroked my hair 'til it was lustrous in the sunlight."

As she stared helplessly at the tangled pile on the floor, she had to acknowledge that her once shiny mane was now more ashen than copper.

"Stand up," the crone commanded, "and remove your gown." She became impatient when Prudenza fumbled with the fastenings of her dress and, with no concern for modesty, pulled away her shift and in its place slipped over her head a shapeless sack-like garment. The rough weave of the fabric scratched as it settled on her shoulders. As the crone tied a coarse rope loosely about Prudenza's waist, she stood back and, with arms akimbo, reviewed her work with obvious satisfaction. "A fine example! Now you are ready to go to your reward, *Madama*. It is your shroud!" She laughed a fiendish cackle and then called the turnkey to allow her to exit. As the door slammed shut noisily Prudenza stroked the roughcut stubble that now crowned her head. "It requires yet another tercet for my *commedia,* Father."

> *Ecco il mio corpo pronto, e preparato,*
> *a sopportar la vera penitenza*
> *secondo l'error mio del mio peccato.*
> *Ecco colei, che si fa dir Prudenza*
> *benchè prudenza, e senno non mostrasse,*
> *quando offesi d'Iddio l'alta potenza.*
> Lament, Line 106

> Behold, my body, ready and willing,
> prepared to submit to the just penance
> according to the error of my sin.

> Behold her who though she is called Prudenza,
> did not show prudence when
> she offended the omnipotent God.

—ɰ—

In the hall of their meeting place the captain of the Comforters had received word from the Bargello establishing the time of the execution. As directed by the rule of the confraternity, he sent word to the brothers to assemble to fulfill their ritual duties this night. The Magdalene Chapel must be prepared for the vigil that would precede the dispatching of the condemned in the early hours of the morning. Beside their spiritual ministrations the comforters were mindful of the physical well-being of the prisoner as well. The lamps must be filled with oil; there must be fresh candles for the altar, and a straw mattress and cushion must be provided.

Earlier in the day *Fra* Tommaso presented himself personally to the captain to request permission to be a part of the comforting ritual. "I am very familiar with your service, and I know it would be a great comfort to *Signora* Cecchi if you would permit me to participate in it. I feel I owe it to her."

"It is irregular, Father, but I know of nothing in our rule that would prevent you from doing as you request. There must always be a priest in attendance during the vigil to celebrate Mass at dawn and to administer the sacrament. So is it then your wish to fulfill that obligation?"

"Yes, Brother. And..."

"There is more?"

"Yes, if you please. I wish to carry the *tavoletta*."

At this the prior hesitated. "That is a privilege normally reserved for one who has long been a member of the brotherhood. You realize, of course, that to do this you are required to walk backward the entire way as you hold the sacred image before her face. It is very important that the condemned one's eyes should not be diverted from the crucified for even an instant. Do you believe you can do this?"

"Yes. Sir, I believe that my presence will actually assist the *Signora* to concentrate on the crucified."

"You seem very certain of this."

"I am, Sir."

"Then it is so ordained; I give you permission."

"With all my heart, I thank you, Brother."

While the chapel was being prepared, Prudenza toiled feverishly over what she realized must be the last lines of her *commedia*. "I must finish it before they come for me. The time is short, but what yet remains of my life story is brief. I would deceive if I pretended not to fear what I know awaits me. In my troubled sleep I live and relive the moment when they will come for me. And now is the time. It is no longer a dream."

> *Poi senti quella porta che s'apria*
> *dissi alla mia compagna "Iddio m'aiuti*
> *ch'io veggio l' hora della morte mia."*
> Lament, Line 100

> Then you will hear the door open and
> I say to my companions, "God help me.
> for I see now is the hour of my death."

"They are come for me now, I know. No voice, no words, just the quiet footfall of these men *Fra* Tommaso calls 'the comforters.'"

Despite his efforts to prepare her for this moment, she recoiled in fright at the sight of the hooded, black-robed intruders as they huddled in the small cell that she now thought of as her refuge, the one little space left to her in this world. It was as if by their presence they sucked the very air, the last bit of breath, from this place.

In the waning light she was unsure if they were corporeal or phantom. Behind their hoods they were but a faceless presence staring through holes that look like the deep sockets in empty skulls. "Is my mind so weakened that I fantasize? Are they ghosts?"

In an effort to distance herself as far as possible from these faceless predators, she flattened herself against the far wall and cried loudly, "Go away! I am not yet dead. Are you come to pluck out my green eyes? Can you not see that I still live?"

Becoming conscious of her appearance she pulled her coarse robe, her shroud, tightly about her and attempted to cover the remnants of her once glorious hair. At the same time she cried out more loudly, "Please leave me. Go away!"

Behind the comforters the jailor had just admitted *Fra*

Tommaso. As he approached her cell he heard her cry out and, seeing her panic-stricken face, made his way to her immediately. "Prudenza, do not be afraid. They are your friends; these are the comforters I told you of and they are here to help you. *Per l'amore di Dio, cara sorella, sta tranquillo, prego.*" (For the love of God, dear sister, I pray you please be calm.)

The sound of his voice and the glimpse of the familiar white habit that shown beneath his mantle were like a small ray of light in an otherwise murky sea of black. "Thank God, you are here, Father."

At that moment the leader of the comforters stepped forward and in a firm but kindly voice announced, "We are come to support you, *Signora* Cecchi." In the words prescribed in the ritual of the brotherhood, he began the well-practiced formulaic counsel: "I admonish you to accept that this is the will of God for you." They were hollow words, of slight comfort now as the leader continued, "It is time to make our way to the chapel."

"Wait! I must bid goodbye to my companions who have shared my agony in this place." In a voice now loud and strong, seeming to come from some unplumbed inner reserve, her words rang out. "To you, my companions on this journey, I render my heartfelt thanks for your kindness to me, and I give to you whatever poor worldly possessions I leave behind here. I pray you recommend my soul to God. We will meet in eternity. *Addio.*"

In the respectful silence some muffled sighs could be heard from faces pressed close to the bars of their cells, watching to catch a last glimpse of her as she passed. Gone were the coarse comments and obscenities of that first night when she was brought to prison.

Turning to *Fra* Tommaso she said, "Father, these people are my friends; they have a role in my *commedia*. I beg you; allow me a moment to inscribe them in the final tercets." So saying she bent over the manuscript, not even taking time to sit, and wrote:

> *Udendo le miei preci lacrimose*
> *tutti le circostanti m'ascoltero*
> *come persone nobili e pietose.*

Così quel popol mansueto e pio
con il cappello in mano in mia presenza
fecion più che non disse il parlar mio.
Lament, Line 124

Hearing my tearful prayers
all those nearby listen to me
like noble and pious people.
Thus those kind and gentle people
with their hats in hand in my presence,
do more than I have said in my words.

With the skill of one well practiced in the ritual, the captain of the brotherhood stepped forward and quickly bound her hands with a rope. At the same time *Fra* Tommaso stepped closer and whispered, "I am here, Prudenza, and I will not leave you."

So saying, he traced a cross on her forehead, donned the hood that the prior handed to him, and proceeded to adjust it so that he could see clearly through the eyeholes.

"Must you, too, wear this thing, Father?"

"Yes, Prudenza. If I am to accompany you it is required."

With reverence he then grasped the stem of the *tavoletta,* held it close to her face and awaited a signal from the prior indicating that it was time to begin the procession. At the words "Let us go now," he began walking backward, inching cautiously toward the doorway.

She averted her eyes from the *tavoletta* for a moment and looked sadly at the manuscript of her lament. "It is but a few pages—my whole life contained in a few lines of verse—imperfect, like their subject. Here I, Prudenza Beltramonto Cecchi, lay down my pen. But my *commedia* is not yet complete." Turning to *Fra* Tomasso she asked, "Who will tell my sad tale when I am wasted? Although my hands are bound now and I can no longer write, I say to you, only with my voice can I now complete my lament. Hear me!"

"Although this fortress of the Bargello has been my home now for months I have never before seen the chapel. My feet are like lead as I mount the few steps at the entrance to this holy but dreaded place where others before me have spent their last hours. I sense the presence of their spirits. I am met, too, with the blast of a familiar odor that sickens my stomach. It is the heavy stench of oil and smoke. I have smelled it before. O God! It is like the seer's place! *Madonna chimerica.* Dear Lord, must I be reminded of her now in my last hours? I close my eyes tightly to banish the thought, but then I hear *Fra* Tommaso say softly, 'Prudenza, look. Look above, on the opposite wall.'"

"As I lift my eyes I see it and my pulse quickens. There, opposite the entrance of the chapel, I see a depiction of Paradise and, among the blessed I recognize at once the divine poet. I hear *Fra* Tommaso say, 'He is with you in this hour, Prudenza.'"

Given their long friendship, the depth of the joys they shared and the ordeals they endured together, *Fra* Tommaso could with ease now read her soul. A blessed calm had descended upon her, and every effort must be made not to disrupt it. She was withdrawn now, even from him, remote and calm. He realized she was completing her *commedia* in her mind, telling her story in her thoughts:

My hands may be bound but my mind is free. I watch now as the altar is being prepared for the friar to celebrate Mass. It is my last Mass. I see *Fra* Tommaso remove the black trappings of the Brotherhood as he dons his priestly vestments—red for maryrdom. I smell the sweet fragrance of melting beeswax, a blessed relief from the smoking oil lamps now sputtering their last, burning out like the last moments of my life.

I hear the brothers begin the comforting chants of the Mass prayers that I know so well from my childhood; the familiar, consoling Latin. I think, How appropriate, for I well remember my first meeting with *Fra* Tommaso when he asked if I knew Latin. I can still hear my terrified response. "*Ad deum qui laetificat juventutum meum.*" How doubly ironic it is now to speak of bringing "joy to my youth," for although I am perhaps old in experience, I am yet young in years, a gray-haired youth of twenty-eight!

At the moment of communion I hear him say the words, "*Corpus Domini,*" and I am comforted by the belief that the wafer on my tongue is the body of the Lord. *Viaticum* they call it "food for the journey."

—◊—

As the Mass ended Prudenza settled silently on her knees before the altar and after some time one of the hooded brothers approached with something in his hands.

"*Signora*, it is for you."

"What is it, Brother?"

"It is a small oil cake, *Signora*, a token from the nuns of the church of San Niccolò. It is an old custom of theirs to comfort the afflicted."

"It seems, Brother, that I have come full circle. The church of San Niccolò was the first place I visited when Matteo brought me to Florence as his bride."

Breaking off a small piece she tasted it. "Please thank the kind sisters for me, and give the remainder to your brothers in token of my gratitude for your ministrations."

The fright that she had experienced at their first appearance had by now vanished as she continued her *commedia* in her mind:

I can hear the bells of the *Badia* just across the way. Soon the monks will be singing the Office of Matins. But their sweet-sounding peal is interrupted by the ominous deep boom of the *Montanina*. I know that sound too well now; it calls me by name. "Prudenza, Prudenza Cecchi it says; it is time."

I see the captain of the Brotherhood signal to *Fra* Tommaso to again don the black robe and hood like the others and to receive once more the *tavoletta*. It is just as *Fra* Tommaso had told me it would be—a small painting of the crucified one. He tells me to kiss the image on the cross, which I do, and as the *tavoletta* comes closer to my face its broad frame blocks my peripheral vision—a kindness of sorts!

He starts to walk backward, cautiously feeling his way as he goes, and whispers quietly to me as we begin that final walk of my last act. "Think, my child, '*in manus tuas*…Into your hands I commend my spirit.'"

His proximity to me makes it possible now to carry on this last, quiet, comforting conversation unheard by the other brothers as they continue chanting their prayers and litanies. How kind of him to arrange to do this: I know it is difficult for him…this last tender expression of friendship.

In the distance now I hear my sentence being read. That dreadful piece of doggerel that speaks of *femminile errore*. I know it is meant to be a warning to wives. I did not write that!

Anticipating the roar that will go up at the moment when we pass through the prison gate and come into the field of vision of the crowd I hear him say, "*Coraggio, cara sorella. Coraggio.* Let the welcoming songs of the angels drown the cries of the crowd. Know, dear sister, that your *commedia* is nearly completed. Do not be distracted now; I beg you."

Although my demise is to be public, I am almost grateful for that, for the distance from the prison to the *palco* in Piazza Sant'Apollinare is short, much shorter than the way to the Prato della Giustizia. At least it will be over sooner.

We have reached the steps that ascend to the *palco*—my stage, we had once jestingly called it—and I recognize that he is struggling with his long habit as he moves slowly backward up the steps. When we have nearly reached the top of the platform I make my last request: "Father, There is yet one last tercet that I would have wished to write."

"Tell me, child, what is it that you would say?"

"I would write:"

Ero fra tutte l'altre una fenice,
or son un'animal posto al macello
per quel peccato mio che dir non lice.
Lament, Line 73

Among all the others I was a phoenix,
I am now an animal taken to slaughter
for that sin of mine that may no more be
spoken of.

We have reached the platform now and he holds the *tavoletta* ever closer to my eyes repeating over and over, "*Deus adiuva me…*" I know the *tavoletta* is meant to block my vision of the *mannaia* and of the simple bier that lay on the ground ready to receive my body. But I know it is there. Even though I cannot see the brothers now I know, too, that they have fallen to their knees at the foot of the *palco* and I hear them chant their solemn prayers imploring mercy on my soul. And I, too, implore the Lord.

> *Dicendo Padre, Io vengo al sacrificio*
> *piacciati per la tua gran misericordia*
> *donare a l'alma afflitta il grato ospizio.*
> Lament, Line 145

> Saying, Father, I come to the sacrifice.
> In your mercy may it please You
> to grant welcome shelter to this afflicted soul.

But I do the unthinkable—that which *Fra* Tommaso warned me not to do. I know he will object, but I must. Just as we reach the platform I turn abruptly from the *tavoletta* and search the crowd with my eyes. As I do so I hear the horror of disbelief in his voice: "No, Prudenza, No! Do not look away, I beg you."

There is an audible gasp from the crowd as well. After a few moments my eyes come to rest: I see her standing at the edge of the crowd and in a feeble voice I cry out, *"Mamma, perdonami!"*

We are face to face now, my friend and I; and it is time to say goodbye. Looking directly into his eyes, I hear myself say, "Thank you! You have taught me well, Father."

With the divine poet I can at last say:

> *Tu m'hai di servo tratto a libertate.*
> Paradiso, Canto XXXI, 85

> You have led me from my bondage and set me free.

"We meet in Paradise. *Addio, Padre.*"

...AND MY BEGINNING IS MY END.

"It is over!" But no, that generous, loving heart cannot be stopped so summarily. It continues to pump as blood gushes from my headless body.

I see him now standing cold and frozen like a stone statue, sickened by the sight of my blood. It now covers the *palco* and even stains the hem of his habit. Only the solemnity of the promise that he would close the eyes of my severed head, could sustain him to fulfill this last ministration. My heart is filled with love and gratitude.

Although there is no time here—only the eternal present—from this place of bliss that knows the measure of neither day nor millennium, it is given to me to see that on the corner of the very *piazza* where I met my death there stands a balladeer in shabby pilgrim's weeds, a dark stain on the cloak its only insignia. Yet I see that from the pilgrim's neck there hangs a gold ring that I recognize—the symbol of fidelities from my past. It is hers now as she fulfills her last service to me. In woeful demeanor, measured cadence, and mournful sound the singer intones my sad tale:

> *O fratelli e sorelle*
> > *levate gli occhi e resguardate.*
> > *piangiamo e narriamo--*
> > *il pietoso lamento della Donna Prudenza.*

> O my brothers and sisters,
> > lift up your eyes and see.
> > Let us weep and tell the
> > piteous lament of the Lady Prudenza.

Some say that on the tenth day of August, the day I surrendered my spirit, a small voice can be heard to say, "They cheered as they cut off my head, but I still live! The phoenix has taken wing!"

AUTHOR'S NOTE

The flood that devastated Florence in 1966 was indirectly responsible for this book. As a result of it Prudenza took up residence in my imagination, prompting me to abandon a serious archival study, to explore instead an otherwise obscure life. I was not the first to make such an abrupt and unexpected detour from a major research project, lured into unforeseen territory. I was encouraged by such successful books as Gene Brucker's *Giovanni and Lusanna Love and Marriage in Renaissance Florence* (1986), and Judith Brown's story of the nun, Benedetta, in *Immodest Acts* (1985). Both were the result of their authors temporarily abandoning their original purpose, seduced by the real-life stories of their subjects. But as theirs are truly descriptive historical works, Prudenza's story as told in *The Trophy Bride's Tale* is historical fiction.

Anyone who has worked in the State Archives and the great libraries of Florence can attest to the recordkeeping obsession of the Florentines who were precise not only in the preservation of significant legal, financial, and political data, but also in the keeping of household records, inventories, and letters that frequently reveal details in the private life of a segment of society that is often otherwise poorly recorded. Beguiling stuff to seduce one into a veritable mine field of distractions!

My odyssey with Prudenza began when I was engaged in musicological research on the elusive repertoire of popular religious music of the renaissance, which is poorly documented since most of it was transmitted orally, under the guise of sacred parodies (*travestimenti spirituale*) that were printed without music. Only the texts were given with the directive (*canta si come…*) "to be sung like…" the popular song whose title followed. These tunes were obviously so well-known that there was no need to provide the music, the printing of which would have been an unnecessary and costly endeavor.

In the course of my work I repeatedly came upon references to a certain Prudenza immortalized in one of these popular hymns contained in a collection first published in 1675 by a Florentine priest, Matteo Coferati (1638-1703), under the title *Corona di sacre canzoni*.

Further searches revealed references to a woman named Prudenza who was executed for having poisoned her abusive husband. Was this the same Prudenza? Although her story was apparently well-known at the time, finding the actual text was serendipitous. While working at the Biblioteca Nazionale on something completely unrelated, I stumbled upon the real mother lode—a poem entitled *Il pietoso lamento che fece la Signora Prudenza anconitana pria che fosse condotto alla giustizia*. (The Pitious lament made by the Lady Prudenza from Ancona, before she was taken to justice.) Here Prudenza's story is told in 148 lines of verse, said to be written in her own hand while she was in prison awaiting execution.

The Italian language is rich in this type of literature. The lament had become a genre, a kind of "set piece" that can be traced to traditions and conventions of antique rhetoric. More important to my work, however, was the knowledge of how this literature was disseminated after Prudenza's death in 1549. The later-sixteenth century witnessed a proliferation of such popular literature, at first published in the form of loose pages that circulated among peasants, shopkeepers, and daily laborers and were sometimes recited in the *piazza*. The lament served as a kind of dark chronicle reporting news that was increasingly taken up with descriptions of executions, as well as predictions of dire events in the coming year. The *Lament of Prudenza*, in fact, became the prototype of such literature that continued to be printed well into the nineteenth century in inexpensive leaflet form.

But was this Prudenza a real person or merely the creation of some poet's imagination? I found the answer in the documents of the Compagnia dei Neri del tempio, a pious brotherhood that ministered to condemned criminals, prepared them for death, accompanied them to their execution and buried their remains. At the Biblioteca Marucelliana I located the brotherhood's meticulous record of the condemned attended by them from 1500 to 1817. The entries are often embellished with details of the crime, the method of execution and the location where it was carried out. There, in just one brief sentence, the truth of Prudenza's existence was confirmed, stating that she had been beheaded publicly on 10 August 1549 in Piazza Sant'Apollinare (now Piazza San Firenze) for having poisoned her husband, Matteo Cecchi.

With that knowledge my quest turned into an obsession. I could not pass through that busy *piazza* or visit the Museum of the Bargello, a prison in her time, without being seized by a growing compulsion to find the details of her existence so briefly acknowledged here. Further searches turned up more archival documents confirming her existence as well as her husband's abuse, which drives the plot of the story.

Even with archival proof of Prudenza's actual existence, there still remained the problem of the authorship of the poem. Did she actually write it as the title of the *Lament* alleges? Where would a young woman in mid-sixteenth century learn to write in *terza rima*, the style of Dante, which was by now surpassed in popularity by Ariosto and Castiglione? Hence the need to create for her a tutor who very early in her life introduced her to the beauty of the *Divina Commedia* and urged her to try her hand at such poetry.

Seduced by the amount of information contained in her *Lament* I chose to treat the poem as her creation. As a result *The Trophy Bride's Tale* uses authentic archival documents as the basic scaffolding of the story and, if one accepts the *Lament* as Prudenza's own writing—as I have chosen to do—the poem provides a wealth of material to flesh out the story. It is with apologies to the "pure historian" (but with no regrets) that I have elected, rightly or wrongly, to leap into fantasy feet first and draw on both sources to create a fictive biography. Out of respect for historical integrity I have attempted to incorporate into the narrative actual personages, facts, and events of the world Prudenza inhabited. At the same time, in order to provide connections in the narrative, it has been necessary to invent situations and characters, to create conversations and to endow Prudenza with both ancestors and descendants.

Her *Lament* is rich in details. From it we learn that she was from Ancona, was married to a Florentine man of means, and was the mother of four childen. She was twenty-eight years old at the time of her death, and her own mother was present at her execution. She speaks of confraternity members who visited her in prison and, perhaps most striking of all, she never denies her guilt. (It is a frequent theme of later laments that the condemned woman confesses without threat of torture, but rather in despair.)

In stanza 28 Prudenza speaks of a trial during which doctors and lawyers argued her case for seventy-five days. The logical course of action was to study the court records—which is where my intention to write a scholarly essay came to an abrupt halt. The documents I needed perished in the flood of 1966.

Perhaps even more important than the authenticity of the *Lament* is the question why Prudenza's story was perpetuated over several centuries. The earliest published version found thusfar appeared in Florence in 1557 and it continued to be published intermittently in other Italian cities as late as 1866. (See Bibliography.) To date I have found eleven different editions, five of them in the British Library alone. The longevity of the poem invites speculation.

Was Prudenza perceived as a warning and an example to disenchanted wives? The fact that her execution took place in an important public *piazza* seems to suggest so. Moreover, the misogynistic tone of the so-called sonnets attached to some of the later editions of the *Lament*, which speak of *femminile errore,* lend credence to that theory. Or was Prudenza possibly venerated as a popular folk heroine/quasi martyr. Her story takes the reader from Prudenza, the innocent convent-schooled adolescent caught in a marriage arranged by her adoring but misled father, to Prudenza the courageous mother being led to the scaffold as a criminal for having chosen to sacrifice her own life to save her children.

The sixteenth-century scenario of this genre often places the ultimate reason for the outcome of such tragic events, squarely upon destiny, *Il destino*. Indeed, the opening lines of Prudenza's poem seem to suggest that there was no escape. *Fuggir non si può mai quell che'l ciel vuole*. "It is never possible to flee from that which the heavens have ordained."

I ask only that the reader consider this. On 10 November 1549, exactly three months to the day that Prudenza died, the Farnese Pope Paul III met his creator. He left at least two bastard sons and a mistress jocularly referred to as *sposa di Cristo*, yet he was eulogized by Guicciardini as "a man adorned with learning and of unspotted character." He may have had his moment of encomium, but there were no popular utterances such as have survived over the centuries to tell the sad tale of the Lady Prudenza. Perhaps we will never know the secret of her story's longevity. I leave it to the reader to ponder.

BIBLIOGRAPHY

PRIMARY SOURCES

MS II, I, 138 *Libro di Varie notizie della venerabile Compagnia di Santa Maria della Croce al Tempio* (Folios 71r – 143v, marked *Libro dei giustiziati*) record executions attended by the brotherhood from 1420 to 1745. For 1549, the year of Prudenza's death, there are two recorded, one hanging and one decapitation. Biblioteca Nazionale Centrale Firenze, (Hereafter BNCF).

MS N 85, Passerini, *Libro di Ricordi*, (BNCF).

MS IT.Iv 337, ff. 80. *Notizia della Compagnia dei Neri di Firenze, e catalogo dei condannati quali la compagnia prestava la supreme assistenza*, (BNCF).

MS D 202 *Pazzienti della Compagnia del Tempio dal anno 1500 fino al presente (1817)*, Biblioteca Marucelliana, Firenze.

EDITIONS OF THE LAMENT

Il pietosa (sic) lamento che fece la Signora Prudenza Anconitana prima che fosse condotta alla giustizia e di nuovo quanto disse e scrisse da sua propria mano. Florence, 1557. London: British Library.

Il pietoso lamento che fece la Signora Prudenza Anconitana prima che fosse condotta alla giustizia, con la aggiunta di tutto il caso di nuovo quanto disse, e scrisse da sua propria mano. Lucca and Pistoia: no date. (BNCF).

Il pietoso lamento...Bologna: 1614. Biblioteca Archiginnasio.

Il pietosa (sic) lamento...Florence: 1623. Biblioteca Marucelliana.

Il lacrimoso lamento...Venice: 1625. London, British Library.

Il lacrimoso lamento...Bologna: 1627. London, British Library.

Il pietoso lamento...Lucca: 1818: London, British Library.

Il pietoso lamento...Lucca: 1823: London, British Library.

Il lacrimosa (sic) lamento...Treviso: no date. BNCF.

Il pietoso lamento...Bastia: 18??. Yale University Library.

Il pietoso lamento...Prato: 1866. Studio Bibliografico Orfeo, Bologna.

SELECTED SECONDARY SOURCES

Berners, Elija. The Dyers Companion. New York: Dover Publications, 1973.

Brackett, John K. Criminal Justice and Crime in Late Renaissance Florence, 1537-1609. Cambridge: Cambridge University Press, 1992.

Brucker, Gene. Florence, the Golden Age, 1138-1737. Berkeley: University of California Press, 1998.

————. Giovanni and Lusanna. Berkeley: University of California Press, 1986.

————. ed. The Society of Renaissance Florence. New York: Harper and Row, 1971.

Calisse, Carlo. A History of Italian Law (trans. Layton Register), New York: A. Kelley, 1969.

Capelli, Eugenio. *La Compagnia dei Neri: L'arciconfraternità dei battuti di Santa Maria della Croce al Tempio*. Florence: Le Monnier, 1927.

Delamare, François and Bernard Guineau (trans. Sophie Hawkes), Colors: the Story of Dyes and Pigments. New York: Harry N. Abrams, Inc. 2000.

Edgerton, Samuel Y. Pictures and Punishment: Art and Criminal Prosecution during the Florentine Renaissance. Cornell: Cornell University Press, 1985.

Eisenbichler, Konrad *"Lorenzo de' Medici e la congregatione dei Neri nella Compagnia delle Croce al Tempio,"* in Archivio storico Italiana,150, 1992: 343-70.

Feltwell, John. The Story of Silk. New York: St. Martin's Press, 1991.

Frick, Carole Collier. Dressing Renaissance Florence. Baltimore and London: The Johns Hopkins University Press, 2002.

Guccerelli, Demetria. *Stradario storico bibliografico della città di Firenze*. Rome: 1985, rprt. of Florence, 1929.

Klapisch-Zuber, Christiane. Women, Family and Ritual in Renaissance Italy. (trans. Lydia G. Cochrane), Chicago: Chicago University Press, 1985.

Martines, Lauro. Lawyers and Statecraft in Renaissance Florence. Princeton: Princeton University Press, 1968.

Natalucci, Mario. *Ancona attraversi i secoli*, vol. 2, Città di Castello: Unione arte grafiche. 1960.

Origo, Iris. "The Domestic Enemy: The Eastern Slaves in Tuscany in the 14th and 15th Centuries," Speculum, 30, 1955, 21-6.

Prosperi, Adriano. *"Il sangue e l'anima, Ricerche sulla compagnia di giustizia in Italia"* in Quaderni storici, 17, no. 3 (1982): 959-99.

Siraisi, Nancy G. Medieval and Early Renaissance Medicine. Chicago: University Press, 1990.

Sobrero, Albert M. *"Crudeli e compassionevoli casi: La cronaca nera nella letteratura popolare a stampa,"* in La Ricerca folklorica 15, 1987: 19-26.

Stannard, Jerry."Medieval Herbals and their Development," in Clio Medica 9:12-33.

Stevens, Serita Deborah and Ann Klarner. Deadly Doses, a Writer's Guide to Poisons. Cincinnati: Writer's Digest Books, 1990.

Trexler, Richard C. The Women of Renaissance Florence, vol. 2, Power and Dependence. Binghamton: Medieval and Renaissance Texts and Studies. 1993.

Uccelli, Giovanni B. *Istruzione universale della Compagnia dei Santa Maria della Croce del Tempio*. N.p., 1861.

Wilson, Keith D. Cause of Death: A Writer's Guide to Death, Murder and Forensic Medicine. Cincinnati: Writer's Digest Books, 1992.

Zorzi, Andre. *Amministrazione della giustizia penale nella republica fiorentina*, Florence: Olschki, 1998.

NB quotations from Dante's *Divina Commedia* appearing throughout the work are from the rhymed translation of John Ciardi. First
New American Library Printing, New York, 2003. Free transla-
tions of excerpts from Prudenza's *Lament* are by the author, based
upon an undated version of the poem published in Lucca and Pistoia, located in BNCF.

ACKNOWLEDGMENTS

Many debts have accumulated in the years since I began this journey with Prudenza and it is a pleasure now to acknowledge the individuals and institutions that enlivened the trek. First among them is Gino Corti who set me on Prudenza's path at the outset of my work and shepherded me down ways I could probably never have discovered or traversed by myself.

This study would not have been possible without the support of a Fulbright Scholarship to the University of Florence, an I Tatti Fellowship to Harvard University's Center for Italian Renaissance Studies, and various grants from the American Council of Learned Societies and the National Endowment for the Arts. These have made possible extended periods of research in Italy: in Ancona at the Biblioteca comunale Luciano Benincasa; in Florence, at the Archivio di Stato, the Biblioteca Nazionale Centrale, the Biblioteca Marucelliana and the Biblioteca Riccardiana; in Bologna at the Biblioteca Archiginnasio, and in London at the British Library. Additional work was done at the Library of Congress, and the Mullen Library of The Catholic University of America in Washington, D.C. I am indebted to the many staff members of these institutions for their assistance.

Among those who graciously read portions of the manuscript at various stages and offered helpful criticisms, I owe special thanks to Gail Armondino, Thérèse Bard, Mary DiQuinzio, and Mary Ellen Larson. For technical assistance I thank especially Imre Bard, Randy Hoelzen, Geraldine Rohling, and Andrew, my

434   THE TROPHY BRIDE'S TALE

"Mac guru." To the staff of Mill City Press for their patience, pro-
fessionalism, and commitment to the project I am deeply grateful.
Their collective encouragement along the way has been invaluable.
And finally, for that best of all gifts to a writer, an editor with patience, good humor, and the midas touch, Marly Cornell.

On a more personal level it is a joy to remember the summer spent in Bar Harbor, Maine, in the home of Ann Sears and
William MacArtor—a summer of revisions and rewrites rescued
from the grind only by my hosts unfailing hospitality and the always enthusiastic interruptions of Seji and Kiri, the resident ca-
nines.

Among the many individuals without whose patience and
encouragement this book would not have been realized, I am especially indebted to Christina and Anthony DelDonna who so often
and on so many levels came to the rescue. *Grazie.*

ABOUT THE AUTHOR

Cyrilla Barr has lectured and written widely on the popular religious music of medieval and renaissance Italy. Her early work, *The monophonic lauda and the lay religious confraternities of Umbria and Tuscany in the Late Middle Ages*, is well known to musicologists and historians of the period.

She is equally known and respected in the area of women's studies, having written a noteworthy biography, *Elizabeth Sprague Coolidge: American Patron of Music*, as well as a monograph, *The Coolidge Legacy*, published by the Library of Congress. With Ralph Locke she co-edited and co-authored *Cultivating Music in America: Women Patrons and Activists since 1860*.

With *The Trophy Bride's Tale* Barr's musicological scholarship and dedicated interest in women's issues come together in an intriguing historical novel based upon authentic archival records that document an actual case of abuse, murder, and criminal justice in sixteenth-century Florence.

She holds a Ph.D. in musicology from The Catholic University of America where she has taught and later became chair of the Musicology Department.

She now makes her home in LaCrosse, Wisconsin, where she continues to write.